Now Is All There Is
by
Sarah Catherine Knights

About the Author

Sarah Catherine Knights and her husband have lived in Malmesbury, Wiltshire since 1985. Peter was in the RAF, so the family had moved every few years: to northern Scotland, down to Lincolnshire and eventually to Wiltshire. They bought a house in Malmesbury to try to put down roots and to be near the base at RAF Lyneham, but then were posted to RAF Akrotiri, Cyprus in 1991. It was here that the seed of an idea for a novel was planted.

Returning to Wiltshire after the three year posting, Sarah taught English as a foreign language and started a photography business. She dabbled in writing, but it was only after doing an MA in Creative Writing at Bath Spa University, that she realised that she had a passion for both photography and writing. The story that had lain dormant since the Cyprus posting came pouring out and resulted in the debut novel, *Aphrodite's Child*.

Following on from the success of *Aphrodite's Child*,
Sarah continued the trilogy with
Now Is All There Is and
Shadows in the Rock

This book is dedicated to my family

Contents

Prologue

October, 1994

I sat on a seat in a picture window, overlooking the narrow street. It was quiet; only cars that needed access drove here and just the occasional passer-by walked down to the harbour, or trudged back up the hill.

This was my favourite place to sit.

Seagulls were swooping above the cottage, their mournful cries making me feel nostalgic for the past. I'd climbed Brae Hill on the opposite side of the estuary so many times as a child; my parents had always insisted we climb right to the very top. Now, remembering those days, I saw us running and chasing, skylarks singing, seagulls plunging … a never-ending childhood dream.

The sky was dark and gloomy; the clouds, charcoal grey in places, interspersed with blackness. The wind was gusting – I could see some of the seagulls now, as I looked up, being pushed and shoved by it, almost losing control of their flight.

I loved this place, even in this weather. The harbour, time-less in its space.

I glanced at my watch, ran my hand over my ripening stomach and felt both a little anxious and annoyed. He was often late these days, so why was I surprised, this time? But this was to be a special day, one for planning our future … and dreaming.

I'd give him another half and hour and then I'd go for a walk and leave him a note.

I continued to sit there, occasionally checking my watch. Twenty-five minutes went by and so I put on my coat and hat, prepared to be blown by the wind along the coastal path. I found a scrap of paper and wrote:

'I waited ages. Have gone along our usual path towards Hawkers. Meet me there!'

The phone rang. I picked up the receiver and without waiting to hear who it was, said, "Where are you? You're late."

It wasn't him. A voice said, "Is that you, Emily? Are you alone?"

The disembodied voice sounded odd; I heard a cough.

"Yes … who is that?"

My mind was confused. I was so sure it would be him, I couldn't understand.

"You better sit down, I … I've got some … terrible news."

I sat down obediently, feeling like a child.

I knew … in that moment, I knew.

Chapter One

January, 1995

I lay spread-eagled on my back, propped up on a pillow. I'd lost all sense of time, my mind was drifting on a sea of nothingness. Not knowing or caring who was in the room with me, I had a sense of people coming in and out, talking above my head; machines were making beeping sounds, regular rhythmical blips. Before each crescendo of pain that rose and rose and rose, I lay exhausted but then the pain would rise from somewhere deep inside and I could feel it invade my body again. It was as if my back was shattering into a million pieces and my belly was being squeezed by an unknown force; it was resisting by becoming so hard I could feel every muscle straining, every tendon pulling, every ligament breaking. Tension radiated down my legs, reaching my feet propped up, miles away from me.

Someone wiped my brow.

"Get off!" I shouted and I pushed the hand away with as much force as I could find.

Did I shout then? Was that me?

"You're nearly there now, my darling. Keep going, keep going..."

"I can't do this... I can't..."

"Yes, you can. You're doing brilliantly... it won't be long now..."

Someone was shouting and screaming in the room.

I could see the black night sky towering over me. I was a tiny speck, floating in the warm sea, a pinprick in the vast expanse of sky.

*

The thing I was lying on, was shifting, rolling ... lights ran above my head, like passing houses through a window on a train. People were running, doors opening.

"Don't worry, dear, we're going to Delivery now..." a voice said.

Between the lights, the doors, the running lights and the running people, I scanned the space around me for those eyes.

I was in a bright room. They were saying – breathe, push, don't push, wait, pant, stop, start.

I want to stop all this ... right now.

"Another one is coming and this time I want you to push as hard as you can. Try not to make so much noise, dear, you're wearing yourself out ..."

Then the blackness of pain landed: the searing heat, the flesh tearing, the knife slicing through, the hammer blows, the needle piercing, the electric shock, the pressure – and I was pushing, pushing, pushing. This thing inside me was breaking out; it had to get out, its life depended on it.

"That was brilliant, Emily, just amazing. One last push, and your baby will be here."

I drifted outside myself again, up to the ceiling, looking down. There I was, plain to see, a woman in the ocean. Floating ... my hair streaming in waves behind me, lights flickering through the blueness, turtles swimming by, watching. Lying on my back, I let the water cradle my body – I could almost feel the pain floating away into the ripples.

Then, a wave engulfed my body from nowhere – it hit me headlong with a rush of white water – and I was pushing, pushing. Someone said, "The head, the head…" and I wondered what they meant. "Pant, dear, pant … one last push and then Baby will be born."

There was hardly any time left now.

"Now we've just got to get Baby's shoulders out; one last, big push, dear…"

And suddenly I felt a slithering, a sliding, a gliding, snake-like surge and then … a quietness.

"It's a girl."

All around, people were moving. That voice I'd been searching for was crying near me, saying, "She's beautiful. You're beautiful." And he kissed my face.

In the far away distance, I could hear the sound of the first few angry cries of a new life.

*

Lying there on that strange bed in that foreign place … it was as if I'd been shipwrecked and thrown up onto an uninhabited island, bloodied and bruised. My body felt used, ripped. I was numb, in pain and … euphoric.

My eyes were closed – I couldn't bear the brightness – my mind closed down and disappeared down a tunnel. I could feel someone touching my arm, gently rocking me and saying, "Emily. Wake up – here's your baby. She wants a cuddle with her Mum".

I dragged my eyes back up the tunnel and opened them, slowly. A woman placed a wrapped bundle on my chest – masses of dark hair was sticking up above the blanket. I lifted my arms and held her.

I stared into the azure eyes that were staring back at me and … I felt an overwhelming sense of having met her before. Her eyes pierced my soul – we gazed at each other, like long lost loves across an ocean of time.

And then I remembered.

Chapter Two

Christmas Day, 1992

"Happy Christmas!" shouted Amy down the phone, her face bright with excitement. "What are you doing, Daddy? Are you lonely, all on your own out there? We've had masses of presents; Granny says we can eat some chocolate before lunch!"

I stood next to Amy, watching her face light up every time Luke said something. I was hovering near, so that I could speak to him. His disembodied voice sometimes reached me and I felt a huge need of him.

"Can Mummy speak to Dad now, Amy?" I said, reaching for the phone.

Amy turned away from me almost aggressively, keeping the phone pressed to her head, fearful of losing contact with him.

"When are we going to see you, Dad? I've got your Christmas present here and I want to give it to you – you're going to love it."

I waited to see what was said to that question.

"Oh okay … okay …I'll hand you over. Byeee, I love you too …" She blew three kisses into the mouthpiece and shouted, "Did you get them?" I heard Luke laugh.

Amy turned back towards me and thrust the phone at me.

"Here's Daddy," she said, scowling.

Amy was such a sweet girl, but since coming to England, I could detect a small amount of animosity towards me. She didn't understand what was going on consciously, but she'd picked up on something, I was sure of that.

Amy ran off, back into the kitchen, leaving me alone in the hallway; my heart was beating fast and I took a deep breath before saying, "Hello … Luke, it's me." My voice sounded small, timid even; I could think of *nothing* to say.

There was a short pause and then he said, "… is everything okay that end? Amy sounds good." His voice was flat, lifeless.

"Yes, everything's fine … the children are having a lovely time and that's the main thing."

There was another long pause. I wanted to talk about the future, but didn't know where to start.

"That's good … the children have got to be our priority. How's your mother?"

"She's much better, thanks; she's loving having the kids to stay – I keep having to tell her to slow down. The latest test result was good – they're confident that we've got all the cancer."

"Well, that's good."

Our chat was stilted. We were talking – we were listening to each other, but – it was as if we were acquaintances making polite conversation, not a married couple, with years of history.

"What are you doing today? It must be odd …"

"Sophie and I are making the best of it. We're going to the Mess for drinks soon and then to the hotel in Pissouri for Christmas lunch – they're doing a deal and you get all the works: five courses, champagne and afternoon tea thrown in. We thought we'd treat ourselves."

Jealousy exploded in my chest; I had no right to feel it but it flew through me like a flame, singeing my heart.

I couldn't help myself, I said, " Well, that sounds very cosy, Luke, I hope you both have a lovely time."

"Well, what would you have us do? Sit here in the house, eating beans on toast? Thank God she's here, otherwise I would've probably done just that, but Sophie insisted we get out and celebrate Christmas. You're the one who's left the family home, Emily. You're the one who broke the family up."

"You TOLD me to go, Luke ... I would've stayed. You wanted me out of the house, you said. So I went. Don't make out it's ..."

"Look, we've been through this ..." he said, too wearily. "I don't want to talk about it any more ... you asked, so I told you. I'm sorry if you don't like what you hear."

He was right – what was the point of going over the same old ground? What did it matter if he and Sophie were going to the Columbia Beach? I was here ... he was there.

"When's Sophie going home?" I asked in a voice that I tried to keep neutral, but sounded like a petulant child's.

"She's going back to the UK soon after new year. By then, her tenants will have left and she's going to try to make a life for herself there, without Sam. It's not easy for her, Ems. Just be grateful to her for staying with me – I don't think I could've coped without her, to be honest ... she's kept me sane and out of the bar."

"I know ... I am pleased she's with you. I'm sure you're company for each other. I'm sorry ... what will she do when she goes back – has she got a job lined up?"

"Well, I've persuaded her to go back to modelling. She's still got contacts and it's something she's good at. She's made a couple of phone calls and it's looking promising."

"That's good. Maybe she can use those pictures I took of her all that time ago." I thought about the beach at Buttons Bay when I took pictures of Sophie there; she was so beautiful and happy, then – Sam was alive and life was full of possibilities.

I stared out of the window across the front garden of my parents' house. The trees were covered in a heavy frost which hadn't dissipated during the morning. It was a perfect

Christmas scene – there was even a robin sitting on the branch outside the window, its red breast standing out against the whiteness. I'd never felt so un-Christmasy in my life. The children's excitement, the smell of turkey that had been slowly roasting since eight o'clock and the tree in the corner of the hall, twinkling and glittering, had only served to emphasise my emptiness.

"Luke ... what did you say to Amy about seeing her – just so I know?"

"I said I'd see her soon – I wasn't specific."

"Oh. Okay. Well, I better go ... say hi to Sophie for me and – have a good time, Luke."

And I meant it.

We said goodbye and we said we'd speak again the next day, at the same time; I'd get Charlie to speak to him, next time. He'd been too engrossed with playing with his Granddad – they were setting out a new train set and there were grand plans for family fun after lunch.

I stood alone in the hallway. My eyes were damp – I hadn't even realised I'd been crying. I stared at the phone and vowed to speak to him properly tomorrow.

I was going to put forward a proposition.

*

I'd told Mum the whole story, the day after we'd arrived. At first, she hadn't questioned Luke's absence at all; she'd accepted my explanation that he had to work over Christmas. My mother wasn't stupid, though – she'd known something was wrong and she pressed me to tell.

It came as a relief.

Dad had taken Charlie and Amy down to the park and I'd opted to stay with Mum to help cook. Mum had been amazing; she'd put her arms around me and hugged me. I cried in her arms and it released a torrent of tears that had been building inside me for months. I couldn't stop. I made Mum promise not to tell Dad the truth; I knew he wouldn't be so understanding.

"So ... do you love this James, then?" Mum asked. "I suppose you must do, for all this to happen."

"Yes, I do Mum. It's like ... I love them both, which is impossible, I know. I'm an idiot – I've ruined everything."

"You're not an idiot, don't say that. These things happen ... it's called Life," said Mum. "Perhaps you see different qualities in them. I'm not condoning what you've done, but I do understand. I've never told you this ... but when I'd been going out with your father for about a year, I met a chap at a dance. Dave, his name was. He took a shine to me and me to him. Your dad was completely oblivious to it all, but I was in turmoil – he had such a wicked sense of humour, Dave, and we laughed all the time. It never went anywhere ... he eventually moved away and I heard he'd married a South African woman. But I could imagine if I'd been in a romantic setting like you were, away from real life, that things might have turned out differently ..."

This surprised me; I'd never heard the story before and I couldn't imagine my mother in this situation. She had a knack of making me feel better about things.

"Why did you stay with Dad?"

"Well, there's a question. I think I realised that Dad was also my best friend. Dave was funny, good-looking and a great dancer ... and I think I loved him ... but ... your father was ... I don't know ... my soulmate, I suppose."

"Oh Mum, I just don't know what to do. What shall I do?" The word 'soulmate' was one word I often thought about, these days.

"I can't help you there, love. Only *you* can decide. I didn't have any children when it happened to me – we weren't even married, as I said. It's different for you. You've got to put Amy and Charlie first."

"I know …"

The tears were still coming. I heard the children's voices coming down the path, so I scuttled up the stairs before they could see me. I'd left out the bit about the miscarriage – I felt that was too much for Mum.

I looked at myself in the mirror and all I could see was someone I didn't like much any more. I ran the cold tap and cupping my hands, threw water at my face.

*

Now, leaving Luke's voice behind, I went into the kitchen with a forced smile and said, "Anything I can do? Shall I do the sprouts?"

"How was he?" said Mum, with a quizzical raise of the eyebrow.

"He was good … I think." I looked across at Amy who was using some new paints at the kitchen table. "Daddy was okay, wasn't he, Amy?"

"Yes," she said without raising her eyes from her painting. "Sophie's keeping him company, he said. He said we'll see him soon."

Mum and I exchanged looks across the kitchen.

"What time are David and Steve coming over?"

"They're going to try to arrive around twelve-thirty," said Mum. "We'll sit down around one. Dad will want to watch the Queen at three, you know what he's like … and then we'll open the rest of the presents."

We were following the normal ritual of Christmas Day that we'd done ever since David and I were small children: a few presents for the children before lunch, along with our stockings, of course. Charlie still believed in Father Christmas; Amy, on the other hand, knew it was me delivering the presents to her bed, but pretended not to. I was pretty sure Amy had been awake when I went in last night. I'd looked across the darkened room and her eyes were squeezed tight shut.

It was comforting being in this childhood routine, surrounded by my family. All the Christmases before lined up like a pack of cards behind this one, giving my life some meaning and continuity – I needed this now, when my life felt so fractured.

David and Steve duly arrived with armfuls of presents wrapped in brightly coloured paper. The greetings, the hugs, the placing of the presents beneath the tree, the pre-dinner drinks, all added to the normality that I was trying to feel. I'd already spoken to David on the phone about everything – he'd listened to my night time confession all those months ago, so wasn't surprised by the turn of events. He'd said 'things'll work out, they always do,' in his usual calm way ... and I'd almost believed him.

Dad, of course, was wonderfully ignorant of everything. He and Charlie had renewed their bond over trains and cars and he carved the turkey, making rather a mess of it, as he did every year. I wondered if Mum had, in fact, told him ... but I decided she hadn't; I didn't think Dad would be able to keep quiet and Mum had promised she wouldn't.

This was the first time I'd seen Dad with Steve; I'd heard about previous meetings between him and his son's boyfriend and wondered how it had gone. David had said he was okay, if somewhat formal and I could now see him making a huge effort to be friendly but I knew, deep down, it wasn't easy for him.

So here we all were – a strange collection. Two gay men, a separated wife, my parents (one recovering from cancer) and two little children. We enjoyed our Christmas Day together: the traditions and the camaraderie – but there was no getting away from the fact that I was going to have confront what had happened and try to resolve it, one way or the other.

Chapter Three

"Do you want to talk to Daddy, Charlie? I'm going to ring him, right now."

"Yes please – I need to tell him about my new train set. I want to know if he'll help me build the station when we get back."

I looked at his questioning eyes. I couldn't face telling him that we might never go back. Not yet; I would wait until the Christmas festivities were over. "Well, come here then, we'll go out to the hall now," I said, my stomach churning.

I let him dial the number and listened patiently to their long involved conversation about every present Charlie had received and about a grievance he had with Amy about the toys they'd received from Luke's parents – Charlie wanted to swop with Amy and she'd refused.

When I eventually got on the phone I explained the situation to Luke. "I think your parents have forgotten how old Charlie is. It was a bit of a babyish present, to be honest, and he thought Amy could play with it, 'because she's a girl,' he said. She wasn't so keen and I can't say I blame her. Perhaps next year, we'll have to give Nana suggestions to avoid all this arguing." The reference to next year fell on a black hole of sound; neither of us wanted to contemplate the future at the moment.

"Anyway, how was your Christmas meal? Did you enjoy it?"

"Yea, not bad."

"You don't sound too enthusiastic."

"Well … take two people. One, who's just lost her husband in a tragic accident and one, who's just been cheated on by his wife … and put us together for a Christmas meal in a characterless hotel dining room … and you don't get the best of situations, no."

I didn't know how to respond. "Was the food good?" was all I could come up with.

"Yes … it was edible."

"What did you do afterwards?"

"We went home and I got pissed. I couldn't drink at the lunch as I was driving – I did drink a bit – but when we got home, I laid into the Scotch and passed out."

"That can't have been much fun for Sophie."

"No. She went to bed. So you can see, we had a ball."

I could feel my heart kicking my chest.

I was going to say it.

Now.

"Look Luke. I've been thinking … just please listen to what I have to say … you don't have to give me an answer now."

I waited.

"Well, go on then. What?"

"Amy and Charlie are our priority, right? If I stay here, where are we going to put them into school? If I go back to our house, I've got to wait ages before I can get the tenants out. I can't stay at my parents' forever. They're happy to have us for a while but …"

"So, what are you saying?" said Luke, angrily. "You should have thought of all this when you were having your assignations with lover boy. I wanted them to stay here – it was you who said you couldn't possibly go without them, so I let you take my children away. I've regretted it ever since."

"What I'm saying is … is this. For the sake of the children and their education, I think I should come back. The children can go to school and we can talk."

I could hear him breathing.

"I'm not sure I could face you. I need more time," he said.

"But Luke, the children need to go to school. The easiest and best solution is for them to go to the school they've been to for the past year. They love it there, they're doing well there. It's not about us, it's about them."

"Where would you live?" he asked, as if there was an alternative.

"I'd come back to our house – I could sleep outside, in the maid's quarters, if you couldn't bear me near you. I'll do *anything* to give the children some stability. Please … just think about it. We'd be doing it for *their* sake."

"Have you spoken to your lover?" he said. "Have you had any further liaisons?"

"Luke, stop being so …"

"It's a perfectly straightforward question."

"I've spoken to James, yes, of course I have. But I think we've got to put everything to one side and think of the children. Are you prepared to do that?" I said, my mouth dry, my legs shaking.

"I'll think about it. I'm not promising …"

"Thank you. It would only be till July. We need to make the decision quickly, though. The school term starts again in two weeks. I'll ring you tomorrow – okay?"

"Yep."

"Yes, what?"

"Yes, *okay*."

*

I had, of course, been in touch with James, as Luke pointed out. How could I not? I'd been effectively cast out of my home, had flown back to the UK where James was; I needed to hear his voice. We hadn't met, as yet; he'd been in London when I'd arrived, but he was spending Christmas with his parents and was now just down the road effectively, in Basingstoke.

We'd spoken several times after everyone else had gone to bed – long, quiet phone calls where his voice comforted me, but also confused me. He'd said, all those weeks before, that he would set me free to stay with Luke if that's what would make me happy, but I had no idea anymore what would make me happy. I felt as if my body and my mind were on a wrack, being slowly tortured. At the moment, the pull of Luke and the children was stronger, but if I saw James, I knew the balance would once again change.

"I think I've got to go back to Cyprus, if Luke will have me," I said on Boxing Night. I was sitting in the armchair my parents have by the phone. It was dark, except for the moonlight I could see filtering through the curtains. I was speaking quietly with my hand cupped around the mouthpiece, terrified that someone upstairs might be listening. "I've always said, haven't I, that the children come first? And I mean it. They need to go to school and I can't just put them into some random school near my parents' house. Our house is still occupied and it will take six weeks to get the tenants out, so even if I told them tomorrow to get out, there's a gap when the kids have to be schooled. It's impossible. I asked Luke tonight to consider me coming back."

James didn't say anything; I thought he was choosing his words carefully before he spoke. "Okay. Yes … that's good, if he'll have you. Wasn't he adamant that he wouldn't, though?"

"You're right there. He was so angry with me that he couldn't bear me anywhere near him, but after he'd calmed down a bit, he saw that the children should be with me, didn't he? He understood that their best interests were more important. When I put it to him for me to come back, he didn't say no, he said he'd think about it. I'm ringing him tomorrow."

I realised that it must seem to James that I was choosing Luke, so added, "I don't know where this gets us all, the adults, I mean. I've said I'll sleep in the maid's quarters if he wants me to. James … you're very quiet. What are you thinking?" My heart was racing.

"Yes, I think it's sensible to go back, finish the school year, get the tenants out and then go on from there." I was so grateful to him for not pressurising me and realised how hurtful it must be for him.

"When you come back, in July time, we'll see … we'll see what …" his voice tailed off.

"I should go now James. I'll let you know what Luke's decided. Whatever happens, you know I'll always love you, don't you? I'm wearing my Aphrodite bracelet right now, you know."

"Are you?"

"Yes, it's one of the most precious things I own … Adonis! Maybe, one day, I'll get you a matching one … not a bracelet of course – that would be a bit girly, but … how about a signet ring or a something to wear round your neck?"

"I don't know, you choose. A and A intertwined – maybe we should start a new addiction group … AA for people addicted to each other." He laughed as he said it, but there was a sadness underlying it.

"Goodnight James."

*

The whole day following, I kept reliving the phone call with Luke, wondering if I had put my point strongly enough. The more I thought about it, the more it seemed the right thing to do. Part of me really wanted to go back to Cyprus; I'd loved my time there, despite everything that had happened and if I didn't go back, what would I do? Our house wouldn't be the same without Luke. The children would slot back into their old lives quite happily, I was sure of that, but it would be hard for Amy – two terms back at her old primary school and then on to big school; so much better if she completed primary out in Cyprus and start afresh after that. What would I do alone in the house? All my local friends would still be around, but life moves on and I'd been absent for nearly two years – would they accept me, without Luke? Everything was whirling and churning around my head and I had no idea which way Luke would go.

At six o'clock as planned, I phoned 'home' (I still thought of the quarter as home, which I knew was strange) and the ringing tone echoed around my brain. I was just beginning to think Luke wasn't going to pick up when his voice said, "Hello, Luke Blackwell speaking…" In that moment, his voice was warm … soft even – maybe he didn't think it would be me?

"Hi Luke, it's me. I thought you weren't there."

"I was outside on the patio."

"How are you?"

"I'm okay …"

"The children send their love."

"Where are they?"

"They're watching something vital on the telly. I didn't tell them to come and speak to you this time, I knew you'd understand about the film and I wanted to speak to you …"

He didn't fill the gap that ensued; it was almost as if he was forcing me to ask again.

"Well," I said, raising my voice into a question. "What's your verdict?"

"I've thought long and hard," he said and then didn't continue.

"And …?"

"And … I've decided that, all things considered, you're right. I think it's best if you come back for the children's sake."

I could feel tears of relief stinging my eyes and I had to swallow hard to make the words come out. "Thank you Luke, I'm sure that's the right thing."

I gazed around the dark hallway and wiped the tears off my cheeks, as if he could see me. I shook my head, clearing my thoughts.

"I'll go ahead and book the flights tomorrow and let you know when we arrive."

*

With the flights booked (we had three more days and then we were off) I felt something had lifted; it was as if I'd been carrying a dead weight around and had put it down. My body was lighter, my smile unforced. Mum could sense it.

"I knew you'd sort it out," she said, smiling across the table at me. Everyone else was in the sitting room and we each had a mug of tea.

I blew across the top of mine and said, "Don't get your hopes up, Mum. We're both only thinking of the children at this stage. We've got a lot of talking to do."

"Yes, but you're on the right track. You'll be back home with your husband and that's got to be good news."

"We're going to see how it goes, Mum. The kids will finish the school year out there and then I'll come back for us to start school in the UK. The rest of it is ... who knows?"

"So ... are you going to ring that James and tell him? You can't lead him on any more, Emily. He's got to realise that whatever it was, it's all over."

"I was going to ask you Mum – would you mind if I go and meet him and you look after the kids for me? I feel I owe it to him ..."

My mother's face looked anxious and I wished I didn't have to drag her into it, but now she knew the whole story, it seemed daft to lie.

"Well, okay, but I won't tell your father ..."

"No ... God no. He wouldn't understand – I'm sorry to involve you Mum but ..."

"It's all right … just this once. I won't do it again, though. And please tell him, this James, to get on with his own life now." I promised I would and went to arrange the time with him. We were to meet in the same pub, as we had before, all that time ago.

I told Dad and the children that I was going to meet Jen for a girly lunch.

The next day, I set off in Mum's car. I hadn't seen him for what felt like an eternity. I'd spent a long time getting ready (not wanting to dress up too much in case my father noticed) I'd chosen my clothes carefully, trying to imagine the scene and his first impression of me. I'd put make up on (I hadn't bothered all through Christmas – what was the point?) and staring at my face close-up in the mirror, I'd noticed the black rings beneath my eyes. The permanent anxiety I felt was etched on my face; I'd aged ten years since Sam's death. The joy and youthfulness I'd felt on the island had fallen away, leaving a face that revealed as much as it concealed. My short blond hair was losing both its style and its colour and I could detect the ginger roots poking through.

Was I turning back into that woman I was before I went abroad?

*

The pub looked just the same – of course it would. I walked in and looked around, expecting to have to wait, as his car wasn't in the car park, so I was shocked to see him sitting at the same table as we'd sat at before. He stood up and raised his hand.

It was as if we'd never been apart and as if we'd been separated for a million years. He stood there … so familiar … the dearest person I'd ever met, yet I was there to tell him I wasn't choosing him.

I was choosing my children.

"Emily, it's so great to see you," he said, smiling, as I walked towards him. He held out his arms and I walked into them. We kissed briefly on the lips and then he held my shoulders and looked at me.

"You look tired – are you okay?"

I wasn't offended that he'd said that; I knew I looked exhausted and he knew me so well that he was bound to notice.

I pretended to be put out and said, "Oh thanks, you don't look so hot yourself."

I smiled as I said it and ran a finger down his cheek. I'd forgotten momentarily in fact how 'hot' he was.

He stroked my face, kissed me again and said, "Come and sit down. What would you like?"

"Just half an orange and lemonade, please. I've had so much alcohol over Christmas, I'm not drinking any more at the moment … sorry to be boring."

"Don't worry, I feel the same. Mum and Dad think Christmas is an excuse to buy every conceivable spirit and to try all sorts of expensive wines," he laughed. "Won't be a tick," and he turned away. I watched him walk to the bar and wished I knew his family, but his mother sounded so posh and his father was a General; I was sure they wouldn't approve of me.

When he came back with our drinks I said, "How come I didn't see the car? Have you changed it?"

"Yes, you could say that …" he said, smiling like a naughty child. "I didn't mention it before but …"

"What? What have you got? It wasn't that red sports car I saw, was it?"

"No … I've always wanted one and I thought, sod it, you're only young once … I've bought myself the ultimate boy's toy … did you happen to see a Harley Davidson out there? A silver and black beast, parked under the tree?" His face was beaming.

"No, I have to say I didn't, but I wasn't looking for it. Wow … that's … surprising! I didn't know you had a hankering to be a Hell's Angel …"

I couldn't help feeling unsettled by this. I realised I didn't know him at all – had he ever even *mentioned* his love of motorbikes? I was sure he hadn't. I had to stop myself sounding like his mother with comments like, *don't go too fast … are you sure that's sensible?* I mentally bit my tongue and said out loud, "That must be so much fun …"

"Yes, it's the best thing I've ever bought … apart from my guitars, of course. It was expensive, but it's cheaper to run than a car. I have a terrible desire to ride it without a helmet, to feel the wind in my hair, but I won't, don't worry – I'm quite a safe driver, you know." Maybe he could see the worry on my face, but I was *trying* to look excited for him.

"Have you got all the leather gear to go with it, then?" I asked, raising an eyebrow and imagining him in black leather top to toe.

"Yes, for long journeys, but it wasn't far today, so I'm not in it now."

"That's a shame."

"Would you ever come on it with me?" he said. "Have you ever ridden pillion?"

"Can't say I have … not sure about that James. It sounds terrifying." I had a vision of myself, arms round his waist, pressed up against his back, at death-defying angles.

"One day, perhaps?" he said, his eyes looking at me from beneath his fringe.

I looked away and gazed through the window. The weather was cold, but surprisingly bright for just after Christmas; the light hurt my eyes.

"James … Luke said we can go back." I looked at him to see his reaction. The smile he'd had on his face had disappeared and he was staring at me intently. I carried on, not wanting him to stop me.

"It's best for the children and I finally got Luke to see that." I leant forward and touched his hand. We interlaced our fingers on the table top – I still had my wedding ring on and it glinted accusingly in the golden glow of the candle.

"So … what I'm saying is, I leave in two days. I don't know what the future holds for Luke and me. We're going to live together, for the sake of the children." I repeated the phrase, like a mantra, trying to convince myself it was the right thing to do.

His eyes locked mine and he simply drew my hand up to his lips and kissed it. The feel of his mouth was too much; I'd told myself I wouldn't cry, I wouldn't …

"I understand," he said quietly. "If our baby'd lived, I would've sacrificed anything for him, I *know* I would." The ghost of our dead baby lay between us and a pain swept across my stomach, as if his spirit had passed through it. I'd tried so hard to forget him (I still thought of the baby as a boy) and at times had succeeded, but now that James and I were here, holding hands, he was the glue holding us together, forever.

"It's so hard … but I know it's the right thing. I don't know what I feel about going back. Part of me misses the island and the thought of swimming in that sea again makes my spirit lift, but then I think of the atmosphere between Luke and me … and it makes me shudder at the thought. I think it will be like two strangers sharing a house who try and be jolly in front of the children. Sophie's still there, but leaves just after I get there. It's going to be so odd … even odder when she's gone."

We'd finished our drinks already and I got up to fetch some more; I was relieved to have something to do. When I came back to the table, we didn't talk about my departure. It was as if, by mutual consent, we'd decided to leave it to one side. He told me about his Christmas and I began to think his mother sounded a difficult character.

"Mum always has to have everything perfect – it's so stressful – any little thing that's not quite right can start an avalanche of recriminations. Dad forgot to get the Stilton for Christmas lunch (according to Mum he'd gone out specifically to buy some) and you'd think it was end of the world, the way she carried on. Poor Dad, he just takes it, but it must be wearing."

He took a sip of his drink; I stared at his hand wrapped around the glass.

"Has she always been like that?"

"I suppose she has. When we were kids, I found it very difficult to have toys and mess around. She's a perfectionist and a control freak – that and children don't mix well. She's an amazing pianist and nothing else matters to her. Such creative people are difficult to live with, I guess."

"They sound a weird mix, your parents, a creative and an Army general. How did your mother put up with all the disruption of Army life?"

"She doesn't mind where she is, as long as she can play. Dad just had to make sure that we always had a piano in the house. She was frustrated when we were young, as we were always interrupting her, but as we grew up, we learned to leave her alone and we got used to her not being at home a lot. We were only there in the holidays anyway, being packed away to boarding school at eight. It gave her the freedom to do concerts wherever she could."

I thought about my own mother and realised how lucky I was; my mother had always been there for me with love and advice. It sounded as if James' mother had really only tolerated him and his sister.

As we made our way out of the pub, James said, "Will you come on the bike now, just for a short drive? I've got a spare helmet … please?" It would be a way of being with him for a little longer and he looked as if it would make him so happy.

My stomach did a flip at the thought but … why not?

"Well, I'm not really dressed for it."

"It's okay, you've got trousers on, that's fine. We'll just go for a spin for five minutes."

The bike looked mean and powerful, waiting to be let free. James took a spare helmet out of a box at the back and handed it to me.

"Okay, just five minutes then," I said.

It was like when I went on the speed boat for the first time: adventurous, dangerous, thrilling.

He put the helmet on my head, pushing it down and fixing the chin strap. "How come you even look sexy with that on?" he said, as he brushed his lips against mine.

"Sure … I must look ridiculous! Come on, show me what she can do!"

I put my bag back in the car and waited for him to get on. It felt strange to lift myself onto the bike behind him, but intimate and exciting.

"Just lean with me. You might find it a strange sensation but don't worry, just go with the flow. I'll look after you, I promise."

We set off slowly out of the car park, the engine idling, rather like the boat coming out of the Mole. My arms were wound tightly round his waist, my face pressed close to his back. The smell of him, the sheer masculine presence of him, overwhelmed my senses and although I was wary, I was exhilarated – it was so unexpected to be doing this.

Just when my life was weird enough …

He took a side turning that led down a country lane, high banks on each side, trees towering above us, branches almost meeting overhead. He let out the throttle and it was all I could do to hang on – the force of the acceleration pushed me back and I clung on to his jacket with as much strength as possible.

"Oh My God!" I shouted above the roar of the engine that seemed to be penetrating my body. "It's amazing … how fast are we going?"

I felt my voice trailing behind me and wondered if he could hear me.

"Only fifty … this is nothing. You wait!" He shouted through the air and his voice came loud and clear.

"Don't go too fast, James. This is fine."

"We'll just go out onto the dual carriageway in a minute"

"Oh God, really?"

"You'll be fine. Hang on. Here we go," he said and we pulled out onto the busy road. He opened the throttle and we shot forward, slicing through the air like a spear through flesh. My heart was hammering now – it was thumping against my ribs; surely he could probably feel it against his back?

I closed my eyes, gripping tighter and tighter – I could feel the speed against my face. It took me back to a bolting horse I'd once ridden through a forest; the horse had been frightened by a bird and took off through the trees and I'd been completely at its mercy. I was willing him with every fibre of my body to slow down.

It was if he'd heard my thoughts; the bike slowed down and turned left. The feeling of leaning over, unbalanced me.

"How fast was that, then?" I said, wetting my dry lips with my tongue.

"Only seventy-five for a few seconds ... she can go a lot faster."

I felt as if my life was one long rush of adrenalin, events taking over, thrusting me forward. The thrill of the moment, the rush of the wind, the noise of the engine, the pumping of my heart – life was exciting ... but dangerous.

I saw the pub in the distance and my heartbeat slowed down. It was a two-edged feeling – the relief of getting off the bike – but the certainty of saying goodbye.

We pulled up and he stopped the engine.

"Well, that was one hell of a way to say goodbye," I said as I got off; my legs were shaking and weak. I undid the strap of the helmet, lifted it off and put it on the seat.

Running my fingers through my hair, I said, "So ... it's time."

"Yes," he said, turning to me. "Promise me ..."

"What?"

"Promise me that you'll call me if you need to. I mean it. Any time, day or night. I'll always be here. You know that."

"I know. But I've got to go out there and try and make a go of it with Luke. I have to."

I fell onto his chest, my arms round his waist, breathing him in. "I love you, James, but it's not enough. It's not meant to be." He put his hand under my chin and drew his mouth down to mine. The kiss lasted for minutes, hours – I wasn't sure. All I knew was that I didn't want it to end.

We walked arm in arm to the car. "Have you finished that song yet?" I said, remembering the day on Aphrodite's Beach.

"Yes, nearly. I'm still working on the melody, but the lyrics are done. I'll send it to you in a letter."

I felt strangely calm as I got into the car. I'd been expecting to feel devastated, but I knew I'd see him again. I knew it.

This couldn't be the end.

Chapter Four

My parents took us to Heathrow; the children were so excited to be going 'home' and they kept telling me what they were going to do when we got there.

I'd managed to talk to David before he left and he'd reassured me that I was doing the right thing.

"What else can you do?" he said. "I'm sure you love being with Mum and Dad, but could you have hacked being with them for weeks on end? Just from a purely practical point of view, it's the only option you've got. You two didn't really think it through when you left Cyprus, did you?"

"No … we were too caught up in the moment, feeling sorry for ourselves and not thinking."

"Go back, Sis, and sort it out with him. Luke's a good bloke – you could do a lot worse. I'm not saying James …"

"No, I know what you mean."

"Luke's your husband, the father of your children. You've got to find a way to make it work. Give it time out there and if, at the end of the summer, you're both still miles apart, then maybe pack it in *then* – but you've got to give it a go. You really have."

He was right; I owed it to Luke to try.

*

"I can remember the first time we landed here," said Charlie. "It was hot and I didn't like it. I like it now." He was shuffling down the aisle in front of me, Amy behind.

"It's a different airport, Charlie. When we came the first time, we landed at Akrotiri – do you remember? Dad was there and we got to our house very quickly. We're at Larnaca now, so we'll have a bit of a journey back to the camp."

He stopped and looked back and up at me. "Will Dad be here, now?"

"Yes, I'm sure he will," I said, putting my hand on his head.

The thought of seeing Luke was making me nervous. "Go on, keep going. or we'll hold everyone up."

The air was warmer than England, but it was only January and even Cyprus was cool then. The scent, that special smell, filled my head. It wasn't like an oven, as it was in the summer, but there was still that mix of soil, sun and herbs that would be forever baked in my sensory memory. It would always be associated with this strange interlude in my life – this posting to a foreign place – where I'd lost myself.

We made our way across the tarmac into the building; I showed our passports to a weary-looking official, who hardly even glanced at the photos, and collected our bags with no problems. As we went through the 'Nothing to Declare' channel, my heart was beating like a drum.

Luke was standing at the barrier. He raised his hand and looked towards the children, not me. His eyes lit up as Amy ran towards him; Charlie was shouting, "Dad, Dad," above the noise of all the other people.

I hung back, watching … he lifted them both up, laughing. It was as if they'd never been away.

He glanced at me over the top of Amy's head as she clung to him, her arms tight round his neck. Now I could see dark rings under his eyes – he looked unhealthy, tired and worn out.

"Come and give Dad a kiss," Amy shouted, turning round to me. "Come here!"

Amy wriggled down from his arms and ran over to me, pulling me by the hand towards Luke.

"Okay, okay, give me a chance, I was just letting you …"

"Hello, Ems … how was the flight?" he asked as he put his arm round my back and kissed my cheek. His voice was flat, his arm barely touching me. I could smell alcohol on him, seeping from his pores.

"It was good. A bit bumpy halfway through, wasn't it kids?" I could hear the false brightness in my voice, the jollity I'd predicted I'd adopt.

"I like it when it bumps around," said Charlie. "I close my eyes and think I'm on a fairground ride."

"I don't like it at all," said Amy, pulling a face. "I think the wings are going to drop off."

"No, they won't, Silly," said Charlie, "don't be so stupid."

Amy was just about to whack him over the head, when Luke said, "Okay, kids … don't let's argue now, let's get you home. Get your things, the car's just out here."

We walked across the large car park. I couldn't think of anything to say, but the kids were chatting away, filling the space. The light was so bright I was able to hide behind dark glasses. I'd thought I'd never come back to Cyprus when I'd left, so I tried to concentrate on the feeling of being back somewhere I loved, despite everything.

As the journey progressed along the motorway, I let the scenery float by, loving that I'd been given a second chance to visit those places I'd noticed on the journey before Christmas. I was going to make an effort to go to these mysterious names signposted off the road: Zygi, Monagroulli, Germasogeia – there was a dam at that last one, it said. I'd take this opportunity to take photos, to immerse myself in the land and its culture.

And forget James.

Amy was talking enough for all of us put together. I put in the odd comment, glancing sideways at Luke. He was studiously avoiding eye contact with me. Normally, he would have looked at me and squeezed my leg during a journey like this, but the road ahead held a great fascination for him. Sometimes he looked in the rearview mirror to smile and laugh with the kids, but he didn't even glance at me.

As we entered the camp past the static aircraft, past the cinema, I began to have doubts. I wondered how many people knew I'd been home – did they believe the story about me visiting my parents and Luke working?

I realised that without Sophie, Sam and James I had no real friends here, who gave a damn about me. I was going to have to make another huge effort.

We wound our way through the quarters and … there was our house. Despite it being a married quarter, it felt like home.

Amy and Charlie jumped out immediately the engine stopped and in their normal chaotic, noisy way rushed round the side of the house. They were off to look for Tom Kitten, leaving the two of us alone for the first time.

Sophie came out of the door to greet us.

"Welcome back, Emily, it's good to see you. I'm so glad you've come." She squeezed me and I found it comforting.

"Thanks," I said, standing back and appraising Sophie. "You look really well; I probably look as tired as I feel." I stretched and groaned and rubbed my back.

"That was a long day. We had to be up at 4.30 to get to the airport for 7. Oh well, we're here now. Here come the kids. Come and give Sophie a big hug, you two!" They rushed round the corner and flung themselves at Sophie. Tom was walking behind them, like a dog.

"Have you made us a cake," said Amy, "like the one we made for Mum when she came back before?"

"Well, funny you should say that, I have. Come into the kitchen and leave Mum and Dad to get sorted."

I saw a flash of a look between Sophie and Luke, as if they'd pre-planned this. She took the kids' hands and walked through the front door.

Luke was leaning up against the side of the car; taking out a cigarette he lit it, drawing in the smoke, as if it was oxygen.

"So ... you're back, Ems." He stared at me through the smoke that curled round his eyes.

"Yes, I'm back. Let's just try to get on, act normally. The kids are blissfully unaware and I'd like to keep it that way."

"Don't you be so sure," said Luke with a cynical smile. "Amy's not stupid. She knows, even if she doesn't understand ... she *knows.*"

"Well, what are you saying?"

"I'm not saying anything. Just don't underestimate her."

"So what do you want me to *do*? You seem to be implying ..."

"Look, I'm not implying anything. I'm stating a fact – our daughter knows something's up and we've got to try to shield her from it."

"For God's sake, Luke. That's what I've been saying all along. I know we've got to shield them – that's why I brought them back." I paused and then added, "I don't want a lecture."

We stared at each other. Nothing had changed between us. Luke could hardly look at me and I didn't know what I could say or do to make it better.

"Sophie's here tomorrow and then she's off," said Luke. "Thank God she's here," he mumbled, almost to himself, but loud enough for me to hear.

"What do you mean by *that*?"

I couldn't believe he was being so mean. I'd thought we'd be civil to each other.

"Well, at least we have someone here to dilute the atmosphere." With that, he walked off towards the house, carrying the case.

It was going to be much harder than I'd thought.

"So, how's it been, while I've been away?" I said to Sophie later, when Luke was putting the kids to bed upstairs. The remains of the cake Sophie had made was on the table and we now each had a glass of white wine. I kept my voice low – I didn't want Luke to hear, but couldn't resist asking.

Sophie lit yet another cigarette (she seemed to have one permanently attached to her hand these days) and let out a long breath. "It was okay, but … you've got to understand how hurt he is. He hasn't come to terms with it at all. I tried to be there for him, but often he wanted to be alone and an awful lot of alcohol's been consumed. I'm worried about him, to be honest." She took a long drag and blew the smoke up to the ceiling. "When we went to the Mess on New Year's Eve …"

"You went to the New Year party? Luke didn't mention it …"

"Yes, we did. It seemed too depressing to sit here on our own, but it wasn't a good idea … everyone kissing and talking about the future – wasn't the best thing for either of us. We both got very drunk."

"Why didn't he tell me?"

"I don't know … maybe …"

"What time did you get home?" The thought of them, both drunk and vulnerable, made me feel queasy.

"God knows … about four, I think. I don't remember much about it. I know we both felt God-awful the next day. I think we've just about recovered now," she said.

Luke strolled through the door and she smiled at him saying, "Haven't we, Luke?"

"What?" he said, picking up his half-empty glass. "What are you two talking about?" he added, as he topped up the large glass to the brim.

"I just told Emily how awful we felt on New Year's Day."

"Yes, just a tad." They glanced at each other; I began to feel the outsider. "I have no idea how we got home. Did you carry me, Soph?" he said, laughing across at her.

"No – don't you remember? We walked and it was cold – I had to sit down at one point and then you fell over my foot and ruined your trousers and grazed your knees?"

"Oh God, yes, it's coming back – where are they, the trousers, I mean?"

"I've thrown them out – irreparable, I'm afraid." Sophie glanced at me and I saw that her beautiful face was showing no sign of this recent overindulgence. She'd lost weight and if anything, looked even more beautiful than she did before. Her hair was loose, glossy and shining, like a shampoo advert; her clothes casual, yet fashionable, but hanging off her.

"Well, we did nothing. I spent the night with Mum and Dad – we stayed up till midnight, watched the festivities on the box and then went to bed. Not sure I could have coped with your evening," I said, wondering if I'd heard the whole truth. The glances I kept seeing between the two of them told a different story. Was I being over-suspicious?

Anyway, what right had I to criticise?

*

Sophie spent the next day packing up and playing with the children; Luke went to work and I tried to re-orientate myself.

I wandered around the house, feeling both at home and completely alienated within the space of seconds, but I was determined to make it work. We'd got round the problem of our first night together. Luke had feigned tiredness and had gone to bed early, leaving me to pretend I didn't want to disturb him and sleeping in the maid's quarter with Sophie. No one believed any of it but we all played along.

The next day, Sophie was up early; her plane was at one in

the afternoon at Larnaca, so she was around to say goodbye to the children before they went to school. I was to take her to the airport at nine thirty.

"When are you coming back, Sophie?" asked Amy, clinging on to her. "It won't be the same without you."

"I'm not sure … I've got to go and get a job, Amy … but we'll see each other soon. Maybe next time we see each other – you'll be back in England, who knows?"

"Oh no, that's too long to wait. Come back here …" said Amy, looking towards me for confirmation.

"Yes, come back, whenever you want."

When it came to Sophie saying goodbye to Luke, I observed them carefully. I wasn't sure what I was looking for – a secret look, a passing glance?

"Thanks so much for everything, Luke. I don't know how I would've coped without you," she said. They held onto each other for a long time, like two people clinging to some flotsam at sea; it was too painful for me. Holding her shoulders, he said, "I wouldn't have been able to cope without you, either," and he kissed the top of her head. Emotion seeped through their words and I saw tears in Sophie's eyes.

Luke turned away and striding out of the drive, he raised his hand in a gesture of a goodbye wave; he didn't look back.

The journey to Larnaca was uneventful, but we both, I was sure, were thinking back to the last time we made that journey down the motorway together, when everything changed – when Sophie told me about Luke's secret and I confided in Sophie about my baby. I was sure that we both registered the place we'd come off the motorway, all those months ago.

Soon we arrived at the airport and parked the car.

"So, how are you going to fill your days, now you're back?" asked Sophie, as we made our way across the car park to Departures.

"I'm going to try to live my life as best I can. I know you hate me for what I've done…"

"I don't *hate* you…"

"Well, that's how it feels. I know I've been stupid, but I can't undo the past, so I've got to move forward. Perhaps I feel you hate me, because you're on Luke's side."

"You know what I thought from the start, I never tried to hide my feelings."

We'd arrived at the door and instead of proceeding through, we stopped outside the building. Sophie leant against a pillar and reached for a cigarette. She lit it and inhaled greedily. "I've tried not to take sides, you know, but it's been difficult while you were away. Luke was so upset … I had to do my best to hold him together. He was often in tears, you know."

I wasn't surprised by this; his face looked ravaged but I didn't like having to hear it.

"Did you sleep with him?" I asked. It came out more directly than I'd meant it to, but there was no point mincing my words.

"Pardon me?"

"You heard. Did you sleep with my husband?"

There was a hint of a pause before Sophie said, "Of course I didn't! How could you ask such a thing?"

"Well, it wouldn't be the first time two people, two friends, comforted each other with sex."

Sophie stubbed out her cigarette with force, twisting her foot to the left and the right – grinding it into the pavement.

"I'm not going to dignify that with an answer," she said, picking up her suitcase and moving towards the door. "It's not *me* who's slept with someone else, Emily. Don't tar me with the same brush as yourself!"

"Look, I'm sorry – but I need to know, if you have. Please tell me … I'll understand."

Sophie continued walking towards the desk where she joined the end of the queue. The two of us stood together, close, so that our conversation wouldn't be overheard by other passengers.

She leant in and said, "I didn't, okay? If you *really* want to know, Luke wanted to and I turned him down. I didn't want to spoil our friendship. So … now, you know."

Tears sprung to my eyes and I looked away, over towards the entrance to passport control. Soon, Sophie would go through that gap and be gone. I didn't know what to believe anymore. I could imagine Luke wanting to sleep with her, that's for sure. I'd always thought that Sophie was his type; he liked girls with dark hair and dark skin – I didn't know how he'd ended up with a redhead like me. Why did it hurt so much that Luke tried it on with Sophie?

I couldn't bear the thought of him sleeping with someone else.

Now I understood how he must have felt when I told him about James.

I turned back to Sophie and said, "Well, maybe it's a good thing I came home when I did. Maybe you wouldn't have been able to resist his charms …"

"Look, Emily. I loved Sam … I love Sam … I don't want to sleep with anyone else. I can't imagine ever loving anyone ever again, so please … leave it." She was speaking in a harsh whisper and sounded menacing. I began to wish I'd never said anything; this was an awful way to say goodbye.

In my jealousy, I'd almost forgotten Sophie's grief. "I'm sorry, Sophie, I'm all over the place at the moment."

The queue shuffled forward and then Sophie had to speak to the stewardess and have her bag weighed. When it had disappeared behind the black strips, we walked slowly to the place where we would, at last, say goodbye.

I felt both relieved and sad; relieved that Sophie was going and sad that our relationship had sunk to a new low. When I thought back to that day when Sophie had posed for me on the beach and we'd had so much fun together, I couldn't believe that I'd allowed that wonderful feeling of at last finding a friend, to change to this. I was determined to make it up to her, if it wasn't too late.

"Sophie, I hope you'll forgive us both – you've had to get involved in our mess and you've had so much to cope with yourself. I'm so sorry." I put my hand on my shoulder. "Go back to England and forget all this. We'll sort ourselves out. You must concentrate on yourself, now."

We put our arms round each other and for a while, there was a genuine feeling of friendship between us again.

Sophie was the first to pull away, saying, "Right … I must go. See you soon and good luck with everything."

She gave me a quick kiss on the cheek and walked through the barrier. I watched as she showed the man her passport; she turned, waved and was gone.

Chapter Five

When I got to the house, there was no one home – the children would be back in an hour. I relished the silence and emptiness; it was the first time for ages that I'd been alone. I loved my family, but when I was with Mum and Dad, I never had any time to myself.

Tom Kitten greeted me with his pathetic miaowing; he wound himself around my legs in a figure of eight, purring and pushing his head against my calves. Picking him up, I kissed his head and breathed in that soft sweet smell of cat. I gave him some food, which he consumed as if he'd never been fed before and then with no false affection, disappeared out of the back door, without giving me a second glance.

I went into the maid's quarters to strip Sophie's bed; the room looked bare, almost medical, with its white tiles and white walls. Leaving the other bed made up in case I needed to sleep there again, I threw the sheets outside the door and went to get the hoover. Sophie hadn't worried about the state of the floor, it was covered in dust, fluff and scraps of paper.

Having stripped the bed, I looked at the mattress and on impulse decided to turn it over. As I grabbed it and lifted it up, something blue fell from the head of the bed onto the metal base. I let the mattress crash down again; it was now half off the bed. I negotiated my way round it, curious to see what the blue thing was. My heart did a thump of recognition when I saw what it was – a pair of Luke's boxers.

*

The children were desperate to go down to the beach and as I had the car, I decided to take them and try to forget what I'd seen. Luke would normally have been home by then but he'd failed to appear, so the three of us set off through the camp – Curium was the beach we'd all decided on. I left him a curt, but polite, note.

I had no intention of swimming – it was far too early in the year – but I took my costume (in case I felt the urge when there) and my book and camera. The weather was overcast and windy, not beach weather at all, but there were tavernas there we could sit in and I fancied walking the length of the beach, blowing my mind free, with sea air.

"Wow, Mum, look at the waves!" said Amy, leaning out of the window and pointing. The road turned right but to the left there were windsurfers shooting across the water like sea birds looking for fish.

Instead of driving to one of the tavernas, I parked and we all got out to watch them. I had the long lens on my camera and attempted to capture some spectacular tricks – one guy, in particular, was amazing. It made me realise just how much I had to learn; I was a mere beginner compared to them.

When the children had had enough of watching, we took the car up to the tavernas and based ourselves there. Considering how windy it was, it was surprising how many people were on the beach, scattered around.

"Can we go in, Mum? It looks like Cornwall, the waves are fantastic. Please!" said Amy, who was taking her top off already, to reveal her costume underneath.

"Charlie, do you want to?"

"Only if you come too, Mum. Come on, it'll be fun."

I looked along the beach; there were a couple of other brave souls in the sea, jumping over the white water. The colour of the water didn't look inviting, it was more green than blue, but the waves did look good, so I said, "All right then! We must be mad!"

We all held hands and ran into the sea – that was the deal – no one was allowed to dally on the edge. Once the initial shock had passed, as long as we kept moving, we were okay. We dived through the waves, jumped over them and chased each other – I couldn't remember having so much fun for a long time. We even body-surfed, jumping on the waves and letting them swish us into the shore. We'd end up grounded, with sand and pebbles in our costumes and hair over our eyes, but it was addictive and we did it again and again. Our eyes were stinging with salt, our skin tingling with cold, but it was exhilarating and I had a clear moment of feeling that life was *good*. I'd forgotten everything in that half hour; my mind had been full of enjoyment, of laughter and a feeling of together-ness with the children.

We dried ourselves near the car and then went to the nearest taverna to warm up. We sat in the window, shielded from the wind, with a view of the beach. Sipping our Cokes and eating ice cream, we reviewed our exploits in the surf and looked forward to another Cornish holiday; the children would be older and more capable of dealing with the Atlantic waves than they were before Cyprus.

"How much longer have we got here?" said Charlie, his hair all tousled and his chin dripping with pink ice cream. His eyes looked huge, his skin all red with the weather and the sea.

"Well, it's about six months. We'll go back in July, in time for you to start the new school year in England. So, we've got to make the most of it."

"Will we all go back together? I hate it when you and Dad do different things," said Amy. "It makes me sad." She took a long swig of Coke, looking directly at me.

"Dad'll have to stay on a bit longer than us, I'm afraid."

"Why? It's not fair! I hate it. I'm going to tell him, he *must* come with us."

I found it difficult to think so far ahead – I wondered if, by then, we would've sorted things out, one way or the other. Would I be pleased to leave without him or sad, being separated again?

Only time would tell.

"It's not his fault, Amy. He has to stay on till at least Christmas, but we have to go back to get you into school. You'll be starting big school; it'll be exciting!" I said, with as much upward lift to my voice as I could muster. I knew it would be daunting for Amy to start yet another school. At least Charlie could go back to his old one.

"I don't want to go home, anyway," said Charlie. "I'm going to stay with Dad. I don't *care* if I miss school."

"I'm not sure your teachers would feel the same. Dad and I wouldn't let you miss school, either. Come on, finish up and we'll have a walk down the beach. We'll watch those windsurfers again and then head home. You'll be able to tell Dad all about the waves."

*

That night, I decided I'd go to my 'normal' bed; going to the maid's room now that Sophie had gone was too big a statement and I didn't want to be the one being 'off', so I went upstairs, as usual, and said, 'See you up there' to Luke, who was watching the TV with great intensity. I hadn't slept in this bed since the row, when I'd confessed to loving James, so it now took on a huge significance.

I undressed, took my make-up off and brushed my teeth. Climbing into the familiar bed, I took my novel off the bedside table, but my mind wasn't up to reading and soon I switched off the light and tried to coax myself to sleep. I was beginning to drift off when I heard Luke's steps; I heard him undressing outside the bedroom door as he used to do, in an attempt not to wake me and then he slid into bed next to me.

There was that awful moment when we both knew I was awake, but didn't want to acknowledge it. I was lying on my back; the room was dark except for the moonlight shining weakly through the thin curtains. The outline of the ceiling fan, now still, hung above the bed, like a propeller. It looked heavy and menacing and I wondered briefly, if it was secure in its position.

There was silence, except for the fridge whirring downstairs and an unknown animal in the far distance making an eerie sound; it was probably a fox, I'd seen one on the patio once. It was smaller and less red than an English fox, but it had slunk off, in the same sly way. I'd always found the sound of a fox barking at night disturbing.

"Ems, I know you're awake," said Luke, after a few minutes.

"Yes, I can't sleep. I hate that sound."

"What sound? I can't hear anything."

"That fox – there – it did it again."

We both lay still.

"I ... I want you to know ... I can *never* forgive you. I've thought about it, all the time, while you've been in England and I just can't get my head round it. Did we have such a terrible life together? Was I such an *awful* husband that you had to find someone else? I just don't *get* it."

He was speaking in a hoarse whisper.

"It wasn't anything *you* did, Luke. I told you that. It was *me* ... you've got to understand. I *changed* ... something happened to me, which I don't even understand myself. It was as if I became a new person. It was like I had no control. James was there ... he didn't know the 'old' me ... or maybe he did, at the Ladies Guest Night ... I remember that night, so well. That feeling of shedding my old skin started that night and he just happened to witness it. Don't blame him, Luke, he was an innocent in all this."

"For God's sake, don't be so *naive*. He saw his opportunity and took it, without thinking about anyone else but himself. He didn't care that you were happily married and had two children – he was just out for all he could get."

"It wasn't *like* that, Luke. He didn't set out to seduce me – you've got it all wrong. It just happened."

There was a brief pause. Luke shuffled, the springs creaking beneath him; down the corridor, one of the children coughed.

"You can think that, if you want to," he said, "but you're fooling yourself. He was an opportunist. I'll never forgive you. *Never.* You've ruined my life."

I could hear tears in his words.

"Luke, I'm sorry, I truly am … but we've got to get through this … somehow. Can you imagine how hurt I was when I found out that you'd taken a decision about having another child and hadn't told me? You *knew* I wanted another one, you *knew* …"

"Are you comparing the two things? I know what I did was wrong and I regret it now. It seemed like a good idea at the time. We were starting a new life in Cyprus and I didn't want to be tied down with a baby …"

"But it wasn't *your* place to make that decision on your own …"

"But I did it for the right reasons."

"No, you didn't. It was your own selfish reasons. You didn't give me a second thought."

"Yes I *did* … I thought that if I had a vasectomy, it would take the pressure off you. You always seemed so stressed back in England, with the kids and teaching. I thought you could have a time of freedom in Cyprus, with no more worries. That turned out well, didn't it?"

"But Luke, you can't do that sort of thing without your partner's say-so. Why do you think the Air Force doctor wouldn't do it? For that exact reason, of course. I just don't understand why you can't *see* that."

"We're going round in circles, Ems. What's the point? I'm tired. I'm tired of this discussion and I'm tired of feeling like this."

"Why don't we both agree to try and forgive each other? We've got to, for the sake of the children and if we don't, then there's no point …"

Luke didn't say anything. I could hear him breathing … and then he said, "You're here now. We've got about six months to fill. That's how I'm regarding this time. You do what you like. Ring James, write to James, I just don't *care* any more. Come July, you can go back to our house and then we'll make a decision."

"About what? What do you mean?"

"About our future. Together or apart. I can't even think about it now. I'm too raw, too confused. All I know is, I love our children. I love you too but at the moment, I hate you and I can't think straight. The only way we're going to get through this time is to pretend – and that's what I'm going to do. Pretend. And now I'm going to sleep," and with that, he turned over, away from me.

I stared up at the shadowy propellor lurking above the bed, wishing it would fall.

*

Something happened to me when I woke up the next day; Luke was already up and I lay there thinking about what he'd said and decided I too was going to pretend. Sometimes pretending was good; if you pretend long and hard enough, the pretence can take on its own life and become the truth.

So, I got out of bed with renewed vigour and got the children ready for school. Luke left for work on foot, leaving me the car, so I dropped the children off at school and went out of the camp, my camera on the front seat. I was going to go where the mood took me for the morning.

I was going to impersonate someone having an ordinary day.

Chapter Six

And that's how the weeks and months passed at Akrotiri; Luke worked, the children went to school and played in the garden or on the beach and I learned new tricks with my camera, was a mother, read novels, wrote my diary, wrote letters to my parents, chatted to David on the phone and carried on as if my life was perfectly good.

To an outsider, I was living the dream: sunbathing, windsurfing and swimming, with hours spent on beaches. The Red Arrows came and went in April; I watched their displays with awe, never tiring of their speed and audacity. I made a point of positioning myself on the top of the cliffs at Dreamers, to watch them swoop and dive across the Mediterranean. The red planes darted across the sapphire seas and over the crystal cliffs – their smoke trails making temporary patterns in the sky and then dissipating, as if they'd never been. The heart shape they made daily only served to taunt me with hope but I was determined not to let the sadness of its daily disappearance affect me. All it was, was a phantom, a ghost.

I *did* speak to James, of course I did; I longed for his voice like a desert walker for water. We got into a routine of speaking at certain times in the week. I didn't hide it from Luke, I didn't need to, he simply wasn't interested but I didn't make a show of it, either.

James told me how he'd been posted to Abbey Wood in Bristol, a posting he dreaded: an office job of the utmost tedium. He'd be going at the end of June and would get a flat in the city. It would be deadly dull and the only way to get through it would be to do other things like music, running and riding his motorbike.

And … seeing me.

"At least we'll be near each other," he'd said. I was determined not to think about it.

All the other social events came round; I began to see how it was all just repeated – the never-ending cycle of formal Mess dinners, barbecues at people's house, wives' coffee mornings – just things to fill the void. Without Sam, without James, without Sophie, they'd lost their attraction. We went to a few of them; Luke drank too much, but I ignored that and to be truthful, I too started drinking far too much, drowning myself in gin and brandy sours to deaden the feelings that I'd had before, of living the wrong life.

We'd go together to these things but spent the evenings as far away from each other as was decently possible. It was amazing how easy it was to dupe everyone; we arrived together, as a seemingly happy couple and left together but what people didn't see was the complete lack of communication between us in the intervening hours.

At one such event, the hearty Wing Commander Reg, collared Luke and slapping him hard on the back said, "How's the *other* lovely lady in your life, Luke?"

"What are you on about, Reg? I couldn't cope with more than one woman, this one's trouble enough."

I felt myself bristle with both indignation and embarrassment.

"You know, Sam's wife. God, she's a stunner, that one. Won't be long till she's snapped up, that's for sure."

I couldn't believe how insensitive Reg was being; surely it wasn't politically correct to talk about a dead officer's wife like that? I hated the kind of 'old boys' banter that was common-place, so I answered for Luke.

"Sophie's gone back to the UK and is trying to pick up the pieces of her life. I'm sure she has no intention of being 'snapped up' by anyone, with her husband only being dead for a few months." I didn't make any attempt to soften my abrupt repost.

Reg was taken aback and Luke looked at me somewhat askance.

"I just wondered how she was," said Reg, his face reddening, more than normal. "She and your hubby seemed to get on so well ..."

"She asked Luke to accompany her to England and they became close ..." I said, surprising myself, sticking up for both Luke and Sophie.

"Yes, shame you had to go back to England over Christmas," said Reg.

"Anyway ... Reg, we've got to move on – someone's just bought me a drink and it's calling ..." said Luke, with his hand under my elbow, ushering my away.

"What the hell was all that about?" I said when we were out of earshot.

"Just Reg, stirring. He's got a reputation for it, didn't you know?"

"No, I didn't and quite frankly, he really annoyed me. And so did *you*. I didn't appreciate being referred to as 'trouble'."

"Well, I would've thought that was an understatement in the circumstances."

"Oh, shut up, Luke. I really didn't like the way that conversation was going. You and Sophie obviously gave the gossips something to talk about when I was gone."

"Not really. Don't listen to him."

I had to stop myself from confronting him about the boxers. I was going to bide my time.

"I'll be pleased to leave this do and Akrotiri, for that matter, if that's how it's going to be."

"Please yourself, you always do. Go home if you want, right now."

And that's how our conversations went a lot of the time. A stand-off between two bitterly opposed protagonists, with undercurrents of jealousy and antagonism thrown in.

*

In a bid to appear normal and make the most of our time in Cyprus, back in April, Luke had applied for a pass to the Turkish part of Cyprus. Sam and Sophie had gone and told us how wonderful it was, so we'd decided it would be a good half-term treat for the children. When the end of May came round, the holiday didn't seem quite so appealing – the four of us cooped up together with no distractions, filled me with horror. Still, I agreed that it would be good to see Northern Cyprus and show the children another culture.

We were going for three days; the weather was hot and so we took few clothes; all we'd need were shorts, t-shirts and swimming costumes. We arranged for the neighbours to feed the cat and water the indoor plants and we all piled our cases into the back of the Pajero. The kids were beside themselves with excitement, not knowing what to expect on 'the other side'.

Luke had been told how long it sometimes took to get through the border; he'd made sure he had all our documents and everything was in order, he didn't want any problems with officials. Although Sophie had told me a bit about the life over there, I really had no idea what it'd be like. I was excited to be getting right away from the enclosed life on the camp and to be seeing new places.

We made sure the children had plenty of things for the journey; it was easy to forget what a big island Cyprus was (over 9,000 square kilometres, the third biggest Mediterranean

Island, I'd read). The journey would be long and the children were never very good at sitting still, so we had a supply of books, games and tapes in the back of the car that would, hopefully, keep them occupied for a while. I also had a supply of sweets; bribery was always a last resort, but useful in these situations.

Before we reached Larnaca, we headed left inland towards Nicosia. The temperature gauge on the car dashboard began to creep up; without the sea breezes, this was going to be hot. From the comfort of the air-conditioned car, I looked out at the landscape; there was a shimmering haze, the far away mountain range peaked out through it like ghosts.

We began to approach the sprawling suburbs of Nicosia; I couldn't help thinking back to that day with Sophie when we went Christmas shopping. We hadn't really seen much of the city then, we'd been too absorbed with our thoughts and revelations. I wanted to 'see' the city this time, to observe its buildings, people and busy streets.

I was glad I wasn't driving; as we got more central, the traffic increased with cars pushing in and drivers using horns loudly and incessantly. Motorbikes weaved in and out of cars, cafés full of people sipping coffee in the shade slid by, shops with strange fashions passed in a blur. Luke was unfazed by the strange city and pressed on through the chaos, finding his way through narrow streets, until we got to the border crossing where we joined a long line of cars creeping slowly forward, as each one was allowed through.

After half and hour or so, we reached the officials who were checking documents. Luke had to get out and was taken into a shed-like building to fill in forms. My eyes were drawn to the picture hanging by the door. It was a map of Cyprus, but the part now known as the Turkish Republic of Northern Cyprus was coloured in red and the red was dripping, as if it was bleeding. It was a haunting image. Next to it were photographs of corpses and injured soldiers – I began to realise the significance of what had happened all those years ago. It was easy to live in our British haven in the south and be unaware of the island's troubled past. The Greeks certainly made sure that anybody going through the border was no longer ignorant.

The children were just getting annoyed and fractious, when Luke came back to the car. "Well, we can go through now, but they don't half make it difficult." Sweat was dripping down his face. "We're made me feel guilty for considering going through. There are lots of rules and one thing's for sure, we mustn't be late coming back."

He started the engine, driving slowly away. It was odd to think we were now in a different country, but in the same city. All around us were reminders of the past – areas of No Man's land with UN soldiers on lookout posts.

As Sophie had said, it felt different from the Greek side immediately; this was mainly to do with cars. We'd got used to everyone driving new, or nearly new, Japanese cars in the south; here our car was an anomaly. People stared at us as we drove past, unused to seeing a brand new four by four. The cars here seemed to be well-preserved, but very old Renaults and Fords; I began to feel self-conscious. The people themselves looked poorer, the buildings shabbier. How could the atmosphere be so different, just yards apart?

We drove out of the city and headed across the plains – vast swathes of flat land with acres of crops growing in abundance. There were now oases on the tarmac, which disappeared on approach, as the sun rose higher in the sky.

"Are we nearly there yet?" whined Charlie. His patience was just about at an end.

"How long do you think we'll be now, Luke?" I asked. We hadn't spoken much on the journey.

"I should think we'll be there in about half and hour, Buddy. You've been very good so far – just hang on a bit longer. Let's play I Spy."

That kept us occupied for a while and just when they were beginning to try to kick each other and argue, we entered the pristine, manicured surroundings of our hotel. It was on the outskirts of Kyrenia, known locally as Girne where we were staying two nights. It was a relief to get out of the car, but the heat slammed into us like a car crash as we opened the doors. The air-conditioning in the car had been icy and we'd temporarily forgotten the intensity of the temperature outside. Dragging our cases out of the back, we made our way to reception and registered.

What we were given was more like an apartment than a hotel room – there were two separate bedrooms, a sitting room and a small kitchen. It was luxurious and the children ran around touching everything and shouting their approval. I helped them unpack their bags, Luke made some tea and then we all sat on our balcony, overlooking the large pool below. It was decided that we'd all go for a swim to cool down and then go into Kyrenia for dinner.

It felt wonderful to slide into the cool, blue waters of the pool; it was warm enough for it to be pleasant, but cool enough to be refreshing. I lay back, my legs and arms spread, my head lying on the water, as if on a pillow. Luke was ploughing up the length doing an impressive crawl and the children were screaming and shouting with delight, jumping in and splashing each other. Our voices broke the almost church-like quiet of the beautiful gardens surrounding the pool and I felt sorry for the people lying on loungers, peacefully reading books. It was like a scene from a holiday advert: large groups of noisy sparrows chirruped in a tree, waiters carrying trays of drinks walked around delivering orders to supine sun worshippers and a small fountain tinkled lightly, reflecting diamonds of light from its surface. While the children played, I decided to follow Luke's lead and did some serious swimming; it was great to use my limbs again, after so long cooped up in the car.

The rhythm of my strokes and the regularity of the inhalation and exhalation of air, always comforted me and as I swam up and down, I reflected on my life. This could be the time to get back on track with Luke; nothing had worked so far, but here we were, the four of us, a family unit, away from everyone else; isolated and thrown together. Surely now we could reconnect? Surely now was the time to try to make a go of our marriage?

I determined that tonight, I would try to reach out to him, to find him again.

*

"God, this is absolutely stunning, isn't it?" I said. "You can hear how beautiful a place is a million times but you've got to experience it, haven't you?" I looked across at Luke, who smiled back.

It was dark and we were sitting at a restaurant in the half-moon curve of the harbour. Tables ranged along the edge of the water, with boats almost within touching distance. A road ran along beside the tables in front of the buildings, but no traffic went along it – just people, meandering slowly, some holding hands. A myriad of candles flickered in a line, following the shape of the harbour, street lights glowed, quiet music played. We could hear the clinking of glasses and the tap tap of the masts, as the hulls rocked gently. At the harbour entrance, the castle stood solid and proud, lit up against the night sky.

The children were tired from the long day of travel and fun in the pool and were content to sit still.

Luke said, "Why don't we order a meze?" He was reading the menu card, flicking the ash from his cigarette into an ashtray.

"What's a meze?" said Amy.

"Well, it's lots of little dishes – so if you don't like one thing, you can try the next. What do you think? Shall we?"

"Yes, let's. I'm fed up of always eating chips."

"You can eat chips as well, if you want."

"No … I'm going to try new things tonight," said Amy; she was growing up fast.

"Can I have chips?" said Charlie; he wasn't the most adventurous eater.

"Yes, of course you can, but try something else too," I said. I was feeling relaxed, happy even. I caught Luke's eye and we held each other's gaze for a second.

We duly ordered our meze and the little dishes just kept coming – olives, hummus, fish, chicken, rice, bowls of salad, pitta bread, all washed down with large brandy sours for us and lemonade for the children. The sea breeze picked up a little, but it was still warm; I put my cardigan over my shoulders.

"So what do you think of Turkish Cyprus, kids?"

We'd all eaten huge amounts of food and were sitting back, letting it all go down.

"I like it," said Amy. "Can we live here instead? I don't want to go back to England."

Luke and I looked at each other. A sadness rose up from the pit of my stomach and I said, "Well, it'd be lovely, Amy, but we have to go home sometime. You know you've got to go to big school. It'll be nice to be back in our house. Can you remember it?"

"Of course I can. But I still don't want to go back. I like living by the sea and our house is nowhere near the sea. I like living in a sunny place."

She was expressing what we were all thinking. This time in Cyprus was slowly coming to an end. Very soon, in three months, we'd be leaving for the UK and life would be different.

"What will you do with the car and the boat, Luke? Would you ever think about taking them back home?"

"I'm going to look into the cost. Diesel in England is so much more expensive. Even if we managed to get them on a flight for nothing, the cost of running them both back home would be horrendous."

"It'd be nice for you though, to have the boat, at least." I smiled at him again, wanting him to be happy.

"Yea, maybe." He stared out to sea; I could see him clenching his jaw, the tight ridges rising and falling in his cheek. "Let's pay the bill and go for a walk along the harbour to the castle. Walk off some of this food."

As we walked along the kids ran ahead, happy to be allowed up so late in the dark. The two of us ambled together and without thinking, I put my arm through his, as we used to. He didn't flinch, neither did he react.

We walked on in silence.

"It's been a lovely evening, Luke. Thank you for arranging this holiday. I think it's just what we needed, don't you?"

"I think the kids are having a great time, and that's the main thing."

I looked up at him and said gently, "I'm happy."

"Good," he said, looking ahead.

"Are you?"

"If happiness can be defined as being content at one moment in time," he said, "without a future or a past, then yes, I'm happy. Now. I can't say anything else."

"Maybe that's all that matters …" I said and squeezed his arm.

*

Even though it was a short journey back to the hotel, Charlie fell asleep and had to be lifted out of the car. He stayed flat out while we undressed him and put him to bed, his face still dirty. We stood together, looking down at him; he was lying on his side, his thumb in his mouth (we'd tried everything to stop him sucking his thumb, but nothing worked); his hair was long and his fringe was over his closed eyes, his long eyelashes peeping out. The room was dark, except for the light coming in from the sitting room.

"Do I have to go to bed too?" whispered Amy. "I'm a lot older than him and I'm not tired."

We agreed she could stay up for half an hour; we all sat on the sofa, Amy between us, and turned on the TV. Flicking through the channels, we found a re-run of the 'Sound of Music'. It was in English with Turkish subtitles, so we watched that. Amy and I sang along to 'I am Sixteen', trying not to wake Charlie. It was Luke's idea of hell but as there was nothing else in English, he sat and watched it too.

Sam came bounding into my mind. I saw us dancing down the road to 'I Could Have Danced All Night' and felt a longing I'd almost forgotten. How I'd love to be with him again. I still found it impossible to believe he was dead. It was too final, too awful. Surely he would one day walk back into the room with "Hello Ginge" and throw me over his shoulder? I thought of that day when I threw water at him on the beach; he'd been lying on the sand, sunbathing and when I'd tipped the bucket over him, he'd chased me into the sea.

Luke, despite his hatred of musicals must have been thinking of Sam too.

He said, "Sam would've enjoyed this."

It was as if our minds had touched each other, as if, just for a short time, everything we'd both done had been forgotten and we were reaching out to each other.

"I was just thinking the same thing," I said, looking across at him.

"I remember Sam – he was always singing, wasn't he?" said Amy. She paused for a while and then she turned to me and said, "Do you think Sophie will ever marry another man, Mum?"

"Well, I hope so, but not yet. It takes a long time to get over something like that, but I'm sure she'll find someone in the end. Sam wouldn't want her to be lonely, would he?"

"No. I think Sam would want her to get married and have babies."

The simplicity of her statement hung in the air. Would Sophie ever be able to have babies now? Her maternal clock was ticking.

Wanting to move away from the subject that somehow affected us all, I said, "Right, it's time for bed. Go and do your teeth and I'll come and tuck you in."

Amy stood up and went to the bathroom. The gap where she'd been gaped between us and I stood up too to divert attention away from it.

"What shall we do tomorrow?" I said as I walked towards the kitchen to make coffee.

"I thought we'd go to St Hilarion and climb to the top," said Luke.

"Great idea. I've seen pictures – it looks amazing." It would be a long, hard climb.

Avoiding any deeper conversation than this had become the norm. We both knew that it was superficial, trivial stuff, but anything else was too difficult.

I went to tuck Amy in and came back with the coffee; we drank it in companionable silence, watching the end of the film. Luke was half watching, half reading a thriller he'd bought; I sometimes stole glances at him. His face was the same face I'd fallen for all those years ago – why did he feel like a stranger now? I wanted to recapture those feelings I'd had for him, I really did. I wanted to wipe James from my mind, to reignite our marriage. This was crazy; we were like two lost souls, like birds that mate for life, but who had been separated by the wind and weather and couldn't find each other. I wanted to call for him across the plains, for him to answer me, to come flying back to me.

I'd call to him tonight; tonight I would try to make love to him. If he rejected me, so be it … but I'd try.

"I'm going to bed. Are you coming?" I said, as casually as I could.

"Yea, I'll be in, in a minute. I just want to finish this chapter." He didn't look at me.

"Okay. See you in a minute."

I undressed and got into bed. I tried to read, but couldn't

concentrate. Turning off the bedside light, I lay on my side, trying to remember the last time we'd had any physical contact. It was before Christmas, before the big row when everything went wrong.

After about fifteen minutes, I heard him walking around, switching off the TV and the lights and then the door opened. He undressed in the dark and lifting the duvet, got into bed. We lay still; I was facing him. I hardly dared move. I couldn't tell whether he was facing me or not, it was so dark but I was sure he was facing away.

I reached forward with my right hand, as silently as I could, to see how near he was. My fingers touched his back and having got that far, I decided I couldn't back off, so I let my hand rest on his ribs. I let it stay there, not moving, wondering whether he'd move further away, so that my hand would fall away … but he didn't, he let it rest there. I could hear him breathing; my own heartbeat pumped in my ears. I let my fingers move slightly and I felt the undulations of his ribcage. There was a wide gap still between us, my arm was at full stretch.

Inching forward, I curved myself, spoon-like, around his body, my right arm moving round his stomach. He took my hand and pulled it upwards, so that my arm was now encasing him. We lay like this for a few minutes, our body heat meeting and melding together, our legs following each other's contours.

"I'm sorry," I said. The room was absolutely silent and my voice cut the emptiness with the accuracy of a Stanley knife.

He didn't say anything, but he turned his body so that he was facing me. I could feel his breath on my face, his hand was still holding mine.

"Luke, did you hear me?" I said. "I'm sorry."

"I know you are."

"How can I make you believe me?"

"I believe you … but it doesn't make it any easier. You hurt me too much."

He let go of my hand and putting his hand behind my head, he pulled my mouth to his. He kissed me aggressively and with such force, that all the worries I'd had about rejection dissipated; I knew it would be all right. I kissed him back, finding all the passion I used to feel. We kissed for a long time, our mouths locked together, our tongues touching. Before all this had happened, we didn't often kiss when we made love; it had become mechanical and routine, but now, it felt new and exciting ... but dangerous.

It was as if we were on a life raft being buffeted in a storm of terrible proportions; we were clinging to its ropes for fear of falling off and drowning in the depths of the ocean. We made love passionately as if it was the first time; there was an element of desperation too – our lives depended on this simple act.

We lay back after, exhausted, overwhelmed by the physical act that had at last reunited us.

Was it enough?

"Can you *ever* forgive me, Luke?"

"I don't think that's what the problem is."

"What do you mean?"

"I mean, you love me, I know you do. But I'm not enough for you any more."

"Luke ... didn't you see, tonight? You *are* enough ..."

"I may be enough tonight, but, if James was here, who would you choose?"

I couldn't answer, I knew I couldn't.

"Can't we just deal with tonight? As you said, *now* is what matters. Now, you *are* enough, Luke. Now, I love you. Now, you love me. *Now* is all that matters."

"You didn't answer my question. Who would you choose?"

"I choose the children. And if I choose the children, I choose *you*. You know that."

He turned away. "I'm going to sleep."

"Good night."

I turned towards him, curved my body around him, placed my hand on his ribcage.

He didn't take my hand.

*

When I woke up, we weren't entwined in each other's arms, as often happened in the past when we'd made love; we were right on our own sides of the bed, as if our bodies didn't want to touch. I opened my eyes and looked at Luke's head on the pillow. He seemed vulnerable in sleep, I wanted to roll into him and put my arms around him and protect him.

But I didn't ... I couldn't. The space in the bed was too large.

I got up and went into the little kitchenette to make some tea. There was no sound from the children's room, so I took the two mugs back to our bedroom, placing Luke's on his side of the bed.

He stirred and grunted and I said, "Tea," but he didn't respond.

I propped myself against my pillows, sipping the tea. After a few minutes, Luke sat up and reached for his cup.

I turned to him and said, "How are you feeling this morning? Do you hate me?"

"No, you know I don't hate you. I just wished you loved me ... and only me. Were you imagining I was James, last night? Is that how it is for you now?"

"For God's sake, Luke ... I was making love to *you*, not James. How could you say that?"

"You know why ..."

"Look, we're here ... together. Let's just *be* together ... please?"

"It's hard. The moment I woke up I thought of you and him, you and him rolling around together ... it makes me feel physically sick. I can't get the picture out of my head."

"Well, I've been seeing a picture in *my* head recently, if you must know."

"What do you mean by that?"

"When I was clearing out the maid's room after Sophie left, I found your blue boxers – they fell out when I turned the mattress. You both categorically denied that anything happened ..."

I looked at his face; at least he had the decency to look embarrassed. I hadn't meant to bring it up but ...

"It didn't ..."

"Don't deny it, Luke, give me some credit ... "

"What I was going to say, if you'd let me finish, was it didn't mean anything." He looked at me with such sad eyes, I felt sorry for him.

"So you're admitting it? You seem to be making lying to me rather a habit, aren't you?"

All the bitterness about the vasectomy came back. Surely now he could see that we were as bad as each other? I'd slept with James, he'd slept with Sophie.

We were quits.

I didn't blame Sophie, somehow.

"Look, I didn't tell you because ... because it was just mean-ingless. We were like two friends, that was all. You were gone, Sam was gone ..."

"You've always fancied Sophie, I know you have. You just waited till I was out of the way ..."

"That's unfair ... *you* left me."

"You told me to go."

We looked at each other. The fact that we were sitting in bed together, holding mugs of tea, was not lost on me; it was ironic, funny even. We were bickering like children – you said this, you did that.

The door opened and Charlie came in.

"Can I get into your bed, like I used to when I was little?" said Charlie.

"Of course, Buddy," said Luke and Charlie jumped on the bed, like an excitable puppy. He did a forward roll between us and ended up facing the headboard. Turning around and lying down, legs straight out, he said, "Can we have a diving competition today? I'm much better than Amy."

"I'm sure we can. We're also going right to the top of a very high castle. We'll do that first and then come back and swim," said Luke. He smiled down at Charlie, ruffling his hair. His eyes caught mine. Charlie had single-handedly changed the atmosphere in the room and made our argument seem pointless and nasty.

"Charlie, go and wake your sister and get dressed," I said. "We want to get an early start." He bounced off the bed and was gone through the door, like a sprint runner.

We looked at each other and it was as if we both knew what the other was thinking. Charlie's intervention had worked.

"Let's enjoy today," I said.

Luke got out of bed and strolled towards the bathroom.

"Let's try," he said.

Chapter Seven

"How long are we going to be in the car?" asked Amy as we climbed in. "It's not going to be ages, is it? I'm fed up of driving."

"Yea, so am I. Why are we going to this place, anyway?" said Charlie.

"It's not far, Amy and the reason we're going is because it's going to be fantastic," said Luke.

"How do you know, if you've never been there?" said Amy, grumpily.

"I've read about it. It's called St Hilarion and Walt Disney is meant to have based Sleeping Beauty's castle on it." At the mention of one of their favourite films, the children started taking more interest.

"Hope you're feeling energetic – there are about four hundred and sixty steps to the top and you're about two thousand feet above sea level. It's going to be a real adventure, so sit tight and we'll be there soon." The kids were excited now and chatted happily in the back.

I began to wonder if I had the energy for the climb. It was hot already and the thought of all those steps made my legs feel weak. It would certainly be a distraction from the morning's conversation though and that's what we both needed. I'd seen pictures of the castle; I told myself that this is what I wanted to do in Cyprus – to see the sights, to experience the history, first hand.

As we approached the mountain that grew out of the ground like a huge stalagmite, I could just make out the castle structure winding its way around it. It looked as if it was part of the mountain itself and towered above us. This was going to be a long climb. The children leant out of the windows, looking up with both amazement and awe. There were a few other people in the car park but considering how truly spectacular it looked, even from here, it was strange for it not to be crowded with tourists.

We began the long, slow climb; the first steps were easy and the children skipped up them with birdlike lightness. I could tell it wouldn't be like a British site from the point of view of safety; there were a few hand rails but there were also lots of places where the children could stray from the path and plummet over the edge. The steps were uneven and often slippery.

"Stay with us, you two. Don't run ahead and keep to the path!" I shouted between breaths.

"Don't worry, they'll be fine. Let them run on, if they want to." Luke was always so much more relaxed than me. The moment there was some element of danger where the kids were concerned, I became like a clucky mother hen. I couldn't stop myself. I decided this was going to be one place where I'd have to trust Luke and them not to do anything stupid, otherwise I'd be a nervous wreck the whole way up.

Occasionally, we crossed paths with people coming back down. We'd exchange pleasantries and the passers-by would say things like, "Keep going! Not far now!" "The views are magnificent!" and "Only another two hundred steps to go!" Even the kids were slowing down and asking for sips of water, which Luke was carrying in a rucksack. We had a rest when we reached the middle part; the castle was divided into three distinct areas. There was a tiny shop here and we wondered how the person who worked there could possibly climb those steps everyday. My calves were aching already and my thigh muscles … I wasn't as fit as I thought I was.

The children recovered quickly in the shade and were anxious to get going again. Pulling me by the hand, Amy said, "Come on, Mum. Don't be lazy."

As I stood up, I couldn't get out of my head the idea that this climb was like my situation with Luke – climbing, climbing, feeling as if I was on a never-ending path of hazardous steps. That's what comes from being an English teacher: the ability to see poetic comparisons in things.

The final stage got steeper and steeper. There were parts where my heart was beating, not from the climb, but from the sheer drops on either side and the possibilities for the children to fall; safety seemed to become less and less apparent as we got higher, instead of the other way around.

Eventually, we got to the very top and we looked out across the vista below us. It was covered in a light heat haze; the coastline meandered below like a map – we were so high, it was as if we were viewing it from a plane. The blue of the sea and the sapphire of the sky merged; it was almost impossible to see where one stopped and the other began. The craggy cliffs and promontories around us gave the view some perspective; I tried to feature them in the many photos I took. My pictures wouldn't do the view justice; it would be impossible to convey the magnitude of the scene on a piece of photographic paper.

"Wow – that was certainly worth the climb, wasn't it, kids?" I said. "Are you pleased we came? Charlie, stand still. Please stop jumping around, you're giving me a heart attack every time you do it."

"Don't worry, Mum, I'm fine," he said, deliberately hanging over the edge of a particularly sharp drop. I felt a shooting pain down my legs as I saw the depths below. How come it almost felt like you wanted to throw yourself off and at the same time, felt sick with fear at the height of it? I grabbed him by the arm. I wasn't sure I could take much more of it.

Trying to keep my voice calm, I said, "It would be a shame if you fell off, Charlie. You'd miss out on the lunch we've got planned. Let's make our way down again."

"Before we go, let's ask that guy over there to take a picture of us all at the top. That would be one for the family album," said Luke. He walked over to the man, who turned out to be German; we gathered together, Luke put his arm around my shoulders and the kids stood either side of us, with the view behind us. As the German tourist fiddled with the camera, I turned my head to Luke and placed my arm round his waist. He smiled at me, the warmest smile I'd seen for many weeks. I was still burning hot from the climb but more heat rushed through my body.

"This has been great for all of us, hasn't it?" I said, squeezing him.

"Certainly a day we'll all remember … everyone say Cheese, then."

*

After the long trek down, which seemed oddly worse than going up (the pressure on my thighs, shins, calves, back … everything) we made our way to a taverna where we ate ravenously. Never had barbecued chicken and salad tasted so good.

The afternoon was full of diving lessons, family relay races and finally the promised diving competition where, Charlie and Amy got equal scores from the judges; neither of them were very good losers.

We cooked in our apartment that night and the children were so exhausted, they fell into bed as soon as we'd eaten, with no complaints. Luke and I watched the only thing in English we could find on the TV and drank a bottle of Cypriot wine.

The climb, the games, the sun and the alcohol combined to make us both feel relaxed. We went to bed and fell straight to sleep.

*

Our third and final day in Northern Cyprus was equally successful, if a little more fraught with danger, although I didn't know that until afterwards. We went to Bellapais and wandered around the beautiful Abbey, a twelfth century monastery, set on the side of a mountain. The Gothic architecture with its arches, cloisters and courtyards didn't hold the children's attention as the castle had, but they ran around, chasing each other and generally disturbing the peace (indeed, the name means 'Abbey of Peace'– rather lost on the younger ones of the party).

We found a lovely taverna nearby and sat down to a meal of sea bream, salad and ice cream. While we were sipping our coffee, the children went off to play. They were gone for rather a long time, so I went to investigate. I could hear their voices which appeared to be coming from the top of a high wall.

Following the steps leading up to the top, my heart stopped as I saw what they were doing. Oblivious to the danger, they were both jumping over a gap in the stone, through which they could have fallen to their deaths. Not only that, there was a sheer drop on one side, with absolutely nothing to keep them safe and back from the edge. My instinct was to shout, but didn't want to alarm them, so I said, as calmly as I could, "Hey, there you are. Will you come down now?" my voice trembling in my ears.

"We just want to jump one more ..." said Charlie, preparing himself for another go.

"Yea, we're having fun ..." said Amy. "One more!"

"No! It's time to go now," I said, moving forward to try to gather them up. For once, they did what they were told and dragging their feet, came towards me. When they were with me I said, "Did you realise how dangerous that was? There was nothing between you and hundreds of feet ..."

"Yes, we realised," said Amy, " but that's what made it fun." Her bright little face was lit up.

"Come on, Dad's waiting for us. It's time to head on back to the camp now." My legs suddenly felt so weak, I had to sit down. I hadn't noticed on the way up the stairs that there were no handrails, I'd been so intent on getting up to the top to see what they were doing, I'd bent forward and used the next step to steady me. Going down, was impossibly difficult now; nothing to hang on to, drops each side and wobbly legs. The children skipped down in front of me without a care in the world, while I came down on my bottom.

"Are you all right?" asked Luke. "You're as white as a sheet."

"Yea, I'm okay but I feel a bit sick ..."

"Why? What were they doing up there?"

"You don't want to know. Let's put it this way, if we'd known, we'd never have let them go up there."

As we made our way back along the road to the car park, I thought about the other time when the children had caused me to feel like this, when the land around the house caught fire and I couldn't find them. Being a mother was one long series of incidents where you'd do anything, *anything* to save your children, but at the same time, you felt helpless in the face of ... life.

I thought of the future, when I would have to let them go out with friends at night, for the first time; to go in a car driven by another teenager; to go to parties; to leave home and go away to university. I inwardly shuddered at the road we were on, when I'd have less and less control over their movements. Both the fire and wall incidents, here in Cyprus, I could blame on bad parenting; I was too wound up with James to take an interest in where the children were going when they left the house, all those months ago; too relaxed, too intent on staying comfortably at the table here in Bellapais, to notice where the children were running off to. Soon, however, I wouldn't even be able to take responsibility for their actions; I wouldn't be able to blame myself or Luke for their brushes with danger. It would be all their own choices, their control.

We made our way back across the plains to Nicosia, back through border control and back along the motorway towards Paphos. The car was quiet; it seemed we were all content to listen to the radio and think our own thoughts.

When I turned to look at them, the children were fast asleep. The three day break had worn them out.

We'd been together as a family, away from everyone. We'd survived a few dangers, we'd laughed together, played together.

Surely there was a chance that we could stay together?

Chapter Eight

The children went back to school for the last time in Akrotiri; it was hard to take in that the next time I sent them off, it would be back in the Cotswolds.

Back home in the quarter, Northern Cyprus now a memory, our lives continued as before. There was a distance between Luke and I that couldn't be filled by children's laughter; we functioned as a couple, only so far as we had breakfast and supper together. The sex that night was a one-off event; neither of us made a move again and Luke took to going to bed late, having drunk too much red wine and often ended up in the maid's room. The first time he did this, I asked him why. He mumbled some excuse about not wanting to wake me, but after that, I didn't bother and he didn't make any excuses.

One day at the beginning of June, I took the children down to ARABS for the afternoon, Luke choosing to stay at home and 'sort out his paperwork' whatever that was. The children met up with some classmates and I lay in my normal place, on a sun bed I'd brought down with me. It was two o'clock and the sun was high.

Having spent so long on the island, I was getting sick of the relentless heat. I knew it was foolish and that when I got back to grey, cold England I'd regret feeling this way, but that was how it was. I thought with longing of the variety of weather in the Cotswolds: the drizzle, the sleet, the wind, the snow, the cool spring sunshine, the showers, the blustery, dull days. Every day was the same here: heat, blue skies, no clouds – relentless heat, heat, heat. I was beginning to think my skin would shrivel and die; I'd never been so brown, but it had its consequences. When we lived in England, I yearned for the sun; Jen wouldn't believe it if I told my how I was feeling now.

I lay under a sunshade on my stomach, reading Sebastian Faulk's novel, 'Birdsong'. I loved it the moment I'd started it and I knew it was one of those books that I wouldn't want to finish. I'd found it in the only good bookshop in Limassol; the beach and the heat now disappeared as I fell back into its atmosphere and story. Glancing up occasionally, I'd check on the children but they were playing happily a little way away.

I read the line 'But you must live your own life eventually. You have one chance only.'

I suddenly felt such a longing to see James, my body ached. Is he my one chance of happiness? How I'd love it if he walked out of the sea right now, a male Aphrodite, brought to me, not on a shell, but on a windsurfer; I could see him …his red trunks, his tattoo, his smiling eyes, his dark hair, water dripping down his face in shimmering droplets. I looked up. He wasn't there of course but it was as if I could touch him.

A ghost-like figure emerging through the heat haze.

To distract myself from my daydream, I turned my head to the right towards the sailing club and sitting nearby, under another sunshade was a young girl with a baby. She cut a lonely figure, cradling the small baby in her arms, gently rocking it as she stared out to sea. I thought how difficult it must be to have a baby in these temperatures.

The girl, at that moment, turned her head; we smiled briefly at each other and I raised my hand in a half-hearted wave. She turned back to her baby.

There was something about her that made me want to go over and speak to her. I never did that sort of thing normally;

I was reticent to put myself in a position where I might be rejected but something about her made me want to befriend her.

I got up and went the few steps required to stand by her.

"Hi there. I saw you … your baby's so tiny … how old is it?" I was aware of calling the baby 'it' but it was hard to tell whether it was a boy or a girl. "I'm Emily, by the way."

The girl turned again and on a closer look, I realised how young she was. She couldn't be more than twenty-three or four. Her eyes were sad; she smiled and said, "She's two months old. Her name's Grace."

I bent my knees to get a clearer look and reached forward to touch the baby's cheek. "She's gorgeous," I said. "Was she born here, on the camp?" The baby was indeed a cherubic vision – round, rosy cheeks, long white eyelashes and a shock of auburn hair.

"Yes, she was."

"How was the birth?"

"A long labour but …"

"How are you feeling now? Have you recovered?" I was still crouching by her side, so I sat down on the sand next to her. I wanted to ask all the questions that a recent birth experience demands.

"Yes, sort of …" she said and looked away; I was sure she was trying not to cry.

"Is she sleeping at night?"

"No, not really."

This was hard work – the girl wasn't going to engage in a conversation, but still I persisted.

"What's your name, by the way?"

"Bethany … Bethany Hughes."

"How long have you been at Akrotiri?"

"I came out when I was six months pregnant. I hate it here."

Her bald statement shocked me. I'd heard about people who didn't like the life, but had never met anyone like her before.

I'd always scoffed at the idea of people not liking it; how could they *not* enjoy this life of sea, sun and enforced indolence? But seeing Bethany, so young and so alone, despite the baby, sitting on a beach in temperatures of twenty-eight degrees or more, I began to see how lucky I'd been to have children the age they were. With a baby, I wouldn't have been able to do any of the things I'd done.

Was Luke right about the third baby I'd wanted? He'd said he was acting in my best interests when he'd had the vasectomy. Then I looked at Grace again and anger seared through my veins.

"Oh dear. Why do you hate it?"

"I miss my family back home. Gary's always working and when he's not, he's with his mates in the bar, getting pissed on cheap booze. And I don't have any friends." Her eyes filled with tears; she had a pretty, round face with grey eyes and her hair was a wonderful burnished gold colour, long and wavy. She wasn't traditionally beautiful, but had something that made you want to look at her.

She brushed her tears away, shook her head as if to stop herself crying and said, "Sometimes, I wish I'd never had her." She looked out to sea and then down at the baby.

Grace started to cry at that moment and Bethany stood up, put her on her shoulder and started bouncing up and down, up and down.

"She never stops crying," she said with desperation in her voice. "I don't know what's wrong with her. Why won't she stop? I feel so useless." She looked at me almost pleadingly.

"Are you feeding her yourself?"

"I tried but I gave up in the end. Now she gulps her bottle and often projectile vomits it all back up. I don't know what to do. I wish babies could tell you what they wanted. How are we meant to know?" Her face was contorted. "I only came down here to get out of the house. A beach is a stupid place to be."

I remembered feeling just the same. Charlie, particularly,

was so difficult to feed at a similar age and all he did was bawl. At least I had support – Mum and Dad, David, Jen, Luke – I had a fantastic circle of people who helped me all the time. What would it have been like if I'd been here? I thought back to how isolated, lonely and downright depressed I'd felt in those early days on the camp too. Imagine if I'd been feeling like that *and* had a baby to deal with?

"May I hold her?" I asked, stretching out my arms.

"Do …" said Bethany, handing over the little bundle. I took her and was amazed how light she felt; I was so used to picking up Charlie and Amy, who now felt like giants compared to Grace; she felt as if she might float away.

The baby carried on crying and I did what I'd done with Charlie, I put her face down on my arm, with her arms and legs each side and bounced up and down, bending my knees. It seemed the most natural thing to do and whether it was that or simply the novelty of the position, Grace stopped crying.

"How did you do that?" said Bethany.

"It's just something I used to do when Charlie was little. I think the pressure on the stomach helps."

"I've never even tried that. You see … I need *help*. I don't know what I'm doing."

"I'm sure you do. You're her mother … and that's all she needs."

I lifted her from that position and cradled the baby in my arms. I could smell that wonderful smell that only babies have; I breathed it in, my miscarried baby coming to me out of the past. I saw my own imagined baby clearly now and it was as if I was holding him; he hadn't died, he was here, right now.

For a moment I was lost in my fantasy but soon I was back on the beach with this stranger. The baby started crying again.

"Have you got a bottle here?"

Bethany reached into a bag and offered me the bottle.

"Would you like to feed her?"

"I'd love to."

I took the bottle and placing the teat in the baby's mouth, I watched as Grace sucked hard. She did indeed gulp and feed too quickly, so after a short while, I took the teat out and sat the baby up and rubbed her back vigourously. She did a loud burp.

"That's a good girl," I said, stroking her back again.

"Do you think I should stop her, like you did? She always seems so hungry, I let her go on."

"I don't know, maybe … just try different things. I know it's hard, but try to be confident. *You* know what's best for your baby. Don't follow any rules you've been told. Follow your instinct."

It was easy to say, but harder to do. I could remember all those books I'd read when I was pregnant and how difficult it was to ignore their warnings.

I handed Grace back and Bethany started feeding her again. She settled down and fed quietly for a while and we smiled at each other.

"Call me Beth, by the way. That's what my family call me."

"Where do you live, Beth? I could come and visit."

"In the Airmen's quarters."

"Well, if you'd like, I'll come round tomorrow for a coffee." It was a gamble – would Beth want me to come? I remembered how great it was to meet Sophie and how it changed my life. Perhaps I could help Beth and Grace.

"Yes, I'd like that. How about 11? I can't guarantee that we'll get any peace, she's got absolutely no routine, but you never know, we may be lucky …"

"Okay. That's a date. I better go and find my two."

"I wish Grace was old enough to enjoy it here."

"Well, we've had our ups and downs, but you're right, it's a lot easier than having a baby. Maybe I could babysit for you one evening and you and Gary could go out together?"

"That's kind, but I'm not sure …"

"Well, maybe sometime in the future. There's no rush."

"Thank you."

We said our goodbyes, I got the address and I walked away towards the children.

*

I walked round to Beth's house the next day; it took me a long time – I'd forgotten how big the camp was and didn't often come down this way. The airmen's quarters were in a completely different part of the camp and this was the first time I'd have ever gone inside one. I still hated this segregation of ranks, but this is how the Air Force operated. It was no worse than different areas of my village in the Cotswolds but it was more marked here.

The houses were all attached and smaller than ours; I found the one I was looking for and knocked on the door. After a few seconds, I could hear movement and Beth opened the door; she looked tired and her naturally pale complexion looked even paler than yesterday. We exchanged greetings and I was shown into the kitchen. It was messy, with stuff everywhere and piles of washing up in the sink.

"Is Grace asleep? It's all very quiet," I said.

"I've just got her down. I've been feeding her for the last hour; she finally gave in and fell asleep. I kept stopping her so she wouldn't throw it all back up again. Your method seems to work. She's upstairs. Coffee?"

"I'd love one. So … we can have a good chat, hopefully."

Beth made a couple of mugs of coffee and we went into the sitting room, again cluttered with everything to do with the baby: empty bottles, nappies, talcum powder, scattered everywhere. I moved a teddy off a seat to sit down.

"How was last night? Did you get any sleep?"

I smiled encouragingly across at Beth, who didn't smile back. She rubbed her eyes and pulled her hair back off her face into a pony tail in her hands.

"I was awake at eleven, two, four and six. Gary's going mental. So am I."

"Does Gary get up at all?"

"Gary? You must be joking. He's never changed a nappy, even. He wouldn't have a clue."

"So, you do everything?"

"Yes, just about. Gary's out on patrol all the time or with his mates and when he comes back he's either pissed, knackered or …"

"He's Regiment, then, is he?"

"Yes. He's bored most of the time here, so he drinks … what does your husband do?"

The whole officer versus airmen thing embarrassed me. I'd been dreading having this conversation. "He's in ops here, but he's a pilot …"

"Oh … how long have you been here?"

"We've been here a long time – I'm going back to the UK soon."

Beth looked across at me and the realisation that any friendship would be short-lived, registered on her face. She said, "Where are you going back to?"

"We've got a cottage in the Cotswolds; I think Luke's going back to the same camp we were at before. What about you? Where are you from?"

"Until I came here, I'd lived in Cornwall all my life. My Dad's a fisherman in Padstow and my Mum runs a little shop on the harbour."

"How lucky are you! We go to Cornwall every year. We know Padstow really well. What did you do before Grace?"

"Not a lot. I didn't do very well at school – that's where I met Gary – I left school at sixteen and worked in shops in the summer and cleaned houses in the winter. Every spare minute I had I was in the sea, surfing …"

"Wow, I'm so jealous … we just belly board when we go down – do you do proper, stand-up surfing?"

"Yes. I love it. It's my life."

"You must miss it here."

"Yea ... I haven't done it for so long, I'll probably have forgotten ..."

"Of course you won't. It's like riding a bicycle. Does Gary surf?"

"God, no. He hates the sea."

"That's a shame when you live in Cornwall."

"He's just into football, that's all. Here I am, with my board." She handed me a photograph: Beth was standing with the Atlantic rollers in the background, holding her board that was considerably longer than her. She was wearing a wetsuit and her hair was in wet tendrils, framing her face. She was smiling broadly into the camera; I hadn't seen her smile like that at all.

"I'd just won a competition at Watergate – it was so brilliant. I wish I could go back. I'm not sure I can stand two and half more years out here. If Gary carries on the way he's going, I'm going home."

I didn't know what to say. I didn't want to encourage her to leave her husband, but I wondered how she'd cope here with no help.

"Didn't you meet anyone when you had Grace in the hospital? What about mother and baby groups? There must be some, surely?"

"I met an older mum when I had Grace and I've been to a couple of groups, but all the babies were crying, the noise was awful. I met a girl called Sadie who lives down the road and we sometimes get together but ... I haven't met anyone I can really talk to. Sadie's all right but ..."

"Well, I know I'm going back soon, but maybe we can get together?"

"I'd like that."

"We could go out and about and I could show you some of the local sites. Have you been off the camp?"

"Not yet, no. I haven't been anywhere – Gary's not interested and it all seems too difficult with Grace in tow."

"We'll do that, then. I'll get the car one day this week and I'll take you and Grace to Curium. We'll take my kids too. I'll help you with Grace and you can have a bit of a break. There are sometimes little waves at Curium; I could look after Grace and you could have a body surf. It won't be like Cornwall, but it'll be fun."

We heard a short muffled cry from upstairs.

"Here we go again," said Beth, with a look on her face of resignation. "I wonder what she wants this time?"

"Babies are hard work, aren't they?" I laughed. "Why don't you go and sort her out and I'll make a start on the washing up? I can remember what it's like – there never seems to be enough time to do any housework, does there?"

"I couldn't ask you to do …"

"You didn't ask me, I offered. Go on, I'll make a start."

I remembered Mum and Dad coming to stay when Amy was small; they did all the mundane household chores like cleaning, washing and cooking, leaving me to deal with the baby. I was so lucky, I realised now.

I made a start in the kitchen. Beth came down a few minutes later, we heated up the bottle of milk and she settled down to feed Grace, sitting at the kitchen table. I carried on washing up.

"So … how about you? Have you enjoyed your stay here?" said Beth.

I thought about this – had I enjoyed it? 'Enjoyment' was rather a bland word for the kind of experience I'd had here. It had been a life-changing, mind-blowing, heart-stopping, gut-wrenching time but I wasn't going to go into details now. Maybe in the future, if it was appropriate.

"Yes, I have. I have to admit I didn't at first, I felt like you do now, except I didn't have a baby. It was like I was a fish out of water; I hadn't lived on a camp for years and I was so lonely. The men don't understand, do they? They just think they can drag you halfway across the world and everything will be hunky-dory. It's easy for them, they have a job and a ready-made circle of friends."

"I thought it would be better for you officer lot somehow?"

"Not really. Maybe it's okay if you like socialising with the wives at coffee mornings and arranging flowers in the Mess, but it just wasn't my scene at all. Everything changed for me when I joined a windsurfing class. I loved the sport and I met a girl called Sophie, who became a really good friend. Everything changed then ..."

"Is she still here? Sophie, I mean?"

"No ... her husband was killed in a helicopter." I stopped what I was doing and gazed out of the window.

"Oh my God, that's terrible. It puts my life into perspective. Are you still in touch?"

"We supported her a lot after Sam's death, but she had to go home in the end. It all got a bit complicated though, as you can imagine." I didn't want to tell her; I'd learnt my lesson about putting too much onto a new friendship with Sophie.

I thought about Sam and tears sprung from nowhere. I wiped them away and Beth said, "It must have been awful. I can't imagine ..."

We lapsed into silence; there was just the sound of Grace drinking milk.

I finished washing up and then dried it all, piling the clean crockery on the side. It was satisfying. I felt as if I was really helping someone for a change, instead of constantly thinking about myself.

I suggested Thursday afternoon for our outing and said I'd collect her around two o'clock.

"Thank you so much," said Beth. "Are you sure? It might be a disaster, she might cry the whole time ..."

"It'll be fine. Amy will love looking after her, and so will I."

Chapter Nine

Beth sat in the back with Grace on her lap, next to Amy. Charlie sat proudly in the front. Amy kept up a constant chat with Beth, asking all about Grace. Beth looked noticeably brighter today and that smile I'd seen in the photo kept appearing.

"Are you going to take Grace in the sea?" said Charlie.

"I think she's a bit young for that," said Beth, "but I might go in ... if your Mum doesn't mind holding the fort."

"You're going to love it, isn't she, Mum?" said Amy.

We turned left and onto the small road leading down to the beach. It was a windy day and there were a few windsurfers strutting their stuff over the waves, which were some of the biggest we'd seen there.

"Let's go to our favourite taverna and whoever's in charge of Grace can sit behind glass, out of the wind. I volunteer to look after her and you three go in first."

"Are you sure?" said Beth.

"Absolutely!" I said, pulling on the hand brake.

Having been given all the paraphernalia that goes with a baby, I went into the taverna and found a seat by the window, leaving the children and Beth to strip off and go straight in the sea. I ordered a Nescafé – Grace was still sound asleep.

I watched the others run down the beach and they kept on

running into the surf; the light was so bright I had to squint and wished I hadn't forgotten my sunglasses. They were all holding hands and jumping over each wave as it reached them. The sea was aquamarine and the white horses frothed forward in chalky rolls, engulfing them with bubbly cotton wool. I could see them all laughing and shouting, Beth turning her back to the rollers and letting them bash her back, the spray framing her; she lifted her arms above her head and I could see the sheer joy on her face. How lucky that there were waves today, it could have been a calm day.

They were quite far out, Charlie must have been out of his depth by now. He was a competent swimmer, after hours spent in the outdoor pool on the camp having swimming lessons. I wasn't worried about either of the children.

I looked down at Grace who was sucking an imaginary teat in her sleep. How sweet and vulnerable she looked; I wondered if she looked like her dad. Gary sounded like a bit of a jerk to me; perhaps they'd drifted into marriage far too young? I couldn't wait to meet him and make up my own mind.

I felt a tap on the shoulder.

"So, who's this? Have you had a secret baby, or what?" Not realising how near to the truth that question was, the speaker said, "She's gorgeous!"

I recognised Alice's voice, the Wing Commander's wife, who I knew quite well by now and liked, despite the impression I got on that very first day. She was a bit of a busybody and liked to organise everything, but her heart was in the right place. How she could stand Reg, I'd never know.

"I'm just minding her for a friend, who's swimming with Amy and Charlie."

"Oh, who's that, then?" said Alice, ever the nosey one.

"Bethany Hughes. Her husband's in the Regiment. They haven't been here long."

I could sense disapproval coming from Alice.

"Oh ... I see. How long have you known her?"

"Only a few days. We met on ARABS and she seemed very lonely and a bit lost, so I thought I'd help."

"Mm ... well, I must be off. Nice to see you again, dear. You must come round before you go. How long is it now?"

"About six weeks. I can't believe it."

"Well, I'll get Reg to arrange something with Luke." The thought of having my personal space invaded by Reg again made me shudder.

"That'll be lovely," I said, determined to turn down any invitation.

Alice wandered off with a backward wave and I looked out of the window once more, scanning the sea for the children. I couldn't see them at first and a feeling of panic swept through me, but then I saw they'd been taken down the beach by the current. As I saw them, Charlie's head disappeared under a large wave; I waited for what seemed like a lifetime for his head to reemerge, but it didn't. Bethany was there and I saw her dive under the wave and was out of sight for a while. She came up, holding Charlie under his armpits; he appeared to be all right, but was coughing and spluttering. They all came out, soon after that. While they were changing, Grace woke and I started giving her a bottle. I found that all my attention fell on her face; she was so intent on drinking and her eyes stared up at mine.

"Wow, that was brilliant," said Bethany, bouncing into the taverna, changed, but with wet hair, which was now the colour of wet seaweed. The children dragged in after her, with tousled hair and red cheeks. They all sat down.

"We nearly had an accident, didn't we, Charlie? But it was fine in the end."

"Yes, Beth had to pull me up. I nearly drowned," said Charlie, proud of himself.

"I saw. Thanks for your quick reaction, Beth. I owe you one."

"No, you don't. I've loved this day. It's been the best day

I've had here. Thank you." Her eyes were bright and her face looked quite different. All the stress and tiredness seemed to have been wiped out by the waves. "How I wish I could get back on my board."

We all had an ice-cream while Grace finished her bottle. I would've liked to linger on the beach and maybe have a swim myself, but now that Grace was awake, Beth wanted to get home. It was too windy for the baby on the beach.

We pulled up at Beth's house and as we were getting everything out of the car, a man came out of the front door. I assumed, rightly, that this was the famous Gary.

"Where the hell have you been? I came back and when I found the house empty …"

"Gary … this is Emily," interrupted Beth, trying to distract him.

He ignored both the introduction and me and said, "I told you I'd be back for lunch today …"

"Did you? I don't remember …"

"There's nothing in the house to eat … if you've got time to go out, God knows where, you've got time to go to the NAAFI."

He was short and thick set; his whole being, was aggressive and demanding. It didn't take much imagination to see him picking a fight with someone and I wasn't even sure he wouldn't push Bethany around. I felt uncomfortable and facing Beth said, "Shall I carry Grace in for you?"

"That won't be necessary," he said, his face red with anger. He snatched a bag out of the back of the car and started walking away, towards the house. "Get everything in the house, Beth …"

The children were sitting quietly in the car, taking it all in. They weren't used to adults speaking like that and they looked worried.

Beth was standing at the passenger door holding the baby, all the joy of half an hour ago gone from her face.

"I'm sorry about him," she whispered. "He doesn't like me doing things on my own." She pulled a face at me, bent forward and kissed my cheek and said, "I should've told him where I was going, I suppose. I didn't think he'd be home till later – he's usually not back at this time." She looked towards the front door; he was standing there, looking impatient.

"Bye, Emily. Thank you."

She walked into the house and the door closed.

"Why was that man being horrid to Beth?" said Amy.

"I don't know … I really don't know."

*

As I drove the short distance home, I couldn't help thinking about Beth. Why did Gary react the way he did? Even if he didn't know where she was, it wasn't that big a deal, was it? He must be a control freak. I kept remembering his angry face, Beth had implied he was difficult but she hadn't said he was violent. Perhaps I was reading too much into it? He was just being rude and macho – throwing his weight around, wasn't he?

We hadn't made any arrangements to meet up again – there hadn't been the chance – so I decided to go round in a couple of days.

Luke was there when we got back; I told him I'd met a new girl and taken her out for the afternoon. He didn't seem that interested and just thrust a letter at me.

"I went to the Mess for a drink and this was in our pigeon hole." He looked around to make sure the kids were out of earshot and then said, "From lover boy, I assume?"

I took it and it was indeed from James. His handwriting leapt off the blue airmail.

"Yes, it is."

"Send him my undying love, won't you?" he said.

"Look, I haven't tried to hide the fact that we write to each other. Since we got back from the North, you've hardly looked at me anyway, never mind spoken. I realised as soon as we got home that nothing had changed. For a few days in Kyrenia, we seemed to be getting something back, something changed but now we're here, it's all gone ... I'll be leaving in a few weeks and you'll be able to get on with your life without me."

I hated it when we spoke to each other like this. It was all so pointless.

I slumped down in the armchair, still clutching the letter. I stared into space and Luke busied himself in the kitchen. With my mind turning to my imminent departure, I said, "Have you heard from Hugh? Have the tenants left? Weren't they meant to be out this week?" Hugh was the agent who was looking after our house.

"No, it's next week. I'll give him a ring." It was strange the way our relationship could lurch from bitter argument to mundane conversation within the space of minutes.

"Have you no idea where you're posted yet? Surely you should've heard by now?"

"Nope. I won't hear for a while. I expect I'm just going back to my old job. Just think ... we can go back home and continue with this charade in the comfort of the cottage, as if nothing has changed. Can't wait."

I looked down at the letter. I wanted to read it, but with Luke now out on the patio, I didn't dare. Luke was standing with his back to the house, smoking. His whole body looked tense. He turned round and said to me through the open French windows, "So ... how do you see this panning out?"

"What do you mean?"

"Well ... us? Now that you've done your duty – the kids will have completed their schooling out here. So, you can go back to our house and then what? Do you expect to just go on seeing James? I don't think so. It'll be decision time when I come home, Ems. Me or him. Simple." I came outside and sat down on one of the patio chairs.

"Keep your voice down," I said. "The kids'll hear."

"Well, maybe it's time for them to know the truth," he said. "They're going to have to know soon, anyway."

"Not necessarily."

"Why, not *necessarily*? What are you implying? That we're all going to live happily ever after? Says *she*, while holding a letter from her lover. God, you make me sick."

I looked at him, trying to remember how he used to look, before all this. He was older, thinner now ... his face reflected all our problems back at me.

He turned back to gaze at Mount Olympus in the far distance, blowing smoke rings up into the air. That view had held so much hope for us both when I first arrived – the possibilities for our future on the island had been encapsulated in that far-off mountain, surrounded by heat haze. Now, it was forever bound up with memories of that day when we'd all gone up there and I'd lost James' baby.

Funny how that scene, this house, Curium, Limassol, Aphrodite's Rock – would all soon be confined to memories. I'd return to England, to whatever my future held for me, and this posting would become something that had changed me; had changed my past and changed my future. It would be an interlude in my life when all sense was lost, all logical thought forgotten ... when I allowed myself to fall in love.

Is it possible to resist the temptation of falling in love? Did I consciously go looking for love, or did Fate have its own plan for me? I've read so many books about Fatalism and Pre-determinism; Thomas Hardy was one of my favourite novelists – I'd studied both Tess and the Mayor of Casterbridge. I remembered a famous quote from one of them, I couldn't remember which ... 'Character is Fate' . You can believe cruel forces are forcing you to do things against your will ... but, you can also believe that you are the author of your own downfall ... your own actions determine your future.

Sometimes, I felt as if all this was set in the stars; we were always going to come to Cyprus … things were always going to go wrong between me and Luke. Perhaps my life was already mapped out for me when I was in my mother's womb? Maybe Aphrodite just simply gave Fate a helping hand. Other times, I thought it all came down to me.

I looked up from my reverie; Luke had disappeared – I didn't even see him go, I was so absorbed in my thoughts. How would I feel if he disappeared from my life forever?

I couldn't even contemplate it.

*

Later, I opened the letter. I was upstairs, sitting on the bed; Luke was playing football outside with the children, their shrieks and shouts were coming through the window.

I always felt nervous when I read James' letters. Was he going to end it, this time? Had he got fed up with my constant wavering?

His handwriting was sloped and messy, not efficiently clear, like Luke's. I imagined him sitting at a desk somewhere, perhaps at work in his office, when he was meant to be doing something else. I could see his hands so vividly.

My Emily

Thank you for your last letter. Sorry I haven't replied very quickly, but this new job is full-on and incredibly boring. I have this General breathing down my neck all the time – he doesn't miss a trick. This is my lunch hour – I can't be bothered to go anywhere, there isn't enough time. So I thought I'd write to you, instead. Your letters are the only things that keep me sane.

I'm glad you had a good time in the North; I wish I'd gone when I was in Cyprus. Still, no point regretting.

I wonder how life is for you now you're back home on the camp? I'm counting the days till you get back to the UK. Even if we don't see each other, it will be so good to think we're in the same country again. I hate that we're so far apart – I'll just feel more relaxed when I know you're back on the same soil as me. I know that things can't go on like they were in Cyprus. I know you're reading this, wondering what to do. I understand, Emily, I really do. Your children are your world and I can't compete with them, but I suppose, if I'm honest, there's part of me that hopes somehow we can work this out. That you can come to me and have the children too. I know it's impossible, but a man can dream ...

I've found a few like-minded souls, nothing to do with the Army, and we've started jamming together. There's four of us – a drummer, Keith; a bass guitarist, Paul and Mike, on keyboard. We've only had a few sessions together, but it's been great – I think it might work out better than Brigade in Cyprus – we all seem to like the same stuff. The guys in Cyprus and I were always arguing about the set list.

You might be wondering how 'your song' is coming along? Well ... I've got a cracking melody, very soulful. I think my strength lies in the music, words are more your thing than mine. I've been working on the lyrics, but to me, they sound more like a poem than a song. I thought you could cast your expert eyes over them. Be honest, tell me what you think – they're on a separate sheet I've enclosed.

I'll sign off now. Try to enjoy your last few weeks, Emily. It'll be so tough, I know but ... the future is an unknown quantity. Enjoy what Cyprus has today. When you get back here, everything will sort itself out. Believe me.

You know I love you. James xxx

I read the letter through twice, not wanting to look at the song yet. I could hear his voice, see his eyes. I loved getting his letters, they were like having a really intimate conversation with him that I could have again and again.

I put the letter down on the bed and unfolded the thin piece of paper. I read it through. Time stood still. I could hardly breathe.

A Song for Aphrodite
Her rock stands alone.
Solid, against the dusky sky.
Cobalt seas painted crimson,
Mandarin clouds.

She rises from the foam.
Hair, glistening strands of sun.
Goddess, in human form,
Floating, ghost-like, to earth.

Fate brings me to you.
Woman, in goddess form,
Thigh deep in azure waters.
You come to me on Cyprus.

Here, now with you,
We leave stone hearts in dunes.
Letters entwined with love,
Our destiny fulfilled.

Hands linked through time,
We walk barefoot over eternity.
Through the sands of existence,
Beyond the universe.

You are she,
She is you.
Both, forever spirits,
Dancing through ripples,
Flying through infinite sunsets.

My heart was beating so fast, I felt as if I'd faint. My mind was in turmoil; I read it again and again. I thought it was the most romantic thing anyone had ever done for me, to write words like that. How could I possibly compete with a gesture like that? I couldn't and didn't want to; I couldn't begin to write like that. I had no idea that he could write; he'd been so modest about his song writing, I hadn't really given it much thought. He was right, it did sound more like a poem to me, but it didn't matter.

It was perfect.

Perfect.

I folded the piece of paper carefully in two. It was so precious I didn't know where to put it; I went to my chest of drawers, found the bracelet he'd given me hidden beneath my clothes and placed the poem in its box.

I went to bed that night with my head full of love for him again. My dreams were like an enactment of the poem: I was floating and swimming, flying and diving through the night.

Chapter Ten

"So, what's this new friend of yours called, then?" said Luke.

"Beth, Bethany Hughes. Why?"

"Well, I was taken to one side at work today. It's been noted."

"What on earth do you mean?" I genuinely hadn't got a clue what he was talking about. "What's been noted?"

"Your friendship with an airman's wife. It's not approved of."

"Oh, for God's sake, that's ridiculous. I just met her on a beach one day, she seemed really down and lonely and I got chatting. I thought I was being kind and caring – is that wrong?"

"No, of course it isn't. I don't see anything wrong at all, but the powers that be, do. It's up to the Regiment to look after her, officially. They don't like other officers' wives interfering. If you're interested, I told them my thoughts, which didn't go down too well, either. I stuck up for you."

"Thank you, Luke. How did anyone find out anyway?"

"God knows. Someone must've seen you."

"Hang on a minute … of course, it was Alice. I met her at Curium, when I was holding Grace and Beth was swimming. She looked a bit bemused when I told her who the baby was.

She must have relayed the information back to Reg. For *heaven's sake*."

"Well, I told them I'd speak to you – so regard yourself as having been spoken to. If you want to carry on being friendly to her, it's fine by me."

"To be honest, I think she could do with some help, at the moment. When we got home from Curium, her husband, Gary, was really horrible to her and blanked me. She says he's always off with his mates and getting pissed. I didn't like the look of him at all, he seemed aggressive."

"So I'm not such a bad husband, then, compared to him, am I?" said Luke.

I felt instantly guilty; he was brilliant compared to Gary.

"She's really struggling with the baby too. I just thought I could give her some moral support."

"If Alice says anything to you, just ignore her. It's your life, as we all know too well."

*

When the kids went off to school the next morning and Luke was out, I sat down and wrote back to James; I wanted to tell him how I felt.

My James
Well, I don't know what to say. Your song is so beautiful – I read it again and again and I love every word. How clever you are to capture the magic of that place so well and link the past and the present. I feel unbelievably flattered that someone has written words like that for me. Thank you so much.

You're right, it does sound more like a poem to me – not that I'm an expert or anything, but maybe you could adapt it to your melody – you'd need to add choruses and hooks, I suppose? Listen to me, I sound like a know what I'm talking about! I love it the way it is, though. I've put it in the box with your bracelet and I'll read it every day.

I feel in limbo here, now that we're back from the North. I did enjoy seeing the sites and experiencing the culture. Luke and I got on well too; we seemed to be able to forget everything that's happened, for a few days. Maybe being away from the camp helped; the moment we got back though, everything reverted to how it was before.

The one good thing that's happened is that I've made a new friend, a girl called Beth. She's very young, with a tiny baby and I've tried to help her. It seems to have caused some trouble though, as she's an airmen's wife.

God, how I hate the Air Force, sometimes.

I can't even begin to imagine what will happen in the future, James. I've got through this phase and that's all I can say. When I get back to our cottage, maybe I'll be able to think more clearly. I feel as if the heat has addled my brain.

All I know is that I love you. I'm trying to live each day as it comes. If Fate has a plan for us, so be it. Although Aphrodite and I are the same person in your poem, I am just a divided human.

Thank you again for your words. Whatever happens, I'll cherish them forever.

Yours, always,
Emily.

*

I went round to Beth's the next day on the off chance that Gary wouldn't be there. Fortunately, he wasn't. Beth answered the door with Grace in her arms, a cloth over her shoulder, her face weary and drawn.

"I thought I'd pop round and see how you are."

"Come in," said Beth, "perhaps you could make us both a coffee and I'll carry on feeding." She ushered me into the kitchen and pointed to the Nescafe jar.

Beth sat down at the table and Grace continued drinking milk, making contented baby sounds. I brought the two mugs of coffee to the table and sat down.

"I'm sorry about Gary the other day. He can be really rude."

"Don't worry about it. I was just concerned for you. Was he okay in the end?"

"No, not really. It seems he's allowed to go out with his mates whenever he wants, but I'm not. He went out soon after and I didn't see him again for hours. We used to get on all right. It's awful now ..."

"What are you going to do?"

"I really don't know. I've just got to concentrate on Grace and try and get through this. I just wish I had my family round the corner; I wouldn't be so dependent on Gary then. Maybe I've never realised how little Gary and I have in common because I've always had Mum and Dad there."

"Yes, Cyprus certainly brings relationships into the foreground ..." I sipped from my coffee and said, "I've discovered a lot about myself and our relationship, since coming here." I wanted to confide in Beth – maybe we could help each other? I wanted to be honest with her; Beth probably thought I was leading some sort of ideal life. I learned my lesson before, when I'd told Sophie everything, but James' letter kept popping into my mind and I wanted to talk to someone.

"Beth, if I tell you something, can you keep a secret?"

And the whole tale came flooding out.

I told her everything.

Beth listened intently, occasionally sitting the baby up to rub her back and finally laying her down in the cot. Still the story went on. Unlike Sophie, Beth didn't give any opinions or show disapproval; she simply asked a few questions and nodded sympathetically.

"Do you want to be with James?" said Beth, standing by her daughter's crib.

"Yes, I do. But ... now that you've got Grace, you can

understand. It's like you have two lives – before and after children. Children change everything. I can't bear the thought of hurting Amy and Charlie, ripping our stability apart. How could I live with myself?"

Beth stared down at the sleeping baby. She stretched her hand down and gently stroked her head. "It would be terrible at first, but maybe in the long term, it would be better for the children to be living with one happy parent than two miserable ones."

"But Luke would never let me take them …"

"Has he categorically said that?"

"Well, yes. He's a fantastic dad too …"

"That's the difference … Gary wouldn't care if I took Grace away with me. He just can't connect with her at all."

"Some men find it hard when they're babies …"

"I know, but somehow I can't see Gary turning into Dad of the Year when Grace is a toddler. You can tell, can't you?"

I thought I wouldn't want Gary anywhere near my children.

"Maybe when you get back to the UK you can sort out joint custody. It works for other people," said Beth.

"It's so disruptive for the children, though. They need both of us. And who's to say James wants me with two children in tow?"

"If he loves you as much as he seems to, he'll want you and everything that goes with you."

Perhaps she was right. Perhaps we'd be able to sort it out like grown-ups.

"Enough of me … you've had to listen to all my problems. Sorry to burden you – life's hard, isn't it? I wish I could turn back time, but … anyway … I have a proposition for you. I'd love to practise my photography on you and Grace; some mother and baby, black and white shots – are you up for that? I thought it'd be good for both of us, a distraction."

"I'd love it. We've only got some awful pictures Gary took; most of them are out of focus."

"How about if I come round tomorrow morning? Same time? I've always wanted to take mum and baby pictures … you'd both be perfect models."

*

The next day, Luke confirmed that the tenants were leaving this week and that the date for our departure was set. It was unreal. There were just three weeks left of the school term and then I'd have the children around everyday; we'd do as much swimming, windsurfing and sunbathing as possible. Once we were back to our UK house, it would be sorting, gardening and settling the children into school.

Beth was looking more relaxed than she had the day before. When I opened the door, I noticed she had make up on and her hair was brushed.

"I thought I'd make a bit of an effort, if I'm modelling. In between nappies, feeding and vomit, I managed to find a moment to wash my hair and bung on some makeup," she laughed.

"You look lovely. I thought we'd stay indoors with the fans on, as it's so hot. Any preferences as to where we go?"

"Well, nowhere's very tidy, but we can clear the rubbish as we go."

Grace was sleeping and it was with trepidation that Beth reached down and picked her up.

"I hope she stays asleep," she whispered. "Grace screaming the place down won't make such a good pic." We laughed silently above her head.

We managed to get some nice shots of them both on the sofa, but something was missing; it looked too homely, too conventional.

"Is there anywhere in the house where there is a plain white wall you could pose in front of?"

"I could move this," she said, pointing to an armchair. "If we slide it along, I could sit on the floor here?"

"Perfect. Would you be up for taking your clothes off? I know it sounds odd, but I'm sure you've seen those sort of photos? You don't show anything but the closeness of the mum's and baby's skin looks wonderful and intimate. Especially in black and white. Timeless."

Beth hesitated and I wondered if I should've asked.

"I'm not sure Gary would like it …"

"He needn't know; it could be our secret."

Beth brightened and said, "Okay, let's do it. As long as you don't show anything … I've got awful stretch marks."

"All you'll see is perhaps your bare arms and shoulders. I'll zoom right in."

I moved the chair and then held Grace, while Beth undressed her top half. We lay the baby on her changing mat and took off her baby grow. She woke up, but for once didn't cry, liking the feel of her mother's skin.

"Maybe I ought to do this more often," said Beth, kissing the top of Grace's head.

She sat with her back to the wall, cradling Grace, their heads were to be close, their bodies touching, skin to skin. Beth soon relaxed and I clicked away. I knew I was getting some wonderful shots – tiny hands against her mother's chest; the intense gaze babies give their mothers; the look of love on Beth's face. I even tried to get one of Grace's hands in Beth's, the difference in size emphasising the mother and baby bond and the child's vulnerability.

I heard a key turning in the front door and then it banged shut. I looked at Beth with disbelief. Gary barged through the door and stood stock still in the doorway.

"What the hell's going on? Get your bloody clothes on."

We were both frozen to the spot, incapable of movement.

"We're just doing some photos …"

"Get up, for Christ's sake. Parading yourself like that," and he came forward, trying to pull her up roughly. Grace started to cry.

"Stop it, Gary. Let me get up myself, you're frightening her."

"Shut up. Give her to me."

"No, I won't ..."

At this point, I thought I ought to do something. I put down my camera and went towards them saying, "Hey, Gary, I'll get her ..."

"No, you won't – piss off!"

"Gary, for God's sake, she's just trying to help," said Beth, who had now stood up and was holding onto the baby.

"Look, I'm sorry, but it was my idea, not Beth's. I just wanted to practise ..."

"I bet you did," said Gary, his face twisted with anger. "Clear out of my house and don't come back. I don't want you here. You come here with your fancy car, your posh officer wives' ideas. Just leave us alone." I could smell alcohol; it was emanating from him and each time he opened his mouth in my direction, I got a full blast.

"You'd better go," said Beth, who was standing clutching Grace to her. They looked a forlorn sight; the baby crying and Beth, her eyes full of tears, still naked from the waist up. I couldn't just leave her in this situation.

"Look, Gary. I'm not going until Beth has got dressed and Grace has stopped crying. Beth, you take the baby upstairs," and without any more encouragement, Beth disappeared. Gary and I squared up to each other. I wasn't going to be intimidated by him; I was going to stand my ground.

"Gary, Beth is struggling a bit out here and I was just trying to help. I thought it would be a nice thing to do, to take some pictures of the two of them. I wasn't doing anything wrong ..."

He turned his back to me, went out onto the patio and lit a cigarette. I was left standing there so I followed him.

"It's really hard out here for wives, you know. You guys have loads of instant friends. The wives feel isolated and lonely. I know, because it happened to me. Give her a bit of slack."

He didn't answer at first but then turned round and said, "If I wanted your help, I'd have asked. But I didn't. So, I won't ask you again. Get out."

I decided I was probably making things worse, so I went out into the corridor and called up the stairs, "Beth, I'm going."

There was no reply.

Chapter Eleven

Despite what had happened, I took the photos to be developed; I certainly wasn't going to give Gary the satisfaction of winning that argument but I decided to leave it for a few days before going round again. I'd write a note and drop it in with my address and phone number and leave Beth to contact me. I was worried for her but didn't want to make matters worse. My mere presence seemed to anger him.

I took the photos to my favourite shop on the outskirts of Limassol and instead of going home, I took myself to Germasogeia Dam, just past the city. The name had taunted me every time I'd driven past it and with such little time left, I decided to go there and take some pictures.

It didn't take me long to get there; I parked up and got out, gazing at the deep blue waters. Cyprus relied on dams for its water supply, but I could see that it wasn't full to capacity. Every year, they hoped for enough rain to see them through.

It was far bigger than I'd thought it would be; it nestled among the moon-like hills like an inland lake. It was tranquil, the only life being a few birds flying overhead. I took some pictures, but somehow the majestic stillness was difficult to capture. The blueness of the water was mesmerising; it was different from the sea, perhaps a greener blue in places and almost sapphire in others. It stretched as far as the eye could see, without a ripple.

The heat was feverish, bearing down on me, making me feel like one of those African women you see carrying huge weights on their heads; I was burdened and tired of it. Soon, it would be a thing of the past, this heat. It was as if I couldn't bear it any more, it was too intense, too all-consuming. I'd been standing against a rail that went around the top of the dam; the metal was too hot to touch with my bare skin and I went to sit in the shade of a tree.

I listened to the silence, which was as much as a presence as the heat. It was peaceful and I felt an overwhelming solitariness. It was at times like these when I was utterly alone that I had to truly face up to myself. The quietness invaded me and with it, a sense of loneliness. However many relationships I'd had – with children, parents, brothers, husbands, lovers … I was separate, a tiny spot in the universe that was of no consequence. I live, I die. I leave the world alone and even if memories of me linger in some people's minds, when they and our memories are gone, so too am I.

That's the reality.

I shuddered at the thought; the surrounding silence didn't give me any answers; the water sat there, like a solid piece of nothing, into which I would go.

Like Sam.

*

I wrote the note to Beth and dropped it round early one morning, hoping that Gary wouldn't find it first. I then went round to the school where we were having our sports day. It was strange to have running races at eight o'clock in the morning but any later and it would be too hot for the children and indeed for the adults standing on the sidelines.

Luke managed to get an hour off work and we both stood together, shouting encouragement when Amy or Charlie were taking part. Amy was a sporty child and managed to win a couple of races; Charlie, however, wasn't so athletic and was definitely a bad loser, so had to be consoled.

"Never mind, Buddy, you did very well to come fifth," said Luke, trying to see the bright side after one particular race. "The other ones were much bigger than you."

"No, they weren't. It wasn't fair, they all started before me."

"I don't think so ..." said Luke, stroking his hair. "There was a whistle ..."

"But they all started before the whistle, Dad."

"Well, let's go and get a drink, so you'll be ready for the next race, old chap." He took Charlie's hand and went towards the refreshment tent.

"He's telling lies. They didn't start before him. He's just a slow coach," said Amy.

"He's not 'a slow coach' Amy. Don't be unkind. He's doing his best," I said. "Shall I go in for the Mother's race?"

"Yes, go on. It'll be fun. You'll beat all the other mothers, won't you?"

"I doubt it. I can't remember the last time I ran any distance." I was secretly dreading it, but thought I ought to. I didn't want to make a fool of myself, but I'd come in trainers and shorts in anticipation and the look on Amy's face made me want to do it, for her sake.

The time came; the tannoy asked for volunteers and I looked at Luke for encouragement.

"Shall I?"

"Yea, go on. It'll give me a laugh, before I go back to the office."

"Thanks. I'm glad I'll keep you amused for the rest of the day."

There were about ten mothers lined up. I wasn't the oldest, but there were some who looked like girls, in comparison to me. Suddenly, all my competitiveness came to the fore and I really wanted to win. We lined up and at the whistle, I set off as fast as I could, but I could see straightaway that some of the others were much faster. I was in the middle – some of the older, fatter ones were trailing behind me – I could hear the kids and other parents shouting, but all I could see were the disappearing backs of the ones in front. The finishing ribbon was still a fair way off, when without warning, I crashed forward and landed in a heap, head first on the grass.

I lay there, dazed with the suddenness of it for a few seconds and then I could hear Charlie's voice saying, "Mum! Mum! Are you okay?" I lifted my head, pushed myself up and sat up. My knees were bleeding, but I had no recollection of how I fell, so didn't remember landing on my knees. I stood slowly up, bent forward with my hands in the small of my back, feeling the aches of a fall and the humiliation of everyone looking. I hardly dared look up, but when I did, I realised that no one was really looking at me, they were more interested in the finish. The only people concerned were my family.

Luke put his arm round my shoulders and said, "That was quite a fall. Are you sure you're okay?"

"I'll survive. My pride's hurt, though." He withdrew his arm.

He gave me a knowing smile. I felt an utter failure. "I'm sorry to let you down, Amy. I've no idea what happened."

"Don't worry, Mum. At least you tried." This was the sort of thing I said to the children and it was odd to hear it coming back to me. "A lot of the other mothers were younger than you."

"Thanks, Amy." I wasn't sure that it made me feel a whole lot better, but Amy meant it well.

"You've got blood all down the front of your legs," said Charlie, proudly, as if it was a badge of honour.

"I better go and find a tissue; I'm going to feel it in the morning."

Luke went off back to work and all the children were gathered up and taken back to school. I went home in the car, limped upstairs into our bedroom and was just about to take off my grass-stained shorts when I caught sight of myself.

There I was: blood congealing down my legs; sweat and dust lining my face; my white t-shirt with spots of blood and dirty marks on it. I stared long and hard. What a sight.

It was time to go home.

Chapter Twelve

Our last week in Cyprus was fast approaching. We'd spent most of the school holidays enjoying the beach; the temperature reached an all-time high for a couple of days of forty-one degrees and so on those days, we stayed indoors from eleven until four, taking regular cold showers just to keep cool.

Luke and I had one more social event to go to before my leaving date, an open-air concert at Curium Amphitheatre. I'd heard about these, but we hadn't been before; from various reports it was a fun thing to do. It was a military band playing and although I loved most music, this didn't appeal. Brass bands were not my thing at all but I remembered the band at the Summer Ball – they were brilliant, so maybe this would be okay? I wasn't sure how it would be, the two of us going out together, but Luke wanted to go.

We got the babysitter settled and left the camp at six o'clock. I'd dressed up a bit for the evening and felt good. I'd bought a short, floaty dress in Limassol, one I'd probably never wear in England; it was brightly coloured with swirly flowers on it. We had a cool box full of drinks and snacks.

We parked the car; the temperature was still high, despite the time of day and as we walked from the car park towards the amphitheatre, I could feel sweat trickling down my back;

the cicadas were shouting their song from the bushes. This was one thing I'd miss about the hot climate, these evenings when you could be bare armed, bare legged, until midnight. Luke had on some beige trousers and a white short-sleeved shirt; I looked at him and thought he looked handsome with his tan and aviator glasses.

"Where shall we sit?" he said as we entered the stadium. It was huge, with rows of stone seats ranging in semi-circles. It was already quite full.

"Oh, I don't mind, you choose." We hadn't really spoken for days and the tension between us was getting worse as my departure loomed. I wanted to reach out to him but didn't know how.

He set off down some steps and we sat in amongst some noisy people who were already drinking champagne; the low sun was lighting the bubbles.

I sat down and looked around. The view was spectacular; the amphitheatre was facing the sea so we'd be able to watch the sun set, over the horizon. Whatever the music was like, I'd soak up the atmosphere.

I glanced at Luke, he was getting our wine out of the cool box. With ease, he extracted the cork and poured me a glass. Handing it to me, he said, "Cheers," without smiling and we chinked glasses, for all the world as if nothing was wrong. I watched him as he sipped the wine; he normally drank red, but we'd only got white in the house. Its cool temperature was refreshing and light.

His familiar profile, the way he held his glass, his wedding ring, everything … made my realise how much I'd miss him. I was mentally ready to go back to the UK, but was dreading leaving him.

Soon the seats were full; the dignitaries from both Epi and Akrotiri were seated; down at the front and from the side, the musicians started to file onto the stage. After a short introduction, the band began playing a mixture of styles, ranging from classical to music from the West End shows. The acoustics were amazing, the sound that was generated was crystal clear and loud.

I went into a sort of trance, losing myself in the music, the moment. As they played on, the sky reddened, casting an orange glow over the whole scene. I gazed at the sea, watching as it darkened.

I became aware of a noise that was not part of the concert and saw other people looking up. There, above us, was a powered hang glider flying right overhead, silhouetted against the crimson sky. Wondering what it must be like up there, I imagined myself looking down, seeing hundreds of people seated in tiers, the amber light warming the scene like a filter on a lens.

He must truly feel like a bird, swooping and gliding up there, alone in the sky.

The fiery sun was moving relentlessly towards the sea – how quickly it descended. There was an explosion of colours: yellows, every shade of orange and red. I stared so long at the sun, in the end I had to look away. Soon, it was half submerged in the ocean and with a final plop, disappeared. It was as if the band was performing to accompany the sun's beautiful display; they were playing a peaceful classical piece I recognised, but didn't know the name of.

I would remember that sunset for ever. Everything good about Cyprus, was here.

There was an interval when everyone got up and stretched their legs; the stone seats were uncomfortable but I hadn't noticed until I stood up, so absorbed I'd been in the scene.

Luke had wandered off and was talking to someone I recognised from the camp; there was no one here I wanted to talk to and I was perfectly content simply observing everyone. The light had now all but gone and the flood lights were turned on, lighting up the stage.

Everyone sat down as the musicians filed in again. We all

sat quietly waiting for the music to begin. There was a hush of anticipation and I wondered why there was a delay.

Suddenly, from behind me, there was the most incredible sound; a sole musician was standing at the top of the stadium, playing a hunting horn. It made me jump when he started but then I turned around, like everyone else and watched as he played. He was silhouetted against the night sky, his instrument pointing towards the sea and the sound he made reverberated around the stone circle. The rest of the band joined in and he made his way down the steps. It was magical.

The more they played, the more I realised how talented they all were; I'd definitely maligned them in the past. As they progressed through songs I loved from the musicals, memories of Sam flooded back; I could almost see him skipping down the steps in front of me. I missed him so much, it hurt.

I reached across and took Luke's hand. He didn't look at me but he took my hand in both of his.

We sat like that until the end of the concert. I had to take my hand away in order to clap and he made no move to reclaim it. The band did an encore and when they finally finished, the whole audience stood up and cheered. The musicians filed off the stage and people started collecting their belongings and making their way out.

"There's no hurry," said Luke, staying seated. "It'll take ages to get everyone out of the car park. Let's just wait here a while."

"Okay. Did you enjoy it?" I said, wondering what to say. His face was as hard as the stone we sat on.

"Yes, I did. Unusual for me." Luke never really enjoyed anything to do with music. He continued sitting there, with the remains of his wine, staring ahead, his jaw twitching.

"It was amazing. Thank you for bringing me."

"Well, we're almost there now," he said. "You can go and forget all about me and Cyprus and start your new life back home."

"Don't say that, Luke. You know that's not how it is." My

stomach clenched; I couldn't bear to have the conversation that I knew was coming.

"Do I?"

"You *know* I'm never going to forget you. I'm going to go home and you're going to come back soon after."

"And then WHAT?"

He turned to me, his eyes glittering.

I honestly didn't know the answer to that question.

"Well, that depends on your posting. I wish they'd let you know." I knew he wasn't referring to the practicalities of postings and jobs, but I pretended he was.

"They will soon." He looked down and put his hands over his eyes, resting his elbows on his knees. His shoulders were shaking and I realised that his eyes had been full of tears. A wave of heat and panic passed through me and I rested my hand on his back, rubbing it up and down, like I would with the children.

"Luke … Luke … it'll be okay. Please …"

"How will it *ever* be okay again?" he said, into his hands. I looked around – most people had now left; a few stragglers like us, were dotted around. I was aware that I didn't want anyone to notice Luke's distress.

I sat down right next to him and put my arm around him.

"What do you want me to do?" I said.

"I want you to love *me*, not him," he whispered. "I want you to be with me because you want to be with *me*, not just because you want to be with the *children*. I want it to be how it used to be …"

I squeezed his shoulders and lent into him.

What could I say?

"Maybe when we get home, it *will* be how it used to be. Maybe we'll be able to forget Cyprus …"

"That concert felt like the end … the going down of the sun on our marriage … the grand finale … the one last song …"

"Look Luke, I know this feels like the end. It *is* the end, in a way. I'm going back to the UK, I've got to go, the children …"

"Yes, it's always the children …"

"It *has* to be about the children, you know that – we agreed. We've both behaved terribly out here – it's not just me. You took a decision on your own; you should've considered me too. I wanted another child, you know I did and now I never can. You've slept with Sophie. It's not just me that's …"

"It's you that's fallen in love with someone else. YOU. It would never have happened with Sophie, if you hadn't left me. I blame YOU."

His voice was cracking and so full of emotion that I put my own head in my hands.

He was right. Everything was my fault. I knew that. I was a bad person, a thoroughly bad person.

We sat together in complete silence for what felt like an eternity. Now we really were the last ones still sitting on the stone steps.

"Come on, let's go home, Luke. We can't stay here all night," and I reached forward to pull him up. He refused my hand and stood up, wiped his face and walked up the steps into the enveloping darkness, away from the flood lights.

The sky was a mass of stars, the moon was gold. It should have been a magical ending to the evening, but instead we walked in silence to the car and went home, with neither of us saying another word.

*

I was beginning to get everything ready for the journey. The cases were out and each time I thought of something, I put it in. The children were told to sort out which toys they wanted to take and which they would leave, to come back in the container.

Two days before the big day, the children had just gone to bed, Luke was watching TV and I was upstairs, sorting clothes. We'd hardly spoken since the concert.

I heard a knock on the door, which was unusual – we didn't

have many visitors these days. I didn't feel like being sociable, so let Luke answer it, hoping whoever it was would go away. I could hear Luke talking to someone, a female, their voices were quiet and I couldn't make out what was being said. Then I heard the door close and the person was this side of the door.

Luke came upstairs and poking his head round the door, he said, "Emily, I think you better come down. Someone's here."

"Who?"

"Your friend, Bethany. She needs help."

I jumped up – this was odd; something must have happened.

I ran downstairs and there she was, standing in the hallway with Grace sleeping in her arms. There was a small bag beside her on the floor.

Her face said everything; she'd obviously been crying and there was anguish written all over it.

"Beth, what's happened? Come in here," I said, ushering them into the living room. Luke turned down the telly and Beth sat down on the sofa.

"Shall I go?" he said.

"No ... I think you both need to hear this. I don't know what to do."

"So ... what is it?"

I knew before she opened my mouth what it would be. I'd sensed it.

"Gary, as you know Emily, is ... very difficult. He's always been volatile but here ... here, he's got completely out of hand. I don't know what it is. He hasn't coped with the new baby, at all. He drinks too much. He's angry all the time. And tonight ... he hit me." Her voice tailed away.

"Oh God. Are you okay? Do you need a doctor?"

She laid Grace down on the sofa and pulled up her sleeve to reveal a huge bruise on her arm. "He just lost it. I hadn't got round to making anything for dinner. He was drunk again and when I asked him if he could walk round to the chip shop, he just sort of lunged at me. He hit me and then pushed me so hard, I fell over and banged my head on the side of the oven." She touched her scalp. "Then … he just walked out." Her foot was jiggling up and down in a nervous movement.

"I'm frightened of him – I'm frightened for myself … and Grace."

I looked to Luke; he was always so good in a crisis and I was at a loss as to what to do.

"You must stay here tonight – you're not going back there. I'll go round and see Sally, the Families Officer in the Mess and ask her advice. She should be there, I'll go straightaway."

"Thank you. I'm sorry this is your first introduction to me … Do we have to involve …"

"Yes, we should. It's not my area and I'm sure there's protocol. I'll go now – you two have a cup of coffee," and he went out.

"Have you got all you need for Grace?"

"Yes, I grabbed everything for her, I've probably forgotten things for myself. I'm so sorry … I didn't know where else to go."

"Don't be daft. That's why I left you that note."

I put my arm round her and tried to reassure her, then went into the kitchen and made two mugs of coffee. When I got back, Beth's eyes were almost closed; she looked exhausted.

"When you've had this, why don't we go and sort out your bed. You look done in."

"We better wait and see what Luke finds out. I don't know what to do."

I could tell she had no energy for chatting, so I suggested we watch TV. It wasn't long before Luke was back with the Families Officer in tow. He introduced her to Beth and indicated to me that we should leave them to it.

After about twenty minutes, Sally called for us and we all reconvened.

"Well, we've had a chat and Beth has decided *not* to press charges but Gary's Squadron Leader will be informed and I've heard that you've kindly said that Beth can stay here tonight."

"Yes, that's fine," I said, smiling across at Beth. "We'll look after her, won't we, Luke?"

"Of course. I think I better inform my Wing Commander, so that everyone's in the picture."

"Yes, that's probably for the best," said Sally and took her leave.

While Luke made his phone call, Beth and I went out into the maid's quarter and sorted out the beds. Grace would sleep in one of the single beds with lots of pillows around her to keep my safe.

"I thought you might like to see these," I said, handing Beth the photos from our shoot. "Some of them are lovely. Let me show you my favourite." I found a black and white picture of Beth holding Grace, their faces touching. There was something about Beth's expression that made it a perfect shot.

Beth gazed sadly at it and said, "That's beautiful. Thank you so much. What a shame Gary can't see it for what it is." She placed it back in the pile. "I'll look at the rest of them properly in the morning," she said and lay back on the bed, exhausted.

"If there's anything you need, just let me know."

"Thank you. I'll be fine." She didn't look fine, her face was drawn and there were black rings under her eyes.

"See you in the morning. I hope you get some sleep."

When I went back into the sitting room, Luke was there and I said, "What did Reg say?"

"Well, as you know from before, it's not really approved of, your friendship, but he understood that there was no alternative. I'm glad I rang. The Regiment will have to sort it in the morning."

"What will happen to Gary?"

"It's a domestic so unless she presses charges, he'll just get a warning."

"He won't get sent home or anything?"

"No, we need him here. The two of them will have to sort it

out between them. The Air Force can't interfere with all their guys' marriages, can they?"

"No, I suppose not." There was a pause and then I said, "What do you think she should do? Is it safe for her to go back?"

"She's a nice girl and all that, but it's her decision and only hers. I can't even sort out my own marriage, never mind hers."

"I'm worried about her."

"There's no point worrying, Ems. You're leaving, so you won't be able to do anything about it."

"Could you keep an eye on her for me?"

"Me?" His face looked as if this was the last thing he wanted to do.

"Would you?"

After a hesitation, he said, "Okay, okay – if you really want me to. I'll do it for the baby, not for you, not for her."

"Thank you, Luke."

Chapter Thirteen

After consultations with Gary's squadron leader, Beth decided to go back. There was no alternatives – no parents to run to, no friends (we said she could stay on, but we all knew this wasn't the solution.) If she wasn't going to pursue the situation and get Gary arrested, she had to go back. She told me that as much as she hated Gary right now, she didn't want him to end up in a military prison. It was agreed that Luke would go round the next day to see her; I thought it best that I keep my distance, in case Gary was there. He wouldn't dare to be like he was with me, if Luke appeared.

We only had one day left. Our Tristar was taking off from Akrotiri at midday the next day, so the day was taken up with packing, sorting and reminiscing.

"When will all our other toys get back to England?" said Charlie. "I don't know whether to take this with me now, or wait." He was holding up his favourite car.

"Dad's going to pack up everything soon and move into the Mess. It will take about six weeks for it to arrive, so about the middle of October, I think."

"That's ages!"

"Well, you've got to make the decision. I can't. Try and work out what you can't possibly live without and put those things in the case."

It was easy to say but I was finding it difficult myself. All the stuff had come out of storage in the UK last week and David had overseen it back at the cottage; I'd completely forgotten what I'd even put in there. Mum and Dad were going to collect us from the airport and take us back to their place for a couple of days, then David had offered to come and drive us back to the cottage. I was so looking forward to seeing them all again, but when I got back to my cottage in my imagination, I couldn't 'see' what it would be like at all.

We were going to take the children out for a final meal and after asking them which taverna they wanted to go to, it was decided that Chris Kebab was the favourite. We'd had many meals there since that very first evening out; the kids loved how they were allowed to sit at the bar. Chris still gave them toxic-looking blue drinks, but had also introduced some bright red ones too.

Luke went round to Beth's at six, just before we left for the meal.

I'd written a note to give to her:

Hi Beth,

I didn't come round – I was worried I'd make things worse. I hope today has been okay? I've thought about you a lot. No doubt you've had some meetings with 'officials' and maybe Gary has had a good talking to. Let's hope he's learned from this and you can begin to pick up the pieces.

It's such a shame that I'm leaving tomorrow. I wish I could be here for you. But, as you know, it's probably time for me to go and sort myself out. I feel really sad that we met so near the end of my time here – I think we could have had fun together.

You must try to make new friends. Maybe that nice Families Officer could help you? I'm sure there are groups of mothers and babies that you could join. I know you said you didn't enjoy that one you went to, but it's better than sitting alone in the house.

If you ever need to ring me, my home number is 01285 325478

– I'll be on that number by the end of next week. I promise I'll try to help, whatever it is.

I'd like to think that we can stay friends and keep in touch. I know your address, so I'll write to you as soon as I can.

Good luck, Beth, and give Grace a big kiss from me.

With love, Emily xx

"So how was it?" I said, as soon as Luke came back.

"Gary wasn't in, thank God. I'm not sure I could've stopped myself from hitting him. I hate blokes who throw their weight around and intimidate women. I'd never do that."

I remembered the scene when he'd found out about James. He could have been aggressive towards me, but the only thing he did was pull the door violently – I did hurt my head but he hadn't meant to hurt me and I deserved it; Beth didn't.

"No, you wouldn't."

"Anyway … she was okay. Grace was awake and was calm and contented. Beth looked very tired and to be honest, withdrawn. Apparently, they had a joint meeting with someone and Gary promised he'll never do it again. He's been given a warning; at least it's out in the open. But those sort of blokes always say that and don't really mean it."

Poor Beth. This was going to be a very long posting.

"How did you leave it with her?"

"Well, I said I would be here until December and to contact me if there was any trouble. I gave her your note, of course. I have a bad feeling about this, though."

"Why? What do you mean?"

"I'm not sure but let's put it this way, I won't be surprised if she gets in contact. I like her; she deserves better."

*

The meal was a huge success, for the children. They laughed and ran around and sometimes sat down with us, but mostly sat up at the bar with some other children they knew from school. Luke and I were left together making superficial conversation and often sitting in silence. I drank three brandy sours ; as the brandy seeped into my bloodstream, my mind clouded with memories of lost days. Summer balls, evening cruises, a myriad of beaches … snowy mountains, polo games, barbecues … what an amazing time we'd had.

If only things hadn't changed, if only …

"What are you thinking about?" said Luke, cutting into my dreams.

"I was just remembering all the good times. It's gone so quickly, now that it's time to go. I can't believe it …"

"It could have been the best time of our lives."

I looked at him across the table. I could see a sheen of tears in his eyes and my stomach lurched.

"Let's think about all the good things, Luke. Look how the children have changed and how confident they've become. How many children get the chance for such a great experience? They've learned so much here."

Luke didn't answer; he took a long drag from his cigarette, letting the smoke drift around his eyes.

"Think about what fun we've had," I said, "… me, learning to waterski, windsurf and play polo. You, mono skiing … skiing with the children up the mountain. Summer balls, cruises. All these things … we'd never have done them back home. We've done so much."

"I know, I know," he said. "Cyprus has been incredible … the island has been everything I'd hoped it would be. The people have been the ones who let me down."

It was so true, there was no denying it. Cyprus, with its beautiful coastline and stunning Troodos mountains, its quaint harbours, its food, its history had surpassed my expectations too. It was a wonderful place and it would always hold a special place in my heart. My own experience of it, however, was something separate. Falling in love with James, Sam's death,

Luke's betrayal … these were all things that happened here, here in Cyprus but could I blame the place, this island for them?

It was somehow the mixture of my personality, the heat and the beauty of the place; it had all come together to cause this maelstrom of emotion, destruction and even death. Sam's death couldn't be blamed on my actions, but it was so inextricably wound up with it all, I felt as if I was somehow responsible. Sophie's sadness, the breakdown of our friendship, even Beth's troubles, all these things, such negative things, had one common denominator.

ME.

Luke was right, I'd let him down and everyone else around me.

We drove back, the children falling asleep in the short distance from the taverna. As we entered the drive for the final time, I looked at the house, now dark against the starry sky and felt sad that I'd be leaving it tomorrow. I'd hated it that first day, with its stark white tiles, ancient cooker, its awful breeze block walls, its furniture and horrible coloured suite. But I'd grown to love it; its quirkiness had crept up on me and as we'd stamped our own style on it, it had become a haven, a home.

I carried Charlie in and put him straight to bed, Amy persuading us that she could stay up as it was her last night. We all watched TV and then we went to bed.

Luke and I slept at different sides of the bed, the gap between us as big as ever.

*

"So ring me when you get to Granny's," said Luke, to Charlie. "You should be there around nine o'clock my time."

My stomach was churning; I was nervous about how to say goodbye.

I'd miss him – I looked across at Luke now and wished I could tell him, but was so worried it would sound hollow and untrue. He was in his own clothes, as he'd been allowed to take the morning off. His shorts and t-shirt looked crisp and clean, his hair, short and tidy. His aviator glasses suited his face and gave him an enigmatic quality; he could hide his emotions behind his dark lenses. His voice was upbeat, but I could tell he was trying too hard.

"When are you coming home, Dad?" said Amy.

"It'll be just before Christmas. You must tell me how your first day at secondary school goes. I want to hear all about it."

"We'll ring every day, won't we, Mum?" said Amy looking up with her big eyes.

"Well, perhaps not every day, but every other day, perhaps."

It was time for us to go through to the departures. Luke hugged both the children – they clung onto him, not wanting to let him go. Amy started to cry.

"Don't cry, sweetheart … don't cry. I'll be home before you even realise …" said Luke, crouching down before her; his face was full of concern and love.

I stood to one side, allowing Luke to have all the precious time with them.

My heart was pounding, waiting for the final goodbye. He came slowly to me with a look of utter despair, then, moving forward, he put his arms around me burying his face in my neck. I could feel his arms quivering and I hugged him back, with all my strength.

He whispered, "I love you, Ems. I always will."

And in that moment, I loved him with all my heart and soul. He was my husband, my soulmate, my rock.

"I love *you*, Luke, you know I do. We'll sort this mess, we will. I'm going to miss you, so much."

Tears were running unchecked down my face now, I couldn't stop them.

"Don't cry, Mum, you'll see Dad soon," said Amy, her face full of compassion. Her hand found mine and squeezed it.

"Come on, Mum, we'll miss the plane," she said, pulling at my hand as she was walking away.

Luke stayed rooted to the spot and we all moved away from him. He looked so alone, with all the hustle of people around him.

I felt I was abandoning him, leaving him to his fate, whatever that was.

He blew kisses and waved as we disappeared.

*

We filed onto the plane and sat down. Now that we were on, it felt to me as if the posting was a dream. I looked through our porthole window at the arid, rust coloured earth; the sky, a shimmering arch of blue. Trucks were moving busily, doing last minute jobs, men were signalling; the reality of leaving the island hit.

I felt a longing for Luke, for the island, the sea – my life, unclouded by complications. I had a sudden memory of that very first day when I went to the end of the garden and saw Mount Olympus for the first time; I remembered that feeling of hope, of anticipation and how I went back to the patio and sat on Luke's lap. We'd kissed then, the first proper kiss in Cyprus, the first kiss after such a long time. It ran through my mind – I closed my eyes and relived it.

The plane began moving slowly, edging its way down to the end of the runway. It stopped, waiting for 'go' from the tower. It was as if our lives were hanging in the balance, waiting, waiting. Then, the loud engines roared, there was the thrust of power, the speed, the nerve-jangling wait for the wheels to lift, the tilt and upward movement into the sky. As I looked down, the sea spread out below; the coastline, a map-like line of white.

I imagined Luke watching the plane, a dark silhouette against the sky, getting smaller and smaller and disappearing from sight.

Chapter Fourteen

When we arrived at Brize, Mum and Dad were both there to greet us; as I wrapped my arms around Mum, it really *did* feel like coming home.

Spending time with them, back in the family home of my childhood, was like a little interlude before reality. I went out shopping with Mum the day after arriving, leaving Dad to look after the children and we had a conversation about what Mum called, 'the situation'.

"So ... what's going to happen now?" she said, as we sat in Tescos car park. "Have you managed to resolve your problems? I didn't like to ask in letters, in case ..."

"Well, it's not easy, but maybe we're getting there ... slowly. It's so hard. It's like this awful gaping wound between us. It's as if it'll never heal."

"I'm sure it will, dear, you've got to work at it. I hope you've stopped communicating with that James?"

I felt myself reddening and looked away. "Yes ..."

My mother gave me one of my knowing looks. "Emily ... that didn't sound at all convincing."

"I'm *trying*, Mum, but ... how do you stop loving someone?" My throat felt constricted; I squeezed my eyes.

"You just *have* to, for Luke's sake, for the children's sake and for your own sanity. If you don't ... well, I don't know what'll happen."

This was the only conversation we had on the subject, but when I was getting into David's car to leave, Mum squeezed me tight and whispered, "Remember what I said."

David chatted on the way back up the M4, telling us all his and Steve's news. It was going to be wonderful to have them just up the road, in Birmingham (it wasn't really 'up the road' but it was a lot nearer than Cyprus). We made plans for weekends, when he and Steve would come and stay in the cottage; I'd love having them.

As we neared our village, I felt a lifting of my spirits; I was going back to the house Luke and I had bought and done up in the style we liked. It was our own house, the place where we'd been happy. I hadn't been back for two and a half years; what was it going to feel like, walking through the door and into my home?

Driving along the country road that led from the motorway, I couldn't help being mesmerised by the sheer greenness of everything. It was so lush, so abundant, it was as if the countryside was exploding with life. It was in such contrast to Cyprus; I'd forgotten how beautiful the landscape around our house was. The sun was shining and fluffy white clouds tripped across the sky. Even though the summer was reaching its peak here, there was still a feeling of ripeness and plenty. The fields spread out and rolled up hills into the distance; stone cottages with manicured gardens dotted the scene.

We approached our village, passing the pub where we'd had so many evening meals by the fire; we passed the children's primary school where Charlie would go. There was the war memorial and the duck pond, on the left. How many loaves of bread had I given those ducks? When the children were tiny, we'd go there for something to do.

Soon, we turned into our lane; it was narrow and people often used it as a cut-through, so I'd been nervous of the children getting out of the gate; Luke had put a lock on it, so I'd be sure. Our house was on the right, with a tiny little drive. David pulled in.

"Well, here we are, kids! Do you remember it?" said David, turning round to face the children on the back seat.

"Yea, of course!" cried Amy. "I wanna get out …"

"Okay, okay, hold your horses … I'll just undo the child locks."

With a click, the doors unlocked and undoing their seat belts, the children opened the doors and jumped out.

"It looks different," said Charlie, looking up at the cottage; I wondered if he *did* remember it, as he was so young when he left.

"I think it's because the garden's a bit overgrown," I said, trying to reassure him. "When we were here, I was always gardening. I don't think anyone's been looking after it, like I did."

"Didn't you have someone doing the garden for the tenants?" said David, as he stood by the driver's door, rubbing his back.

"A guy came in once a month, I think, but it was only to mow the lawn and cut the hedge. Maintenance, really. Not like I did."

I too was staring at my house. The roses I'd trained round the front door looked rampant but past their best and lots of petals were browning on the door step. The sitting room window was covered with trailing leaves from some ivy that should have been cut right back.

"So, let me find my key – it's here in my handbag some-where. Here it is, right at the bottom, as always. How come keys disappear into the depths?" I laughed.

"You shouldn't have so much rubbish in your bag, Sis."

"Oh, shut up! You always say that. Us girls need things. It's not rubbish."

"You've always had the kitchen sink …"

"Oh, it's great to be back, being bullied by my brother again," I laughed, slapping his arm.

And it was. I'd missed David. He was like a best friend, brother and confidant, all rolled into one.

I walked round to the side entrance, the one I called the back door, and unlocked it.

"Here we go," I said, pushing the door open. "How did it look when you were here overseeing the storage?"

"It seemed fine to me, but I don't know it as intimately as you do, of course. Nothing appeared to be broken or anything."

I went down the rather shabby entrance corridor (we'd been going to sort it out for years, but had never got round to it; it was perfect for dumping wellies and hanging up coats). I entered the kitchen with its wooden floor, low ceiling and pine cupboards, the kids running past me and on through to the sitting room. It was a dark room, so we turned on all the lights and stood in the middle surveying the scene.

"Pleased to be home?" said David, who'd come and stood next to me; he put his arm round my shoulders.

I turned my head to look at him. Luke's absence was all-encompassing; being back here made me miss him so powerfully, it hurt. I missed those happy days, those pre-Cyprus days that now loomed out of the past.

"I feel such a fool, David. Being here again, with Cyprus gone, it's almost as if it never happened. But Luke's not here and ..."

He squeezed me and I leant into him. "Look, Sis, you'll be okay. Put Cyprus down to a long, drawn-out moment of madness ..."

"A two-year moment ..."

"Well, yes, you always were one for extremes." He pulled my head into his chest. "You'll get yourself back, now – you'll see. Everything will return to normal. He'll be home soon."

"I hope you're right. So ... come on, let's get the stuff out of the car. By the way, thanks so much for sorting it. That was a step way beyond sibling loyalty! I'm sure it took ages ..."

"Yea, it did, but you know me, always a sucker for my ginger sister. Actually, the guys who brought it were amazing."

We walked out to the car together, leaving the children to run up the narrow, steep stairs.

David stayed that night; it took us a while to sort out the beds, unpack the cases and find pyjamas for the children. We had fish and chips for supper from the chippy in the next village.

Sitting round the kitchen table together, with the fish and chip paper still on the plates, it felt as if we were camping in someone else's house. We realised we had no tomato ketchup, which was a disaster as Charlie claimed he couldn't eat it without the necessary dollop of the red stuff. There was *literally* nothing in the cupboards – tomorrow, first thing, we'd have to go shopping. David was going to take me into Cheltenham to buy a cheap car.

That night, in bed alone, it felt so strange to be back in the cosy bedroom with its deep blue carpet and curtains with those familiar flowers. I lay on my back, listening … it was as quiet as the grave; not a sound. I thought about the noises of daytime Akrotiri … the drone of engines, the cicadas, the tinkle of the ice-cream van and visualised Luke, alone in our room in the quarter.

Two people, now separated by over two thousand miles.

I thought about James, now just 'down the road' in Bristol. It was as if, once again, I was being pulled from one to the other. I imagined standing with the two of them each side of me: Luke was trying to reach me but was too far away and couldn't quite touch my hand. James, was closer and I felt the warmth of his hand in mine.

I fell into a deep sleep and didn't dream of either of them.

*

The next morning, I woke up at seven; the light was streaming through the curtains and as I'd left the window open, I could hear the chirrup of noisy sparrows sitting in the foliage, right outside. I got up and drew the curtains; it was a lovely English summer's day – how nice it would be not to be stifled by the heat, to simply enjoy the sunshine.

The house was quiet; it was unusual for the children to sleep in, but they were exhausted from yesterday. David was always capable of a lie-in, so I left them all to it. I crept downstairs and I imagined Tom Kitten here. I could see him, winding his way through the chair legs, meowing for food.

There was a little village store down the road which stocked most things. The man who ran it had been there for years and knew everyone in the village. Stan wore a crisp white overall everyday, greeting people cheerily as they pushed through the door with the 'ping' of a bell. The shop opened early as it also delivered newspapers, so having got dressed, I left a note on the table, *"Gone to the shop, back soon."*

"Morning, Mrs Blackwell," said Stan, as I entered. He'd known us for years, but insisted on using my surname. He was an old-fashioned soul.

"Back then, after your travels?"

"Yes, we got home yesterday, but Luke's still out there. We've got nothing in the house, so I've popped round for some basics and a paper."

"Your two must have grown," he said, stating the obvious. We used to go in there a lot for sweets and lollies; he was always very kind to the children, but I remembered how he would weigh out the sweets from the jar with meticulous accuracy – never one bitter lemon or liquorice over the designated amount. How different from the Cypriots; they were so generous with giving ice creams and fruit away.

"Yes, Amy's off to secondary school next week."

"Goodness me, I can't believe it. It only seems like yesterday she was in a pram."

I agreed with him. Now that I was back it was as if I'd never been away. I picked up a basket and bought milk, bread, butter, cereal and a few other bits. I added The Times – one of the headlines on the front page talked about Michael Jackson being accused of child abuse. This was the first I'd heard of it and felt certain that they must have it wrong – surely not? I loved his music and felt affronted that one of my pop idols should be accused of something so heinous. I put the paper in my basket, took it to Stan and paid.

I walked back the long way, which took my past the church. It was an archetypal Saxon church with ancient gravestones. It looked beautiful this morning, the sun shining through tall chestnut trees, dappling the graveyard. We'd often gone there as a family before even though neither of us was very religious but I'd wanted the children to have the same religious education I'd had and then they could make up their own minds later.

I stood at the arched gateway, remembering when Charlie had fallen off the wall that went around the periphery. He'd hit his head quite badly and even though it had been a nasty incident when I'd been terrified he'd really hurt himself, I looked back fondly … at a more simple time.

I wandered back along the road; everywhere was quiet. There was one solitary dog walker, but all the houses still looked asleep. Our next-door neighbours, a retired couple, were nowhere to be seen.

When I got home, everyone was up. We sat down and when the children had finished breakfast and rushed off again, I showed David the headline.

"I can't believe it. Have you heard anything?"

"It's been on the news a bit; you probably missed it as you've been busy packing."

"Do you think it's true?"

"Well, you never really know celebrities, do you? He might be an amazing singer and songwriter but …"

"It's such a shame. It's horrible, if it's true. I won't feel the same about his music."

It made me think about my own situation: everyone back

here thinks they know me but they'd be so shocked, if they knew what I'd done.

We spent the day, shopping and car-buying; we bought a small Ford. The garage man would deliver it for me tomorrow.

When David left in the early evening, I watched him drive up the road with a feeling of dread. He was such great company and I'd miss his banter and friendship. As much as I loved the children, I was now without adult company.

The phone was going to be connected tomorrow so at least I'd be able to chat to Jen, my parents and no, I wouldn't ring James.

I wouldn't.

Chapter Fifteen

The days went by quickly, despite my loneliness. Once the phone was connected, the children spoke to Luke most days, Mum and Dad rang a lot and I spent hours chatting to Jen; I'd missed her and it was great to talk on the phone without fear of huge bills. We arranged for her and the kids to come and stay in two weekends' time.

I didn't ring James. I went towards the phone many times with the intention of ringing him, but stopped myself at the last minute. Mum was right; I had to stop communication with him and then it would all be okay.

He knew my address though and one morning his familiar handwriting plopped through the letterbox. My heartbeat quickened and I longed to open it, but it was the day of the start of school and so I put it to one side and concentrated on the children. Amy was going on the school bus which stopped at the end of the road. Her new school was in the nearby town, but she'd hopefully know a lot of the children there, from when she was at the village primary.

Charlie and I walked her down to the bus stop and when the bus approached, I hugged her hard and said, "Have a lovely day, Amy. You'll be fine." She looked at me with anxious eyes. Should I have taken her to school in the car? Surely it was better to do what all the other children were doing?

She put on a brave face and went up the stairs onto the bus with exaggerated enthusiasm. There was a girl I recognised sitting on one of the front row of seats and Amy sat down next to her; as the bus drew off, they were already talking to each other and Amy didn't even wave goodbye.

"Well, Amy's off," I said, feeling relieved at the painless outcome. "Now we'll pop home and get your pack lunch ready and walk you round to school, Charlie."

"I wish I was still in Akrotiri ... I won't know anyone."

"Yes, you will. All the children who you knew before will still be there."

"But I don't know them now."

"You'll soon remember them, don't worry. Come on, I'll race you home," and I started running up the lane to divert his attention.

We ambled round to the school and I took him into his classroom to meet his teacher, Mrs Cressman. She introduced him to a boy called Peter, who led him away to where they gather for registration; Charlie looked back and gave a little wave.

Outside, I bumped into someone I used to know before I left; her name was Bella and she had children of a similar age. They lived in a big house at the other end of the village. She was friendly and outgoing, married to the local vet.

"How *are* you? Long time, no see ... how was Cyprus? You lucky things, living the dream out there."

"It was great, thanks."

I tried to sound as upbeat as Bella, but it sounded false, even to *my* ears.

"It's good to be home. I was fed up of the heat, in the end."

"God, I wish I could say that – 'It's been so hot here, while you've been gone...' Ha Ha! Joke. All right for some. It must've been brilliant. Why don't you come round for coffee and you can tell me all about it? I'm dying to hear. It's all been pretty dull here."

"I'd love to … but could I come later in the week, do you think? I've got to get back now …" I was thinking of the letter and couldn't bear not to read it for another few hours.

"Of course! How about Friday?"

We arranged coffee at ten thirty on Friday and I left, wondering why I'd agreed to it.

I got home. The letter was on the dresser, lying there, waiting to be ripped open.

Hi Emily,

So … you're back on UK soil. I can't tell you how good that makes me feel. It was as if the world wasn't turning properly without you here.

As you haven't rung me, I'm assuming … well, I don't know what I'm assuming. Maybe, you and Luke have decided to make a go of it? Maybe, you've decided you don't want either of us? My mind's all over the place with what might be happening to you. I know it must be incredibly difficult to be back in the family home again; I wish I was there to help you. I hope the children have settled in okay and aren't causing you too many problems. I expect they miss their dad.

I've just been working, working. I hate this job! It must be the most boring job ever. It's got everything wrong with it: it's boring, repetitive and pointless – do you get the idea?! And, did I mention, an awful boss? I think I'm going nuts. The only things that are keeping me sane are the bike – how I love to get on it and ride – and the guys in the band. We're getting on so well together now and we've got a great set list. I wish you could come and hear us. We're doing our first gig in a couple of weeks, at a pub in Bristol. It's quite famous for live music and often gets a good crowd. So, we're practising as much as we can.

The other thing that keeps me sane of course, is you … the possibility of maybe seeing you sometime soon.

I hope this finds you happy. All I want is for you to be happy, you know that, don't you? If I felt that by leaving you alone I would achieve that, I wouldn't contact you. But, I think I make you happy, don't I? Or am I deluding myself?

I think of you all the time. I miss you so much, it hurts. James. xxx

I sat at the kitchen table, my fore-finger running over the words, tears stinging my eyes.

James, I'm trying so hard here, and then you go and write me this.

I read it again. And again.

I stood up and looked out at the back garden all overgrown and crying out for my attention. I'd go and attack it with shears and a pruner and hope that the physical activity would shed some light on what I should do.

*

I spent the next three hours in the garden. The sun was out, the birds were singing and in the distance, I could sometimes hear the sound of the children playing in the primary school grounds. Their shouts sounded joyous. I gardened as if my life depended on it, clearing great swathes of weeds and making a huge pile for the compost heap. By the end of the morning, my arms, which I'd left bare, were covered in scratches from wild brambles and my T-shirt was dirty.

I went inside and when I saw my face in the bathroom mirror, I was somewhat surprised to see smears of earth on my cheeks and some blood from my arms had found its way onto my forehead. I looked as if I'd been in a fight. I tried to visual-ise myself as I'd looked at that first summer ball, all blond hair and cheekbones. That woman had gone. The sophistication I'd found in Cyprus had gone without trace and here I stood: back to my old self. This was the person Luke loved all those years ago.

I decided not to do anything about James' letter.
I wouldn't reply.

*

Despite Charlie's worries, he loved his first day at school. Peter had become his best friend and Charlie was already asking if he could come round and play. Amy was tired when she came home but she too was full of enthusiasm about how amazing the 'big' school was. She couldn't find her way around it, but wasn't fazed and just loved the fact that they moved from one room to another between lessons. She'd made friends with a girl who was completely new to the area called Maisie; they had a lot in common as she'd also been away from England, living in Hong Kong.

"Maisie's so pretty, Mum. She's got incredible hair."

"What's it like?" I asked as I stood by the cooker getting the children's spag bol ready for tea.

"It's really long, right down her back to her bottom. She wears it in a plait but she undid a bit for me and it was all kinky and blond. She's got studs in her ears too. Can I have some?"

"I think you're a bit young for that, Amy. Maybe when you're older."

"Why? Maisie's mum doesn't think so."

"Well, I do, so that's it."

I realised that this was just the beginning. The moment they went to secondary school, things changed. She'd soon be a teenager and there'd be boys ... still, that was quite a long way away yet.

"Where does Maisie live, anyway?" I said, trying to divert attention away from the stud issue.

"She went on the same bus as me, but got off a few stops before mine. I think she lives in a big house."

"Oh well, you'll have to ask her round for tea soon."

"Can I? When? Tomorrow?"

"Let's just get this week over with, first. I've still got lots to sort out. Ask me again next week."

Kids were so quick to adapt to new situations. Who would ever have thought they'd both settle in so well? I knew it was very early days, but it would be okay, I could see that.

"We've got some English homework to do," said Amy. "I have to read a bit of *Charlotte's Web,* our teacher read the first chapter in class."

"I love that book, lucky you. Go and read it now and I'll call you when supper's ready."

*

Life for the children settled down well. The first day of school for them both proved to be indicative of how the days would follow. There were no complaints, no dramas; just excited re-telling of things that happened at the end of each day and they even did their homework without too much fuss. Peter came round to play one evening and Maisie came the next; it was interesting how different the two sexes were – the boys, running noisily around the garden kicking a ball and the girls, giggling quietly up in Amy's room.

My life wasn't quite so easy, but considering the upheaval I'd been through, it went by without too many problems. I had to get a plumber in to look at a leak, my new car broke down and I had to call the AA, but apart from that, everything on the outside, was okay.

Now that I was back, I began to wonder what I'd do with the rest of my life, from a job perspective. I certainly didn't want to go back to teaching, of that I was sure ... but had I really got the confidence to set up a photography business? It had all seemed so simple in Cyprus, but now that I was back in the UK, I wasn't convinced I had the skills or experience. I wouldn't do anything until after Christmas anyway. I needed these months to reorientate myself. I knew I was lucky to have the luxury of Luke's salary; I didn't actually need to work for the money, but I needed to work for my own state of mind. I'd had enough of leisure … maybe that was why everything went so wrong; I'd had too much time on my hands.

I liked Bella; the coffee morning went well and I'd in fact, quite enjoyed recounting my exploits in Cyprus, leaving out all the gory details. I just told her about the balls, the boat, the expeditions to the mountains and the North; if only it had been like that – I almost convinced myself that our posting had been an unqualified success. Bella's children, Fred and Pippa, were fun and at other get-togethers, the kids played and the mums drank coffee, tea and sometimes, wine.

By not replying to James, I told myself that I was moving on. I didn't need him, or Luke for that matter. Who needs men, I said to myself? I'm coping fine on my own. They are complications that us women don't need.

Jen and the children came to stay for the weekend. John didn't come as Luke wasn't here; he'd made some excuse about work, but I was sure he didn't want to come. I was glad he didn't as it gave me and Jen time to chat like the old days and talk about 'the situation', an expression that Jen too had adopted, like Mum.

I'd never shown anyone the bracelet James had given me and I certainly had never let anyone read his letters, but almost to prove to Jen how serious he was about me, I gave them to Jen to read. The kids were asleep and we were drinking a bottle of Sauvignon Blanc.

"Oh my god, that poem …" said Jen, taking a large swig of wine. "That's amazing. No one's ever written anything like that to me."

"I know, it's … beautiful, isn't it?" I looked across at Jen. "How am I meant to forget it and move on? I've been very good, I haven't replied to his last one. It's been nearly three weeks since I got that. I haven't heard from him. Maybe he's got the message and isn't ever going to contact me again."

"I doubt that very much …" said Jen, holding a letter in her hands and turning it over to see his name. "He's probably just confused, wondering what to do. How do you see things panning out, once Luke gets back?"

"God knows …"

"Any idea of his posting yet?"

"No, it's just a formality, though. It'll be back here. That side of it is easy. It's the rest … I haven't contacted Sophie since I got back. Ever since the revelation about her and Luke, I just haven't wanted to speak to her. She was so adamant that nothing happened. I don't know how she had the brass neck to deny it to my face at the airport."

"Maybe there really was nothing in it and she felt it best to spare your feelings. I hate to say it, but I can almost see how they could have done it, thrown together like that, when they were both so … lost. Perhaps it was just sex."

"Maybe … but it's a bit two-faced after all the stick she gave me over James."

"Why don't you ring her now you're back? Clear the air?" said Jen.

"I might … I'll see."

I wasn't at all sure I wanted to.

I told Jen all about Bethany. "I do wonder how it's going for her out there, poor thing. It must be awful. I asked Luke to look out for her, but at the end of the day, she's stuck in a house with a baby and that terrible husband."

"Why do you think she married him in the first place?"

"They were very young and … you know how things are, she fell into marriage without thinking it through. Like us all, I suppose! None of us really understand what we're doing, do we? Anyway… how are you and John? We always talk about me, me, me! Are you two okay?"

"You know us, boringly happy! He gets fed up with his job,

often having to stay up in London but, generally, we're fine. Nothing very exciting happens to us, not like you. Your life is like a soap opera, compared to mine. I can't wait for the next episode to brighten up my day."

"Oh shut up!" I laughed and pushed Jen on the arm. Suddenly, I wished I was like Jen. *Really* wished it. "I'd love mine to be normal. I never asked for this. It just happened." The atmosphere which had been light-hearted, changed and Jen could sense it.

"Look, whatever happens, we'll still be friends. I won't judge you. I like them both, Luke and James. Someone's going to get hurt, though. Be sure you're making the right decision for *you*, for no one else. There's no point you staying with Luke for the sake of the children. I know it's an awful thing to say, but tons of children have survived divorce ... yours are no different."

No one had ever mentioned the 'D word' before and the stark reality of it hit me hard.

Divorce.

That's the reality. Divorce Luke, live with James and see Luke sometimes, because of the children.

Or ... live with Luke and never see James again.

Chapter Sixteen

I was home alone one afternoon. The kids were both going back for tea with friends: Charlie to Peter's and Amy to Bella's daughter, Pippa.

I was cleaning the windows – a job I hated with a passion – when the phone rang. I picked it up without thinking and Luke's voice said, "Hi, Ems. How are you?"

I was so surprised to hear him at that time of day, we always spoke in the evenings.

"I'm fine. The kids aren't here – they're still at school and then they're …"

"I know … I need to speak to you."

His voice worried me. Why did he sound so serious?

"What's happened?"

"My poster's been in touch …"

"Oh, at last. That's good. What did he say?"

"Well, it's good news. I'm getting promoted."

"That's brilliant, Luke. Well done, Squadron Leader Blackwell," I said, still thinking there must be something else. "What about the posting?"

"Well, you know I've always wanted to fly helicopters?"

"No … not really … you mentioned it ages ago but … Sam dying changed that, didn't it?" Sam's face flew into my mind with complete clarity.

"Not for me. That was a tragic accident … but it hasn't changed the way I feel about them, no."

"So … what's this got to do with your posting, Luke?"

"They're giving me what I want."

"What do you mean?"

"Well, I've always asked and now they're letting me convert."

I let his words sink in.

"So, where would you go?"

"To start with, to Valley for conversion and then Chivenor."

My heart was racing, my mind was jumping all over the place. He'd said it was an absolute certainty that we would be staying …

"But you said we'd be here, Luke. You *said* that it was almost a hundred percent sure that …"

"Nothing's ever a hundred per cent sure in the Air Force. You know that. It's an amazing opportunity for me, Ems."

"But it's not just about *you* …"

"You know how important my career is. And this is something I've always wanted."

"Can't you say that the kids have just settled into their school?"

"No, I can't. They've given me what I've been asking for. Why would I quibble with that? I'm in the RAF and you have to accept that these things happen. If you wanted someone like John, who's going to be in the same job, in the same place, working nine to five every day until he drops, you shouldn't have married *me*. Try and look on the positive side. You love Cornwall and Chivenor is just up the coast in Devon. We've often talked about how we'd love to have a house down there."

"For GOD'S SAKE, Luke. Going on holiday somewhere and living there, are completely different things. You were the one who talked about buying a cottage down there, not me. I love this house and I've just settled down in it again. The children are really happy in their schools. I don't believe this."

There was silence at both ends of the line. I could hear

Luke breathing; my own heartbeat was racing still and I felt breathless.

"So, what are you saying, then?" he said, quietly.

"I don't know what I'm saying. I can't think straight," I said, feeling both guilty for not being excited for him and angry with him for just accepting the posting without talking to me.

"How long's the posting?"

"They implied that I'd definitely get a second tour there, so maybe … six years."

"Christ."

"That's a good thing, though. It means that we can see Amy through secondary school there. Charlie'll be okay too. Kids are adaptable, Ems, don't worry about them so much. We'll love living down there. Think of all the fun … and I can have the boat …"

"I'm not interested in your bloody boat, Luke. There's more to think about …"

Again, there was another pause. I slumped down in the chair next to the phone and pulled my hand through my hair.

What on earth was I going to do?

"The timetable as far as I know is … me, back home at Christmas. Quite a lot of January off as I've accumulated leave and I get disembarkation leave after Cyprus and then I'll do the Flying Supervisors Course at the beginning of February and a few other courses. They think I'll start at Valley towards the end of March."

"So … are you saying …"

"I can live in the Mess, for a while … you get food and accommodation free but … it's not something I'd want to do for long. I'm past living in the Mess."

"Well, I'm past all this *fucking* upheaval!" I shouted. "Why did I bother to come back here on my own to get the kids settled into school? I should've stayed out there."

I was getting more and more upset as the conversation went on. There was just *no* thought of me and my life. Wives just had to up sticks and follow their man around.

"You went back because we thought we were going to be posted back there. I didn't know, any more than you did, what was going to happen, did I? Perhaps this is just the excuse you needed. You can run to James now, can't you? God, he's going to love this, isn't he? He's just waiting for you to go to him. You can say, 'Oo, Luke's so horrible to me … he's forcing me to move' and he'll be all sympathetic and say, 'Come here and I'll make it all better'. I can just see it."

"Oh, shut up, Luke. Don't be so *horrible*. I haven't spoken to him or communicated with him in any way since I got back here, if you must know. Now I wonder why I've bothered, you just don't seem to think of me at *all*. It's your career that matters, nothing else. How long have you been asking for this anyway? It's news to me."

"You know I've always wanted it, Ems. I've asked at every opportunity I've had. I never thought they'd let me, to be honest. Why can't you be *pleased* for me?"

"I am pleased that you've been promoted, Luke but this changes everything for me and the children. Can't you see that?"

"If it wasn't for my salary, you wouldn't be able to swan around doing nothing and you certainly wouldn't have been able to live in Cyprus. They pay my wages and we have to go where they send me. End of."

"I'm hardly 'swanning around', as you put it. It's hard work looking after two young kids and running a house and being uprooted all the time. Why don't you *ever* see it from my point of view for a change?"

This was getting us nowhere. I wanted to end the conversation and … then what? It was all done and dusted; there was absolutely nothing I could do about it.

"Anyway, I've got to go now. Think about it and when you've calmed down, we'll speak again. I know it's a shock, but I think when you've thought about it, you'll see that it's a great move. I'll ring again tomorrow night and I'll speak to the kids. Give them my love."

He put the phone down before I could say anything else. I sat there in the dark kitchen, staring out of the window into my beloved garden that I'd spent hours trying to tackle. The silence of the room hummed around me, the tick of the clock, marking out the seconds, entered my brain with a maddening regularity.

I stood up and went to the bookcase. Some of the books that had been kept in storage were lined up there. I reached for a map book, went to the index and looked up Chivenor. Soon I was scanning the North Devon coastline and when I saw the name, I put my finger on it. He was right; it was just up the coast from Padstow. On the map, it looked a short distance, but I knew it wasn't as near as it seemed. We'd had a holiday once in Bude and that was nearer. We'd also been to Woolacombe before the children were born and that was just north of Chivenor.

But it was all so far from here – my home.

Was I being unreasonable? He was so pleased about it but I couldn't help feeling that I just didn't come into the equation at all – only in so far as he had to tell me what he was doing. No discussion. But then, he was right, he's in the Air Force and this is how they operate.

I should never have married him in the first place. I knew he was in the Air Force when I met him. What did I think was going to happen?

I only had myself to blame.

I looked at the clock. It was five. The kids were due home at seven.

I was going to write back to James. I'd had enough of it all. I'd tried and now this had happened. Look where it got me, trying to move on with my life?

Absolutely nowhere.

*

I sat at the kitchen table and poured my heart out to James; it was like I was off-loading all my resentment towards Luke and the RAF, onto him. It was therapeutic and when I'd finished, I felt calmer. I made myself a cup of coffee and then came back to the table and re-read the letter.

I tore it up and started again.

I couldn't expect James to read all that, it wasn't fair on him. So I wrote a more level, less ranting letter, apologising for not writing before and trying to explain why. I ended the letter:

I'm so sorry, James. I should have written to you before now. To be absolutely honest with you, I wanted to, everyday I wanted to, but I was trying to be 'good'. I have no idea what's going to happen. Luke's news is so recent, it hasn't really sunk in yet. All I know is, I don't want to move again. I'm happy here; the kids are happy here.

I've missed you every minute of every day, but I've been trying to kid myself I haven't. If you still want me, I'd love to see you. I'm going to post this now, before I change my mind.

I love you, Emily x

PS My phone number is 01285 325478

I sealed the envelope, wrote the address, put a stamp on it and walked purposefully down the lane to the postbox by the Church. My hand hesitated as I poked the letter through the gap. I held onto the letter and then, with a thunk, it plopped into the bottom of the box.

Chapter Seventeen

I didn't tell the kids Luke's news, but once they were in bed asleep, I rang Jen, David and Mum in quick succession. They all tried to make me see the positive side. Jen said, "Think of all the holidays I can have down there, staying with you!" David said, "It will be a new start, Sis. It will be good for you both." Mum said, "That's the best thing that could have happened. It'll get you away from that James."

I could see everything they said but they weren't me, were they? They didn't have all the disruption, the packing up, the new environment, another quarter … the Air Force. They were trying to put a 'spin' on it, trying to make me feel good but how would they like to have their world completely turned upside down?

I woke up the next day; it was one of those sickening mornings when you slowly come to and you know something has happened and you can't think, for a split second, what it is. When the realisation dropped into my head, my body reacted. I felt hot and shaky.

I didn't want to go. I didn't.

I knew that my letter would be arriving at James' flat that morning; I wondered if he'd get the post before setting out for work. I tried to 'see' him opening it.

How would he react?

"Are you okay, Mum? You don't look very well," said Amy

when I came downstairs. "You look as if you're going to be sick."

"I'm okay, thanks Amy. I didn't sleep very well, that's all."

I certainly wasn't going to worry the kids with it all until we'd talked again and decided what to do.

I needed to get away from the house, so once the children had gone to school, I went into the local town. I'd been meaning to join the gym and today, I was going to do it. I needed the distraction. Having paid my dues, the staff insisted on showing me how to use the machines and checking I did the exercises correctly. I tried to burn up some of my pent up frustration, doing more repetitions than was advised. I left feeling a little calmer, but completely exhausted.

When I got back to the house, as I walked in the phone started ringing. I picked it up, expecting it to be Luke again.

It was James.

"Hi! I got your letter this morning, so I thought I'd ring and see how you are. I won't be able to speak for long as I'm at work but I wanted to hear your voice."

I sank into the chair, a warm feeling passing through me; his voice always had this affect. I closed my eyes and saw his face as clearly as if he was right there.

"I'm sorry I didn't write back to you, James. I thought I'd …"

"Don't worry, I understand."

"It was lucky, I'd just got in when you called. I've been to the gym."

I didn't know what to say. Somehow, whatever I said, seemed wrong. He must think I was only turning to him because things had gone wrong but that was far from the truth.

I continued, "Luke's news has thrown me."

"Yes, I can imagine. Was it completely out of the blue?"

"He says no, but it is for *me*. According to him, he's been asking for this for years. As far as I knew, we were coming back here."

"It must be so hard being married to a military guy. It's even worse in the Army, you know."

"It is hard, James. Luke just doesn't see it, though. To him, it's his career … nothing else matters."

"As I said to you that day on the beach, I realised that and that's why I haven't had a serious relationship. You weren't part of the plan. I was going to leave the Army and then start real life."

The implications of his last statement struck me. I was something that happened to him. He hadn't planned falling for me, any more than I had, him. Fate had found a way of putting us together, for better, for worse.

He said, "Let's meet. I need to see you. You're so near now. We can't *not* meet."

"When were you thinking?"

"Why don't we meet when the kids are at school? Then there's no problem. I can take some time off here; I've got a meeting on Friday up in London, but I could sort it and send someone else … how about Friday?"

The thought of actually seeing him, having his arms around me was so good.

"Friday's good."

So we arranged for him to come to the house at ten. I felt sick with excitement.

The deed was done.

*

Luke and I spoke again that evening. We decided not to tell the kids yet until something had been finalised. He told me that all the stuff from Cyprus would arrive soon and that he was making arrangements for the boat and Pajero to be sent back. Sometimes, it was possible to get them on a Hercules and that's what he was hoping for.

So ... the boat's on its way; important stuff, I thought.

The time till Friday seemed to drag, even though there was a lot to do in the house. I'd decided to repaint the kitchen; the walls looked dirty and fat-splattered and I wanted to give it a lighter colour. We'd painted it terracotta before and now I was painting it magnolia which was brightening the room and making it look bigger.

I was constantly staring out of the window from quarter to ten onwards; every car that came down the lane, I thought it might be him. So it came as a surprise when I heard the throaty rumble of a motorbike; I'd forgotten he rode one, of course he'd come on it.

I stood at the window watching as he drew up, put his feet down on the ground and turned off the engine. As he strad-dled the bike, unaware of me looking at him, he took off his helmet, running his fingers through his hair. He was wearing his leather gear that I'd heard about; now that he'd stopped and the wind wasn't cooling him, he'd be hot in the sunshine. He unzipped the jacket and took it off, revealing a pristine white t-shirt beneath. Lifting one leg over the saddle to stand by the bike, he put the helmet in the pannier at the back. I saw him check his face in the little mirror; he rubbed something on his cheek and then, with the leather jacket slung over his shoulder, he walked towards the door.

I took a deep breath, swallowed hard and before he had time to knock I'd opened the door.

"I saw you arrive," I said, holding the door open for him. He strode through and I closed the door behind him.

We stood looking at each other, for what felt like a long time; our eyes drawn together, the tension in the room palpable. He walked slowly towards me and putting his arms around me, pulled me into him.

Neither of us spoke; I felt weak, vulnerable even. His arms felt strong and protective. I lay my head on his chest, the softness of his T-shirt like a pillow; the smell of him was a mixture of clean clothes and engines. With his right hand round my face, he tipped my chin upwards and lowered his lips onto mine. Our mouths rested together; we didn't kiss – we simply let our lips find each other, at last.

I was home. This was where I was meant to be. All doubts were gone and in that instant I knew what I had to do about my life, my future.

I drew my mouth away from his, took his hand and led him upstairs.

*

We lay together on the bed. I was acutely aware that we were in our room, it seemed the ultimate betrayal of my marriage but at the same time, it felt right too. James was on his back and I was snuggled into him; he had his right arm under me and I was on my side with my head resting on his chest. I could feel the vibration of his heart – it was beginning to slow now.

"I love you, James. This is where I want to be."

"I love *you*," he said and kissed my hair. "You know I do." His right hand was gently stroking my back.

"I think I know … I think I know what I should do."

"What do you mean?" he said, turning to face me.

We were now both lying on our sides, our faces centimetres apart, looking into each other's eyes.

"I mean … I must tell Luke the truth. Tell him how I feel about you, once and for all. I must leave him."

He kissed my nose and then each eye-lid. "Are you sure? I don't want to pressure you …"

"You're not … this is *my* decision. I know it's the right thing to do now for everyone concerned. Jen said, and she's right, I can't stay with Luke just for the children. Other kids have survived their parents' marriage breaking up. Amy and Charlie will."

"Do you want …"

"No, James, I don't want to think about it any more. I've thought about it for too long already. I've only got one life and I want to spend the rest of it with you. I know it's going to be incredibly difficult … I know I'm going to hurt people … but … I know it's right for me. And for you."

We kissed and it was as if I could see my future at last.

With James.

The kiss went on and on; the present turning into an eternity of love and kisses where we could be together forever. The light was streaming through the curtained windows, little streaks landing on his skin. I thought of the ocean when I was swimming that time with Amy off the boat. How the light had streaked through the surface to the bottom of the sea bed, how I'd felt like a mermaid, drifting.

I was adrift now, but the ocean was beckoning me, to swim out, not to come ashore. To swim and swim … to never return.

Chapter Eighteen

When he left, we said our goodbyes inside the house. Even though my mind was made up, I didn't want prying neighbours seeing us. Conclusions would be drawn, rumours started and ... I didn't want that. I wanted to face it head on but on my own terms.

I felt remarkably calm as his motorbike drew away from the house. We'd kissed knowing that it *wasn't* the end, but the beginning.

Luke would be hurt, angry, sad but he would hardly be surprised; he'd already predicted it. He could move on with his life and not be tied to me; I just made him unhappy these days. He deserved to find someone else. When I'd tell him, I wasn't sure. It was too soon; my mind was still reeling and I wanted time to let it sink in.

I felt utterly convinced now that it was the right decision.

I went upstairs to our bedroom, sat on the bed, re-read James' letters and the poem and then lay down and fell into a deep sleep. I didn't dream; my mother sometimes referred to sleep like that as 'a short portion of death' – a sleep so deep that it was on another level. I had to drag myself up from the depths of unconsciousness but then, I felt refreshed, happy and calm.

Why had it taken me so long to reach this conclusion? I *did* feel guilty that we'd made love on this bed, where the history of our marriage was almost engrained in the wooden frame, but it would be a secret between me and James.

I stripped the bed, throwing the linen down the narrow stairs and then went to the airing cupboard and got out some clean sheets. I made up the bed, smoothing down the sheets so that they were flat, creaseless and pristine.

*

Each time Luke rang that week, I avoided speaking to him; Amy would try to force me onto the phone, but I always found an excuse. We were just going to have to get through the next few weeks somehow and I was going to put off having the conversation for as long as possible. I didn't want Luke to think I'd made the choice purely because of his posting. That had initiated things, but ...

When all our things arrived from Cyprus the following week, life back in England was complete; Akrotiri was a dream that had faded. Unpacking the boxes, I could still smell that Cypriot smell on our things; I put a jumper to my nose and breathed in deeply. Sitting on the floor, as I had in the quarter all that time ago, unpacking my CD's, I turned each one over, savouring the list of songs on the back. I put them back in the rack, put my books back on the shelves each side of the fireplace and it was as if we'd never been away. That interlude away from our home was a myth, a forgotten time.

I found my photo albums and started flicking through the ones I'd compiled in Cyprus. There was Sam, smiling into the camera.

My heart lurched. I'd never see him again. I still couldn't believe it. His laugh echoed round my mind and I snapped the album shut. I resolved to ring Sophie – I didn't know why I hadn't rung her before. It simply didn't matter about her and Luke anymore and I no longer felt I had to justify myself to her.

One evening the phone rang at ten o'clock. It was later than usual for one of Luke's calls and I'd already spoken to James; we spoke every day now.

"Hello, is that Emily?" I immediately recognised Beth's voice.

"Hi, Beth. It's lovely to hear from you. How are things?"

"Awful. I'm sorry to call you so late like this, but ..."

"Don't be silly, you know you can always talk to me ..." I could hear her trying to suppress tears at the other end of the line and I said, "Beth, Beth ... are you okay?"

"Gary's not here, he's out again, so I can talk. I can't stand it any more, Emily. He's been pushing me around a lot and today was the final straw. I was holding Grace and ..."

"What did he do?"

"He was drunk and I tried to shield her from him. He was shouting at me and that was making her cry and ..."

"Did he hit her?"

"No, but he grabbed her from me and stormed off upstairs with her, saying he was going to put her in the cot; that I spent too much time with her and not enough with him. I ran after him and as he got to the cot he virtually threw her in it and shouted at me to shut up crying. I grabbed his arm and he swung round and hit me in the face." I could hear her crying. "I just can't take any more. I want to come home."

"Do you want me to call Luke?"

"Yes ... I haven't wanted to bother him before now, but I think it's reached the stage when ... "

"Look, I'll ring him right now. You stay where you are and I'll call you straight back."

"Would you? Tell him I want to go home, back to the UK, will you? Soon?"

"I will, Beth. Don't worry."

I rang Luke. It was two hours later over there and I could tell he'd been asleep. I explained what had happened.

"Could you go round there now?"

"Now?" he said, sounding both sleepy and annoyed at being woken up.

"Yes, I think Beth really needs someone. I'd go, if I was there, but I'm not. Please go! What if he comes back and does some real damage this time? It's got to stop."

"Okay ... okay ... I suppose you're right. I'll sort it ... I'll try and get her on the next flight home."

"That's brilliant, Luke, thank you. I knew I could rely on you."

Realising that I'd not spoken to Luke about Beth at all in the past weeks, I felt guilty. I'd been so busy and preoccupied since I'd got back I hadn't even asked him if he'd been round at all.

I phoned Beth straight back and told her to expect Luke in the next fifteen minutes.

"Thank you so much. I didn't know who else to turn to. I haven't met anyone else since you left and it's just got progressively worse. I've really missed you."

"Luke says he'll get you on the next plane out of there. If you like, I can meet you at the airport, it's not far from where I live. You can come and stay with me for a few days and then I can put you on the train down to Cornwall."

"That would be amazing. Are you sure?"

"Absolutely. I'll speak to Luke tomorrow morning and find out what's happened. Don't worry, we'll sort it."

*

Luke did everything he'd been asked and when I rang the next day, he promised me that it was all done. It'd been difficult; Gary denied any wrong-doing but, this time, there was no getting away from it. Luke arranged for Beth to stay somewhere else, Gary was charged and the plane was booked.

"So, it's happened. I'm on my way home. This was never

home – I can't wait to see England again," said Beth when she rang from a pay phone, later the next day.

"How do you feel about Gary? What's going to happen?"

"At the moment, I just want to get away from him. Ever since we got married, I've secretly worried that I'd made the wrong decision but … then Grace came along and I thought it would all be okay, but children don't help a broken marriage; they make it worse. I feel I just don't know him any more; he's changed here."

Cyprus had taken its toll on another marriage. Maybe the isolation of camp living, the loneliness of being away from everything familiar forced people to be who they really were and created situations that wouldn't happen back home. Whatever it was, the heat had burned a hole in another relationship and I was sure, this time for Beth and Gary, it was permanent.

"It will be so lovely to have you and Grace here. We can talk everything through and then you can go back to your parents and you'll be able to start surfing again!"

"I know. Now I've made up my mind, I'm so excited. This whole posting has been a disaster for me. The only good thing that came from it, is Grace … meeting you … and your family. Luke's been amazing."

Hearing someone praising Luke like that, made me proud and sad. He was the sort of guy you needed on your side in a crisis. He was good like that.

I had a moment of panic, thinking about what I was giving up.

"I'll see you on Friday, Beth. I'll be there. Luke says you'll land at Brize at three. I'll get the kids sorted with friends …"

"Thank you. I can't wait."

*

Beth looked so young and worn out when she came through from her flight that I felt motherly and protective towards her.

I gave her a hug and offered to push Grace while Beth wheeled an enormous case.

"Your husband is fantastic, Emily, he really is. I don't know what I would've done without him. He arranged everything for me and was down at the terminal when I got on the plane. You're both great."

"I'm pleased he was there for you," I said, wondering when and if to tell Beth about my decision. "Let's get you back to the cottage and we can relax with a bottle of wine when Grace is asleep."

The kids were excited to see Beth and the baby again and when they eventually went to bed, we settled down with some Pinot Grigio. Grace had had her last feed and was fast asleep.

"I have absolutely no regrets coming home," said Beth. "When the plane took off, I felt a weight lifting off me. Gary didn't even apologise; he just kept denying that anything was wrong and said we'd 'sort it out' but ..."

"What do you think you'll do?"

"It's too early to say but I can't see us getting together again. We were too young; Gary likes being with his mates, he's not mature enough to be a dad. I'll be happy on my own, with my parents to support me."

"Beth, I think you should know something; I've also made a huge decision. I'm leaving Luke."

"Oh ..."

"It's the right decision for me ... and everyone. I haven't told Luke yet, but he won't be surprised."

"It's just that I hadn't really got to know Luke when you were out there and he's been so kind to me these last few days. I know you're in love with James, but are you sure you want to?"

"Yes, I'm sure."

I couldn't cope with Beth questioning me; I'd had enough of Sophie judging me and I just wanted to be able to make up my own mind.

"I'm sorry, it's not really my place ... I shouldn't have said anything. Luke told me about the posting."

"Yes, it's weird isn't it? He was convinced he was just going to carry on as before. At least this means that I'll be coming down your way a lot, even though I won't be living down there, I'll visit and take the children down to stay with Luke. It's not far to drive on from Chivenor to you."

"And I could come up; Woolacombe is an amazing beach for surfing. Mind you, how I think I'm going to get back into surfing now that I've got Grace, I don't know!"

"I'm sure you'll find a way and if you come to Devon, we can look after her for you."

This talk of the future seemed odd. I hadn't even told Luke yet and here I was planning visits.

I resolved to tell him next time he rang.

Chapter Nineteen

"So, you're telling me, that you're prepared to throw everything away, everything, for some bloke you met on a prolonged holiday? I just don't understand you, Emily, I really don't." He paused and then blurted out, "Is it because I've been posted to Chivenor?" I could hear his voice shaking with anger, or maybe emotion, I wasn't sure which.

"No, of course it isn't. I won't lie, though, I don't want to go. I've had enough of constantly moving around, never knowing where we're going to end up next. It's no life, Luke, for me – it might be for *you*, but there are two of us in the marriage, you know."

"And James being in the Army doesn't strike you as the same situation, then? God, you're more stupid than I thought."

"I know it's … but he's leaving the Army soon."

"And you know that for sure, do you? What's he going to do then? It's not that easy in civvy street you know. Perhaps he can busk with his fucking guitar … what a joke. You can sing along too …"

"I know he's leaving, because he told me and I believe him. He doesn't know what he'll do yet, but I'm sure he'll find something … he's not obsessed with his career, like you. He doesn't care what he does …"

"Well, I hope you'll both be very happy living off benefits."

"Oh, don't be so ridiculous, Luke. He's got plenty of skills."

"His main one being … seducing other people's wives." I could hear him breathing deeply and felt sick – I knew he'd react like this and didn't know what to say next.

"So where are you two lovebirds going to live, then?"

"We haven't talked about that, or anything practical yet. I'll stay here …"

"You will, will you?" he spat. "Why should you stay in our family home? If you think he's going to move in …"

"I wouldn't dream of him moving in. I just mean I'll stay here for a while until we know what we're going to do."

"Well, we'll have to sell it …"

"What? Why? You'll be in accommodation during your training and then you could live in the Mess …"

"We'll sell it because we're going to get divorced, Emily or isn't that part of your plan? Would you like to stay married to me for convenience sake, so that you can stay in the home we built together? Life's not like that. You've made your decision. We get divorced. We divide everything up. We live separate lives. That's how this works."

With that, he slammed down the phone, leaving me breathless; my heart was thumping so hard, I felt as if it might stop.

But was there ever a 'right' moment to say something like that? Surely it was better that he knew now, so that he could get used to the idea. By the time he comes back, he will have accepted it and we can all plan our futures, I thought.

I lent forward in the chair, hugging my stomach; I sat for a few minutes, wondering what to do. The children were in bed asleep. Beth and Luke were the only ones who knew my decision; maybe it was time to tell Mum and Dad. I sat up and my hand hovered over the phone; the thought of breaking the news to them was awful. I withdrew my hand. If Mum had kept my secret, it would come as a complete shock to Dad and I wasn't sure how Mum would react, either. Mum loved Luke and clearly wanted me to distance myself from James.

Deciding to face her, I picked up the receiver, dialled the number and waited for someone to pick up. After an eternity of ringing, I heard my mother's voice.

"Hello, Mum. It's me."

My mother was always tuned into my every emotion and mood and her response was, "Emily, what's wrong?"

She knows me too well …

"Mum, I'm ringing to tell you something …"

"Yes, dear I can tell that. What's happened? Are the children okay?"

"We're fine, Mum. It's me …"

"What do you mean?"

"Mum, I've made the biggest decision of my life … I'm leaving Luke."

There was a long pause at the other end of the phone, then Mum said simply, "Are you going to that James?"

"Yes, I am. I love him and it's time to stop trying to have them both. I can't go on like this. Mum, I don't want to move again, I really don't, but no, that wasn't the reason. I think if I'm honest, it made me make my mind up, though. Luke didn't even consider my feelings or what I wanted to do, he just accepted the posting without even telling me …"

"But you've always known he was in the Air Force, Emily. That's how it is. He can't just say 'no' to postings, you know he can't. He's often told us that's what he dreamt of, so I'm not surprised he's accepted it. You should be more supportive, you really should, Emily."

"But Mum …" I wished my mother would stop using my name; it sounded so formal and I felt like a child again.

"No, Emily … this time I *can't* stick up for you. Your father is going to be so disappointed in you."

"Will *you* tell him, Mum?" reverting to childhood tactics.

"I suppose I'll have to, if your mind's made up. What are you going to do?"

"I don't know, Mum … all I know is that James and I want to be together and …"

"But it's not just about *you and James*, is it? What about those poor children of yours? Where are they going to live?"

"With me, of course."

"And is Luke happy about that?"

"I don't know. He slammed the phone down on me."

"I'm not surprised. Well, he won't be happy at all. He's such a good father. He won't want them to live with a stranger."

I could feel myself getting more and more upset as the conversation went on. Mum was voicing all the things I'd been trying to ignore in my head. I knew she was right. Luke would *never* agree to me and the children moving in with James.

What was I thinking?

"Look, Mum. I don't want to talk about it right now. I'm tired and I want to go to bed. I'll ring you again in a few days. You tell Dad. I'll ring David and tell him. I think he'll be a bit more understanding ..."

"Emily, dear. We love you, you know that. But we can't condone this behaviour. We don't even *know* this man."

"Well, you'll have to meet him soon, then, won't you? Mum, I love you. Bye."

I put the phone down and cried.

*

The following days went by in a blur. Luke didn't ring at all, not even to speak to the children and although Amy kept asking, we didn't ring him. I went through the motions of life; I had coffee with Bella and was even invited round one evening for dinner. The kids were at sleepovers, so I didn't have to get home for the babysitter. Bella's husband, the vet, Simon, was friendly and fun to be with – he plied me with drink and by the end of dinner, I was pretty tipsy and had to be walked home. It wasn't the same as walking back through the camp at night with the star-filled sky; it was pitch black, with owls hooting and foxes barking; it took on a melancholy atmosphere.

"Are you okay now?" said Simon, as he waited while I struggled to find my key at the bottom of my handbag.

"I'm fine, I think. Thank you for a great evening and … sorry I drank too much."

He put his hand on my arm as I turned to put my key in. "Don't worry. It must be difficult living here on your own with two young children and your husband, thousands of miles away. I know Bella wouldn't be able to cope like you. It's good to let your hair down, sometimes."

"Yes … it's hard," I said, realising that Luke never praised me for coping, never acknowledged how I got on with life without him.

I opened the door, found the light switch and kissing him on the cheek said, "Bye and thanks again for walking me home."

"Bye, Emily."

I stood in the door and waved as he turned down the lane. Closing the door, the silence of the house engulfed my befuddled head. It was the first time I'd been completely alone in the house for years and it was now evident that every creak, every noise from the plumbing system, was going to sound like a cacophony. The clock said ten past midnight – how come the night had gone so quickly? Was it too late to speak to James?

I dialled his number and he picked up.

"James?"

"Are you okay? Why are you ringing so late? Is something wrong?"

"No, no … nothing's wrong … I'm all alone and a little drunk … and I wanted to hear your voice."

He laughed. "You sound very sexy when you've had too much to drink."

Ignoring his joke, I said, "James … what are we going to do?"

"How do you mean?"

"About everything. Luke's so angry with me, he hasn't spoken since our row. Mum says he'll never let me and the kids live with you. He says we'll have to sell the house. I haven't spoken to Mum again; she's very cross with me."

"You've had a bit too much to drink and it's late …"

"And I'm completely on my own in the house. I hate it!"

"Where are Amy and Charlie?"

"They're at friends'. I was invited to Bella and Simon's for dinner. He gave me loads to drink and he had to walk me home …"

"Do you want me to come over?"

"What, now?"

"Yes, now."

"Would you do that?"

"Of course I'd do that for you. I'd do anything for you, you know that."

I suddenly felt guilty for burdening him with my petty worries in the middle of the night. "No, don't be daft. You can't do that."

"I will if you want me to."

I wavered. How I would love him to be there, but no, I couldn't ask him to. It would take him at least forty minutes.

"That's really sweet of you, James. But I'm okay. I'm happy just to hear your voice. I'm sorry if I woke you."

"I was watching TV in bed, just beginning to drift off. I'm pleased you rang. When can we see each other?"

"Well, I have a plan. David's coming over next weekend, with Steve, and I thought I'd leave the kids with them for a night and come and visit you. David knows everything and he's even suggested it … he's such a good brother. Does that sound like a plan?"

"It certainly does. Next weekend it is. I'll cook you a romantic meal, how about that?"

My mind visualised a candlelit table in a dark room and James sitting opposite me, his eyes shining.

"Wonderful."

*

A few days later, Sophie rang. The moment I heard her voice, I knew that Luke had told her. Her voice was brittle and unfriendly.

"Emily. How are you?" she said with no upward lift, a formality only.

"I'm okay. How are you?"

"I'm good. Modelling again. Living back in my house. Trying to move on." Her staccato, abrupt sentences indicated that she had something else to say. I didn't want to discuss my life.

There was a pause and then she said, "Luke rang."

"Oh."

"Yes, he's told me your 'news', Emily and quite frankly, I just can't believe it. Why ... why?"

"What do you mean, why? You've never liked James, Sophie but I love him and I want to spend ..."

"Oh, please," she interrupted, "don't give me all that crap again about ..."

"It's not crap, Sophie. I've made my decision. People know now – join the queue of the disapproving ... David is the only one who's been understanding."

"Well, I'm sorry but I think you're making a huge mistake. Luke's a good man, a wonderful father. Cyprus was an unreal place ... a place where bad things happened."

To Sophie, Cyprus must always be associated with death and grief, I understood that, but why was she so against me? I wanted to stick up for myself.

"I know about your little dalliance with my husband, which you denied. I found evidence and Luke admitted it."

There, *that* told you.

There was silence. I was fed up of Sophie; she'd been judgemental right from the start.

"I'm sorry you had to find out …" she sounded taken aback; maybe Luke hadn't told her I knew.

"So, *none* of us are perfect, are we? We're just human beings trying to make our way through this messy thing called life, Sophie. I never went into this whole thing deliberately to hurt Luke or to break up my family. It happened … like it just happened with you and Luke. I've forgiven you both, because I can see why it happened. I just wish you could do the same for me."

"Look, I know you didn't mean to do any of this. I'm sorry if I'm blunt with my opinions. I've always been the same. When I think something, I say it out loud. Can we still be friends? I want to be friends with you both … I don't want to take sides, you know."

Her voice had softened, her tone, gentle. I saw it suddenly from her point of view. Maybe Luke and I were the only stable things left from her life in Cyprus; perhaps she was hanging on to us, trying to hang onto her memories of Sam and all the fun the four of us had together. Imagine how I would feel if say, Jen and John broke up and one of them went off with someone else – how difficult it would be.

"If we're going to be able to move forward, Sophie, you've got to forgive me. You've got to stop blaming James. I know Luke's probably been telling you he's a serial wife seducer, but he's not, Sophie; he's just a nice person who's muddled up in someone else's family mess. Blame me, not James."

"I'll try to understand," she said. "Why don't I come and see you and the kids, sometime?"

"That'd be lovely, Sophie."

I knew that neither of us meant it – our friendship was over.

*

168

"Hey you two, come and give your uncle a big hug," said David as he walked into the sitting room. Amy was drawing and Charlie was on the floor, playing with his trains.

They both loved David and seeing him, they jumped up and rushed over to him. They were less effusive with Steve, but all four of them chatted away. I looked on, loving having my brother in the house again.

"So, Steve and I are in charge tonight – your Mum's going out and we're looking after you two so you better be on your best behaviour."

"Can we stay up late?" said Charlie, ever hopeful.

"Maybe … we wondered if there was anything on at the cinema you'd both like to see?"

There then followed shouts and arguments and reference to the local newspaper and arrangements were made to see something they could all enjoy. Copious amounts of sweets and ice creams were promised.

"You two are complete pushovers," I said, laughing and pushing Steve on the arm.

"Well, if you can't spoil your sister's children, who can you spoil?" said David, kissing me on the forehead.

I was so happy to be leaving them with David and Steve; I could go off without any worries and enjoy my night. The only bit I didn't like was that I was lying to the children.

When it was time to leave I said, "Now be good you two – do what David and Steve tell you to do. And you two," I said, turning to my brother, "you two, don't let the kids dictate what happens. You're in charge, not them!" I kissed them all and saying I'd be back tomorrow lunch time, I left.

James had given me instructions and I found his flat relatively easily. It was in a house on a quiet road on the outskirts of Bristol. I pulled up outside; parking was allowed after six and I went up to the front door and rang the bell, marked Flat 2C.

"Hey, you're here," came his disembodied voice. "I'll open

the door, then come up the stairs opposite you and I'm on the left."

A loud buzz sounded and the door clicked open. There was lots of mail and flyers on the floor that no one had bothered to pick up. I went up the dingy staircase, noticing the scuff marks on the walls and made my way to his door.

He was already standing inside the open door, with a glass of white wine in each hand.

"Welcome to my humble abode."

He kissed me on the cheek and handed me a glass.

"Cheers, my love," he said and chinked his glass on mine. I took a little sip and looked round to put it down somewhere, so that I could take off my coat. He took it and hung it on a hook in the corridor where we were standing.

"Come into the sitting room – well, I say, sitting room. It's also the dining room." I followed him down the corridor, glancing through the door on the left that led into a very small galley kitchen. The room he led me into was square and had a small table and two chairs in one corner, a rather shabby sofa, an armchair and a television.

"Come and sit, you must be tired after the drive. Are the children okay with David?"

"They're fine. They've got him and Steve wrapped round their little fingers." I sat down and James popped out into the corridor to collect my forgotten glass. As he handed it to me, he kissed my lips. "It's so good to have you here at last. I've waited for this."

I felt strange. I didn't know why exactly, but I supposed it was because this was the first time I'd been in his 'territory' and I had to admit, the smallness of the flat, the shabby entrance hall and the old furniture gave me a bit of a shock.

"Sorry about the flat," he said, as if he could read my mind. "It's just somewhere to sleep. None of this stuff's mine. It's a furnished flat, which was ideal for me as I don't own anything. It's convenient for work too, I can park the car and the bike outside, with a permit. It's nothing special, but it does at the moment."

"Can I go to the loo?" I said, wanting to hide in the bathroom for a few minutes, to pull myself together.

"Sure. Down the corridor, just past the kitchen."

I hadn't noticed the other door. I opened it and there was a simple, white bathroom: a bath with an old-fashioned shower over it; a rather grubby looking shower curtain, a basin and a loo. I brushed my hair and talked silently to myself in the mirror. Why was I worried about where he lives? What did I expect? What difference did it make?

It brought it home, I suppose, that he was a bachelor, leading a bachelor's life. Where would we fit into this single man's existence? It was absolutely impossible to imagine myself and the children living here; there was only one bedroom and the flat was totally unsuitable in every way. Why was I even thinking like this? I'd stay put, in our house. The children would continue going to school where they are. I'd see James when I could.

I leant forward until my nose was virtually touching the mirror. All I could see was a fool.

When I came out, he was busying himself in the kitchen.

"I'm doing a lasagne from first principles, everything's homemade, even the cheese sauce. Hope you're impressed?" He had on a butcher's apron and was chopping onions.

"What? Even the pasta?"

"No … I have to admit I bought that; that would be a step too far, I'm afraid. But I'm making the mince for the layers and I've already done the cheese, so it's just an assembly job. Hope you like Pavlova for dessert?"

"Did you do that too?"

"Yup, it used to be my mother's favourite pudding and she taught me. I'm very limited on the cooking front, though. Pasta and mince in various guises and Pavlova and eggs … that's it!"

"Well, it's very impressive. Luke's never done any cooking at all." I wished I hadn't mentioned his name. I went up behind James and put my arms around him and put my face against his back. "It's great to be here, James. I feel like a normal couple. Us here, in the kitchen …"

He put down the knife, and turning round, he wiped his hands on the apron and then put a strand of hair behind my ear.

"This will be our life together from now on. Domesticated bliss," he said, kissing me on the mouth. "This is just the start. I wanted to cook for you, I don't know why. Maybe we should have gone out to a restaurant?"

"No, this is perfect," I said, meaning it. "I love it, just you and me. No one else."

A picture of the children flashed into my mind.

*

The evening went by in a heartbeat. The meal was absolutely delicious, even if the lasagne was a little burnt; we'd been so engrossed in each other and he'd almost forgotten to get it out of the oven. We sat at the little table; he'd lit two candles, so my vision earlier was accurate. We talked about our plans: he said of course we'd eventually find a bigger place where we could live together; he said he realised this place was totally unsuitable. I told him all about Luke's reaction and my parents'. I'd told him briefly before, but now I told him every little detail. He held my hand across the table and even sympathised with Luke.

"I'm not surprised he reacted like he did. I can't imagine what he's going through. If I lost you now …"

"You won't, James, you won't. I'm yours now. Forever."

We talked about having a baby together. We figured if we were going to do it, we should get on with it; I'd always wanted another child … Luke had known that and he had decided to kill that dream for me. James would now fulfil my wish instead; we'd have a baby together, a brother or sister for Amy and Charlie.

We left the plates and the debris from the meal on the table and drifted into the bedroom. He lay down and pulled me on top of him.

"You're here, Emily. In my bed. You've come to me at last."

"Yes, I'm here, James. I'm here."

"Let's start making babies," he laughed, rolling me over, so that I was now under him.

"Perhaps it's a bit too soon …" I tried to say.

*

When I woke up early next morning, nothing was as straight-forward as it had been the night before. I lay on my side, watching James sleeping and thought back to our conversation: new house, new baby, new life. But the reality was I had my old life, my old house and two children who didn't even know of James' existence. I was going to have to tell them and soon. Before Luke came home.

James opened his eyes and said, "Morning, Beautiful …" and stretched his hand over to stroke my head.

"Morning, James."

"What's wrong?"

He was like my mother, he was so tuned into my moods.

"I was thinking about how I've got to tell Amy and Charlie. I can't *not* tell them. I have to face up to the reality of every-thing … they're going to be devastated."

"Why don't you wait until Luke gets home and tell them together? It shouldn't just be you."

"Yea, maybe you're right, we should do it together and show them that their life won't change."

"You should tell the truth, Emily. Children are quick to understand if they're not being told the whole truth. They'll be very upset to start with, but ..."

"James, you haven't got any children, so please don't tell me what to do."

I felt angry – I didn't want his advice. It was *my* problem and I was going to have to find a way to deal with it.

"Sorry ... I was just trying to ..."

"I know, you're right, James, about telling the truth. Who am I trying to kid? Our lives are going to change dramatically. Oh God."

I turned over, away from him. He put his arm round me and pulled me back to him, so that we were lying like spoons.

"It'll be okay, you'll see. It'll take a while to sort it all out, but they'll be okay. They have two parents who love them very much and they know that."

"But two parents who don't love them enough to stay together."

"Don't be so hard on yourself. You've tried to make it work and now it's time to try another way. They'll understand, eventually."

He kissed the back of my neck and held me while I lay there thinking about my children. We both lay in silence.

Soon we got up and he made me scrambled eggs on toast.

"I didn't tell you about my breakfasts, did I?" he said, handing me a plate piled high.

"Wow, are you trying to feed me up or something?"

"I'm trying to impress you ... is it working?"

"Maybe ... of course, I'm impressed. It's lovely to be waited on hand and foot. I'm not used to it."

After breakfast, we went for a walk in a local park. We saw couples pushing buggies, but neither of us alluded to them; I was sure we were both thinking back to last night's conversation.

When it was time for to go, he walked me to my car. "I

don't feel sick any more when you leave," he said. "When we were in Cyprus, we were always saying goodbye. Always. Now we don't have to. Well, we do, but you know what I mean."

"Yes, I know exactly what you mean. No more tears, no more sadness. No more goodbyes, James."

"I love you."

"I love you," I said.

Chapter Twenty

James' advice about telling the children together whirled around in my mind; I decided to speak to Luke about it and agree a plan. So, late one night, I rang him. It was the first time we'd spoken since he'd slammed the phone down. He sounded flat and detached as if he couldn't be bothered to speak to me at all.

I started off by asking if he had a date for coming home.

"Why do you want to know? It's not really relevant any more."

"I thought we ought to talk about what we're going to do for Christmas."

"Christmas?"

"Well … yes. I know the last person you'd want to spend it with is me and … I thought you'd like to have some time with the kids on your own. I'll go and spend a few days with my parents and you can be in the house with the children." I thought that if I was reasonable, helpful even, it would make things easier.

"How kind," he said with heavy sarcasm. "Allowing me to stay in my own house."

"Luke, don't be like that. I thought …"

"And how are you going to explain your absence to the children?"

"Well, we need to … I thought when you get home, we should sit down and tell them what's going on." I could hear my mother's voice, talking about the 'situation'. There was a long silence, at the end of the line; he'd hate having to tell them, I knew that.

"Luke?"

"Yes … okay then, if your mind's made up. What a lovely Christmas present for them."

"It's never going to be the right time, is it? At least if we tell them together, we can reassure them that everything will be okay."

"And how do you propose to do that?"

"By telling them that we both love them very much and that they'll live with us both, but in different houses. We don't have to make any huge decisions yet, do we? You talked about selling the house, but until you're down in Chivenor, which won't be for a few months yet, we don't have to do anything, do we?" I said, hoping the answer would be negative.

"No, I suppose not but we'll have to sell up next year, so that we can all move on." As much as I hated the idea, I had to agree.

"So, from their point of view, nothing need change – now. You're away at the moment and you'll just 'be away' after we tell them."

"God, you're a hard bitch, sometimes."

"I'm sorry, I didn't *mean* it like that … I just meant that …"

"You just meant that I'm a crap father …"

"NO! I didn't mean that at all. I meant that they are *used* to you not being here now, so it won't be any different, *then*. You're a brilliant father, Luke, you really are."

"Thanks for that little crumb of comfort."

"I mean it. I've always envied the way you are with the kids. They love being with you. You're so much more fun than I am. I will never get in the way of you seeing them; I want you to see them as much as possible, I really do."

There was no getting away from the fact, though, that I would be the main 'carer' due to the nature of his job but I'd make sure they saw him on lots of weekends and most of their holidays when he wasn't on duty.

"Anyway, I've got to go now," he said. "I don't want to speak to you any more. I'm due home on 12th December, so …"

"I'll tell my parents about Christmas."

He put the phone down.

*

Mum was downhearted when I told her about the plans for Christmas. Christmas just 'wouldn't be the same' without the children she said and she was absolutely right, it wouldn't. I couldn't imagine having Christmas away from them but I thought it was only fair. Luke had missed out on months of being with them, it was the least I could do. He wasn't very close to his parents, but maybe he could invite them down? He wouldn't have to cook the meal; the local pub did a brilliant Christmas dinner; we'd gone there the year before we went to Cyprus.

I explained all this to Mum, hoping that she'd see it from my point of view but she just kept saying, was I sure that there was no way we could get back together?

"Your father is so disappointed in you," she said. He probably was (I hadn't dared speak to him since he'd heard the news) but Mum always said that, when she really meant it was *her* who was disappointed.

"I suppose you'll go and see that James, when you're here?"

"Mum, can you *stop* calling him 'that James'? He's James."

"I'm sorry, dear, but I can't get used to the fact that there's another man in your life, who we've never even *met*."

"Well, maybe he could come over while I'm with you?"

"Oh, I'm not sure about that … your father wouldn't approve."

"Mum, you've got to meet him sometime. Maybe Christmas is a good time; David will be there and …"

"I'll run it by your father …"

"Thanks, Mum. I know it's difficult but I think you may like him."

"I'm not sure, Emily. Any man that can break up a lovely little family like yours …"

"Mum. *Please.* It wasn't his fault. He said he'd walk away if that's what I wanted. He just wanted me to be happy and if that meant us not being together, he was prepared to lose me. But I wanted this. It's *my* decision."

"Okay, dear, don't shout."

"Well, I get very upset when you blame him. It's not his fault. Please see that."

The conversation ended with Mum promising not to blame James, but I wasn't looking forward to our meeting.

*

When Luke eventually walked through the door, I found it hard to deal with; seeing him in our house, it was as if three years had evaporated. He was so familiar, so part of my life that I had to convince myself that everything had, indeed, changed and my old life had gone forever.

It was six o'clock when he arrived. He'd flown with the Pajero and speedboat in a Hercules and had landed at Lyneham. All the paperwork for the car and boat had taken a while, but it was all sorted and he turned up in the car, leaving the boat to be stored on the camp, until he took it down to Devon. Amy and Charlie were so excited to see him and watching him pick each one up in turn and smother them in hugs and kisses, made me feel sad knowing what they were soon to be told.

We both did a good job at acting; the kids didn't suspect anything and went up to bed happy. Luke spent at least an hour upstairs with them and when I crept up to see why he was taking so long, I saw through the crack of Amy's open door that she was reading to Luke. She was sitting, propped up against the pillow and he was lying on her bed, with Charlie cuddled in too. The room was quite dark, the bedside lamp giving out a warm orange glow. They were a solid little unit, oblivious to my presence. Suddenly, they all laughed at something Amy said and it made me feel an outsider, an 'extra' in a film, someone on the periphery of a family. I was moving onto another partner, another life, leaving these three in the life we'd built together. They'd manage perfectly well when I wasn't there, I knew that, but seeing them there, snuggled in together, I felt very much alone.

I crept back down the corridor and downstairs, making sure I didn't tread on the creaky floorboards. I sat at the kitchen table, wondering how the evening would progress.

*

"So, are you going to ask your parents down for Christmas?"

I'd made him some supper and he was sitting on the sofa with his plate on his lap, watching the News.

"My parents? No, why would you think that?"

"Well, I just thought you might want to."

"They don't even know you're leaving me yet, so I'd hardly invite them down and anyway, I haven't spent Christmas with them for years, I don't want to start now. I've invited Sophie."

"Sophie?"

"Yes, Sophie."

"How did that happen?"

"She's on her own. She doesn't want to spend Christmas with her parents. We're friends. I thought it would be nice. We've done it before … remember?"

The fact that they were obviously in recent communication with each other, really hit me in the guts.

"Does it matter who I spend Christmas with? Do you care?"

"Of course I care, Luke. I'm pleased she's coming. The kids will love her being here."

I said this without any conviction. I was hoping by saying it out loud I'd convince myself.

"She's been amazing to me."

"Oh."

We both ate our meals, the silence between us broken only by the newsreader's voice.

"I'll sleep on the sofa, Luke. I don't mind, I'm sure you're tired after the journey," I said.

He was staring at the screen and I was taking surreptitious glances at him. He looked thinner but at the same time he had that wonderful Cypriot golden glow that made everyone look healthy. His hair was slightly longer than normal and sun streaked, his cheekbones more prominent. His loss of weight actually suited him: his jeans were looser, his t-shirt moulded to his chest; I could even see the outline of his ribs. I noticed his hands; his right hand on the arm of the sofa, his left clutching a wine glass. Something about them looked different and with a lurch of my heart, I realised he'd taken off his wedding ring that he'd worn every day of our marriage.

He didn't respond; he lifted his ringless hand upwards and took another swig of red wine.

*

"Why are you on the sofa, Mum?" said Amy, standing by my head, looking down.

"You're up early. What time is it?"

"Half past six, I think. I woke up and was hungry, so I thought I'd get a bowl of cereal. Why are you here?"

"I couldn't sleep, so I thought I'd move down here, so as not to disturb Daddy."

That seemed to satisfy her for now and I wandered off to the kitchen. I lay there, looking at the room, wondering if this was the day we'd tell them. Maybe I should have hinted then, but it didn't seem right somehow. When Luke came down, we'd discuss it.

*

"So, kids, we've got something we want to tell you," said Luke, looking over at me with a look of disbelief on his face. We'd decided to talk about it over lunch; we were sitting round the kitchen table eating a lunch of soup, cheese, biscuits and fruit. Charlie was tucking into his third cracker, his favourite food, he claimed.

"Yes, Mummy and Daddy have …"

"Why are you saying Mummy and Daddy? You always say Mum and Dad. It sounds funny," said Amy. "We're grown up now. It sounds babyish."

She was right. I always used the shortened form. It's probably the formality of it, I thought to myself. My stomach was churning; I couldn't face any food and was just picking at a dry cracker. Luke, too, had an empty plate.

"Mum and Dad," I said, correcting my mistake, "love you both very much …"

"We know, we know …" said Amy.

I looked over at Luke for some help; I didn't know what to say next.

Luke reached across and squeezed Charlie's shoulder and said, "Mum and Dad are going to live in different houses …" His sentence petered out, without reaching the nub of the point.

"You always do … Dad's always away, working. We know." Amy said it as if she knew exactly what we were getting at. Charlie wasn't taking much notice. He reached for yet another cracker.

"What Dad's trying to say, is that we don't want to live together any more."

They both looked at us, their faces brimful of questions and incomprehension.

"Why don't you?" said Charlie, his mouth full of cracker. "Do you mean, like that film we saw? When the dad moved out and the children had to keep going to his house? The mum threw all his clothes out of the window, didn't she?"

"Well, not like that, no. I won't be throwing Dad's clothes out of any windows, but a bit like that, yes. Dad will live somewhere else and you'll go and see him whenever you want."

This took time to sink in. Amy's eyes filled with tears and said, "Don't you love each other any more?"

A tear trickled down her cheek; she became a tiny child before our eyes.

"We'll always love each other, Amy, but we don't want to live together any more."

"But why? *Why?*" she said. She got up from the table and went and sat on Luke's lap, wrapping her arms around his neck, hanging onto him like a limpet.

"Sometimes grown-ups love each other but want different things … you'll understand when you're older, poppet," said Luke, stroking her hair. "Come over here, Buddy," he said, opening up one of his arms. Charlie got down and went and sat of Luke's free knee. "I'm going to go and live by the sea," said Luke, "so, you can come and see me and we'll go swimming and surfing and I'll even have my boat there, on an estuary. It'll be like Cyprus, without the hot weather."

"But Mummy won't be there," cried Amy into his chest. "Where will Mum be?"

"Mum will stay here, with you two. Nothing will change. You'll keep going to school and come and see me at weekends and in the holidays. It'll be fun." He squeezed them both hard and looked across at me above their heads. I felt utterly devastated, knowing that I'd caused this, I'd made this happen. I could feel my own tears welling up.

I shook my head, wiped my eyes and said, "And what's very exciting is that you're going to have Christmas here with Dad … and Sophie's coming too."

"Where are you going?" said Amy. "Why aren't you staying for Christmas?"

"Granny and Granddad want me to go there, with David and Steve and I said I'd go and help do all the cooking. They're quite old now and need some help, don't they? I'll only be gone for a few days and you, Dad and Sophie will all go out to the pub, like we did before – do you remember?" I was trying to make my voice sound light and fun.

"No, I don't," said Amy. "I want *you* to be here, with us."

"Well, I can't, I'm afraid but you'll have great fun." My sentence fell into the silence and sounded bleak; it all sounded anything but fun.

Turning to look up into Luke's face, Amy said, "Why are you going to the seaside?"

"The RAF has given me the chance to fly helicopters, something I've always hoped for. I'll be rescuing people who are in trouble on cliffs and at sea. It'll be so exciting, won't it?"

A look of sheer terror flashed across her face. "But Sam was killed in a helicopter, Daddy. You won't die, will you?"

Luke bent down and kissed her cheek. "Of course, not, Poppet, I'll be as safe as houses. That was a terrible accident; it won't happen to me."

He glanced across at me with a look of 'See what you've done?' written on his face. I twisted my wedding ring round my finger, and said, "Daddy's the best pilot in the world, you know that, Amy. He'll save lots of people and …"

Charlie hadn't said anything for a while. He suddenly said, as if it was part of this discussion, "Where's Tom Kitten, anyway? I want him."

Luke said, "He's in a cattery at the moment, Buddy. He has to be there for a few weeks to make sure he hasn't got any diseases or anything and then he can come home. Back to this house."

"Can we go and see him?"

"Maybe, I'll find out. Now, I thought we'd go swimming," said Luke, "so, why don't you go and find your swimming things? Go on, off you go!" and they both got off his lap and went upstairs.

"That wasn't too bad, was it?"

"I'm glad you think that," he said. "You go on deluding yourself. That's fine."

Chapter Twenty-One

The days leading up to Christmas seemed odd in every way; we did our own thing, but at the same time, I was trying to maintain the family unit as I had always done in the past. We went to Charlie's nativity play together; we got the tree from the local garden centre and the kids decorated it. I wrote cards to all the usual people – normally I'd have written some 'news' in the cards, but I simply wrote 'Love from the Blackwells' in all of them, except Jen's and Beth's; I wrote long letters to both of them, which I tucked inside the cards. I bought all the stocking presents for the children and realised I wouldn't see them open them. I agonised over whether to buy Luke a present. It was a silly thing to worry about, but whatever I did, it would be wrong. Not to, looked churlish, unfriendly – mean even, but to give him a present was two-faced, hypocritical and ... but I decided to give him a new mono-ski – a generous present. He'd probably think it was to salve my conscience, but I really wanted to give something to him I knew he'd get a lot of pleasure from. His old one was past its prime and I knew he wanted this state of the art one. I gave it, wrapped, to Amy to hide in her cupboard.

I left on the morning of 23rd December. Sophie was arriving that evening I was told; I was relieved not to see her.

"Now, you two have a brilliant time, won't you?" I said, as

the children hugged me. "You help Dad as much as possible and I'll be home very soon."

Neither of them said anything, they just clung onto me harder, willing me to stay. "Come on, now … I've got to go … Granny's expecting me for lunch. I'll ring you when I get there."

"I don't want you to go …" said Charlie, stamping his foot. He'd been quiet since we'd told him and Mrs Cressman, his teacher even had a word with me at the end of term, asking if there was anything wrong. I'd felt it my duty to tell her the truth; I'd found myself blushing when I told the story; the teacher said she'd keep on eye on 'the situation' – that word again.

"Charlie, I'm only going to be gone a few days, you'll be fine … Dad's got all sorts of things lined up for you. Luke, would you like to show Charlie that thing, you know," I said, winking at him over Charlie's head, "that outing you've got planned to the panto?"

Luke said, "Come here, Buddy," as he extricated Charlie from my legs and picked him up. "I'll show you this leaflet all about 'Aladdin' – we're going to see it on Boxing Day."

He mouthed, "You go," at me and said, "You come here too, Amy. Mum's got to go now." Amy reluctantly let go and walked slowly after Luke.

"Bye, Mum. Give my love to Granny."

I put all my things in the car; I had a bag full of presents for everyone and at the last minute, Luke had added some more. He'd said they were from the children; I didn't look at them, so I had no idea whether he'd given me a present. I almost hoped he hadn't.

I didn't deserve one.

*

I was going to spend Boxing Day with James' parents. He really wanted to introduce me to them and they were keen to meet me. I was absolutely dreading it. It was such an important progression in our relationship – what if they didn't like me? What if I didn't like them?

Christmas Day passed, that's all that can be said of it. The atmosphere just wasn't the same without the children. What was the point of Christmas without them, I wondered? It was just adults, sitting around eating and drinking too much, watching the same old stuff on TV. It was lovely to see David and Steve; Mum and Dad were completely relaxed with Steve now and, as I'd blotted my copybook, David was now the blue-eyed boy, despite being gay.

I was a far worse sinner.

I tried to talk about James and even showed my parents pictures of him, so that they were prepared for the meeting, due on 27th, just before I went home.

"He's got nice hair," said Mum. "When was this taken?"

"Ages ago, on a beach in Cyprus … Aphrodite's Rock, where the Goddess of Love is meant to have emerged from the sea." I left that hanging in the air, the significance of the place being difficult to convey to someone who hadn't been there.

"You don't believe in all that nonsense, do you?"

"Well, it may be nonsense to you, Mum, but it's a magical place. You have to be there, to understand."

"I'm sure you do, dear." I put the picture down on the kitchen table and went over to the sink to continue washing up.

After the long Christmas lunch, we all opened our presents. Amy had given me some perfume; Luke knew what I liked and it was my favourite. Charlie had given me lots of things to put in the bath, again one of my favourite brands.

I saw a small present tucked away at the bottom of the bag. I reached in, looked at the tag. It read, "To Ems, with love from Luke x" I opened it, my heart beating fast. I hoped the others weren't watching me – Mum had just opened her present from

Dad and we were all admiring some special book he'd found.

Tearing the paper open, I saw a blue box. Inside, was a delicate gold locket on a chain. I took it out and in tiny writing on the back, he'd had engraved, 'Love you, always'.

I stared at it. The weird thing was, I loved him too, yet I was leaving him.

What's wrong with me?

How can anyone be 'in love' with one man and 'love' another?

*

James had told me how to find the house and as I went down the long tree-lined drive, I felt like a schoolgirl about to take an important exam; my palms were sweaty, my pulse racing. I pulled up and parked. My hand went to the locket round my neck – I held it between my thumb and forefinger for a few seconds, before opening the door and getting out.

They lived in a small, neat village east of Basingstoke and the house was typical of some of the more expensive houses in the area: red brick, black beams criss-crossing the gable ends. It was evidently very old, sitting on its land with grace and permanence. A plant grew abundantly up the walls around the windows and had done so for years, judging by the twisted, gnarled stem laid bare in the winter months. The house wasn't huge, but it was certainly large, comfortable and immaculate. As Mum would say, the lawns 'looked as if we'd been cut with nail scissors'; the hedges, clipped to within an inch of their lives.

I stood looking at it all, taking in the sweeping lawns to the left and the small pond to the right. The air was crisp and a light hoarfrost decorated the vegetation with crystalline whiteness. It was indeed a Christmassy scene and in other circumstances, I would have enjoyed it but I was too nervous today.

Having got some flowers, a bottle of Merlot and a bottle of Moet out of the boot, I made my way to the front door.

I wished James had come out to greet me but with a house like this, you don't see people arriving.

I rang the bell; I could hear it, reverberating through the house. After a few seconds, the door opened and there he was, looking far smarter than I'd ever seen him before; he was wearing a suit and tie.

"Wow, you look posh," I said, feeling rather underdressed. I'd just thrown on a dress I'd had for years and some long boots I was rather fond of.

He kissed my cheek and said, "Come in and meet the parents. We're in the drawing room and here are Ruben and Roscoe." Two wiggly Springer Spaniels came through a door, bounded over to us and James bent down and stroked one of their heads.

"This one's Rubes and that's Ross; they're brothers and as stupid as each other," he laughed. I fondled one of them, loving his soft fur.

"These are some presents for your parents," I said, brandishing the booze and flowers.

"That's really sweet of you," he said and took my coat. He led me down the wide corridor out of the entrance hall. Opening the door at the end, he stood aside to let me in. "Mum, Dad, here she is … this is Emily. Look what she brought us."

They had both been sitting, reading newspapers and stood up together.

"Hello, Mrs Fox," I said, holding out my hand to an elegant lady in her mid-sixties, "nice to meet you." My hand was dismissed quickly.

"Are these for me?" she said, taking the flowers from the crook of my arm. "How kind."

His father, a florid, portly man, held out his hand, and said, "Nice to meet you too, Emily. Call me George." His grip was incredibly strong, I could feel my hand being crushed. He had a friendly face though and when he'd finished shaking my hand, he put his arm round my shoulders and said, "I'm sure we can polish off those bottles you've brought with our lunch. Thank you very much indeed. What are you having now, for a little aperitif? Gin and Tonic? Sherry? We've got most things."

"G and T please. That would be lovely."

James was busying himself collecting up the newspapers, folding them neatly and putting them on a small side table.

"Frieda, have we got some nibbles? I'm sure Emily will be hungry after her drive. Come and sit by the fire, dear," said George, "warm yourself up."

"James, Darling, will you go and see what we've got in the kitchen?" said Frieda. I could hear the faint German accent which had seemed more pronounced on the phone, all those months ago.

James left and the three of us sat in an awkward silence, for a few seconds. I cleared my throat, took a large swig of my drink and was about to say something, just to fill the silence when Frieda said, "So … where are your children today, then? It's a shame you can't be with them."

I took this as a jibe – it was certainly delivered as such. Frieda was sitting opposite me and I appraised her. She was very straight-backed, her legs together and to one side. She had on a pair of sensible shoes with low heels, thick stockings and a tweed skirt. Her ivory blouse looked crisp and around her neck were a string of pearls; her glasses dangled on a chain. Her grey hair had not one hair out of place; it was in a rigid perm that gave her face a severe frame. Her penetrating eyes looked directly at me. There was no ducking the answer.

"They're with their father today. He hasn't seen them for weeks, so it's nice for him to have them to himself."

"It's usually nice for children to be with both parents, I feel. Especially at Christmas." She said this with great emphasis and continued to look directly at me. "But I gather you're leaving your husband for our James. And where will the children live?"

Fortunately, at that moment James came back into the room and rescued me from the interrogation.

"Mum, give her a chance. She's only just arrived. Nut, anyone?"

"Yes, Frieda, let the girl finish her G and T first," said George.

I took another large swig and sat back in the chair, trying to relax.

"James tells me you too were out in Cyprus?" said George. "I've visited the island lots of times in my career – Episkopi, you know. Gorgeous place. I expect it's changed a lot since the seventies?"

"I expect so," I said lamely, wondering how much they knew. I now wished I'd been briefed by James before I came here. "It's such a wonderful place. I really miss it."

"So, what does your husband do?" said Frieda, determined to confront the fact that I was still married.

"He's a pilot, although he didn't fly in Cyprus, he had a ground job. But he's going to be on helicopters now down in Devon."

"A very worthy job," said George, "saving people. Well done him."

"He's got quite a bit of training to do first, but…"

"And what do you intend to do, when he goes down there?" said Frieda. "I'm assuming you're not going with him?"

I looked to James for moral support. "I …"

"She's going to stay put, in the family home, for the moment, Mum. There's no need to disturb the children's education, yet." He smiled across at me.

"That's right. Once Luke's established down in Devon, maybe next April or May, we'll rethink and perhaps we'll sell the house and …"

"Move in with my son?" said Frieda.

"We haven't got that far, yet, Mother," said James. "I live in a very small one bedroomed flat, as you know. We'll eventually look for somewhere …"

"And what do the children think of all this?" said Frieda. "Do you get on with them, James?"

"They don't really know me …"

"What? They don't know you at all?"

"Well, no, Mum, we thought it best to keep our relationship …"

"Your affaire, you mean," Frieda interrupted.

"Our *relationship*, separate from the children, at the moment. I'll meet them properly in due course," said James, beginning to look less relaxed than he had.

"I'm sure you'll sort things out," said George. "If you love each other, it'll work out in the end." He and James were standing together in front of the fire. His father thumped him gently on the back, in a genial way.

"Love's not the be-all and end-all of everything, dear, as you well know," said Frieda, making me wonder what she meant. "The practicalities of life, usually come to the fore. It's all very well being 'in love' but at the end of the day, there are other people involved." Although she was completely different from my mother, she was effectively saying the exact same thing as Mum, although with less politeness and more aggression.

"Get me another sherry, George," she said, handing him her glass.

"Look," said James, 'we haven't worked out all the details, but the most important thing is, we want to be together."

"And bugger everyone else," said Frieda.

"Frieda, for goodness sake, leave them alone," said George. "Poor girl came here for lunch, not the Spanish Inquisition. Let's go through and tuck in. It's a lovely cold collation; the turkey from yesterday. I hope you're not too fed up with turkey by now, Emily?" He was doing his level best to change the subject and divert the conversation elsewhere.

"That sounds lovely – I think Boxing Day leftovers are better than the main Christmas meal."

"Good girl, my thoughts entirely. I love the pickled onions," said George, ushering me through into the dining room.

*

"Your mother hates me."

"No, she doesn't. Don't take it personally. She's like that with everyone, including Dad. Poor thing, even though he was a General in the Army before he retired and faced lots of awful situations in the past, he's had to deal with Mum for *forty* years – he needs a medal. At least you weren't forced to listen to her playing the piano for hours. I've known her play after dinner and give a kind of concert, which has gone on interminably. At least you were spared that."

"I think that would've been preferable to all those questions."

We'd taken the opportunity to go for a quick walk after lunch, with the dogs. George and Frieda had wanted to have forty winks thank goodness and James suggested we walk round the village.

It was such a relief to get out of the house. The sky was already beginning to darken and the temperature had dropped. I'd bought a large white scarf which I wrapped round my neck and face, to keep the cold air out. We walked hand in hand up the drive, with the dogs scampering around chasing unknown smells.

"Your father's really nice, though. I think at least *he* likes me."

"They both like you, Emily. It'll take Mum longer to get to grips with it all. Don't worry about it. I don't care what they think, so why do you?"

"I'm sure you *do* care what they think, James. We all want our parents' approval, don't we?"

"It would be nice, yes, but it's our lives, not theirs. If she can't give us her blessing, well, so be it," and he put his hand behind

194

my back and pulled me into him. "You're more important to me than anyone in the world. If they can't see that, then they don't deserve to be part of our lives."

"I hope she'll come round in the end. It's your turn tomorrow. You'll see what it's like being scrutinised and interrogated."

"Before we go back, I just wanted to give you this," he said, reaching into his jacket pocket and coming out with a small, square present, wrapped in red paper.

"Go on, take it …"

We were just outside the old church. I smiled at him through the dusky light and reached for the box. Undoing it, my heartbeat quickened.

"I hope you haven't spent …"

"Go on, open it," he said, grinning.

Inside, was a ring, as I'd expected from the size of the box. It was an eternity ring, diamonds encircling it. Light from the amber street lamp reflected from it as it sat cushioned in its velvet.

"Oh my goodness, James … this is beautiful," I said, running my forefinger over its surface.

"Try it on," he said, lifting it out. He put it on the ring finger of my right hand, pushing it down with his forefinger and thumb. It fitted perfectly. "For now, it must be on this finger … but one day …"

"James, I don't know what to say. I love it." I straightened out my arm and stretching out my hand skywards, I stared at its sparkling roundness. It made me think of the star-studded Cyprus sky.

"It's gorgeous. I'll wear it always," and I leant forward to kiss his mouth. "I've got your present at Mum's house. I'm going to give it to you tomorrow."

"What is it?" he asked, lifting my hand up to the light.

"You'll have to wait and see," I said, kissing him again.

It was almost dark now and as we walked back down the drive; the lights were on, making his house look more welcoming than it was.

"Shall I come in or do you think I should go now?" I said, not at all sure whether I could stand another encounter with Frieda.

"Come in and have a cup of tea. She won't bite!"

"Are you sure?" I said, kissing him on the lips.

*

The next day, James' motorbike drew up outside my parents' house at 12.30 precisely; not known for his punctuality, he'd obviously made an effort to be there at the allotted time.

"Goodness, who's that?" said Mum, peering through the window, knowing full well who it was.

"I told you, Mum, James has recently bought a motorbike. He loves it and finds it much easier and cheaper for getting around Bristol."

"Well, I hope you won't be going on the back of it? Dangerous things."

"I've already had a short ride; he's a sensible driver."

James, meanwhile, was taking off his leather jacket and helmet and placing them in his pannier. We watched as he walked to the front door and I waved to him through the kitchen window.

"You go and let him in, Mum," I said, hoping to force her to like him. I'd shown her the ring when I got home, but this hadn't helped the antagonism she felt towards James. My father and the boys were in the sitting room and when they heard the bell, they all came out into the hall and I came out of the kitchen to join them.

"You must be James," I heard Mum say, stating the obvious, as she opened the door.

James kissed her on each cheek, french style, which rather took the wind out of Mum's sails.

"It's lovely to meet you at last … these are for you," he

said, handing her a small bunch of flowers. "And you must be Emily's Dad. Mr Williams, I've heard so much about you all. Hey, David and Steve. Great to see you again." He bear hugged them both.

It was all so easy and friendly with James; he had a way with people, making them feel relaxed and glad to be in his presence. I stood back, watching him greeting my family, knowing that his charm would be hard to resist.

He turned to me and hugged me. "It's not far at all from my parents' place to here. I had to drive a bit slowly as there's some ice on the road but …"

"There, I told you he was sensible, Mum," I said, grinning. "Come through."

We all trooped into the kitchen. "How was your Christmas, then?" asked James, generally.

"Nice, but we missed the children, didn't we, dear?" said Mum, turning to Dad.

"It was a real shame they weren't here," said Dad. "Not the same, without them."

"Still, it was nice for them to be with Luke, wasn't it?" said James, smiling encouragingly across at me.

"Yes, Mum and Dad know why they didn't come, don't you?" I said, trying to glare at them both. I'd always known it wouldn't be easy, but I'd hoped that Mum and Dad would at least make an effort.

James opted for a coffee and we went through to the sitting room; he made all the right comments about the house and furniture.

"So, how's the new job going?" said David. "Not the same as Cyprus, I'm sure?"

"No, it's as boring as hell. Mind you, the job I had out there wasn't the most exciting, but somehow it didn't seem so bad, with sunshine on tap. Here, you get up in the dark, struggle to work in the dark and get home in the dark. Not the same as Cyprus at all."

"We loved it out there, didn't we?" said David, turning to Steve. "It must be one hell of a shock coming back. Hard to adapt."

"How's life with you two?"

"Not bad. Teacher training's going well and Steve's got a placement. We often talk about our holiday though; that cruise when everyone jumped off the boat. Apart from Steve nearly drowning, that was such a good evening."

I rather wished we'd change the subject. "Cyprus was certainly a magical place, if a bit mad sometimes," said James. "I, for one, am glad I was posted there. I wouldn't have met this beautiful girl, otherwise."

He was standing next to me and he put his arm around me and kissed my cheek. I was embarrassed in front of my parents, who looked somewhat taken aback by his direct statement of the facts.

"Well, you're back to reality now though, aren't you?" said Mum, pointedly. "Things might have seemed straightforward out there, but ... there are consequences. Life's not all about sunshine and the Mediterranean. The trouble is, you're not facing ..."

"I love your daughter," James cut in, "with all my heart. The fact that we met in Cyprus makes it seem more trivial than it is. This is the real deal, not just some holiday romance, Mrs Williams. I promise I'll look after her and cherish her forever. We could have met in a supermarket queue, as far as I'm concerned ... I'd feel exactly the same. Please don't worry."

He said all this with such simple conviction and sincerity that he was met with stunned silence. Mum and Dad weren't used to people making declarations of love so openly.

Mum stammered, "That's as may be. I'm sure you love our Emily, dear, but neither of you seem to have thought about how things will work out from here. It's those children we worry about. We love our grandchildren and we hate the fact that their lives are being torn apart."

"I understand what you're saying, I really do," said James, looking directly at her. "I haven't got children, as you know, so I'm not in a position to have an opinion. All I do know is that I offered to walk away, to let Emily be with Luke and she's chosen this course. Emily and Luke love the kids so much – they won't let their lives be 'torn apart' – they'll do everything in their power to make it work, so that the children see them both, as much as possible. But surely it's better that Emily is happy with me, rather than living a lie with Luke? Surely that's better ultimately for the children? They will, in time, realise that it was the brave thing to do."

Mum and Dad looked at each other, unsure of what to say. James' frankness was a shock. I thought I could detect a dawning of understanding in my mother's eyes, though, and that made me glow. If Mum could just see a little of what I saw in James, she'd begin to comprehend how and why I'd made this huge decision.

We escaped for a walk, as we had the day before. I showed him my old childhood haunts: my primary school; the place where I used to wait for the bus to secondary school; the village hall where I'd had my first kiss. It seemed impossible to think of a time when he wasn't in my life – when I was spending my days oblivious to him, even though he was just a few miles away. Maybe we'd even passed each other, some time in the past? Now, our lives were inextricably linked; our paths had led us to Cyprus, on a collision course.

"This is for you – I'm afraid it's not as generous as yours," I said, taking out a small, flat present, wrapped in Christmas paper. "But ... it's with all my heart."

He unwrapped it, revealing a picture in a solid silver frame. "I went back to Petra Tou Romiou just before I left and our hearts were still there, James. No one had disturbed them. They sat there, in the sand, just how we'd left them."

"Wow ..." he whispered. "It was so long ago, but I remember that day like it was yesterday. I thought someone would have kicked the stones and destroyed them but ... I'm so glad they didn't. Thank you. I'll treasure this."

"I'm glad you like it."

"One day, we'll be able to tell our child the significance of it."

"One day ..." I said, holding his hand.

Chapter Twenty-Two

"Well, what did you think?" I said, as we watched his motorbike drive away.

In some ways, I didn't care what my parents thought; I'd made up my mind. But in other ways, I wanted them to like him. I'd always sought my parents' approval …

My mother was standing at the kitchen sink, washing up and cleaning all the surfaces around her.

"He's very good looking, dear. I can see why you fell for him."

That wasn't the answer I was looking for; I wanted her to like him for who he was, for his personality. I could tell my mother was being cagey, not saying what she was thinking.

"I didn't mean his looks, Mum, I meant *him*; what do you think of *him*?"

"It's difficult. I feel disloyal to Luke, saying anything about James."

"What do you mean?"

"Well, Luke's my son-in-law. I've grown to love him like another son. I haven't got the advantage you have, or being 'in love'. I'm not seeing James through rose-coloured spectacles. I can see he's a nice young man, yes, but is he worth … all this?"

She stood with her back to the window now, her hands in blue rubber gloves, her arms outstretched in a gesture of all-encompassing tragedy. Her face was etched with sadness and her eyes were full of tears.

I saw how my actions had ramifications far beyond myself and the children. This would affect my parents deeply. I felt so sorry for her in that moment and for a second I thought about Amy's future. What if Amy married someone who we grew attached to and then she just dumped him?

It would be devastating.

I went up to my mother and put my arms around her neck. My mother's gloved hands went round my back and we stood together for a while.

"I'm sorry, Mum – for everything. I don't think I realised how this would affect you and Dad. I know you love Luke but it doesn't mean you won't see him any more, you know. That won't change."

"It will, Emily, it will," she said quietly. "You're kidding yourself if you think differently. Why would Luke have any reason to visit us, now? It will be like losing a son."

"Of course he'll visit you, Mum; you'll see the children just as much, too."

We pulled apart and sat opposite each other at the kitchen table; Mum took off her gloves.

"Was Luke so bad?" she said, reaching across the table and touching my hand.

"No, of course he wasn't. He's a lovely man, a great father. I'll always love him, Mum. I've always had issues with his obsession with his career, Mum. He can't see much beyond the Air Force – I definitely come second. I've hated being in quarters, being forced to be part of an organisation I didn't join. You've no idea what it's like to be surrounded by the military. They rule your life."

"But James is in the *Army* – don't you see how illogical you're being?"

"I know it seems that way, Mum. But, unlike Luke, he doesn't live and breathe the Army. He has other interests; his music is far more important to him than his job. And anyway, he's leaving in under five years. He wants to get out, to get on with his life."

"And what'll he do then?"

"I don't know, Mum but we'll find a way together. I'll work. The thing is – he puts me first, not his career."

"Well, I hope you're right. You haven't lived together, you haven't had to pick up his dirty laundry from the bedroom floor. You haven't had to face each other across the breakfast table on a cold winter's day in February. Life is about all those mundane things – not swimming together in the Mediterranean."

"I know, Mum, I know it's not going to be easy. But it feels right – when I'm with him, I feel I'm in the right place, with the right person. I can't explain."

My mother got up and switched the kettle on. "I did like him. I can see he's a very thoughtful person."

"Thank you, Mum. I know it's hard for you. I really do."

"When your children have grown up, you'll understand how difficult this is. All you want is for them to be happy. You have to watch them taking their own path, making their own decisions and there's nothing you can do to stop them, even when you know it's the wrong choice."

I didn't answer. I stood up, went round the table, squeezed my mother's arm, kissed her cheek and went upstairs.

*

James was due to play a gig at a pub in Bristol on New Year's Eve and he wanted me to be there; I'd go to support him, leaving Sophie and Luke with the children. When I'd driven back to the Cotswolds the day before, it had been with a feeling of dread. How would it be with Sophie in my house?

I'd spoken to the children every day while I was away. They always seemed very bubbly and excited on the phone. 'Sophie said this.' 'Sophie did that.' I was pleased for them, but part of me resented the fact that she'd slotted in so easily.

"Hi, I'm back!" I called as I came through the door. I was greeted by total silence. The house was unlocked, everything looked untidily homely, the central heating was on. There was even something in the oven – the smell of garlic wafting deliciously around the room. I wandered through, sure that they must be somewhere. I called upstairs ... nothing.

It seemed odd to come into my own home and find it so obviously lived in, but with no one there. I wondered what they'd been doing while I was away and indeed, wondered where they were now. I took my case upstairs and stood, looking out of the window. Their cars were parked outside, so they couldn't be far.

I took the locket Luke had given me out of its velvet and let it rest in my palm; I stared at the ring on my right hand. It was as if each man had made a statement of possession. I took the ring off and put it with the locket, in the bottom of a drawer.

In the distance, I heard the sound of children's voices and standing up, I leant out of the window to see the four of them coming down the road. Amy and Charlie were chasing each other and shouting, Luke and Sophie were walking, arm in arm, behind.

Soon, the kids burst through the door, shouting "Mum ... Mum!" and I ran down the stairs and gave them both long hugs.

"I wondered where you all were; the house was open."

"We went to the pub for a drink," said Charlie. "Dad said he'd buy us some crisps and Coke. We played billiards and I won."

"No, you didn't!" said Amy. "Dad let you ... Dad always lets Charlie win."

At that moment, Luke and Sophie came through the door. Sophie came up to me and threw her arms around me. I could smell a mixture of beer, smoke and frosty air as I held her tight.

"It's lovely to see you, Emily – good journey?"

"Yes, fine. How are you all?" We'd both chosen to ignore our lack of communication since the phone call.

Luke was taking off his jacket and hanging it on the back of the door. He hadn't greeted me and didn't even look me in the eye.

"We've had a great time," said Sophie, "haven't we kids?"

There was a chorus of 'yea' and they rushed off to find their Christmas presents to show me.

"Luke, the door was unlocked when I got here. I wondered what had happened."

"We didn't bother to lock up – we were only down the road."

"But anyone could've walked in. You ought to lock up; it's not like Cyprus here, you know."

"Look, I was in charge and I decided not to lock the door, okay? You can't dictate what we do when you're not around. The house was perfectly all right, wasn't it?"

"Yes, it was but …"

"Well, then … leave it. We were fine. We had a quick drink, that's all."

The warm welcoming atmosphere had chilled and Sophie tried to warm it by saying, "The kids loved their presents. They've done non-stop playing while you've been gone."

Amy and Charlie came back into the room, laden with new things which they proceeded to demonstrate.

*

I didn't like to think about where Sophie had slept when I was gone, but that night, she slept on a camp bed in Amy's room and I slept on the sofa.

I was awake, staring up at the darkened ceiling when, at about two in the morning, Sophie crept downstairs.

"Hey, I'm awake, too," I whispered as Sophie made her way past. "Can't you sleep?"

"It's not the most comfortable thing I've ever slept on; I thought I'd make a cup of tea. Do you want one?"

"Please …" I got off my bed and joined her in the kitchen.

"Thanks for looking after Amy and Charlie so well, Sophie. They've obviously had a brilliant time."

"I've loved it. Christmas is so much better with children. When Sam was alive, it was like having a big kid. He loved Christmas."

I could just imagine it. I ached when I thought of him, but was glad that Sophie said his name so easily; I found it difficult to mention him, for fear of upsetting her.

"I so miss him, Sophie, I really do. I think about him all the time."

"They say it gets easier with time, but I still wake up and don't realise he's gone. It's horrible when the realisation hits me. It's like a recurring nightmare."

Sophie was standing by the kettle, in a knee-length white nightie. She looked so young, so fragile, it was hard to take in that she was a widow.

"I don't know how you ever come to terms with it, Sophie. You've been so brave. Sam would be proud of you."

He'd loved her so much; I remembered the way his whole face lit up whenever he looked at her.

Sophie sat down at the table. I joined her and we sat in near darkness, with our hands around the steaming mugs.

"I wonder what Sam would say about it all?" said Sophie

"What do you mean?"

"Well, this – me here, with Luke – you, with James."

There was a long pause before either of us spoke. I thought back to all the conversations I'd had with Sam about James, his protectiveness and concern and concluded that he wouldn't like my decision at all.

"Are you with Luke, Sophie? I know about you sleeping with Luke last Christmas, as I said before. Don't worry, I'm not going to interrogate you, or shout and scream. If you can believe it, I understand … I'm not angry with you any more."

I didn't realise it until I said it. I wasn't angry with either of them. I had been, but now I knew I had no right.

Sophie stared ahead; I waited patiently for her reply.

"I've slept with him, I sleep with him, but you know, it means nothing. Can you understand it? He knows when we're together, I'm thinking of Sam. I know, when we're together, he's thinking of *you*. He talks about you all the time and only yesterday said to me, 'I'll only ever love *her* … Emily's the love of my life.' We know that we're simply friends clinging to each other, for comfort. Maybe … maybe it'll develop into something else, but I doubt it. There are two ghosts in bed with us."

To be classed as a ghost, struck me forcefully. I put down my mug and put my head in my hands. That was it. I was now a ghost in my own life; a spirit who'd passed on, leaving a misty presence that flitted and flirted around Luke, leaving him unsettled and unable to move on.

I was pleased that he had Sophie.

"Well, I'm pleased we've talked about it. It's in the open, it's not niggling away. I'm pleased that you've got each other, Sophie. I really am."

Sophie stood up and stood looking out of the window. There was a cat fight outside, an eerie sound that sent shivers down my spine. I tried to ignore the caterwauling and stood up too, determined to try to go back to sleep.

"Night night, Sophie. I hope you manage to get back to sleep."

"Night. Before you go, can I ask … did you like the locket?"

"I loved it. Why? Did Luke tell you he'd bought it for me?"

"He asked me to help him with it. So, you see, we really are just friends and he loves you, Emily … very much. He wanted something that might make you change your mind."

"Thank you. It's lovely."

"It didn't have the desired affect though, did it?"

"No, I'm afraid it didn't."

"He tried – now let him live his life without you," and with that, she walked past me and went upstairs.

*

The gig was in a pub in the centre of Bristol; one of its bars was in a large room with a stage at one end. I'd driven straight there and it was only when I arrived that I realised it would be an odd evening for me, as James would be heavily involved with setting up and playing and I'd be left to my own devices. This wasn't something I was used to; I'd been part of a couple for so long now, that being 'single' would be a different experience. Still, he was playing two sets and he'd be with me in between.

"Hey, Emily – you're here. You found it all right?" he said as I walked into the crowded bar. He was at a table, looking very relaxed considering the fact that he was on in half an hour. He stood up and kissed me on the lips. "You look amazing … come and meet the band."

The guys round the table couldn't have looked less like Army officers if they'd tried; they all had long hair: Keith, the drummer had his tied back in a ponytail and had earrings; Mike, the keyboard player, was blond and wore jeans that were moulded to his legs and Paul, the guitarist, had long frizzy red hair that stood up round his head like an Afro. James looked far too clean cut but as he introduced each one I saw how well they all got on; there was continual banter, lots of laughs and leg-pulling.

The crowd was growing and soon it was time for the band to go and start warming up. I sat at the table looking around, people-watching. They were a mixed bunch, not like Cyprus, a complete cross-section of ages and types. I rather liked the anonymity of it, sitting there, observing.

I heard the instruments tuning and checking; there was even the famous 'one, two, one two' over the microphone. I hadn't heard what they were going to play and looked forward to being surprised. They were introduced by someone as 'four guys from Bristol who only got together a few months ago, but who are already making a name for themselves around the city.' He added, 'So now, put your hands together for … The Legend.' The crowd went mad, shouting and whooping and moving en masse towards the stage. I got up and pushed my way into the crowd, to be near the front; I looked up at James on the stage and was nervous for him. There was no need though; he looked as confident as I'd ever seen him. He owned the stage and looked as if that was where he was meant to be.

The songs they played were far 'rockier' than Brigade's. There was some Bryan Adams, Aerosmith and Meat Loaf – his voice suited the style and I could tell he was loving it. I tried to catch his eye, but couldn't. It didn't matter, I was enjoying being able to stare at him, with no one caring whether I did or not; I remembered Sophie making caustic comments during a song, to the affect that it wasn't *me* he was singing to. Well, now it didn't matter, I could enjoy it and imagine that it *was* me. They ended the first set with 'I'd do anything for love' by Meat Loaf and the crowd went mad; I agreed with the sentiment (ignoring the line, 'but I won't do that).

During the break, I sat on his knee. I felt like some young groupie, proud to be the lead singer's girlfriend.

"That was fantastic, James. They loved it. Did you see me in the crowd? I was right in the middle?"

"I have to admit I didn't. When you're up there, the crowd are just one mass, but I imagined you listening and watching." He had his arm round my back and we leant into each other and kissed, long and hard.

"Get a room, you two," laughed Keith. "You're making me wish Julie was here, so I could get some action."

"You just haven't got it, mate," said James. "This girl's followed me here from across the sea. If fact, she came out of the sea to seduce me, didn't you, Aphrodite?"

The lads from the band looked at each other, not sure what he was on about. "It's a long story, guys – one for another time. Just let me say, she's the best thing that's ever happened to me and if I want to kiss her in front of you, you're just going to have to put up with it."

We all laughed and Mike, getting up to get another drink from the bar, thumped him affectionately on the back and said, "You go for it, mate … you're a lucky man."

"I am … I'm a lucky man," he said, kissing me again.

*

The next set started on an upbeat note with some Rolling Stones' numbers. The atmosphere in the room was electric; there was cheering and stomping of feet after each song and the band grew more and more confident. James became a different person, strutting around, jumping even and playing to the crowd. I watched him, mesmerised by his energy and charisma. Whatever 'it' was, he had it on stage. He had the crowd eating out of his hand and when he did 'Dark End of the Street' by the Commitments, he made it his own. There was just a simple spot light on him and as he sang the words about us stealing away together, it was as if the words fell from his mouth straight into my head. I knew he couldn't see me, even though I'd told him roughly where I'd be, but it didn't matter. If there'd been a Disney animation of the scene, the words would have danced and twirled above the crowd, music notes bouncing and twisting around us. I too would have been lit, the two of us bright in our own light, linked by music. I envisaged us walking away together, into the darkness.

They went on to do 'Try a little Tenderness' and finished with 'Treat My Right'. The crowd went mental and were yelling the 'hey, hey, hey' for all they were worth, punching the air with their fists.

I felt exhausted at the end; I'd virtually been holding my breath throughout. I wasn't used to someone I knew being the centre of attention. I felt a sneaking jealousy that James was so admired by all those other girls.

"I'm sorry we didn't do your song, it's not ready for public performance yet," said James as I met him off stage. He was wet with sweat, his hair looked as if he'd been in the shower and his T-shirt was clinging to his chest.

"I hadn't even thought you would play it. I think of it as 'our song' – maybe it should be just for us," I said, reaching forward to kiss him.

"I shouldn't come too close, I'm hot and sweaty. God, I loved that! It was our best yet. Far better than anything I ever did in Cyprus. It was a great crowd. I get such a buzz when people react like that."

"Well, there'll be no stopping you, now. I'm sure you're going to get booked a lot after tonight."

He was like a little boy who'd won a running race. His grin was wide, his eyes twinkling. "I hope you're right. I love it. Almost as much as I love you," he laughed. "Come on, let's pack up and go home."

"Don't you want to stay till midnight and celebrate with everyone else?"

"No. Do you know what? I can't think of a better way of celebrating the New Year than being in bed with you. We'll get a bottle of champagne, count in the new year from the sanctity of our room and then celebrate in a rather different way, not just kissing, if you know what I mean."

"That sounds perfect. I hate all the kissing that goes on with complete strangers at these sort of things. I only want to kiss one person and that's you. Can we get back in time for midnight?"

"If we leave now, we've got plenty of time. We've got the whole of '94 ahead of us – the rest of our lives, in fact."

"I can't wait for our future. It's going to be amazing."

Chapter Twenty-Three

"**D**id you ask Luke to ring me after our conversation at Christmas?" said Mum, one evening at the end of January.

"No, why do you ask?"

"Well, he rang and said he was coming this way soon to visit Sophie and he promised he'd bring the kids to see us. It was so nice of him. He's such a lovely man. When's he starting his training?"

"He's in Wales now. He'll move down to Chivenor at the beginning of April. We've talked about what to do with the house here, but house prices are dire at the moment; it's hardly worth putting it on the market. So, the good thing, from my point of view, is that we'll stay here for now. Thank God. I really don't want to move."

"And how's James?" my mother added, in the disapproving tone of voice that she always used when his name was mentioned.

"He's fine, Mum. He's going to come and stay at the weekend and I'm going to tell the children about him."

"Oh …"

"Well, it's got to be done. They'll be fine, Mum, you'll see. Children adapt much easier than adults."

"I hope you're right."

*

James' visit to our cottage went remarkably well. We didn't make a big deal of it – I simply told the children that James was my new 'friend' and did they remember him from Cyprus? Of course they did and seemed to accept his presence without too many questions. He did sneak into my room late at night, when we were sure the kids were fast asleep, but in the morning, he was back on the sofa as planned.

He brought his guitar and impressed Amy by playing it and singing. She immediately asked for guitar lessons, which I agreed to. Charlie wanted to learn the drums, but I was sure it was only to 'keep up' with Amy; if he was still keen in a few weeks, then I'd review the situation.

James was a natural with the children; he didn't try to endear himself by acting the fool or spoiling them, he was just himself. He kicked a ball around with Charlie, built lego and admired Amy's artwork. He set up running races round the playground and even made up a funny story at bedtime.

Uncle James was a hit.

*

"So how was Luke's visit, then?" I said to my mother on the phone, a couple of weeks later. I too was impressed that Luke had gone out of his way to visit them.

"It was so lovely. We had a super time." My mother wasn't one for pauses, but there was a long one now and she seemed to want to say something. I heard her start to say something, and then stop.

"What Mum? Did something happen?"

"No nothing happened as such … but we had an interesting conversation."

"Really? What about?"

"Well, he told me something that I didn't know ..."

"And?"

"He told me that it wasn't *all* your fault that you'd split up."

"What do you mean?"

"He said ... he told me what he did about the snip. He realises it was the wrong thing to do, Emily and he's very, very sorry, you know. He told me that he blames himself for what's happened."

I was stunned that Luke had told my mother and that he'd defended my actions. My mind whirled.

"It was a very hurtful thing, Mum. To go behind my back like that. I couldn't believe he was capable of being so deceitful."

"I'm sure. I wish you'd told me ..."

"He knew I wanted another child, Mum and he still went ahead."

"He realises that now, dear and he wishes he could change it."

"It's too late, Mum ... it's all too late."

There was another long pause. "Are you going to have a baby with that James?"

"Please don't call him '*that James*' Mum!"

"Well ... are you?"

"Maybe ..."

"I think that would be very silly, dear. You're not as young as you were ..."

"Mum! There's plenty of time. I want another baby. And James wants a baby."

"Luke's very sorry for what he did."

"Mum, I don't think it changed the way I felt about James. I'd already met him when I found out. I'd already fallen in love with him."

"Well, I thought you should know. He'd have you back in a flash, you know that, don't you?"

"I'm not so sure, Mum."

"He would. He loves you. Despite everything, he loves you, Emily. I just thought you should know."

*

I'd been in constant contact with Beth since I'd been back; we rang each other a lot and out of all my friends, Beth was the one I could talk to. Even though my friendship with Jen went so far back, she hadn't lived in Cyprus, wasn't involved with the military and just didn't quite 'get' it. Beth, however, despite her age, got it; she'd experienced everything first hand. She'd settled back into life with her parents and they loved having her, spoiling both her and Grace rotten. She and Gary weren't communicating at all.

"Didn't they mind you walking out on your marriage?" I asked one day on the phone.

"They were worried about me, of course, but when they heard what had been going on, they backed me all the way. They know Gary well but it now turns out they were never that keen and thought we were far too young."

"It's different for my parents; they adore Luke, he can do no wrong, so they really disapprove. I can see where they're coming from but sometimes I wish they could give me some support."

"It must be hard for them."

We'd been talking about me going down to visit and it was during this phone call that the plan became a reality. Luke was coming home for a long weekend at the beginning of March and James and I had talked about having a weekend away. Cornwall seemed like the perfect place; not far down the motorway from Bristol and the chance to catch up with Beth.

So, it was arranged; we'd stay in a rented cottage in Padstow.

"It'll be so good to meet James. I feel as if I know him already," said Beth.

"Yes, you'll see that he *does* exist after all and isn't just a figment of my imagination. Any suggestions for places to stay?"

Beth had plenty of ideas and said she'd ring again with definite prices and locations.

On the morning of the Friday that Luke was due to arrive, I briefed Amy as to what was happening. Charlie had had a sleepover and wasn't there. We were sitting, 'the two girls' together, having breakfast.

"So you're going to Cornwall with James?" said Amy, the light suddenly beginning to dawn.

"Yes we thought it'd be nice to go and see Beth and Grace."

Amy ignored that piece of information and continued, "Why would you go with James? Wouldn't it be better to go with Jen or something?"

"Jen's busy. Anyway, James is looking forward to going down there. He doesn't know Cornwall like we all do."

I could see Amy thinking; thought bubbles drifted round her head as plain to see as a cartoon. "So ... is he your boyfriend?"

I wasn't taken aback by this; in fact, I'd been waiting for this conversation. Amy was now at an age when she and her friends discussed boys all the time; that period in her life when relationships with the opposite sex became something more than 'boys are horrible' 'boys are smelly'. So, pouring myself another cup of coffee I said, as calmly as possible, "Yes, he is, Amy."

"So does that mean ... you and Daddy will never get back together?"

Her face had a look of amazement, tinged with fear. We had tried to explain everything to them but I saw now that Amy hadn't believed the finality of it or perhaps didn't want to.

"Mummy and Daddy love each other but we don't want to live together any more, poppet. James and I are just seeing how it goes. It's not serious or anything."

I didn't want to give the impression that I was jumping from Amy's Dad straight into the arms of another man, even though that's exactly what I was doing.

"Does Daddy know?"

"Yes, he does."

"Does Charlie know?"

"No, Charlie doesn't know. Perhaps it's best if we don't say too much about it to Charlie. He's been upset by Dad not living here and maybe he's a bit too young to know. Shall we keep it as our secret? What do you think?"

"Yes, Mum. You and I will keep it a secret. Can I tell Maisie, though?"

"Well, in time, yes but maybe at the moment, let's keep it between you and me. Do you want some toast?"

"Yes please, two. I like having a secret with you, Mum."

"Good. We girls must stick together," I said, so glad I had a daughter.

"I really like James, Mum. He's brilliant on the guitar and I love his voice. I want to be like him when I grow up. Can I come to one of his gigs, one day?"

"Of course! I'll ask him which one would be good for you."

"Really? Can it be soon?"

"I'm sure. Now, here's your toast. Eat up, it's nearly time for the bus."

Amy came round the table to where I was standing and threw her arms round my waist.

"I love you, Mum."

"I love you, too."

*

We arrived in Padstow at eight in the evening. The journey had been good; nothing like the traffic problems we used to have in the school holidays. Beth had told us the address of the cottage she'd found for us and where to find the key and we'd meet her in the morning.

We wound our way down the steep hill and round the

corner at the bottom. It was dark and there was just a faint orange glow lighting up the harbour side.

"The tide's huge here. It's in at the moment but tomorrow you'll see how far out it goes. That bit there, is just an expanse of sand."

We passed the long car park and turned left along the narrow street leading to the centre. Beth's parents' place was somewhere along here but we meandered on, turning up a little road leading to the church. Our cottage was somewhere up there and we could park outside.

"There it is!" I said, pointing to a pink, terraced house. "Park up there on the left."

Having located the key we let themselves in, coming straight into the sitting room. It was clean and tidy and there was even a plate of scones, strawberry jam and clotted cream on the table.

"This is lovely," said James, looking around. "I'm starving, I think I'll have a scone, right now."

"Let's unpack first, James – come upstairs," I said, going up the tiny little steps leading to the two bedrooms. Our room was on the left: small, but pretty with a sky-blue bedspread, seascapes on the walls and shells on the windowsill. There was a compact wardrobe and I began to hang up our clothes. James had had to duck as he'd come through the door.

"I love it. I've always wanted to live in a cottage like this, it's so cosy and friendly. There's even an open fireplace downstairs – did you notice?"

"I know. Me too. Our house is nice, but there's something about this. Just imagine being in here when the wind's howling and the rain's coming down outside. It'd be like being in a little haven of peace and safety."

We put our arms around each other and kissed.

"What shall we do for supper? The scones won't be enough."

"There's a fish and chip shop round the corner. Let's just have that."

"Perfect. Tell me where to go and I'll go and get them."

After he'd gone, I sat in an armchair downstairs. I felt so happy, so content. The thought of a whole weekend together in this magical place was well, it was just *so* good. The children were happily with Luke, so I could relax about them.

I looked around the room: there was a basket of logs to the right of the fireplace; a dark wood dresser with some pretty plates and a little vase of flowers on it, stood opposite. On the walls, there were photographs of Atlantic rollers crashing ashore; vistas of rocky outcrops and of course, the harbour that was just a stone's throw away. I stood up and went into the galley kitchen to find the plates and cutlery ready for James' return.

How ironic that we're down here in Cornwall, together, I thought. This was where it all began, back when Luke rang about the posting to Cyprus. If I knew then what I know now, would I have jumped at the chance to go, like I did?

*

Next morning, we walked down the lane towards the harbour. There was a distinct nip in the air and the streets were quiet; I was used to them being full of tourists. I'd never been here when it was so peaceful. We walked slowly, hand in hand, admiring the tiny cottages we passed, tempted to look in through the windows.

As we neared the centre, the houses became shops selling pasties, gifts, fudge, shells and ice cream. There were several estate agents and we stopped to peruse what was on offer.

"I'd love to buy a cottage like the one we're in," said James. "I've reached an age when I really should be investing in property. Look at that one," he said, pointing to a white, detached cottage. "Three bedrooms, sea view, parking … God, it's perfect."

"They always look perfect in agents' windows. When you get inside you see they're not quite as described," I said, squeezing his hand.

"When did you become so sensible?" he laughed. "I'd still love to buy one."

We arrived at Beth's parents' shop. It was in a prime position and sold everything a passing tourist might want on a whim: post cards, sweets, bat and balls; there were even plastic shoes, flip flops and bucket and spades. I wondered how much they sold during the winter months.

Behind the counter, was a middle-aged woman. I smiled and said, "Good Morning," as we entered.

"Can I help you?"

"Well, we're looking for Bethany – are you Bethany's Mum, by any chance?"

"Ah, you must be Emily and James," she said, coming round the counter. "Lovely to meet you both. I'm Jill. Beth's told us all about you. Is the cottage okay? It belongs to a friend."

"Wonderful, thanks."

"Beth and Grace are upstairs. Come through to the back and I'll show you up."

I couldn't get over how much Grace had changed. She'd grown into a small person and greeted us with a gummy grin. Beth, too, was different. She looked younger if that was possible. Her face wasn't etched with stress, her eyes were brighter and her smile, relaxed. Even though they'd not met, James and Beth chatted away as if they'd known each other for years; having the common experience of Cyprus helped and I could see they were both making a huge effort on my behalf.

"So have you been in the sea yet, or is it still too cold? Maybe you pro surfers don't get put off by the fact that the Atlantic's freezing at this time of year?"

"Yea, loads of times. It's great; Mum's only too willing to look after Grace, even when she's manning the shop. She loves showing her off to all her friends and complete strangers. They let me borrow their car and I go off to Trevone, Constantine and Booby's Bay. There's a gang of my old friends that go but sometimes I go on my own. I *love* it. The waves are better in the winter, to be honest; the surf's often disappointing in the summer when the weather's good. Do you fancy going surfing today?" She asked with so much enthusiasm, it was hard to resist.

"Today? I haven't got a wet suit or anything ..."

"God, that would be amazing, Emily – let's do it!" said James. He came over to me and gave me an encouraging hug.

"Won't we be freezing?"

"I know a guy who can hire you a winter wet suit and gloves and everything. You'll be fine. You'll love it. A bit different from the Med, but much more exhilarating," said Beth. "I'll check with Mum and find out when it'd suit her to look after Grace," and she ran off downstairs.

She was a completely different person from the Beth I knew in Akrotiri – bright, bubbly and full of life. I looked around the room and saw one of my photos that Gary had so disapproved of, now standing proud on the mantlepiece.

"Are we mad?" I said, looking at James with slight trepidation.

"Completely, but we knew that, didn't we?"

*

"All sorted!" said Beth, bursting back into the room. "No excuses. I've even rung my mate and he's going to lend you all the gear, we've just got to pick it up from his shop on the way."

So there was no getting out of it. We set off at midday and headed along the coast. It was so good to move along the narrow Cornish roads so easily, without the constant stream of traffic. We turned right, off the main road towards Constantine and wound our way down a narrow lane, past a golf course. We ended up at the bottom of a no-through road and parked. You couldn't see the sea, even though it was just over a small rise but according to Beth who was an expert on these things, the surf and the tide were 'perfect'. The waves were always better when the tide was coming in, 'on the push' as the surf experts said and this was how it would be now.

We'd already collected the gear; it was piled in the boot.

"Right," said Beth, "now the fun begins. You've got to get into this lot," she said, reaching in and hauling out a mass of black rubber. The clouds were scudding across the sky, a mix of charcoal and grey and the wind was beginning to pick up. As I got out of the car, I pulled my jacket round my body, trying to protect myself from the cold.

"Do I have to?" I said through gritted teeth.

"Don't be a wimp! Once you're in, you'll know why you're doing it."

There were two empty cars parked up near us. At that moment, two guys came over the little hill, carrying boards. Their hair was stuck in tendrils to their foreheads, they'd pulled down the top of their wetsuits and the sleeves were hanging down by their legs. Despite the time of year, their faces and torsos were brown; they looked every inch the surfer: hardy and toned with long, blond streaked hair.

"Hey, Dan," said Beth, as the first one reached us. "How's it out there?"

"Pumping. Caught some real heavies." They walked on to their car and looking back, Dan said, "Have a good one."

We were in real surfing territory here.

I started to feel nervous; windsurfing and water-skiing on the smooth waters of the Med seemed infinitely preferable.

Trying to get into the wet suit proved to be the first challenge. First, I had to take off my clothes, struggling against the wind, holding a towel around myself for grim death. The suit had to fit snugly, otherwise it would lose its affect, so pulling it over my limbs and up my body was hard, making me sweat despite the goosebumps on my skin. James made less of a deal of it and was zipped up and in his way before me. Beth helped me lift the long zip at the back and tucked it neatly under the velcro fastening. Now I was in it, I felt trussed up like a fish in a net, my arms were tight inside the rubber and the bit around my neck cut in. I marched my legs up and down, trying to loosen the suit.

"It'll be fine once you're in the water," said Beth. "They're meant to be tight. Now, here are your boots and gloves."

The three of us laughed at each other when we were all kitted up.

"We look ridiculous!"

"No, we don't," said James. "We look as if we know what we're doing."

"Shame we don't!"

I'd done a bit of body surfing in the past but very half-heartedly and in the small waves, in order to be near the children. James had never done it at all but I had no doubt he'd be good at it.

Beth had her malibu, a board as long as her and we each had a belly board. Beth looked the part.

"You can have a go on my board, if you like," she said, as we began our long march to the waves.

As we crested the little hill, the sea was spread out before us. Gone was the sapphire blue of Cyprus; here, the rolling waves were of the dark green Atlantic, making their constant crashing way inshore. The bay was huge, with golden sand edged with grassy dunes. It was a spectacular bay that went into the far distance, ending in black rocks.

"We have to walk right down the beach toward those rocks," Beth said, pointing. "This end is dangerous, there are loads of rocks where the tide comes in. The other end's great and if you go even further, past those rocks, you get to Booby's, where the surf's better. I think we'll stay on this beach today, though."

We made our slow way along the beach, our feet sinking

into the dry sand above the tideline. In the distance, we could make out a few other mad fools in the water. They looked like black sea birds in the vastness of the ocean.

We started to walk diagonally across the bay onto the harder sand, eventually getting to the part Beth was aiming for.

"Okay, guys. Here we are. This – is – it!"

Without warning, she started running in, making light work of carrying a big board and jumping over the small waves.

"Come on! Follow me, it's lovely and warm, ha ha!" she cried running on.

James and I arranged our boards so that we could hold hands and started running into the water too. "Oh my God, it's freezing," I screamed, looking across at James.

"At least you've done this before," he shouted above the noise of the waves and the wind. "I haven't got a clue what I'm doing."

Beth was already way out, lying on her board, using her arms to paddle out. As a wave rolled towards her, she expertly dipped into it and let it slide over the top of her. We, on the other hand, were still standing and as the water rose higher up our legs, we were jumping, in a vain attempt to rise above the freezing water.

"It's just got into my wetsuit and it's creeping down inside," I shouted. "It's agony." We let go of each other's hands; the waves were too big now not to have both hands free. I decided to throw caution to the wind and as the next large wave approached, I jumped on my board and let the wave take me. I timed it just right; the wave was on the verge of breaking and I shot towards the shore riding the wave as it broke, leaving James behind. It pushed me forward with such force as it broke, I had to hang onto my board hard to stop it being wrenched away from me. I was attached to it by a length of cord to my wrist and as I eventually fell off, the board continued until it reached the end of its tether and stopped, bouncing and twirling. I stood up, pulling the board back towards me;

water was stinging my eyes and was in my ears, but I felt *alive*.

My wet suit now had a layer of water inside it and would hopefully warm up.

I looked out to sea and James was still where I'd left him. I saw a large wave approaching and I willed him to jump on it. Whether he was a natural or there was luck on his side, I don't know but he caught the wave and came speeding towards me, engulfed in cotton-wool foam. As he neared me, he deliberately fell off.

"I thought I was going straight into you," he cried, water pouring off him as he stood up. "That was brilliant. I think I've got the bug already. Let's go."

He started running back out again, fighting the incoming rollers with me, just behind.

"Look at her – Beth's fantastic at it," he cried. We could see her standing on her board way out riding a huge wave, weaving up and down to keep the momentum.

"Let's go out a bit further and see if we can join her."

As we made our way out we got out of our depth. The waves were towering above us and as I realised I couldn't put my feet down, unease took hold. The strength and power of the water was pulling me towards the rocks. Beth appeared by my side, lying on her board.

"You okay? Do you want a go on mine?"

"No thanks. I'll stick to this," I said, holding on to my board like a buoyancy aid, as another wave hit me on the head. "I'm going on the next one."

I tried to get organised; I looked across at James; he, too, was lining himself up, or trying to. We launched ourselves on the wave and miraculously we both got on it. James was grinning from ear to ear, looking for all the world, as if he'd done it forever.

"Amazing!" he shouted through the roar. "Why didn't you tell me how much fun this was?" and his voice faded as his part of the wave rushed him further on.

Suddenly, without my being able to stop it, the front of my board jerked down below the surface. It was a split second movement that took me with it, hurtling me down. I was turning and spinning, rolling and reeling in a underwater circle. Something hit me in the stomach hard. Just as I was beginning to think I'd never get out I popped to the surface, spitting and heaving. I tried to find the sand and there it was, just within reach. I tried to calm my breathing, grabbing the board that was now by my side, recognising it as the thing that had stabbed me. Another wave swamped me from behind; I hadn't recovered from the first one and was still gasping. It submerged me completely and again I was tumbling under the water, not knowing which way was up. I tried to find the sand, my lungs were burning, I almost blacked out. It was as if I was caught in a whirlpool; I was disorientated, desperate for oxygen, blind and frightened. The water was in my mouth, my nose; I could feel the tug of the tether on my wrist. I was a piece of flotsam at the mercy of the ocean's power.

I was giving up hope when I emerged from my watery grave; a hand had grabbed one arm and was hauling me to the surface. I inhaled, taking in a gulp of air and choked, coughing up water.

My feet were now firmly on the sand and through my hair, which was over my face and in my eyes, I saw James. I felt my legs shaking, my breath was rasping, my eyes tingling with salt. Pulling the tether, my board came back to me like an obedient horse; I leant on it, as smaller waves still washed over and through. I tried to steady my breaths, breathing in through my nose and out through my mouth.

"Are you okay?" he said, trying to steady me against the onslaught.

Between breaths, I managed to say, "I think so … oh my God … fuck, that was awful. I couldn't breathe, James. I was under for so long."

"It's okay, you're okay now. Hold my hand. We'll go in and sit on the sand."

He walked slowly towards the shore, now supporting me round my shoulders. We flopped onto the sand and I lay back, exhausted. I was cold too but I couldn't move so I lay looking up at the clouds, trying to slow my breathing.

"I really thought I'd had it. I couldn't get out of the wave. It was like being tumbled in a washing machine, round and round. And then, just when I thought I was okay and managed to get my feet down, I was hit by another one and it happened again."

"You went under twice?" said James, rubbing my arm.

"Yes, it was awful. My board dipped the first time and then I got hit from behind by another huge wave."

"I didn't realise," he said and lay down beside me. He reached for my hand, squeezing it. "What do you want to do? Shall we go back in, get back on the horse, so to speak? We'll keep in our depth this time, though."

I thought about it for a few seconds.

"Okay … you're right, I love it really. It was unlucky. I need to prove to myself that I won't go under again. Let's go, then. Thank you for rescuing me."

"My pleasure, fair Aphrodite."

"Some sea goddess I turned out to be," I said, smiling across the wet sand at him. He stroked my face. We sat up and scanned the waves for Beth: there she was in her element, shooting down the barrel of a wave, arms outstretched.

We spent the next half an hour, surfing the smaller waves and there were no more mishaps. The wind picked up and flecks of white foam flew in the air each time a wave broke. My head was beginning to ache and my eyes were hurting. I indicated that I was going in to James and he said he'd come with me. We both waved our arms at Beth and she waved back; we pointed towards the shore.

She came towards us, still standing on her board, as if she was standing on solid ground and hopped off into the shallow water.

"How did you two get on? Enjoy it?"

"Well, yes, either side of nearly drowning!"

"You'll have to get used to it, if you want to go 'out back' with the big boys."

"I'm not sure I do. I think I'm happy on the small waves, in my depth."

It had shaken me up. People ask you if your life flashes in front of your eyes in that sort of situation and from my experience, the answer is 'no'. My mind was just a flashing light of panic, pain and survival.

All I knew was that I wanted to live, to rise up, to emerge into the oxygen of life.

To breathe James into my lungs.

*

We dropped Beth back at the house and went to our cottage. We'd sat in our wetsuits in the car and all I wanted to do was to sink into a hot bath.

I peeled off my rubber casing, while the hot water cascaded into the steaming bath. Climbing in, I noticed a large bruise on both my thigh and my stomach. I ached everywhere and with relief I sank down, lying back with my head against the porcelain side.

"Do you want a cup of tea?" said James, his head popping round the door.

"Mmm ... please," I said, hardly opening my eyes. My mind travelled back to the time in Cyprus when I lay like this in the bath after we'd made love for the very first time. Soaking in warm water can heal mental and physical ills. Today, it was more of the physical sort, but being caught under waves had made me realise how precarious life is.

One minute, you're riding a wave with your lover laughing next to you and the next, you're in a situation that may end it all.

Everything can go in a second, be swept away, erased.

"Do you fancy going for a walk, before it gets dark?" asked James.

My limbs were still tired but I thought that it would be good to get out, so we set off up our lane and into the fields above the town. The light was leaving the sky, the town was slowly turning on the amber glow of street lights. We walked along a long path, past row after row of wooden benches. In the dusky light, we started reading the metal plaques that were screwed to the back of the seats.

'For Maisie. She loved this view. 1945 - 1988.'

'Jim loved to sit here and watch the seagulls. RIP. 1952 - 1980'.

There were lots of them with similar sentiments. It was so sad to think of all those people who like us had walked this part of the earth, looked at this view and felt this happy.

We sat down together on one of the seats, staring at the dark scenery.

"Do you remember the time at Dreamers, when we looked out across the sea like this? We talked about marriage – do you remember?" said James.

"Of course I do. How could I forget?"

"It's a reality now. No more fantasies, no more dreams. Will you marry me one day?"

He turned to me, took my hand and brought it to his lips; he then surrounded it by both his and pulled it into his chest. I leant into his side and we sat in silence, for a few seconds.

"Emily?"

"Of course I will, you don't even need to ask," I said, withdrawing my hand to touch the eternity ring on my right hand. As I said it, I was thinking of all the obstacles along the way: divorce; care and custody of the children and houses ... it seemed a long way off.

He took my left hand and kissed the finger that would wear the ring. I still had Luke's ring on. "There, a kiss for now will do, I hope," he said. "If I'm going to be all grown up and get married, I must start planning our future. I'm serious, you know ... I think this would be a great place to buy my first house."

"But you hardly know it down here."

"I don't care, I love it already and that's all I need to know. Look, I don't know where I'm going to be for the next few years. If I had a house down here, it'd get me on the property ladder and we could come down whenever we could. It'd be our bolt hole, a place to escape from the Army and all our problems. No parents' disapproval, no superiors telling me what to do."

"If you're serious, maybe tomorrow we should have a bit of tour around, I could take you to see other possible places."

"Well, we could, but ... I like it *here*. I'm impulsive, you know; I know what I like immediately, as you well know. I saw you and ... and ... I just knew."

I felt a warm glow and my face flushed.

How can I feel *this* happy?

"Why don't we ask Beth and her parents if they know of any properties coming on the market? It's always good to have personal recommendations?"

"Good idea," he said. "Come on, let's go back, we'll have dinner in that pub on the harbour side."

I took one last look at another plaque. This one simply read, 'Our parents Harry and Rose Foxwell loved it here. Gone, but never forgotten.'

"Goodness, look at this! Their surname is a mix of ours - Fox and Blackwell. How weird. Maybe one day, there'll be a plaque here, dedicated to us."

The thought made me shiver.

"I can't think of a better place to be remembered. The place where our life together really began. I'd love to be on a plaque with you one day," he laughed.

"What a depressing thought. I don't want to think about it."

"We've all got to die sometime. What's that expression? Nothing is certain, but death and taxes?"

"I had my fair share of near-death today, thank you and taxes are a pain in the …"

"And who was your saviour? Me! Come on," he said, dragging me back along the path, "let's forget everything and eat, drink and be merry in our own inimitable way, if you know what I mean?"

His eyes twinkled at me through the near darkness and I knew exactly what he meant.

*

Next day, James insisted on staying in the area; he wanted to walk further along the coast. We asked Beth if she'd like to come too. We went past 'our' plaque and on, reaching a war memorial at the top of the hill; we paused there, reading the inscriptions and then walked on. We had the coast on our right and as the tide was out, there was an expanse of sand stretching smoothly away, leaving jagged patterns where the water hadn't quite gone.

It was a bright day with blue skies and bulbous white clouds, warmer than yesterday, but the wind had a chill. Beth was a fast walker and we warmed up as she strode quickly ahead of us. The path took us down through a wooded area and up again along the sand, but high above it. Eventually, we went down onto the beach, running completely out of control, our feet slipping and sliding down a huge dune. The sand on this part was fine and powdery and we kept walking.

"You see, over there," Beth said, pointing, "that's the old Lifeboat Station. It can't be used any more as the tide is too far away from it now. The sand's shifting, they're always dredging the channel so that boats can keep going out to sea. My dad's a fisherman and he says it's changed so much since he first started working here."

"Can we walk over there?" said James. "I'd love to have a look at it."

"Let's cut across the sand then, that's the shortest way," said Beth. We came off the dry sand and taking off our shoes and rolling up our trousers, we walked onto the ridged sand; I could feel the coldness of the water on the bottom of my feet. The ridges were hard and after a while they started digging into my arches. The sea was so far out that the edge of the water seemed far away.

"It comes in really fast when it comes," said Beth. "People can get a bit caught out here, but at least it's an easy beach to get off."

We got to the Lifeboat Station; it rose out of the rocks as if it was part of them. It was almost the same colour too, dark rusty browns and weather-beaten tones of red and steel grey. The ramp, that once took the lifeboat into the sea was now stranded on the sand, emphasising its redundancy. The shell of the building looked both spooky and majestic, growing out of a rocky outcrop. There was a bay the other side of it, with six fisherman's cottages sitting snugly on the rocks and a white cottage at the top of the cove. We walked around, seagulls weaving and screaming above us. One solitary boat was marooned on the sand, waiting for the rising water to float it once more.

"This is gorgeous, so peaceful. What's it called?"

"Hawker's Cove. One of my favourite places," said Beth. "I often come here and sit on the ramp. I do my best thinking here."

"Now if I could buy one of those ..." said James, pointing to the cottages.

"Why? Are you thinking of buying a house down here?" said Beth, looking surprised.

"I am. I love it and it's about time I got on the ladder. We were going to ask you if you knew of any good cottages for sale, actually."

"I shouldn't think any of those cottages ever come on the market but, funnily enough, the one you're renting is coming on the market soon. The owner's wife's just died and he doesn't want to be bothered with renting it out any more."

James and I looked at each other.

"Are you sure?" said James, his face a picture of excitement and anticipation.

"Yes, quite sure. He was in the shop the other day and said just that. Do you want us to have a word? Are you serious about it?"

"Yes, absolutely. God … that could be perfect! What do you think?"

"It's a gorgeous cottage … it seems almost as if it's *meant* to be. I wonder what it would go for?"

"I'm sure I could afford it, judging from prices in the agents' windows. I can't believe it, Beth; you are sure, aren't you? You're not just kidding?"

"No, of course not. I'll find out about it for you."

We walked back to Padstow along the sand; the tide was on the turn now, but there was still plenty of sand to walk on. We picked our way through some rocks, covered in spectacular seaweed that hung in tendrils of vivid green hair. It was here that the ferry went across to Rock on the opposite side of the estuary and there were several people waiting in line for the next one. We, however, made our way up the steep steps that took us back up to the war memorial and then down the long path, back into the town.

Beth had to go back to see to Grace and we said we'd call in, just before leaving for home.

*

"Well, I spoke to him and he's definitely selling. He just hasn't had time to put it on the market yet. I've got his phone number here; he's expecting your call."

We'd packed up the car and had just called in to say good-bye. The cottage had taken on a different feeling now that we knew James might buy it. We'd spent the final hours there, examining every nook and cranny, opening cupboards and trying to imagine it as ours.

We left it with Beth and her mother that we'd ring the owner the next day and let them know the outcome.

"It's been so lovely to see you both. It's exciting to think that you might be coming down here more. It's brilliant news. I hope it all goes smoothly."

"So do I. I can't believe how happy you are here, compared to how you were in Cyprus. You're like a different person."

"I know, I feel it. I've got to move on. I'm going to file for divorce."

"I'm not surprised, to be honest. I'm sorry if we didn't talk much about you, while we were here. There was so much else going on: surfing, walking ... buying houses, I didn't sit and have a proper chat with you. I'm so sorry. I'll ring you next week and you can tell me your plans."

We kissed again, James hugged her and we were gone. Back up the familiar A30, past Bodmin, Launceston and Okehampton and onto the M5 at Exeter. I thought that this journey, so familiar in the past, was now going to be part of my future.

Chapter Twenty-Four

James bought the cottage, everything was done by the end of April. No agents involved, no chains, it couldn't have been easier. He couldn't believe how straightforward it all was and he even bought most of the furniture as the owner was only too happy to get rid of it. I pointed out that house-buying wasn't usually this simple, but he just put it down to luck and a good omen for our future together. We foresaw endless holidays, long weekends and Christmases down there; it'd be a bit of a squeeze with the children, they'd have to share but that didn't matter. It wasn't as if we were living there. It was a holiday home.

At the beginning of May, Tom Kitten came out of quarantine and filled the house with his constant meowing, demands for food and his figure of eights around our legs. He adapted to the new environment quickly; the children loved having him home, insisting on letting him sleep on their beds. He had to learn to share his favours around and spend a night on Amy's bed and then a night on Charlie's.

"I really think it's about time that you got yourself a job, Emily," said Luke one day when he was visiting the children. "You can't expect me to support you. We don't live together any more – we're going to have to come to some arrangement. Maybe James should start chipping in?"

"What? You expect James to support us?"

"No, not the children; *you* if you're never going to work."

"Look Luke, it hasn't been easy for me. I don't want to go back to teaching, you know that and I'm not qualified for anything else. I want to be a photographer, but it's hard to start a business when everything's so complicated. I don't know where I'm going to be in six months, do I?"

"Get a temporary job – work in a supermarket, you could do anything if you wanted to. You just don't want to, that's your trouble."

We were sitting in the kitchen, facing each other across the table. The training was finished and he was on his way to Chivenor in the next couple of days. Things were coming to a head; his departure for Devon was more final – this time, it was the beginning of a three year posting and decisions had to made. I knew that he was building up to saying we needed to sell the house and sort out our finances. I knew I should have got a job, but somehow the months had flown by. What with looking after the children, the house and the garden on my own and then rushing off to see James as often as I could and going down to Cornwall to finalise things – time had disappeared.

"I've been in touch with an agent, by the way, and he's coming round to value the house on Tuesday," said Luke.

"*What?* You could have told me you were going to do that. So, you're going to sell up and chuck us out of our home, are you? I don't believe it."

"I'm just having it valued at the moment, Ems. Don't be so dramatic. But you've got to face facts. I'm going down to Devon; you can't expect me to beansteal forever, down there."

"What does that *mean?* Can't you speak normally?"

This was how our conversations always went these days. We were like two bickering children, constantly jabbing and jibing at each other, hiding behind this continual argumentative talk so we didn't get remotely close enough to each other to really examine our feelings. Well, that was how I saw it, anyhow.

"You know what beanstealing is. God, you've been an RAF wife for long enough. What I mean is I can live for free in the Mess for a while but eventually, I've got to live somewhere. Why should you swan around here in our house, while I have to live in one room? It's not on, Ems. Christ … I'm off for a smoke," and with that, he pushed his chair back with a loud scrape, walked to the back door and wrenched it open. I watched him prowling around the garden, blowing smoke rings up into the blossom on our cherry tree.

He was right; we were going to have to address the situation (that word again). I sat at the table, staring into space.

This was crunch time.

Luke came back into the kitchen; he obviously had something he wanted to say as he prowled round the kitchen finding things to do. He turned on the kettle, banging and crashing plates and cutlery as he emptied the dishwasher.

"Look," he said, when he'd made just himself a cup of coffee, "I don't want to disrupt the children any more than you do, but something's got to give. I've been thinking, if we carry on as we are, pretending that we're still together, I could get a quarter down there after three months or so. You'd have to come down and stay there, as if we're still married, otherwise I wouldn't get one. Meanwhile, you could stay put for a while, nothing would change for months. I could stay in the Mess at the start, then a quarter; we'd have to sell this and move the kids down to Devon schools."

I let this sink in. Was this a not so subtle way of saying he was going to get custody of the kids?

"So … are you saying, you get a quarter and the kids come down to live with you?" I said, my voice rising. "What about me? What do I do?"

"Well, you can be with James and now that you've got this love nest down there, you'll be near enough to spend lots of time with the children. I think it's the best plan. There isn't an endless supply of money, you know. I can't afford to have a quarter and not let out the house here. What alternative is there?"

I had to agree that there wasn't one; the children living with me and James in the Bristol flat wasn't an option. We needed somewhere permanent and by all accounts, helicopters would be at least two postings. That would see Amy through till the end of secondary school. But how did he expect me to get a job when I'd be flitting from place to place?

"So, I stay here for a few months; we sell around Christmas. You get a quarter, the kids come down and go to school there. I come and 'pretend' we're okay initially and then I bugger off and live with James?"

"Yea, that's about it."

His face was deadpan, his eyes looking straight into mine.

"That's great, Luke, just great," I said, my eyes filling. "You've forgotten one major thing, though."

"And what's that?"

"I love my kids and want to be with them."

"You should've thought of that when you fucked lover boy," he said, with a sneer on his face. "You ruined my life, the kids' lives and apparently your own life ... you've only got yourself to blame."

I'd never heard Luke be so horrible before (except during the row when he found out about James, back in Cyprus). I knew crying annoyed him but I couldn't stop myself and tears welled up and spilled over.

"Oh God, here we go ... tears again. It's too *late* for tears, Emily. Too late. I've no sympathy for you; you've brought it all on yourself."

He drained his cup, stood up and said, "I'm leaving now to see Sophie. I thought my plan was a good one. I don't see why *you* can't."

"Did Sophie suggest it?" I said, wiping my mascara-streaked eyes with my two forefingers.

"No, of course she didn't; I thought it would be the best

thing for the children. You really have got to stop being so fucking selfish. It's not all about *you*. I'm going and I won't see you for a while. I'll ring with my contact number in Chivenor. Think about what I've said."

I heard him go upstairs, his feet making the floorboards creak above me, opening drawers and slamming cupboard doors. He thumped down the stairs and without saying goodbye, slammed the door and was gone.

I heard the Pajero start up and listened with a sense of foreboding as the engine got quieter and quieter and disappeared. The house was now as silent as an empty church. His presence hung over the kitchen, taunting me with his words.

'It's not all about *you* ... you've only got *yourself* to blame.'

*

"So, you see, I'm a selfish, nasty person," I said.

"Look," said Jen, "he can say that, but you're only human. We all do stupid things, we all make mistakes, we're all selfish, sometimes. You didn't set out to ..."

"But if I hadn't let myself fall for another man, Jen ..."

"You can't 'stop' these things, can you? It does 'just happen', doesn't it? Don't beat yourself up so much. Luke's hurting at the moment and he's just focussing all his frustrations and feelings on you. He doesn't really feel like that. He told John he'd have you back in a heartbeat."

"Oh, don't say that, Jen. It just makes me feel more guilty. Mum said he said the same to her. *Why* would he want me back?"

"Because you're a lovely person, Emily. He loves you, like we all do."

I was sitting in the dark; the kids were asleep and I was talking quietly, so as not to wake them. Since he'd left, I'd been very tearful; even Charlie had noticed and given me one of his sweets. I'd told him I was just a feeling a 'bit sad' and he'd given me a hug. I'd rung Jen to get some reassurance; she was such a good friend, never judging, always supportive.

"Look, why don't you and the kids come here for the weekend? Just to get away …"

"That'd be good, Jen. I think I need to have a break from everything. Can we *not* talk about it if I come, though?"

"Of course … we'll just take the kids out, shop and relax. It'll be like the old days."

So, the following weekend, we went to Jen's; the kids enjoyed seeing each other again, John kept a low profile and let us girls go out shopping while he looked after the four kids. It was the tonic that was needed and I came back home with a lighter heart and determined to get a job, any job, just to prove Luke wrong about me.

*

"Why don't you put up a notice in the local shop for your photography?" said James, as always the practical one. "There must be loads of people who could do with a family portrait?"

"But I haven't done it for ages and I've lost all my confidence."

"How will you know, if you don't try?"

"I suppose you're right, but it won't earn me much, will it?"

"I don't think that's the point and anyway, it could snowball. I think you ought to offer to do it for free at first and then you won't feel so nervous. If they like the photos, they can pay for the prints and frames."

"Yea, that's a good idea and then I could try to get a part-time job, doing anything that pays me something."

"Sounds like a plan. Give it go. Say something about trying to build up your portfolio or something."

So that's what I did.

The notice read: *Photographer seeking to build my portfolio*

– free sittings – family portraits, mother and baby, pets. Contact …

I went round to the shop and asked Stan to put it in his window.

"Starting a new venture, then?" he asked, squinting at the postcard.

"Trying to," I said.

"Well, I'll point people in your direction," he said with an encouraging smile.

I also told Bella what I was doing at the school gate later that day. She said she'd love to have a family photo done; they'd been meaning to do it for years and hadn't got round to it. I wasn't sure whether she was just being kind but we arranged to do it at the weekend in the park.

I was on a roll now and with my newfound confidence, I went round to the local pub to ask for work. Jim was behind the bar, as usual. He looked like the archetypal landlord: red-faced, overweight and jovial. The pub was popular, mainly due to his friendly approach; he was always laughing and joking and welcoming everyone, no matter who they were. He'd built up a solid reputation for good food over the years.

I was prepared to do anything if it fitted round the children. I explained when I could come (mainly lunchtimes in term-time) and left my number. The chances were slim, he said, as he was fully staffed, but people sometimes let him down or were sick, so if I was prepared to come in at the last minute, he'd bear me in mind.

Chapter Twenty-Five

The estate agent, a smooth twenty-five year old in a well-cut suit, duly came. He walked around the house with a superior air, saying things like, 'I'm sure we could find someone who'd like this' and 'Have you thought of updating the bathroom?' As far as I was concerned, he could think what he liked; the ruder he was about the property, the better.

I didn't want to sell.

I tried not to sabotage Luke's plans, however, and was polite enough but didn't lead or drive about dates and kept telling him to ask my husband, as if I was a poor, helpless wife without an opinion.

The photo shoot with Bella went okay. I was nervous when I walked down to the park; the weather was perfect, but it was so long since I'd done any photography that I wondered whether I'd remember the basics. As it turned out, it all came back and I kept thinking, even if they're no good, I'm not taking any money. Once I got into the session, I began to enjoy it: I got the kids coming down the slide; found a perfect tree for them to pose under and even had them all running towards me. As I walked back home, I thought of that day with Sophie on the beach. In a way, I had Sophie to thank for today; she'd really helped me.

When Bella saw the photos she was really pleased (I didn't

think she was just being polite) and she ordered a large framed print, a smaller one and some prints. I didn't make much of a profit on them but it was a start and if I got some more clients I'd put up my prices. Bella said she'd tell her friends and other mums.

The summer holidays were fast approaching and Luke asked if he could have the children for a week immediately after school broke up. He was going to hire a cottage with Sophie and use the boat for the first time. James and I would take them down and then go on down to the cottage for a week. I couldn't imagine what that encounter would be like, the four of us all making polite conversation, but I was trying to be helpful and it seemed the easiest way.

Out of the blue, the pub rang at ten o'clock one morning, asking me to come in for a shift; someone had the flu and could I help out? Of course, I'd said immediately, abandoning my lunchtime swim at the local pool. I'd never waitressed before but how difficult could it be?

Well, more difficult than you'd think. The chef turned out to be a tyrant who shouted a lot and made me nervous; I got two orders muddled up; I dropped a glass and very nearly deposited a plate of food on someone's lap, but I smiled at everyone and Jim was pleased with me. He said he'd ring me again if the waitress was still sick the next day, which she was so I ended up doing three shifts that week and getting quite a few tips on top of my rather pathetic pay.

*

"Are you excited, kids?" said James, as he got into the front seat. I'd driven to Bristol to collect him and we were going to share the driving down to Devon.

"I can't wait," said Amy. "Dad says we're going to go out in the boat every day. And Sophie's going to be there."

"I want to learn to waterski this time. I'm not a baby any more," said Charlie, pulling rather a babyish face.

"Well, I'm sure Dad will teach you, if you want to have a go," I said, secretly hoping he wouldn't. I hated the thought of them doing things without me, especially something potentially dangerous.

The journey down the M5 went well and we arrived at Luke's cottage at five o'clock. The Pajero was parked outside, so we knew we were in the right place.

"Do you want me to stay in the car?" said James. "I don't mind."

"No, that's all right. We've got to be adults about this, haven't we?" I didn't want the two of them to meet but it would look really 'off' if James stayed put.

"Why do you want to stay in the car?" said Charlie.

"Because he's Mum's … because … they're not staying," said Amy.

"I think it would look a bit odd if you don't, James. We won't stay long, just settle them in."

We all got out, the kids dragging their cases out of the boot. I gently knocked on the gnarled wooden door.

"Hi there," I said, as the door opened, with as much lightness as I could muster. Luke looked through me with dead eyes. James was out of the car but hanging back, as if there was an electric current going round the house that might shock him if he moved forward.

"Hey … kids … come in and have a look. The cottage is really old," said Luke, standing back to let us go through the door. He hadn't, as yet, acknowledged James.

"Hi there," said James, venturing beyond the space round the car. He went to extend his hand towards Luke, but he ignored it.

"How's the new job?" enquired James.

By this time, Luke had retreated into the dark interior of the house and had his arms firmly round each of the kids' shoulders. Without even turning round, he mumbled, "Fine."

"Where's the boat?" said Charlie, oblivious to the tension.

"Down at the estuary. We're going there tomorrow."

"Where's Sophie?" said Amy. "I thought she was going to be here?"

"She's coming later tonight. She was working today and couldn't get away till later." He took both the cases and started walking upstairs, leaving us in the kitchen.

"Oh good," said Amy. "I'm going to unpack," and ran upstairs after her father. Charlie followed.

"I think we'll go," I mouthed at James. "I think it'd be better if we let them get on with it."

"Okay, fine by me." James pulled a face and whispered, "I tried!"

"I know you did … sorry about Luke." I could understand Luke's attitude but at the same time felt sorry for James, who at least had made an effort.

"We'll go, then," I shouted up the stairs.

"Okay," said Luke. Nothing else.

"I'll leave our phone number on the table. Ring me if you need to."

Nothing.

"Bye, kids," I shouted.

"Bye, Mum. See you in a week," said Amy.

Charlie came rushing down the stairs, hugged me and then ran up again. I wrote down the number on a piece of paper and put it on the table.

"Bye then," I said.

I walked to the door, got in the car and we drove away.

I didn't speak for a long time and simply looked out of the window at the passing scenery.

*

We'd rushed down twice to the cottage since the first time to talk to the owner and negotiate over the furniture, but this was our first proper visit.

As we drew up outside, James said, "Our first home, together," and he leaned over the gearstick to kiss me. The journey had helped a little with the feelings of rejection I'd had and now I realised how lucky I was to have a whole week with James alone. I kissed him back, putting my hands each side of his face.

"I love you, you know. I'm sorry if I've been a bit …"

"It was tough back there, on many levels. Leaving the children, Luke being so cold … I know. You don't need to explain."

"It's just that I'm not sure I'll ever get used to this."

"You will in time, promise. The kids are going to have a wonderful time. Don't worry about them. Luke's a great father, anyone can see that."

"I know."

We were still in the car. "Come on, let's get inside. There's loads to unpack." We'd brought all sort of things that we knew the house was lacking, things to make it our own.

That night, in the cocoon of the cottage, with the silence of the stars and distant presence of the ocean, we lay in our bed, entangled in each other's arms, completely at one with each other.

Our lives had led us to this place, to this time; our destinies, forever bound together.

After we'd made love, I lay awake thinking back to the first time I'd set eyes on James; that vision in a red uniform, all spurs and shiny buttons. That side of him, the formal side had made my heart skip a beat, but it was *this* James that I fell in love with. The James that I could rely on totally and trust with my life.

He was already asleep; I could see his outline in the darkness and hear his rhythmic breathing. His legs were wrapped around mine and he'd fallen asleep holding my hand. I closed my eyes and as I drifted off, we walked together across the beach at Petra Tou Romiou and built pebble hearts that lay in the shallows, washed lightly by the warm waters.

Chapter Twenty-Six

Our week was perfect. The weather was typically Cornish, no two days were the same. A couple of days were warm, bright and blustery, but we also had some drizzle. It didn't matter what the elements threw at us though, we didn't care. Having surfed in the cold waters of March, the sea was now positively Mediterranean in comparison and we simply enjoyed our time together.

We saw a lot of Beth, but she was now teaching surfing; there were a lot of children wanting to learn during the school holidays and she'd been asked to join the surf school at Constantine. So we saw her in the evenings, meeting for a drink and once, cooking her a meal at the cottage.

She said she was going to ask Luke down to Padstow and teach him to surf; he'd been so kind to her in Cyprus and she wanted to repay him somehow.

The only thing that blighted our week was that I didn't feel well. I'd relaxed about the children and Luke's attitude, the Cornish air had blown the sadness away and my mind was free. My stomach, however, was another matter. I'd noticed how tired I was in the mornings (putting it down to all the walking and surfing I was doing). Waves of what felt like nausea kept overwhelming me. On the morning of the fifth day, James handed me our normal strong filter coffee and the smell made me want to heave. I put it down on the table and the penny dropped. A tingle went down my body, my hand went to my breasts and yes, they were tender. James had his back to me now, washing up at the sink. I couldn't suppress my smile.

"James …" I said, with questioning intonation.

"Yup, love of my life … what can I do for you? Toast?"

"James, come here a minute."

He turned round, looked at me quizzically and came over to the table.

"Are you okay?" he said, stroking my hair before he sat down.

"Well, I don't know. That coffee made me feel sick."

"I'm sorry, madam, I'll do better next time."

"No … I mean … the smell made me feel nauseous and I keep feeling like that. I've noticed it quite a bit lately, but I haven't said anything because I put it down to …"

"Are you saying what I *think* you're saying?" he said, flicking his fringe away from his eyes.

"My breasts are tender and …"

"Are you late?"

"Yes … and I'm *never* later. Like clockwork, normally. Do you think I could be?"

"Well, we've been practising a lot, haven't we?" he said, laughing. He reached across the table and touched my hand. "That would be the best news …"

We stared at each other, hardly daring to think it could be true.

"Shall I buy a test, right now? Or shall we wait and see?" I said, hoping he wouldn't want to wait.

"God, I can't wait. Let's go and get one."

*

Of course I was pregnant. It had been inevitable right from the start, from the moment I saw him. From the moment we kissed at that first summer ball; from the moment I dived from the boat on the cruise and he found me in the sea; from the moment I saw him on stage; from the moment we made love on the beach. When I got pregnant before and had the miscarriage, it wasn't the right time for us. It was a terrible secret then; now we could shout about it and tell the world our news.

When the result of the test revealed itself, I knew this time it would be okay, I just knew. The baby would be born, a perfect mixture of the two of us, a half brother or sister for Amy and Charlie, the longed-for third child of my dreams. Perhaps Luke having a vasectomy behind my back had somehow made it possible.

We decided to keep quiet about it for now, though. It was early days and I needed to visit my GP to see how far along I was. When we were certain that it was all right, we'd tell our families.

The miscarriage before had been so awful, I was terrified it would happen again but there was no reason, this time.

It was right. It was perfect.

The rest of our time in Cornwall was spent in a haze of happiness. The baby's presence hovered over every conversation, every walk, every touch. I'd place my hand on my stomach, which was still the same shape as always and feel a contentment I had only dreamt of.

As a precaution, surfing was off the agenda; I didn't want any thumps in the stomach like before. We walked along the coastal path, finding little coves and inlets we'd never seen before. Hawkers Cove was rapidly becoming our favourite place and sitting on the rocks there, watching the seagulls whirling and screaming overhead, we talked of our future together. Time stood still; I could imagine smugglers coming ashore, dragging their booty up the beach; I could see the galleons off shore and hear cries of long lost people. As we sat, huddled together on the hard, black rock with its vivid green seaweed and huge rusty old chain that went into the sea, it was as if we too were part of the landscape, forever merging with the sea and the sky.

I was so tempted to tell Beth but we'd vowed not to tell a soul until the due date was confirmed and we'd passed the three month landmark. Beth commented on my 'healthy glow' and I had to suppress a knowing smile.

As we drove back towards Chivenor to pick up the children, we talked about how Luke would react when he knew.

"He'll be angry and hurt; all the guilt he felt about the vasectomy will boil over, I think."

"It'll be difficult for him, I guess," said James, "but he's going to have to come to terms with it. This baby is going to be Amy and Charlie's half sibling; but we'll have to tread very carefully and pick the right moment to tell him, if there is ever a 'right' moment for that sort of news."

Our welcome from Luke at the cottage was no better than before, he had a knack of looking straight through me as if I was a ghost. With James, he could barely suppress his hatred and refused to enter into a dialogue with him. The kids, however, were as excitable as always, shouting and running around, dissipating the adults' passive aggressive stances. Sophie, once more, wasn't there; I began to think that she was avoiding me. Luke said she had to go back to work but it seemed too much of a coincidence that she wasn't there a second time.

In a bid to make conversation, I told Luke about Beth's offer to teach him to surf. I gave him her number and told him he should go down.

"I will …" he said, looking away from me. "I'll take the boat and do some skiing on the Camel. I'll teach her to ski and then we'll go surfing; I like Beth a lot, she's had a rough deal and she's a genuine person," he said, looking at me as if he thought the exact opposite of me.

"That'll be nice for you both," I said. "Her mum's brilliant. She loves Grace, can't get enough of her, so Beth can do all the things she loves now. I'll tell her you'll call."

When we left, Amy hugged her father so hard, he had to prize her off him.

"I love you, Dad, I don't want to leave …"

"I love you too, Ames. I'll phone you tomorrow and your Mum and I will arrange the next visit, okay?" he said, stroking my face.

"I don't want to go …" she said again, tears in her eyes.

"Come on, try to be a big girl … show Mum what I bought you … you know …" and he whispered in her ear. She went off and unzipped the bag that was by the door.

"Look, Mum. Dad bought me this," she said and held out a box. Inside was a charm bracelet. "He's going to buy me a new charm every time I come down."

"Wow, that's lovely." I picked it up out of the box and held it up to look at it closely. I was always amazed at how good Luke was at being a father. This bracelet was like a link between her and her father and could be added to, each time they saw each other.

"Dad bought me a camera," said Charlie. "Look," and he too unzipped his bag. "He's showed me how to use it and we're going to make an album of photos next time I'm down."

"That's lovely, Charlie. You'll be just like me, a photographer." I looked at Luke, whose face was stoney. "They're great presents, Luke."

"I thought they deserved something special," he said.

*

When we got back home, I made an appointment to see the doctor. He, of course, knew nothing of my circumstances; he'd been both mine and Luke's GP for years and assumed the baby was Luke's.

"How's Luke these days? I haven't had cause to see him for a long time."

I felt myself blushing. "Actually, Luke and I aren't together any more."

"Oh, I see. Does he know about the baby?"

I wondered whether to gloss over the child's parentage, but then realised I couldn't. What if James had a blood group that caused a problem with mine?

"The father isn't Luke, Doctor Lake," I said, feeling like one of those awful women you read about in the tabloids with multiple partners. I couldn't read his face; it was inscrutable after years of practice.

"Luke lives in Devon," I said, almost by way of explanation.

"Well, you seem to be in good health with Baby due at the end of January. Your blood pressure is a fraction higher than normal, but nothing to worry about. Sometimes people's blood pressure rises just because they're at the doctor's," he said, his eyes smiling.

"Anyway, I'd like to keep an eye on you, so make your next appointment at the desk when you leave; I'd like to check your blood pressure next week and then make another appointment for a month today."

"Doctor, when I was in Cyprus, I had a miscarriage. Could it happen again?" I knew he couldn't possibly know, but ...

"Well, it would be dishonest of me to say no, but this all looks fine at the moment. Sometimes miscarriages just happen but we'll keep a close eye on you. And don't worry – relax and enjoy it."

His kind, avuncular face reassured me. I'd thought he was judging me but saw that it was my own guilt complex.

"Thank you, Doctor. I will. I'm so excited."

I stood up and as I went to the door, he said, "Look after yourself, won't you?"

*

It felt strange keeping such a major piece of information to myself. I so wanted to tell the children, my Mum, David and

Jen. It was all I could do to stop blurting it out every time I spoke to any of them. But we'd agreed we'd keep quiet until the end of August, then we'd plan who to tell first.

The summer holidays were a blur of activity; I thought that if I could keep the kids busy, they'd miss Luke less. It worked to a certain extent, but every time Amy spoke to him on the phone, she'd cry.

The kids were good at occupying themselves though and now had lots of friends in the vicinity but on top of the usual play dates, I arranged things like, sailing lessons at the Cotswold Water Park; trampolining at our local gym; children's art classes in the village hall. You name it, we did it. I wondered if I was trying to occupy myself, more than them. I was worn out by the end of the holidays; there'd been a couple of photo shoots from other mums at the primary school too, which had turned out to be quite lucrative.

The nausea continued, but as long as I avoided coffee, I was okay. It eased off during the morning and as the holidays went on, it got less and less. My breasts began to get bigger and more painful; when Charlie cuddled into me, I had to try very hard not to say anything.

One evening Beth rang. Her voice sounded happier than ever.

"Hey. You'll never guess. Luke came down yesterday and we had such a good time."

I tried not to sound peeved but for some reason, I was. He never spoke to me when he rang the children, but I thought he'd have at least mentioned seeing one of my friends.

"Yea, he came down with the boat … and he bought a friend."

"Really? Who?"

"Well, a young pilot called Josh. They're on the same squadron or something and we've been out together on the boat. Josh is an ace water-skier, you should see him. He mono skis and virtually lies down, he's at such an angle. Have you ever met him?"

"I've never even *heard* of him, never mind *met* him, Beth. He must be a new friend." It was strange to think that Luke now had friends I didn't even know. During our marriage, we'd known everything about each other and now he was leading a life I knew nothing about.

"So, am I getting the impression that this Josh is rather …»

"Oh my God. He's gorgeous. I think I'm in love!" she laughed. "Not really but … he's the sexiest thing I've seen for years. Don't say anything to Luke though, will you?"

"No, of course not. We're not on very good terms to be honest and anyway, we hardly speak. How did he seem to you?"

"He was okay. He and Josh get on really well and we had so many laughs."

"So is Josh single?"

"I'm not sure. He didn't mention anyone else. I'm hoping … they're going to come down again when they've got a free day off together. They loved the skiing here, they said."

"Didn't you go surfing in the end?"

"Yes, it was the most amazing day. We skied in the morning and then went to Connies in the afternoon. The tide was just right and we had a blast. We all had malibus. Luke was a natural and Josh had done it before. He was really good at it."

"Is there no end to his prowess?"

"No, not really! We came back to ours for tea and he was *sweet* with Grace. I always think guys who are nice to children are the good guys, don't you? If he'd ignored her, I would've gone right off him."

I immediately thought of Luke when Beth said that. He was so calm and kind to the children.

"Well, he sounds lovely, Beth. Do you want me to find out more about him, next time Luke's in touch?"

"If you can … maybe … yes, go on then."

I promised I'd try to glean some information without

mentioning Beth's name and said I'd ring straightaway if I found out anything. I could remember that feeling of stomach-churning excitement, those days when everything was possible.

I just hoped my friend wasn't going to be let down.

Chapter Twenty-Seven

"You're past the three months," said James, "I think it's time to tell people."

He'd come up for the evening, just after the children had gone back to school at the beginning of September. He was trying to spend more and more time with me, sometimes staying the night and going to work from here. We'd gently told Charlie now that he was 'Mummy's new boyfriend' and he took it better than expected. Amy smiled knowingly, pleased to be in on the secret before her brother.

"Who should we tell first? It's so difficult … Luke's coming to collect the children this weekend. He's taking them to see 'Oliver' up in London, with Sophie. Should I tell him and the children together?"

"Maybe … it's up to you whether it's best to tell them together or separately. Personally I think it would be better to tell Luke on his own."

"Yes, maybe you're right. Oh God, I'm dreading it."

"Once you've told Luke I'll tell my parents and you tell yours. Should we do it in person?"

"I think we ought to go down together and do one set of parents and then the other. Why don't we do it this weekend, while Luke's got the kids? I'll tell him on Friday."

"Okay, that's a plan. I'll phone the parents to warn them we're dropping in."

*

Friday came; he was due at 7 pm. They were driving on to Sophie's for the night and then going up to London on Saturday for the 2.30 performance.

I knew I was going to have to catch him on his own, so I'd arranged for the kids to go to Bella's until 7.30. Knowing Luke, he'd be on time and it would give me the chance to tell him. I got the kids to pack their bags before they went and we left them at the door.

"So are the kids ready?" said Luke, looking around the kitchen, expecting to see them. He'd just walked in, without even a 'hello'.

"They've packed – look, there are the bags. They're just at Bella's ..."

"For fuck's sake, I wanted to get straight off ..."

"Yes, I know but I need to tell you something and I didn't want them here."

Luke's face changed from being angry to anxious.

"Well, what is it? I haven't got long ..."

I sat down at the kitchen table. "Sit down, Luke." He did as he was told, like a child.

"Well?" he said. "What's so important?"

"H'um ..." I mumbled, pretending to clear my throat, playing for time. "There's no easy way to say this, Luke." My heart was thumping, I couldn't go on. My hands were sweating and I was wringing them together on my lap.

"You're worrying me now ... WHAT?"

"Luke ... I'm pregnant." I looked straight into his eyes.

His face went from exasperation to despair, all the colour draining from it. His eyes filled with tears.

I'd been unprepared for this; I'd thought he'd be angry, sarcastic but not, this.

I stretched my hand across the table to his but he snatched his away, stood up and went and stared out of the window with his back to me. I got up and went and stood next to him, saying nothing. We stood like that for a few minutes; I didn't know what to say or do to make it right.

I looked sideways at him, not moving my head, just trying to see him with my eyes. I could still see the sheen a tears in his eyes and was aware of his body trembling.

"Emily ..."

I tried to take his hand again, but he took it away. "Luke, I'm so sorry but you had to know."

"I knew this would happen. I knew it, the moment you told me about him that day, the moment you told me you knew what I'd done."

All the grief, all the guilt was there before me on his face.

"What I did was unforgivable, Ems. I'm so sorry."

He walked back to the table and sat with his head in his hands. I came and sat opposite him, staring at him.

"Luke, what you did hurt me so much but *I'm* the one to blame for everything else, not you."

"If I could go back and do things differently ..."

"But you can't, Luke, none of us can. We have to live as things are *now* ... that's all there is."

He lifted his head and, looking straight at me, he said, "I know it's too late for us ... but ... I still love you. I know I've made the most terrible mistake." He covered his face with his hands and then spoke through them.

"I'm pleased for you, that you've been able to have another baby. I'm just so sorry that it's not mine ..."

I reached across the table again, this time with both my hands and took his away from his face. We gripped each other's hands tightly, staring at each other with an intensity that we'd both forgotten. In that moment, there was such a connection between us, that it was as if the clocks had stopped. I stared into his soul and found the person I'd fallen in love with all those years ago.

I felt breathless, confused and sad.

"I know this must be really difficult but please don't think I've done this to spite you. It's nothing like that. I just wanted another baby and I'm happy that I've been able to. Can you understand that?"

He squeezed my hands and lifted one to his lips and kissed the back of it tenderly. Outside, we heard the sound of a car and banging doors.

We snatched our hands apart and stood up; the children burst in. They threw themselves at Luke, who managed to pull himself together so they didn't notice his distress.

"So, come on then you two reprobates, we've got to get in the car and get to Guildford. Soph's expecting us and we're going to be late."

They gathered up their bags, kissed me and went out to the Pajero. "Have a great time, all of you," I said. "Tell me all about it on Sunday – remember all the details!"

I was standing on the passenger side; the window was open and Amy, whose turn it was to be in the front, was leaning out. I gave her one more kiss and I looked across to Luke and said, "Take care, see you Sunday," and smiled.

He returned a smile that made my heart jump and I put my hand on my stomach.

I stood in the lane, watching the car drive away, waving until it was out of sight.

*

When they returned on Sunday we tried to act the same as ever, but the memory of Friday evening, lingered over our conversations; the terrible tension that had been building and

260

building between us over the last few months had dissipated. His reaction to my pregnancy had completely floored me and changed everything. I felt tender towards him once more, instead of the seething resentment I'd felt for months and I was sure he felt the same. We didn't speak about it; we let the children shout and take over, as we often did. They told me all about the performance and re-lived the 'Please sir, can I have some more' scene, with acting panache. I shared smiles with Luke over the top of the children's heads and it almost felt like the old days. I was sad when it was time for him to head off.

As I walked to the car, I realised I hadn't asked him anything about Josh. I'd promised Beth I would but it was difficult to bring it up without implicating Beth, so all I said was, "Your day in Padstow sounded fun?" and hoped he'd go on from there.

"It was fantastic. I took a young pilot with me called Josh. We've been out several times on the boat and he's been teaching me how to improve my mono skiing. He's the best skier I've ever been out with. He took quite a shine to Beth, they had loads in common; he's much more her scene than that awful husband of hers. I told him the situation and he's really keen to go down again and not just for the skiing."

"So, he's unattached?"

"As far as I know. He had a long-term girlfriend who ditched him for another pilot but I don't think this is a rebound thing; he genuinely likes Beth."

"Oh well, let me know developments. It'd be nice if Beth could find some happiness."

"That's all any of us are looking for, isn't it? See you in a couple of weeks."

And he was gone.

*

The weekend with James, telling the parents, had gone pretty well as expected. We'd gone to my parents first and it was as if my mother, in particular, knew there was going to be some sort of important news announced. She'd ushered us through to the lounge, made some coffee and then came in, looking expectantly from one to the other. My father, oblivious to it all, sat in his favourite arm chair with the Telegraph on his knee and said, "So, where are the children this weekend?"

"They're with Luke, Dad. He's taken them to see 'Oliver' in London."

"That's nice ... shame you couldn't go with them."

"Well, it's Luke's turn this weekend. We try to get them together with Luke as much as possible. Actually, we have something to tell you ..." I said, grabbing James' hand and smiling nervously at him.

"I knew there was something," said Mum. "I could just tell. What is it, dear? Are you going to sell the house?"

"No ... well, yes, we'll sell it eventually but it's not that, Mum. It's ..." I looked at James for some moral support and he cut in,

"Emily's pregnant."

He didn't say anything further and neither did anyone else. We all looked at each other and I wished someone would say something – anything.

"Oh ... I see," said Mum. "Is that what you want, Emily?"

"Of course it's what I want, Mum. We're not teenagers any more. We love each other and ..."

"This is going to be a much loved, longed-for baby. A brother or sister to Amy and Charlie."

"Does Luke know?" said Mum.

"Yes, he does, Mum and he's pleased for me."

This was met with stunned silence. I put my hand on my stomach and looking at my parents, said, "I've always wanted a third child, you know that. I'm so excited about it and I hope you can be excited for me, too. This will be your third grandchild." I smiled at them, willing them to accept the situation.

"Well, it's not the way we did things in our day but I'm pleased for you, if that's what you want. When's it due?"

"The end of January. I'm past three months now so that's why we're telling everyone. I've got to tell the children when they come home."

Dad, all this time, hadn't said anything. I knew, in his quiet, conservative world, this would be a bombshell he'd find difficult to deal with. Mum was more 'worldly' and adaptable, but Dad was stuck in a time warp; he'd only just got used to David being gay and even now, it wasn't easy for him. What he'd think of my pregnancy with another man other than my husband, God alone knew.

Dad got up and said, "Excuse me a minute," and left the room.

"Oh dear, is Dad upset?" I said, looking at the closed door.

"Probably, but you know your father, he'll come round in the end. He'll need time to absorb it and digest it and then he'll be okay. Leave him to me, I'll sort him out," she said, smiling at us both.

"Thanks, Mum."

"Yes, thank you for being so understanding," said James.

"I'm sure you'll both make wonderful parents," said Mum.

Dad came back into the room after a few minutes and we all talked about other things, pretending everything was as normal. We didn't stay long because we wanted to go to James' parents next; we said goodbye, promising to bring the grandchildren down soon.

On the way to James' parents, we talked about my parents' reaction and how it had been predictable. We tried to anticipate how the next set of grandparents would be.

"I think my mother will be difficult, so prepare yourself. You know how she was before. You've seen her at her best, or worst. Dad'll be fine."

"Oh God, your mother terrifies me. She's going to hate me even more now. I've corrupted her son completely, luring him away from a life of upper-class rectitude, to one of the sluttish working-class."

He laughed. "She's not that bad, Emily; she may surprise you."

As it turned out, after the initial shock, she did surprise us. After a few comments like 'Are you going to get married?' and 'Are you sure, James, that this is what you want?' she softened and as James is the blue-eyed boy who can do no wrong, she quickly began to take an interest – wanting to know if 'we were going to put his name down for Charterhouse' and we had to point out we didn't even know whether it was a boy or a girl yet.

James' Dad was sweet; he clasped James round the shoulders and said, "Well done, old boy," as if he'd achieved some greatness on the battle field. He hugged and kissed me and said how proud he was.

So, we went back to the cottage relieved we'd told them all but tired from all the emotions of the day. It was our baby, but it affected so many other people. I felt as if we were at the centre of a spinning tornado, a circling twister, rotating and funnelling across the land, engulfing other people and swallowing them up, sucking them up into the air and spewing them out, covered in dust and debris.

I lay in bed with James, clinging on to him, afraid I too would be surrounded and swept up in a water spout into the atmosphere above.

*

On the Sunday evening when I was eventually alone with the children, I waited until bedtime and we were all sitting on Charlie's bed.

I said, "Kids, I've got some very exciting news for you."

Charlie, who'd been lying down looking sleepy, immediately sat up and said, "Is Dad coming home?"

"No, Charlie, it isn't that. It's something about James and me."

Amy was leaning against the wall, her legs over the top of Charlie's which were under the duvet and she grabbed my arm and said, "Mum, are you and James going to get married?"

"No … look kids … I've got a baby in my tummy. You can't see it, but it's there and you're going to have a brother or sister. Isn't that amazing?"

Both of them stared at me with big, round eyes. "How did it get there?" said Charlie.

I'd been so wound up about telling them, I hadn't anticipated a 'birds and the bees' question.

I looked to Amy for assistance who said, "Charlie, Daddy's sperm goes and meets Mummy's egg and they make a baby. We did it at school. Does Dad know? He didn't say anything at the weekend."

Her sweet mixture of confidence and innocence touched me; how could I tell them the truth? But I must …

"Actually kids, it's James' … he's the daddy."

"What's sperm?" said Charlie, but I chose to ignore that question.

I let my last statement sink in for a while and then added, "And Dad does know, Amy, but I asked him not to say anything to you."

"Oh …" said Amy. "But if the baby is James' … is he still our brother?"

"Of course, I'm your mother and the baby's, so he'll be your half-brother or sister. What do you think, Charlie?"

"Will he look like me?"

"Maybe. He may be mixture of us all."

"But not Dad," said Amy.

"No, not Dad."

"Will he live with us?" said Charlie, staring hard at my stomach.

"Of course. You'll both have to help me with holding and feeding and …"

"Ugh! Well, I'm not changing his smelly nappies. They're disgusting!"

"No, you won't be doing that, Amy. Let's buy a book tomorrow and we can see pictures of how the baby's changing from month to month in my tummy."

"How long is it going to be till we see him?" said Charlie, slightly losing interest.

"It's ages, isn't it Mum? It takes nine months, we were told."

"Yes, you're absolutely right. So, we get to meet him at the end of January, as he's already been in here for three months," I said, patting my stomach.

I could see Amy doing some mental arithmetic. "Why have you only just told us? You've known for ages."

"Well, it's best to wait until after three months because sometimes things go wrong in the first few weeks but our baby's fine so we don't need to worry. Come on, it's time for bed now. We can talk some more in the morning. Night, night Charlie, sweet dreams," and I kissed the top of his head.

Putting Amy into her bed, I hugged her and kissed her cheek.

"Thank you for helping me there, Amy; I was wondering what to say! You're getting very grown up, aren't you?"

"Mum. I love you!" she said, squeezing me round the neck. "Is Dad sad?"

"No … why do you say that?"

"I just thought he might be feeling a bit left out."

"I think Dad will be okay, Pops. He'll be fine. Night, night."

Chapter Twenty-Eight

It was such a relief that the pregnancy was out in the open and everything progressed as normal. The sickness had tailed off and as I went through October, I got bigger; before that, I could have hidden my bump, but now it was visible for all to see. I would stare at myself naked, in front of the mirror, fascinated by the changes that were being wreaked on my body. I'd stand sideways, my hand gently resting on the top of the bump, then stroking it, in tender circling movements, as if I was massaging the baby itself. The children and I looked at the book I'd bought most days, so we could see the growth of the baby. According to the book, it was now covered in downy hair on its head and body and was about ten inches long.

I was beginning to be convinced my baby was a girl; the pregnancy was following a similar pattern to my first and when I stood in front of the mirror, it was a female foetus I 'saw'. Charlie was sure it was a boy (wishful thinking for a playmate to play football with, I realised) and Amy definitely wanted a girl. We all referred to the bump as 'Bumpy' and at night, the children would insist on Bumpy joining in the night time routine of stories.

It was on one such occasion in the middle of October when I became aware of the fluttering and skittering movements. My hand was resting lightly on my stomach as I read Charlie his story.

"... and as the boy reached for the ball ... oh!" I said, looking at the children with a beam on my face, " ... I think I just ..."

"What, Mum, what?" said Amy.

"I just felt the baby move! Hold on, just be very quiet and still for a moment and we'll see if it happens again." We all sat, looking at my middle.

"Yes, there it is again!"

We all laughed. "Can I put my hand there, Mum?" said Amy.

"Me, too!" said Charlie.

"Okay, one at a time. You may not feel it though, it's very light. When the baby's bigger, you'll even *see* the movements."

Amy gently put her hand on my stomach and looked expectantly up at my face. Nothing happened for a few minutes, then I said, "Did you feel that?"

"Yes, I did ... I think so! Oh, let me kiss your tummy, Mum, that's incredible."

Charlie claimed he could feel it too but I wasn't so sure he did.

After that, the movements became stronger and stronger and were a regular occurrence.

*

Luke hadn't mentioned selling the cottage again, but he did acquire a quarter which he now lived in, with a view to the kids staying more and for me and the kids supposedly (for the official story, anyway) to move to, in the new year. The story he spun was that the family were staying put until then because of school, which wasn't a lie but the bit about the whole family coming to live with him, was.

The children went down to see him in the October half-term, staying the whole week. I drove them down on my way to Cornwall and the arrangement was, that Luke would bring them back up to the Cotswolds at the end of the week. I'd been concerned about how Luke was going to cope with them during the week. He had to work on the Wednesday, Thursday and Friday but he said it was all under control; he had them going to a children's event on the camp on the Wednesday and the other two days, Beth had offered to come up and look after them. She was going to take them to Woolacombe, get them all kitted out in wetsuits and teach them to surf.

"How did that come about?"

"Well, Josh and I have been back down to Padstow a couple of times and I asked her – she was fine about it. I've offered to pay her, but she won't accept any money; she's going to leave Grace at home. I think she's still trying to repay me for helping her in Cyprus. Anyway, she's very happy to come; she and Josh seem to be getting on very well. He's going to ask her out, when she comes. They can go out the Thursday night Beth stays at the quarter so it works well all round."

I had driven down on the Monday morning after the rush hour and we were now sitting in the quarters' rather boring kitchen. The children were racing around upstairs, establishing themselves in their respective rooms. It was a small detached house, very different from our old one in Cyprus; not quite so stuck in the past. There were more modern appliances and slightly fewer garish carpets, but it still had the distinct feel of a military house: functional and characterless. To be fair, Luke didn't have any personal things in it, so it really was without his own style. The garden was a square piece of grass with a few bedraggled plants in unkempt beds, but at least there was space for the children to play.

"How are you feeling now?" said Luke. We'd avoided talking about the pregnancy since I'd arrived, but alone together in the kitchen, it was the inevitable question.

"I feel really well. The doctor says the only thing we've got to keep an eye on is my blood pressure, but it's okay at the moment. Do you remember, I had slightly high blood pressure with Amy?"

"Yes. When's the due date?"

"Around 30th January," I said, feeling how surreal it was to be talking about this to Luke. His face had shut down, I couldn't read it at all. I wanted to change the subject.

"How's Sophie?"

"I haven't spoken to her for a while; she seems to be getting close to some photographer."

"Do you mind that, Luke?" I was still confused about what their relationship was all about.

"No ... why should I mind? I'm pleased for her. She needs to move forward and find someone she can be happy with. That's not me. There's too much history with us, too much baggage. I told you, we were only ever just friends really."

"Are you going to see her again soon?"

"Maybe. She's going on some assignment to Morocco next week so maybe after that. I told her she should come down with Greg, or whatever his name is."

I wasn't sure what to make of this. Was Luke as laid-back as he appeared to be about Sophie 'moving on', or was he just putting on a front? I realised how far we'd drifted apart; we never spoke on the phone any more. Maybe it was a good thing that she'd found someone else, perhaps we all needed to have a clean break from the past.

"Do you want a sandwich before you leave?" said Luke, "I'm going to make some for the kids."

"Yes, that would be lovely then I'll push off."

He started buttering bread and I came and stood next to him and said, "Can I do something?" and he gave me some cheese to grate. It was such a domestic scene and it struck me that we made a good team, or we *had* made a good team in the past and I felt unutterably sad.

After lunch, they all walked me to the car parked out the front of the house.

"Be good for Daddy," I said, "and help him by tidying up after yourselves."

"We will," they said in unison. I hugged and kissed them both and then for the first time for what felt like a lifetime, I hugged Luke.

"Give me a ring if you need anything," I said. "Ring me anyway, just for a chat," I added. I drew away from him and he kissed my cheek.

"Look after yourself."

"I will." I got into the car, put the strap round myself, making sure it sat below the bump and started the engine.

Before, when I'd left the children with him, I'd had James with me. This time, I drove off, feeling more alone than I'd ever felt before.

*

The drive along the coast to Padstow passed in a dream. My auto-pilot kicked in and I was in the cottage before I'd even realised I'd driven all that way.

This was to be the first time I was going to stay in the cottage alone. James couldn't get down until the next day but I decided I was going to enjoy it and not mope around feeling sorry for myself.

I popped into Beth's shop and told her mother I'd arrived; Beth was out teaching but would be back later and her mum promised to send her round to the cottage. I went into the small supermarket and bought something for us to eat for supper. I was hoping Beth would stay for some food.

The cottage was beginning to feel like home. I was getting used to all its little creaks and clicks and was happy to sit in the sitting room, feeling its presence around me. There was a window seat I liked to sit on; I could watch the occasional person walk by and absorb the sea air through the open window. It was mild for the end of October and I sat there now, waiting for Beth. I had a book on my lap, which I looked at now and again, but somehow, just being there was enough. Pregnancy was making me more contented. I was very aware of the baby growing inside; with maturity, I appreciated the miracle of it more this time. When I was pregnant with the other two, I'd just gone through the process without too much thought. This time, I loved every kick, every hiccup the baby had, even every uncomfortable feeling I experienced.

I saw Beth walk up the road and we waved to each other though the window; I got up and went to let her in. We hugged and Beth admired Bumpy.

"Wow, you've grown since I saw you last!"

"Yes, I'm going to be huge, I think. I'm trying hard not to eat 'for two' but this sea air makes me ravenous. Can you stay for supper?"

"Of course, I'd love to." We both went through to the kitchen and in an echo of Luke and I preparing sandwiches together, we started preparing vegetables and grilling sausages, standing side by side.

"I hear you're going up to help Luke, on Thursday? That's really kind of you, Beth. I'd been a bit worried about how he was going to cope, to be honest ..."

"Well, I thought that. I thought it'd be something I could do for you *both*. And I have got an ulterior motive," she grinned. "Josh is taking me out. He rang last night and suggested we go for a meal. I'm so excited. I can't wait for you to meet him."

"I heard about the 'date' from Luke. I think he's really keen, Beth, from what Luke said."

"Is he? What did Luke say?"

"Oh, just that you've got loads in common and you get on really well."

"We do!" Her face was a picture of excitement and hope.

"It's going to work out for you, Beth, I'm sure."

Beth had bought a bottle of white wine to drink and although I couldn't drink it, the evening passed by with lots of laughter and chat and Beth left around nine, promising to see me again before she went to Chivenor.

I watched some television and then made my way upstairs for a long, hot bath. I lay back, with the water hardly covering my bump. I watched intently to see if I could see the movements on the surface that I could feel fluttering below. Suddenly, my bump 'kicked' and then again.

"You're waking up now, baby," I said, "just when it's time for your Mummy to go to sleep."

I smiled to myself; this was the beginning of many a sleepless night.

Chapter Twenty-Nine

James was due to arrive at two o'clock. I'd got up late, a luxury that didn't happen very often. Having eaten my breakfast listening to Radio Four catching up on world events, I took myself back to bed to continue my novel. Why shouldn't I indulge myself, I thought? I justified it by looking at my ankles which were a little swollen; the longer I could elevate them, the better.

I spent the rest of the morning shopping and preparing a meal for him; it felt like a labour of love. I wanted this meal to be special, one that we'd look back on and remember fondly. I'd bought his favourite bottle of red wine and made French onion soup and chicken curry; I also whisked up a meringue nest for his favourite, Pavlova which I'd put together just before serving it. Out shopping, I'd seen some beautiful local blue and white pottery; I placed the two bowls proudly on the table, waiting to see James' reaction.

Having had a quick sandwich for lunch, I looked at my watch. He'd be here soon. I was looking forward to going on our favourite walk along the coast, maybe at a slower pace than before. I could feel myself slowing down; my walk was already taking on a 'pregnant waddle' as he said and I had to sit down regularly. Still, there were all those benches just waiting for me to rest on.

I turned on the TV and got involved in some mindless lunchtime programme which occupied my mind for a while. Two o'clock came and went. I switched off the television, paced around and looked out of the window, hoping to hear the roar of his motorbike coming up the quiet street.

But he didn't come.

*

I knew, in that moment, I knew …

I felt a cold wave of terror travel down my body, the blood curdling in my skin then draining from my limbs, leaving me breathless and shaking.

"What do you mean? Who *is* this?" I shouted down the phone.

"Emily … it's James' father – it's …"

"Why are you ringing me? James isn't here … ring back soon. He'll be here any minute."

I deliberately misunderstood him. Surely if I blocked it out, it wouldn't be true?

"Emily, listen," he said. "James has been involved in an accident. The police have just been here. I'm so sorry … there's no easy way of saying this." His voice broke and I could hear him coughing.

After a few seconds, there was silence.

"He's died, Emily. He's dead."

His words were untrue.

"Emily dear … are you there? Talk to me?"

I could hear the disembodied voice coming out of the receiver that was now hanging down, swinging. I found myself on the floor unable to get up. I wanted the voice to stop, to go away. My body was a prison, I was encased in it, surrounded by it.

I was shivering and lay down on my side, my knees drawn

up. The voice, *that* voice, stopped and soon I heard a noise: a long, beeping sound. It woke me.

What had he said?

James was dead?

No ... it was a lie.

I opened the door and staggered out. A woman walking her dog looked at me and said, "Are you all right, dear?"

I leant against a wall, breathing fast; seagulls were soaring above me, crying their mournful sounds, making me block my ears with my hands, to keep their cries out.

I stumbled on until I got to the pasty shops and went down the righthand lane, which brought me to the harbour's edge. The boats there made no sense to me.

I'm going to that shop ... there. Someone will tell me what to do.

I crashed through a door, a bell shouting my arrival. I looked around at all the buckets and spades, the boxes of fudge, the little flags, the flip flops, the post cards.

"Hello, Emily ..." a woman said. "What's the matter, you look as if you've seen a ghost."

She came over and sat me down on a chair.

"Emily, what's wrong? You stay here ... Beth's upstairs with Grace. Hold on," she said. "I'll get her."

The colours and smells of the shop were circling and twisting around me.

I was going to be sick.

"Emily ... it's Beth. I'm here. What's the matter? What's happened?"

I knew I'd come for a reason ... what was it?

"James ... dead."

"Oh my God ..."

"James dead," I said again, as if to make it true. "James."

"I ... I'm so sorry," someone said, and that's all I remember.

*

276

When I came round, I was lying in a room I didn't recognise. Beth was sitting at the end of the bed with the curtains closed.

She stroked my leg and said, "I've called Luke, I didn't know who else to call."

The fog lifted with the intensity of an explosion.

JAMES IS DEAD.

I couldn't cry. The tears that were flowing inside my head were stuck behind a dam. I felt I was floating, floating on a sea of tears, unable to think, feel or speak.

"Luke's ringing your parents – they'll come down. You'll be okay." She was stroking my leg again. "Don't worry about the children, Luke will look after them. And I can help."

In the distance, I could hear a telephone ringing. Beth walked to the door.

"I'll be back in a minute, Emily. Don't worry."

She came back. "That was your Mum. They're coming down to collect you. You're going back home to their place. You'll be okay now."

Will I be okay? Where's my home?

*

Later, much later, I had a vague recollection of the journey in the back of my parents' car. It was interminable – slow, painful ... like a journey through a tunnel, dark and impenetrable. They'd covered me in something and I had a pillow for my head, but I put it against my bump. I slumped with my head against the window, the cold seeping into my mind. I must have slept a little, but mainly I stared ahead, the tears still stuck.

The next few days were a blank. People came and went – I was lying in my old, childhood room – and people kept coming in, asking questions and going out again.

I couldn't speak.

*

The only person I fully registered was David. He came in, sat on the bed, held my hand and didn't say anything. Nothing at all. I knew what he wanted to say, but he couldn't say it and I was glad.

When he eventually left, he said simply, "We all love you ... so much. It might seem impossible at the moment, but you'll survive this. You'll live on ... with wonderful memories of James. And you have his baby ... you have him inside you, right now. Hold on to that. When the baby's born, you'll be holding part of James in your arms."

I stared at him and at last the tears broke through the barrier. He sat on the bed again, leant forward and lifted me up towards him. My whole body cried, it shook and trembled. The ocean of tears surged and flooded.

It was a relief to feel the tears, at last.

*

I needed to see the children; they were back at the cottage and I had to go to them. Beth and Luke between them were looking after them but they'd be worried about me and I wanted to reassure them. My parents were going to take me and stay.

As we pulled up outside the cottage, it was as if I had been away for years. Nothing was familiar, I was seeing the cottage through cloudy glass.

Amy was the first to come out of the door; she put her arms round my waist and squeezed hard. She was growing so tall now and her head rested on my chest.

"I love you, Mum ..." she said with tears running down her face. "I never got the chance to go and see him play, Mum ... and now I never will." She closed her eyes.

"It's so unfair …" Charlie came up to me too and hugged me from behind; I was encircled by them.

"Is the baby okay?" said Amy, stroking my stomach.

"The baby's fine … we'll all be fine."

"Come on," said Mum, "let's go inside. We need to get you settled in."

I walked through the door and there was Luke. I went up to him and he enfolded me in his arms. I began to cry; I thought I'd cried all the tears there were but they came again like a torrent I couldn't stop.

"Sh … sh … sh …" he said, "you'll be okay, I. You're home now. Everyone loves you."

He took my hand and led me upstairs. I felt like a child as he made me sit on the bed and took off my shoes, lifted back the duvet and made me get into bed.

"You sleep, now … you're home."

I lay back on the pillow and stared up at him. His face was a picture of love and concern; he reached for my hand.

"I've got to go back down to Devon now. I've had quite a few days off, so I need to go. You must rest and try to get strong again. The funeral's next week, on Monday and I just need to ask you something. Do you want me to come? I'll come with you, if you want me to … but I know it's …"

"Come with me. I can't do it without you. I can't …"

"Of course I will. We'll all go together. The children want to go, I've already asked them. Your Mum and Dad and David and Steve are coming too."

I hadn't been told anything about the funeral and now the prospect filled me with horror … but if they were all there it would be possible to get through it, wouldn't it?

"Where's Beth?"

"She's gone back home now that your mother's here to look after you. She's been amazing, Ems. She's been such a good friend."

"Can you ask her to come to the funeral?"

"She's already arranged it. We'll all be there."

He put my hand back down on the duvet and went to the bedroom door.

"Bye, Emily."

For the first time since it had happened, a feeling of peace descended. I was back home – my Mum and the children were downstairs. I'd get through this.

My hand was resting on Bumpy and as if the baby knew, he gave a little kick.

Chapter Thirty

I had done my best to block out the funeral. I didn't want to think about it, couldn't think about it. It was impossible to comprehend that I'd never see that beautiful face again. The funeral would make it real and I couldn't bear it.

His parents had rung me about the arrangements. They said they understood that I would want to have a 'say' as to how the funeral should be.

All I knew was that he was gone and beyond that, I couldn't think. But being confronted by questions, I realised I *did* want a say. No, he wouldn't want a military funeral; maybe a guard of honour, but nothing else. Yes, he would have liked the tea afterwards to be in his parents' home. I insisted that his band mates would be there and that they should play something in his memory. This, I knew, would not be what his parents would want, but his music meant far more to him than the Army. I was sure he'd want that.

They were remarkably kind to me. His father always had been, but with the first encounter with his mother in my mind, I wondered if I would be blamed for his death. But there was nothing like that; his mother talked gently to me, showing great compassion and concern for both me and the baby. I couldn't conceive of the agony they must be going through: to lose a son at any age was horrendous and I admired their quiet dignity.

They had kept me informed about what the police had to say following the accident. It seems that James had been on a dual carriageway at the time. Witnesses said he was driving fast, about seventy miles an hour and had been overtaking a lorry when he'd lost control. It was thought he'd hit a piece of debris that was found at the scene and had veered into the central reservation. He'd died instantly and no one else was hurt.

Hearing the words, so clinical and factual, did not deaden the horror, in fact they made it worse. In my mind, I relived the moment when he must have flown through the air again and again. I saw his poor body gliding, held in a never-ending descent towards oblivion.

Of course I blamed myself – how couldn't I? If I hadn't been down in Cornwall, he wouldn't have been on his bike, on that road, at that time. If I hadn't met Bethany, we would never have bought a house in Padstow. If I hadn't fallen in love with him in Cyprus, he would never have … but it was hopeless to think like that.

He was on a powerful motorbike and was driving fast and he hit something in the road which made him lose control.

That was it.

Maybe his life had been meandering towards that moment, since the day he was born. Maybe his destiny had been mapped out and there was nothing anyone could do to change the course of those events.

Perhaps we were never meant to be happy and live together forever; the stars had given us our chance, our short time of happiness and that was all it was ever going to be.

*

When the day arrived, 5th November, 1994, I woke up with a start.

This was the day. I'd stopped crying now; the tears had finally gone away and now I felt numb … detached, as if I was seeing my life through a layer of gauze. I could see it but it was happening without me.

My mother helped me get dressed; I wore the same outfit I'd worn to Sam's funeral. I stood, like a shop mannequin while Mum lifted the dress over my head and did the zip up at the back.

Placing the eternity ring on my finger and the bracelet on my wrist, I realised I'd never marry him. It had all been a dream that would never be fulfilled.

Why did we ever think we deserved happiness?

It gave me comfort, somehow, to feel the jewellery close to my skin. James had touched both objects with his hands.

We set off in my parents' car. The children were very quiet, understanding the awfulness of the day but not knowing what a funeral would be like. My mother had told them a little about what to expect. I hadn't got the strength. I knew I should, but … I just couldn't.

The church was beautiful; it sat in its surroundings as if it had been there forever. That was where we'd stood when he gave me the eternity ring. I saw us, quite plainly, two spirits from the past. The ring's heaviness weighed down my hand.

As I got out of the car, I saw Luke. He walked towards me, Beth by his side. They both kissed my cheek and each linking arms with me, walked me up the little path towards the porch. My legs were so weak, I needed them both to lean on. I walked, looking ahead, my eyes staring at the line of men standing on guard, outside the entrance.

Somehow, I got to the front of the church and sat down. The organ was playing a piece which filled both the church and my body with its mournfulness.

I could think of nothing, of no one.

I felt myself trembling; my knees were juddering up and down. I'd almost forgotten the baby and suddenly, it kicked, reminding me.

Luke looked sideways at me and said, "Are you all right?" and I thought, if I look at him, I'll cry ... so I looked down, clenching my teeth in a vice-like grip.

I was aware of his family, but couldn't look at them. I was aware of my parents, my children ... but I couldn't look at them. All I could do was look down.

Soon the coffin was there, to my left, sitting solid and real; the flowers, all white. I let my eyes rest on it for a millisecond and then I looked down.

I stood, I sat down, I knelt; I did all the things that everyone around me was doing, but I was an automaton. I was obeying the rules of the ceremony, only because I had to. People sang, people spoke, but I heard nothing. There was a loud buzzing in my ears that blocked it all out.

Just when I thought I couldn't stand it another minute, the boys from the band came to the front. My heart was pounding. I'd said I wanted them there, but how could they? How could they be there without him?

They sang Dark End of the Street, the song I'd loved that night at the gig. I saw him on stage and remembered the way I'd felt then; how I'd imagined the two of us were going to walk off into the darkness, together. As the song concluded there was no cheering, no applause, as there had been before; the church fell absolutely silent and the boys walked back to our seats.

James was walking in darkness alone, now.

His poem came back to me:

Both, forever spirits, Dancing through ripples, Flying through infinite sunsets.

I wanted to die ... to be with him. Now I understood Sophie's actions that day.

The coffin was carried back up the aisle. There was to be a burial this time, not like Sam. Luke and Bethany held me and walked to the grave and I watched, as James was lowered into the ground. I threw in some clods of earth; Luke gave me a single red rose.

"Throw it in," he whispered.

"Why?" I said and then dropped it in. It fell in slow motion, down, down, down.

It fell on top of the box, on top of the white flowers, on top of the umber coloured clods of earth. The red of the rose took me to the moment I first saw him, resplendent in his dress uniform: the red stripe.

A time line had been drawn between that moment and this; our lives had collided, we'd travelled along the road together and now it was time to part. Him to walk away, somewhere unknown; me to walk alone to an unknown future.

I saw myself getting to a fork in the road. He turned left, I turned right.

I waved goodbye, as he disappeared …

Chapter Thirty-One

The following weeks were a mixture of nothingness and something that couldn't be ignored. The baby kept growing and kicking, moving and hiccuping. I felt strangely detached from it, yet in love with it too. It was the only thing that kept me going.

My parents had stayed for two weeks after the funeral, but eventually they'd had to go, to get back to their own lives. That first night, when I was left with just the children, was one of the worst nights of my life. My parents had to go, I didn't hold it against them, but I felt utterly abandoned and alone.

I had a team of people who rallied round me: Jen popped over several times; David and Steve came as much as possible; Bella was always coming round … but there was nothing any of them could do to take the loneliness away.

Beth and I spoke on the phone and I had little chats to Luke when he rang the children, but I felt everyone else had their own lives to lead; I didn't want to burden them with my sadness. I remembered how I'd felt when Sophie came back to Cyprus; it was so difficult to deal with someone who was recently bereaved. I'd felt so helpless and there was nothing I could do to ease her pain. I didn't want other people to feel the same about me.

One evening, the phone rang and it was James' father. I

hadn't realised until then how alike they sounded. His voice was deeper than James', but it had the same inflections, the same tone, even the same way of saying my name.

"Emily, I wanted to talk to you about something. I'm sure this is the last thing you need right now, but I wanted to reassure you. What it is ... James hadn't made a will. He should have done, especially as he'd bought a house, but he didn't ... so everything comes to us."

He paused for a few seconds and then carried on. "Obviously, he had life insurance to cover the mortgage, so the house is now paid for. He had some savings, not a lot, but a little nest egg. What I'm trying to say is ... we don't need his money and we would like to give you the cottage in Padstow. He would've wanted you to have it," he continued. "He loved you so much; he was constantly telling us how you were the only thing in his life that mattered. And with a baby on the way, I know that's what he'd want us to do. All we would stipulate is that you write a will and leave the house to our grandchild. I'm sure you would anyway but you never know what the future will bring. That would be our one wish."

"Of course, of course," I said. The thought of the cottage filled me with longing. I hadn't been back since that awful day and although it scared me, the thought of being there again made me want to go there, right now. To feel James in its walls.

"The savings, we'd invest on the baby's behalf for him or her to have when they reach eighteen," he continued. "To help with university fees or something else. So, Emily, we just wanted to let you know."

"Thank you ... thank you, both. That's so generous of you."

"Not at all. It's what James would've wanted ... now how's that little baby of yours? Everything progressing okay?"

"I went to the clinic yesterday and they said the baby's a good size. They're keeping an eye on my blood pressure; it's been a little raised again recently, but nothing to worry about."

We talked as if this was the most normal pregnancy in the

world; the fact that this child would never know its father, wasn't talked about. James would only ever be a face in a photograph, only a collection of stories told by people, to keep him alive. The baby would never hear his voice, play games with him, see him on stage, singing and playing his guitar. It was a prospect that I found too hard to think about and it seems other people did too. No one talked about it.

I promised to ring the moment the baby was born and he rang off. It was a strange relationship, we hardly knew each other but were bound together now, forever, with a love for James. I knew how special this baby would be to them and felt a responsibility towards them.

That night, I lay in bed and thought about what I wanted to do. I felt rootless, aimless. I was only in this cottage because that's where Luke and I had lived. I'd stayed because of the children's schooling but ... now?

Should I let them go and join Luke as he wanted? He could sell this, I thought, I don't care any more. I could go and live in the cottage in Padstow. What does it matter where I lived? The absence of James haunted my every breath, making it impossible to envision any life at all.

The sea and its dazzling coastline, its pretty harbours and its sandy beaches, called to me in the darkness. It was where we'd been happiest, where we'd planned our future.

*

My mother was getting anxious to arrange Christmas. It was fast approaching and for the rest of the family, there were things to be discussed. To me, Christmas could disappear off the calendar forever. How could I ever celebrate it? I wanted to forget it, to be on my own ...

It was when I was talking to Beth one day that I came up with a plan. Beth had suggested it and I thought it was the best solution all round. The children would spend Christmas with Luke; I knew that's what he wanted and I'd put a dampener on it, if I was there. I couldn't bear the thought of going to my parents; it would remind me too much of last year. They'd be disappointed, but I had to deal with my life without James and they'd have to understand.

Beth said why didn't I go down to Padstow and spend it with her and Grace? I could have the day with her and her family and maybe Luke would come down on Boxing Day and we could all have a blustery walk along a wintry beach?

I made up my mind immediately that this was what I would do. They would all have to accept it.

I'd told Beth and Luke, David and my parents about my being given the cottage and they'd all agreed that it was an amazing gesture and one that James would've approved of. They were happy for me, they said. I couldn't see how it was anything to be happy about. If he hadn't died, there wouldn't have been a need for the bequest.

But that was the trouble with me now. I couldn't see happiness in anything.

So when I told them all my plans, they didn't try to dissuade me, except Mum, who was worried I'd be alone.

"But that's the whole point, Mum. I can't be with anyone. I just can't."

And in the end, she too accepted the decision and I felt a wave of relief; to think of the time alone, away from false jollity. Okay, I'd be with Beth's family and we'd probably do all the normal things, but it would be completely different, none of the same little routines. I'd cut myself off, get through the day somehow.

I was enormous now and just living each day was tiring. Little walks ended with backache and dragging feelings down my legs. I'd collapse into chairs and feel I'd never get up again. The bump was beginning to impinge on sleep; I'd lie on my side with Bumpy resting on a pillow, my top leg drawn up, resting on the pillow too. I'd wake up frequently and then lie awake feeling the baby heaving around. It was the one comforting thing in my life, apart from Amy's and Charlie's love and lively company, that constant feeling of the baby, ever-present, growing stronger and stronger, waiting for the moment to emerge into its future.

Luke's take on my decision was that I'd be better off being with the children, but he didn't press me and admitted that he was looking forward to doing Christmas properly for them. I could hear the excitement in his voice as he described his plans: he was going to collect them immediately after they broke up and they'd spend the lead up to Christmas decorating the quarter together, shopping and going to a pantomime that was on in the local town. I was pleased for them all. They'd have fun together and without me they'd be able to fully enjoy it.

When he came to collect the children, Amy said, "Are you sure you want us to go, Mum? You'll be so lonely on your own here, without us."

"Amy, I'll be fine. I want to be thoroughly lazy and put my feet up. Dad's really looking forward to having you two all to himself, aren't you, Luke?" I said, smiling towards him.

"We'll have lots of fun together. Mum just needs some time to herself. We'll maybe drive down to the cottage on Boxing Day, would you like that?"

"Yea," said Amy. "And we'll ring you every day, Mum."

They left, the car laden with presents, and I went back indoors. It was quiet, with just the tick tock of the clock and Tom Kitten's loud purr. He was sitting on the window sill, his usual place, where he could watch birds from the comfort of a warm house.

Had I done the right thing, shooing the children away? Even if I'd been a spectre at the feast, would it have been better for them to be with me?

I wasn't sure of anything any more.

All I knew was I couldn't cope with Christmas.

I just wanted it over with.

*

The long drive down to Cornwall on Christmas Eve was hard; I was uncomfortable now, sitting for a long period of time. Bumpy felt constricted and I kept having to stop for a break. I'd arranged with Beth that I'd go straight to the cottage and see them on Christmas morning.

As I drove up the lane, the horror of that day came back; it was as if I could see myself leaning up against that wall, nearly fainting from shock. As I pulled up outside, I thought of the meal I'd been preparing. What happened to it? Would I find the soup rotting in the saucepan on the cooker, the curry congealed in a pan?

I unlocked the door, worried the place would be filled with rancid smells, but there was nothing. I put down my case and going into the kitchen, I found it clean and tidy, no trace of the meal, anywhere. The hours and days after the shock were lost to me; maybe Beth had taken the key from me and come round to sort things out? She must have done.

But what would I find upstairs? James had left some clothes in the wardrobe, we had both put some holiday clothes there. We'd brought a few personal possessions down too, things to make it more homely. There were two chests of drawers; I'd had the one in our bedroom and he'd put some things in the one in the spare room.

What would I find?

Taking the bag with me, I went upstairs. I felt exhausted from the journey and lying down on the bed, I fell into a deep sleep almost immediately. It was one of those sleeps that left me feeling overwhelmed by its dreams. I'd dreamt so vividly of James, that when I woke up I was convinced he was lying next to me.

In the dream, he'd been playing his guitar and singing; we were on a beach and I could smell his aftershave. The wind was blowing, it was one of those hot, windy days in Cyprus, when you feel you are inside a huge tumble drier. The smell, what was it? Aramis ... my favourite, was wafting over to me in the wind ... his voice was sweet and his smile, oh his smile, so kind, so sweet.

I woke with a start ... where was he? I could smell him so strongly, feel the heat, the wind on my face.

I sat up, looked around. I was in an empty room ... he was gone ... gone.

I began to cry; I wanted so much to recapture the dream. I lay back down and squeezed my eyes tight shut, hoping that if I went to sleep again he'd come back to me. But sleep evaded me ... he'd gone.

His absence filled the room.

What if I forget his face, his voice?

A sharp stab of pain went through me like a knife tearing at my insides, slowly, jaggedly.

I lay back and thought about his face, his eyes, his hair, the flick of his fringe ... his long brown legs, his toes, his tattoo. But he was ghost-like; I could only just make out tiny features and then, only for a second. They'd flash into my mind and out again, like those shoals of fish in Cyprus, darting in and out of the light in the sea.

I was losing his memory. Losing him.

I went to my case and got out that photo I'd taken on Aphrodite's beach. He was walking towards the camera, smiling shyly. I stared at it. It came to me, that moment when I'd helped Sophie pack; we'd put a special photo of Sam and Sophie in the case. And now this was me.

All that was left was a photo, nothing else.

Nothing.

Sophie had always been so against him. If she'd have known that we'd only have two years together, would she have felt the same? Would she have understood more?

I hadn't heard anything from Sophie. Had Luke told her

what had happened? I was sure he would have done. Why hadn't Sophie contacted me? Maybe Sam's death was still so raw that she couldn't cope with someone else's grief and who could blame her? In her position, I thought, I'd probably do the same.

I stood up and went over to the wardrobe. Opening a door slowly, hardly daring to look, I peeked inside; there were some of his clothes: a rugby shirt, two polo shirts, a denim jacket and two pairs of trousers. On the floor, were two pairs of shoes. I stared at them and then quickly closed the door ... but then, I opened the door again and leaning in, I buried my face in his denim jacket.

That smell of *him*.

I breathed in deeply, inhaling him down into my lungs, holding the material over my face. I took it off the hanger and put the jacket on, hugging it around me. Normally, it'd have been far too big but because of the baby, I couldn't make it reach over the bump.

In the mirror of the wardrobe door, I caught sight of myself.

Pregnancy, despite everything, suited me.

I looked younger but... lost.

*

That night, I slept in my clothes, wearing his jacket. I didn't dream this time, it was as if my mind opted for complete oblivion.

The following day, I woke late and lying in bed, listening to the seagulls on the roof and the wind rattling the window frames, I was grateful to be alone. The thought of the children's excitement was too overwhelming ... Christmas Day was a day for laughter; the children on our bed, presents being ripped open, endless chores in the kitchen ... I had no energy for any of it, I knew that. I was thankful for the stillness.

Beth and her parents were so kind to me and the day passed, that was all I could say about it. I went through the motions: taking little presents round, eating my dinner, watching television, playing with Grace, but I was like a pre-programmed robot, doing what it had been told to do. I got through it.

"Are you going to be all right, tonight?" said Beth, as we walked back to the cottage.

"I'll be fine. I feel safe and ... James is there."

"How do you mean?"

"His clothes, hanging in the wardrobe ..."

"I'm sorry, I wondered whether to move them."

"No, I'm glad you didn't. They help me remember him."

"But one day ..."

"I know, one day they'll have to go, but I'm not ready yet."

We looked at each other and Beth smiled. "When it's time, I'll help you, you know I will."

"I know ..."

"Is Luke coming tomorrow?"

"Yes ... come round at one. He should be here by then and we'll go for a walk."

*

Luke and the children burst through the cottage door like a breath of new life. The air in the rooms until then had been still, the walls silent. I'd breathed there but had not stirred the oxygen around; my steps had been absorbed into the tranquility and left no footprints.

I had existed.

"Wow, this is lovely, Mum," said Amy. "Can I go upstairs?" and she and Charlie rushed up the tiny stairs, clomping around above our heads.

"How are you?" asked Luke. "Were you okay here on your own?"

"I was all right ... as okay as I'll ever be now."

I smiled at him. His eyes rested on my large stomach and then slid away. The baby's presence was filling the room, the unspoken rebuke, James' legacy. My hand rubbed circles over the bump.

"Are you up for a walk?" said Luke. "Don't worry if you'd rather not ..."

"No ... I'd love some fresh air and it would do the kids good to get out and run off some steam." I forced a laugh as I heard them running around above.

"Amy," shouted Luke, "it's time to give Mum that present."

"Oh, okay," she replied and came running down. "Where is it?"

"Don't worry, I'll go and get it, it's in the boot," said Luke and let himself out of the front door.

Amy grinned at me and said, "You're going to love it ... them."

"Wow, what have you got me?"

"Wait and see, Mum ... come on Dad, where are you?" She went to the door and Luke was just coming back in again, clutching three presents.

"So," said Luke, "this one's from Amy, this one's from Charlie and this is from me." He gave the children their presents to give me and continued, "I gave both of the kids some money and they were allowed to choose ... but it's not for you, it's for the baby."

All three of them looked at me.

"We wanted the baby to have a Christmas present too, even though it's not born yet," said Charlie, grinning.

"It was difficult cos we don't know whether it's a girl or a boy," said Amy, "so I told Charlie it had to be something that was okay for both." She came forward and handed me hers. "I hope you like it ... or I hope the baby likes it," she said.

I undid the paper and found a Baby Book for all the important milestones.

"Oh, Amy, that's lovely … thank you Poppet," I said, putting my arm round her shoulders and kissing her cheek. "That's such a good choice. Did you choose it all on your own?"

"I did," said Amy, proudly.

"Now mine," shouted Charlie, "I really like this." The paper on his was a bit torn and dirty; Luke had obviously left him to do it up on his own. I looked over at Luke, who was looked strangely embarrassed.

"Charlie assured me that this was perfect," he said.

As I undid the parcel, I couldn't help thinking how clever Luke was with the children. This was such a peculiar situation for any man to find himself in.

The copious amount of Sellotape was pulled off to reveal a fluffy teddy bear with a cute face.

"It's fine for a boy or a girl, isn't it, Mum?" said Charlie, grabbing it and kissing it.

"Perfect. Another great choice." I hugged Charlie, squeezing him and said, "You're a clever boy."

As I turned to the final present, I realised I hadn't even thought of a present for Luke. This year, I'd been so wound up in my grief I'd completely forgotten him. And now he was giving me something for James' baby.

What was revealed was something Luke knew I'd always liked: Beatrix Potter plates, a mug and an egg cup, plus The Tale of Tom Kitten. The other two had had some similar pottery, but it was now either chipped or completely broken. It was a very thoughtful present.

I put it down and trying to suppress the tears, I crossed the room and kissed his cheek. "Thank you, Luke. You shouldn't have."

"I thought the story of Tom Kitten was particularly relevant now that we've got a real Tom Kitten," he said, smiling at the children.

"Can I be the first one to read it to the baby?" said Amy.

Just then, there was a knock on the door. Beth came in,

all wrapped up for the walk, bringing in the smell of the sea. After hugs and kisses, we all filed out of the cottage and got into the Pajero. We'd go to Constantine and fly Charlie's new kite.

There was only one other car in the little car park. I hadn't been back here since James, Beth and I went surfing and as I got out of the car, I could see James, standing dressed in his wet suit, smiling at me.

He was there, for sure. I could almost touch him. Surely the others could see him, too?

Beth seemed to understand and put her arm around me and said, "Come on, we've got a kite to fly."

I blinked my eyes, rubbing them with my fingers and willed the apparition to disappear.

It was so windy that when we reached the top of the little rise where the beach spread out before us, we were hit with gusts that nearly blew us over. The sea was way out; it was an evil green with huge rollers pounding in. Even though they were a long way off, the size of them was immense: great barrels of power, weight and strength were forcing their way forward, relentlessly crashing and surging, tumbling and roaring. Foam was flying off each one, floating in the air above.

We all stood and simply watched, mesmerised by the violence and movement of the scene.

"You don't fancy going in, then?" shouted Beth, laughing.

"Not today, thank you," I said, making light of my thoughts, but trembling at the memory of nearly drowning here.

James had saved me then.

I looked at the children, their faces bright and full of life. I felt the baby move inside me. I knew I had a lot to live for.

We walked down onto the beach, trudging through the dry sand. It was such hard work walking, each step sinking.

"Right," said Luke, "let's get this kite going." He started to unravel the string, getting Amy to hold the kite, a large red one with a long tail. Charlie and he spent a long time making sure the string wasn't tangled and getting it straight, a difficult job in the wind. Beth and I stood together, watching.

"It's great to see you all together, doing something like this."

"I know … I abandoned them. I just couldn't face …"

"Don't worry, we all understand what you're going through, we do. Even the children."

"I've got to somehow pull myself together. The baby's due so soon now. I can't carry on as I have been, I've got to face it."

Beth squeezed my hand and said, "Come on, let's leave them to it for while and walk down to the water's edge."

We walked, hand in hand down to the sea, across the flatness of the wet sand. As we got nearer, the sound of the waves was thunderous; the sheer unbridled force of nature was over-whelming.

We stood, together, facing the sea. It was good to be out-side, to be buffeted by the elements, assaulted by the physical world. It made me feel alive, at last.

Until that moment, I had indeed felt dead, with no hope.

Suddenly, the landscape invaded me, made me conscious of myself within the environment, made me aware of my place in it; made me think of … now.

"You'll be okay," shouted Beth, still holding my hand. "You'll be okay!"

"Will I?" I cried.

"You'll find a way to carry on, Emily. You will, you have to. Look at the sea … the world's a wonderful place. You'll find a way to live your life."

I turned away from the sea and we both looked back up the beach.

"Look!" I shouted. The kite was flying now, wildly; diving and swirling, rising and falling. Amy was holding it, helped by Luke and Charlie was running and running beneath it. Their voices were blown away by the wind, so we couldn't hear them. It was like a tableau.

"Your children need you, Emily. You must live for *them*."

"I know, I know," I said, and we began to walk back across the beach to join them.

Chapter Thirty-Two

With Christmas over, I went home, determined to face up to my life. I was now a single mum with a baby due imminently.

I had to be strong for everyone.

The children were back at school and as my bump was so big, I often had a rest in the afternoon. When they were home, I tried to be there for them: to help with reading, to hear their stories of what happened at school; to be a proper mother. I wouldn't 'abandon' them ever again.

I'd long ago got rid of all Amy and Charlie's baby things, so I now started collecting all the things a baby would need; when I looked at the little outfits in Mothercare, I couldn't believe how small they were.

As my due date approached, I visited Doctor Lake for another check up. I was feeling so exhausted and wondered if something was wrong. Surely it wasn't natural to feel this way? Think of all those women who carry on working right up until they give birth? It was all I could do to drag myself from the kitchen to the sofa.

The doctor was well aware of the circumstances (of losing James) and had taken me under his wing. He'd been pleased with the progress of the pregnancy up until now but was worried about my being on my own.

"Your blood pressure's too high, Emily," he said. "It's been a bit high, as you know, right through the pregnancy, but it's higher now than it really should be. I think I'd like to admit you, I don't want to take any chances."

"Today?"

"Yes, I think so. Is there anyone who could come and look after the children for you?"

"Well, my parents were on stand-by for the due date, but I'm not sure whether …"

"I'd like you to phone them and see and I'll make the necessary arrangements for you."

It came as a shock. There were still three weeks to go; the other two had been late and I'd just assumed this one would be the same.

As I left the surgery, Doctor Lake said, "Don't worry. It's precautionary … I think you need someone to keep an eye on you. I'll arrange transport for you. You go home and make the necessary arrangements."

Who would be able to drop everything and come over to help? The children were at school till five today, as they had after-school activities, but what then?

As it happened, Bella said she'd have them both overnight and Mum and Dad would come the next day. I rang Jen and David to tell them the news too and managed to catch Beth just as I was going out.

"Are you going to ring Luke? He'd want to know what's happening."

"No, I don't think so … I've got to do this on my own. He doesn't want to be involved in the birth of another man's child."

"I'm sure he'd want to know."

"No, Beth. I'm on my own. I've got to do this alone but I'd love to see you soon, once it's all over."

"Of course, I'll come up as soon as I can."

When I arrived at the hospital, a specialist said that if there was no reduction in my blood pressure within the next twenty-four hours, they were going to induce me.

"This is better for both of you, Mrs Blackwell. The sooner we can get baby born, the sooner your blood pressure will return to normal." This was, of course, logical; I'd had no problems with it before the pregnancy, so there was every chance it would return to normal afterwards. But the prospect of being induced was terrifying; I'd heard a friend's report of labour starting more quickly and being much more intense. I really didn't want it, but felt backed into a corner. If only I had someone to discuss it with but no, ultimately, it was my body, my baby. The father wasn't here, it was solely my decision.

*

"We're just going to break your waters, now, Emily. Try to relax."

I had my legs up in stirrups; the midwife came towards me with a vicious-looking instrument and I closed my eyes tight, trying to block everything out. I clenched my jaw, made my hands into fists and held my breath.

"Relax, dear, it's going to feel very strange but …"

"Now … that's *that* done. Wasn't too bad, was it? Now we're going to see if that starts it off. If it doesn't, we'll set up a hormone drip. We'll leave you now, so just lie back and read a magazine or something. Here's the buzzer. Any worries, just press this," she said, handing me the device. "We'll see what happens now; we'll give it a few hours."

The midwife was so matter of fact, but I didn't want sympathy. The journey had started and all I wanted was it to be over. I watched as the nurse retreated out of the room, saying they were very busy on the ward that day; I wondered how many other women were giving birth. How many were giving birth completely on our own?

Although I felt alone, lonely even, it was something that had to be faced. Only *I* could do this. Even if James had been here I told myself, what could *he* have done? Talk to me, keep me company while I waited for the labour to begin but it was my body that was going to have to push the baby out.

Mine alone.

I tried to read but couldn't concentrate. They said I could get up, so I got out of bed and ambled slowly round the room, looking out at the car park below. I could see cars arriving, people carrying flowers.

I got back into bed. Lay on my side, tried to sleep. Lay on the other side.

This went on and on and on. Nurses came and went, talked to me, took my blood pressure but nothing was happening. So a few hours later, my original midwife came in and having examined me again said, "Your blood pressure is still up too high and baby is a bit too happy in there, I think. We've decided to put a drip up, is that okay?"

What could I say? I wanted it to start, as much as them, so I said, "Okay, fine ..."

The drip was designed to speed things up and that's exactly what it did; but now I felt as if I was part of the bed. I couldn't move, I was stuck on my back. There was a monitor round my stomach to keep an eye on the baby, a drip in my arm and even a monitor on the baby's scalp, which they'd attached causing me what they called 'discomfort' and I called, agony.

I was a living machine, tied to inanimate objects that had a life of their own; flashing lights, paper readouts and bleeping noises dominated the room. Any peaceful, natural birth I'd dreamt of, was gone. Control over the situation was lost. I was in their thrall.

I'd completely forgotten the pain I'd felt during Amy's and Charlie's births. Now, it came back like a bolt of lightning hitting a metal object; the fierce contractions started almost immediately and crashed through my body and mind, leaving me shocked and frightened.

"Oh my God, they're coming too fast," I gasped. "Why are they so strong?"

The midwife, who was standing by the bed, looking down at me, smiled benignly. "The drip sometimes has that effect. I'll turn it down a bit."

Whatever she did, didn't help much. All the pain was focussing on my back and with every contraction, the pain was intensifying. I drank the gas and air as if my life depended on it, sucking at the device as hard as I could.

"I need something else," I shouted. "This isn't enough. I need something else."

"You can have some pethidine, but it sometimes makes people sick, dear. Do you want some?"

"Yes, yes, I want some."

Once they'd administered the pethidine, I started floating, drifting around the room. The pain was still there, excruciating pain, but my head was cloudy, my mind befuddled, my brain dizzy. I was sick, I was moaning, I didn't know what was happening to me. There were just relentless crescendos of pain that were like a form of torture.

*

I was vaguely aware of people coming and going, doors opening, doors closing. There was a hand that held mine, a voice, a presence in the room, that gave me hope. I could hear my own voice, crying a distant cry, like a wolf howling on the prairie. I had no control; my body had taken over my mind, my muscles tightening and tightening, squeezing the life out of me, like an anaconda killing its prey.

After hours of this, the miracle happened. The birth occurred at 11.20 pm, I was told afterwards.

I lay in a darkened room, alone, still shell-shocked from the hours of pain.

A chink of light shone like a beacon, as the door opened. Someone walked in, holding a bundle … my baby.

"Here's your beautiful, baby girl," the woman said, placing her gently on my chest. "She's 7 lbs 6oz and she's got a great pair of lungs on her. A wonderful head of black hair. You might like to try feeding her now."

Despite feeling so exhausted, a wave of euphoria washed over me and every sinew of my body ached to hold that little human. I held out my arms and the baby lay against me. As I looked down at the tiny person lying in my arms, waves of sadness and joy flooded my body.

James would never see his daughter.

His absence overwhelmed me, my loneliness consumed me.

I stared into the azure eyes which were staring back at me and I felt an overwhelming sense of having met her before.

The baby's eyes pierced my soul.

We gazed at each other, like long lost loves across an ocean of time.

*

Abigail suckled happily; it seemed the most natural thing in the world for both of us. The nurses hovered, but we didn't need them.

There was a light knock on the door and another nurse came in and said, "I know it's very late, but there's someone outside who's very keen to come in and see you both. Are you okay with that? I've said he can stay five minutes."

I nodded and smiled again at my daughter, so content, so quiet.

The door opened slowly and there was Luke. He came into the room, quietly and sat down on the bed.

"You did so well in there, Emily ... you were wonderful."

I took in these words and the realisation hit me; the hand was his hand, the voice was his.

"Thank you for being there, Luke. I'm sorry – I was

completely out of it. I'd had so much gas and air and pethidine, I didn't know what I was doing … or saying. Did I swear a lot?"

"No, not really. You did use a few choice words, but we're used to it." He smiled at me. "Is she feeding okay?"

"So far." I stroked the downy hair on the baby's head; the sensation of suckling, so new, yet so familiar.

"Luke, how did you know?"

"Beth rang me. She told me you'd said you didn't want her to ring me, but she did and I'm so glad she did. It was lucky, I'd just finished a shift, so I jumped in the car and came straight here. I couldn't bear the thought of you doing this all on your own. I lied, sort of, to the nurses … I said I was your husband."

"Well, you are still, technically … thank you."

We sat in silence; the only sound, the gurgling noises of the baby.

"They said I couldn't stay long, so I better go. Have you got a name for her?"

"Yes … Abigail."

"That's lovely. Is there a reason?"

"Yes," I said, almost embarrassed to say. "It means … the father's joy. I know James would have been so joyful. And I've always loved the name. We considered it for Amy, do you remember?"

We stared at each other over the top of the baby's head.

"I'm sorry he's not here to witness her arrival, Emily. Life's so cruel, sometimes." He looked down and rubbed his eyes.

Shaking his head, he stood up and said, "I'll bring Amy and Charlie tomorrow, shall I?"

"That would be lovely. Mum and Dad will want to come too."

"I've been in touch. They're all doing fine at the cottage, I'm going there now. See you tomorrow."

He didn't come near me or the baby, he kept his distance, but as he went through the door, he stopped; he turned and looked at us both for a while and then waved and was gone.

*

As I was a third-time mum, I was left to my own devices that night. They were so busy on the ward (two sets of twins were born) that they had no time to help me and fortunately I didn't need help. I slept fitfully for a couple of hours when I put the baby in the little plastic crib next to the bed, but as soon as she murmured, I awoke and was fully alert. Even though I'd had two other babies, I still found it incredible how small Abigail was; she was so light, it was as if she'd float away. Her perfect little hands with their perfect little fingers mesmerised me; the minuscule nails, so pink, so … perfect.

My first nappy change was a challenge; I felt clumsy and Abigail's legs were so small and precious that I was reluctant to try to move them to accommodate the nappy. I'd never got used to the place where the umbilical cord had been with the other two; I knew it was natural and normal, but the sight of it made me uncomfortable. Just simply putting her arms back in sleeves was a struggle; I seemed to have forgotten how to do everything. I knew babies were much tougher than they looked, but Abigail's vulnerability was heightened by the fact that she'd been born without a father.

As I looked down at her, that's all I could think about. This tiny human being, so fragile, so defenceless only had me to protect her. She had a lifetime ahead of her and every parental decision would have to be mine. I gazed at her wondering what her life held for her – what would she become? Would she inherit James' musical talent? Would she become a famous singer-songwriter and fulfil her father's dreams? Or would she inherit my own abilities? She'd inherited her parents' genes, yes, so she'd be restricted by what she was born with but life was journey, full of opportunities and unknown destinations and I was determined that Abigail would seize them all. I smiled to myself when I thought how ironic it would be if, in the future, she wanted to join the military.

That was one course that I'd try to dissuade her from.

*

Charlie and Amy were thrilled with their baby sister. They came the next day, each holding another present for the baby; Charlie insisted on another smaller teddy bear and Amy bought a cuddly dog. Luke had a huge bunch of flowers and my parents came bearing all sorts of things for me, not the baby: fruit, magazines and chocolates.

When Mum held her, she said tearfully, "She's absolutely gorgeous! What a beautiful baby, Emily. You're such a clever girl." Mum gazed at her, stroking her cheek with one finger.

"She looks a lot like you did when you were born but I think she's got her father's eyes."

This made the room 'stop' as we all remembered James. It was so good of Mum to talk about him; I knew it was hard for her but she was right, those eyes were James'.

Luke took pictures of us all but still kept his distance; everyone held her, including Charlie, who sat with a big, wide grin on his face, holding her as if she was a precious glass. He wasn't at all relaxed but she was the first baby he'd ever held. The sweetest thing he did was when I took her back and Charlie leaned in and kissed Abigail's forehead and said, "I love you, baby. I can't wait for you to grow up, so we can play."

Luke ruffled Charlie's hair and said, "It won't be too long, Buddy," and his eyes touched mine.

When they all left, the room was quiet; the voices, the chatter, the movement had been overwhelming. It had been lovely, but all I wanted was to be with my new daughter, alone.

She was asleep, under the hospital pink blanket. I stood next to her, holding on to the plastic sides of the hospital crib. Gazing down, I watched every little movement, listened to every snuffle. I bent down, to smell that indefinable smell.

I absorbed that newborn perfume, drinking it down like the gas and air. The smell of Cyprus, that heady mix of rosemary, thyme and sandy soil, entered my head in that instant, bringing with it all the passion and heartache that had led to this little person.

I sat down on the bed, lay back and closed my eyes.

James' face showed itself to me with absolute clarity; he swam into view across the Mediterranean.

He walked towards me, across the beach at Petra Tou Romiou, smiling shyly and holding out his arms.

"My Aphrodite," he said.

I ran towards him, fell into his arms and said, "She's arrived, our child has arrived."

Chapter Thirty-Three

The next few weeks were a blur of night feeds and nappy changing. Although Mum and Dad stayed with me at the beginning and so many people rallied round, I realised how hard it was without a partner to share it all with. I began to see how integral Luke had been to the smooth running of the home when the other two were tiny. He'd had to go away a lot but when he was there, he'd looked after Amy to allow me time to sleep and when Charlie came along, he'd take Amy off for walks to the park, to give me some time alone with the new baby. He'd been there to discuss all those little worries and when there'd been the odd crisis, he'd been amazing, like the time Amy got croup. She'd been struggling for breath and doing that frightening croupy cough. Luke sat with her under a tea towel to breathe in the steam from the boiling water, calmly talking to her and stopping her panicking.

The children helped me as much as possible, but they had their own routines of school, homework and friends to play with. Between them and Abigail, I had no time. All my energies were focussed on the three of them and I was able to put my grief to the back of my mind. There would be a time, in the future when I could think of James again, but for now, I couldn't.

I knew he'd understand.

Luke kept a low profile. He spoke to the children at least twice a week and came and took them away for the weekend in February, but he tried to avoid talking to me.

I could tell he felt uncomfortable with Abigail; he had a look on his face whenever he was near her ... a look of sadness that swept over his eyes which he couldn't hide.

Jen noticed it. She'd come to stay for the night, on her own, the weekend that Luke took the children away. He'd been very quiet, not his usual self at all.

When they'd all gone and Abigail was asleep, Jen said, "How's Luke coping with Abigail? Has he said anything?"

"I don't know, I really don't; he asks after her on the phone when we're making arrangements for the other two, but when he's around her ... he can't look at her."

"I think it was amazing of him to be with you through the birth," said Jen. "That must have been so difficult for him. Has he talked about it?"

"Not since the night ... I think he's still coming to terms with it. He always looks sad these days."

"I agree. All the fun seems to have gone out of him. I have to say, I was quite shocked, seeing him just now. He looks different. Thinner. Do you think I should get John to talk to him?"

"You could, I suppose, but he's never been very good at talking about feelings. I'm not sure he would be comfortable even talking to John. Maybe I should talk to him? But there never seems enough time ... or we avoid the situation."

We left it that she'd talk to John and maybe, if the occasion arose, he'd discuss things with Luke. We also talked about having a holiday in Cornwall together again in the summer. "We could hire a cottage near yours somewhere – it'd be like the old days," Jen said. "It wouldn't be far for Luke to come down from Chivenor, if he wanted to come and the four older ones could play on the beach again."

"That's a great idea although I can't imagine ever being able to cope with us all on holiday, at the moment. It's all I can do get through the day here at home."

"We could help you; the older two could stay in our cottage and give you some peace with Abigail."

"We'd love that, Jen … let's think of doing it soon after they all break up. Wow, Abigail will almost be eight months by then. Maybe the four kids could have surfing lessons with Beth; you haven't met her yet, but you'll really like her. She and I get on so well together even though there's an age gap. We've supported each other through some difficult times; she's got a really sensible head on her shoulders. It's because of her that Luke came to the birth; she rang him and told him I'd gone in. I don't know whether she *told* him to come up, but all I know is, he did, and it's down to Beth."

"I can't wait to meet her; my kids would love to have surfing lessons. So, is that definite, then? Shall I try and find a cottage?"

"Yes, let's do it. I'll tell Beth. She loves it when we go down. As much as she loves Cornwall, she sometimes feels a bit cut off. She's seeing quite a bit of a friend of Luke's, a young guy called Josh. I haven't met him yet, but it would be so good if that works out. She's really keen."

Jen rang a few days later and said she'd booked a cottage in Harlyn, overlooking the beach. She thought it would be fun to be right near the surf; we could all come out of the sea and straight into the house to change. The kids could be on the beach all day; it would be like Cyprus, without the sun. It slept eight, so there was plenty of room for Charlie and Amy and Luke, if we wanted to stay.

So it was all set. Next time I spoke to Luke, I told him, so that he could put the dates in his diary. The children were ecstatic.

*

One evening, soon after the conversation with Jen, the phone rang. I was so tired that I was tempted to let it ring; I was slumped on the sofa, dozing in front of the TV. Abi (she was now called Abi by everyone) was beginning to sleep longer. She often slept all evening until around eleven; I'd feed her before I went to bed and then she'd wake at four or if I was lucky, five. Life was beginning to get easier, slowly.

When I heard the phone, I swore to myself. Who's ringing at this time of night? And then I looked at my watch and realised it was only eight thirty. I pulled myself up, feeling like an old woman and picked up the receiver.

"Hello, Emily speaking."

There was a pause at the end of the line. I wondered if it was a nuisance call.

"Hello, who is this?"

"Emily. It's been a long time ..."

"Sophie! Yes indeed, it's been ages."

There was another long pause.

"I'm sorry. I truly am. I should've rung you when James died but I just couldn't, somehow. It brought back too much ... I'm sorry. The longer I left it, the more difficult it was to ring."

I didn't know what to say. Yes, I was hurt that she hadn't rung but I understood too. Our relationship was never going to be the same. Too much had happened.

I didn't think I cared any more.

"And not ringing you when you had the baby, that was unforgivable of me," she said. Her voice sounded small, distant. "How are you both?"

"We're okay ... more than okay ... we're good. Abi's such a good baby, she sleeps a lot compared to the other two, but maybe I found it harder then. She's definitely got James' eyes and his dark skin."

I knew I was filling the silences, not really saying anything. I had a knot in the pit of my stomach.

"But it can't be easy without ..."

313

"No ..."

"It must be terrible ... you must miss him so much."

I felt a whole range of emotions; of course I miss him, I thought. What a crass thing to say but then I realised Sophie was only reaching out to me. What else could she have said? And she's gone through the same thing; surely we should be able to share mutual ground?

"How are you, Sophie? Luke told me you are getting lots of work."

"I am, but it's not like it used to be, somehow. I'm thinking of quitting and doing something else. I don't know what, though."

"Could you go to Uni and study something?"

"I've thought of that, yes. I've always had an interest in art history but ..."

"That would be good ... a completely new start." I was struggling to know what to say. The conversation was stilted; I got the impression that Sophie wanted to say something, that she was holding back.

"Luke mentioned that you have a new boyfriend?" I asked tentatively, wondering if I should have said it. "Greg, is it?"

"Well, it's early days. I like him but ... I miss Sam and feel disloyal."

"Sam wouldn't want you to be on your own for the rest of your life, Sophie. He'd want you to be happy."

"I know he would but ... it's hard ... so hard."

There was a sniff and she continued, "Actually, I wanted to talk to you about Luke. I saw him recently and I'm worried about him."

The knot in my stomach tightened, twisting my guts.

"What do you mean?"

"He seems to have withdrawn from himself and ... Life. He's very quiet and pale. I've tried to talk to him but he clams up. He used to talk to me, we could say most things to each other, but now, he says there's nothing wrong and refuses to talk. He's losing weight, too. Have you noticed anything?"

I couldn't help feeling annoyed. She was poking her nose into our business again. What gave her the right to … but no, I wouldn't say that … she was only saying what Jen and I had said.

"I don't see him very often to be honest but … you're right, he's quiet these days. Do you know if he's enjoying his new job? He never mentions it to me."

"I think so but whereas before, he was always so keen on the Air Force and flying, he never talks about it any more and I'm not sure he's made many new friends down there – apart from that young guy he goes out skiing with. He seems to spend a lot of time on his own, smoking and drinking far too much."

"I'll try to talk to him, Sophie, but it's difficult. We only see each other when he's either collecting or delivering the children. We speak on the phone about arrangements and that's about it. But I'll try … are you seeing him again soon?"

"There are no plans at the moment. I'd love to see you and Abi and the other two sometime. When are you next coming up this way to see your parents?"

I couldn't envisage a time when I would. My parents tended to come and see me, rather than the other way around at the moment and … did I *want* to see Sophie? Maybe, sometime in the future, when all this hurt, grief and resentment had disappeared into the ether. So, I made some noncommittal statement about 'maybe at Easter' and said, 'whenever you're coming this way, do pop in' but we both knew it wouldn't happen.

It was just words.

Too much had changed.

*

"Do you think you'll be able to come down to Cornwall in July, Luke? The kids would love it if you did."

It was April and Luke had arrived at the cottage to take Amy and Charlie down to Devon for a few days. I'd thought a lot about Sophie's phone call and was determined to talk properly to him. I'd asked the kids to pop down to the local shop for me, as a way of getting him on his own. Abi was asleep, upstairs.

"Maybe," he said. "It'll be a bit odd though, won't it? I don't know. Not sure."

"Why? John and Jen really want you to come and they've deliberately taken on a big house so you can. It'll be a great opportunity to spend time with the kids. Why will it be odd?"

"Ems – don't you understand *anything*?"

He was standing with his back to the kitchen window, leaning against the sink. He was almost in silhouette; it was hard to see his face.

"*Tell* me, Luke. I'm worried about you. A lot of people are worried about you. Tell me."

He pushed himself away from the sink and prowled round the room like a caged animal. He ran his fingers through his hair.

"I'm going outside for a smoke," he said, and snatched open the back door. I watched him through the window as he lit a cigarette and went to sit on the garden bench. He blew the smoke out, upwards through the branches of the tree and then stared ahead, his left leg bouncing up and down, up and down.

I went to sit next to him and we both stared ahead.

"Luke, I'm so sorry …"

"What for?" he said, turning his head to meet my eyes.

"For … everything. For making you feel like this. For ruining our lives." As I said those words, he stubbed out his cigarette with aggressive, twisting movements of his foot. "But none of this is Abi's fault, we've got remember that," I continued. "She's an innocent by-product of my stupidity, someone who'll have to live the rest of her life with only one parent. We've got to find a way through, for her sake."

"Do you think I'm blaming *her*?" he said.

"No, but …"

"I don't blame her," he almost shouted, his face distorted. "I blame myself."

"Why? You can't possibly be to blame for all this, Luke."

"But if I hadn't done what I did … have the operation …"

"Look, we've said all this before …" I put one hand on his knee and with the other hand round his chin, I turned his face towards me. "You've got to stop blaming yourself. It's done now."

He let me keep my hand on his face and his eyes, full of tears, looked into mine.

"I'm so sorry," he said. "Maybe if I hadn't done it, we could have rescued our marriage. I made everything worse."

I stood up and then knelt in front of him. "Luke … you're living your life with all those 'if's' and 'maybe's'. The past is past. James is dead and all I have left of him is Abi. We've got two beautiful children together. Try to see that we've got more than *so* many other people. Look at Sophie. She never had the child with Sam that she wanted so badly. We've made a mess of everything, both of us, but we have so much." I leant forward and kissed his cheek and and at that moment, the children came bursting into the garden.

"Why do you two look so sad?" said Charlie, coming right up and staring at us.

"We're just talking, Charlie. Sometimes adults get sad, but we'll be okay, won't we, Luke?"

He stood up, patted Charlie's head and said, "Of course. Go and get your things ready you two, we're going in a minute."

They ran back through the door.

"So, you'll come to Cornwall, won't you? We *all* want you to come, including me."

"Okay, I'll come. We can all pretend it's like old times."

"Exactly."

Chapter Thirty-Four

The holiday arrived.

"How was the journey?" said Beth, as we unloaded the car together. Abi was still in her car seat, beginning to protest.

"It was okay but I had to stop a few times to deal with Abi. Amy and Charlie tried to keep her entertained, but she's at a difficult age; there's not a lot she can do in the car. She slept a bit and we all sang songs."

"Sounds stressful," said Beth, unlocking the front door. "Let me go and get the kettle on."

I followed her in; the cottage had a rather neglected air about it. No one had been in for weeks, although Beth and her mum did pop in now and again. There was a layer of dust over everything and a smell of damp. Still, it was to be expected; houses need to be lived in.

"So this is your new home, Abi. The one your Daddy bought for you ... you're going to love it here," I said, kissing her cheek. "Beth, can you just hold her for a minute while I get the rest in? Amy, you can help me and you too, Charlie."

I handed Abi over to Beth and we went out to the car and grabbed bags; it looked as if we'd come for a year, never mind two weeks. It didn't seem to matter how many days I went away for, I still needed so much for Abi.

Once everything was inside, we started putting cases upstairs. "You're going to spend most nights over at the other house, so don't bother to unpack, you two. I'm going to take you over soon. You don't have to stay there, but we thought you'd have more fun with Holly and Jake. What do you think?"

"Yea, that'll be great, Mum. Are you sure you'll be okay here on your own?"

"Amy, I'll be fine, honestly. It'll be easier for me to be here, quietly with Abi. We could have stayed too but it would be quite crowded with me there and I think it'll be easier to get Abi to go to sleep here. Don't worry, though, we'll spend all the days and early evenings together. And Dad's coming down tomorrow, so he'll be there."

"And I can always help your Mum, if she needs anything," said Beth, smiling at Amy. Charlie didn't seem too concerned; he was just excited about spending time with Jake, doing things that boys like to do.

"Are you ready to learn to surf, you two?" said Beth. "I'm determined to get you standing on boards by the end of this holiday."

"Yea, we can't wait," said Amy. "When can we see Grace? I haven't seen her for ages."

"Don't you worry, I'll bring her down to the beach. She'll love playing with you all."

I was so pleased that Luke had decided to come but was nervous about spending so much time in his company. We hadn't spent any prolonged periods together since ... well, for a very long time. I'd almost forgotten how to *be* with him and he, with me. Our lives had gone down such different roads ... thank goodness that there'd be other people; the chaos of the four older children, plus Abi and sometimes Grace, would make it easy to hide from each other. We could be together, without having to communicate.

After a cup of coffee, Beth had to get back to Grace. I tried to sort out a few things in the house, but gave up and decided to do it later, when Abi was asleep.

"Come on you two, let's get over to Harlyn and get you settled in," I said and we got back into the car. It was four o'clock when we arrived at the house; Jen and the family had only been there since two, so were still sorting things out. There were shouts of excitement as the children renewed their friendships. Jen and I hugged and John admired Abi; this was the first time he'd met her.

"I can't believe you've got another one, Emily. It's bad enough with two, how do you cope?" he laughed.

"I don't know really, we muddle through somehow," I said, wondering how I did 'muddle through'. It was exhausting, that was for sure and I was looking forward to having other pairs of hands to help on this holiday.

"This house is perfect, Jen. What a brilliant choice. I don't think you could have got one any nearer the beach if you'd tried! It'll be great – we'll be able to sit up here on the lawn and watch the kids on the sand, like we did before Cyprus. God, that seems a lifetime ago, doesn't it?"

"Yes, a lot's happened ..." she said. "I'm glad you like it. When I saw it, I thought it ticked all the right boxes."

It was one of those typical white-washed Cornish houses overlooking the beach, with a lawn that led almost to the edge of the rocks, bordered by a prickly hedge. It was comfortable, yet functional; the furniture had seen better days and the carpets looked ancient; there was the ubiquitous whiff of dampness that permeated most Cornish holiday lets: an accumulation of empty, unheated weeks in the winter and damp clothes. But at least it meant that when everyone trooped off the beach, there was no need to worry about damaging the floors; there were generations of previous tenants who'd already tramped inside the house with wet costumes and sandy wetsuits. Any damage had been done years ago. This is what these houses expected, somehow.

We all gathered around the scrubbed pine kitchen table and ate huge, soft scones with mountains of clotted cream and strawberry jam. I'd managed to make one of my 'chuck all the ingredients in a bowl and mix' chocolate cakes a couple of days ago, which I now proudly produced and it was gone in one sitting. The tide was up and we could hear the waves through the open window; the cries of people enjoying the surf or simply running around on the sand, drifted in too.

I could smell the sea.

As I looked around the table, at the children talking animatedly to each other, at Abi sitting in a high chair, her face covered in jam; at Jen doling out glasses of juice and John sitting quietly drinking his tea, I thought how lucky I was to have such good friends, who accepted me, despite everything.

And that made my think of James. He was always there, in my mind, every minute. Anything could bring back little moments I'd shared with him: a smell, a sound, even a colour (the red of his trunks). Meringue made me think of his Pavlova; a song on the radio, a windy day, a stranger's smile, a seagull's cry, a motorbike exhaust, a guitar riff, a Spaniel ... anything could jolt me out of the present, straight into the past and for a brief moment, I'd be with him again, hearing his laugh, seeing his smile.

Tears sprang to my eyes and I had to blink and look down, to hide it from the others. He'd already missed so much of Abi's life, her little achievements that were so important to all parents. Every day, I could see more and more of him, in her face. There would be little fleeting expressions that would flit across her face for just a second and they'd bring him back so forcefully it would take my breath away.

I was brought back to the present ... to now. The children were shouting, crumbs were scattered everywhere, scraping chairs and for the first time for months, I felt the beginnings of something I could almost call normality. I was in my favourite place, Cornwall, with my children and my best friends.

I must cherish this time, this moment of happiness.

Would I have had this holiday if he'd still been alive?

Despite how good John and Jen had been about 'the situation', I doubted whether we'd have all gone on holiday together.

John and Jen were our friends, not James'.

And I realised that it was right that Luke was joining us, even though it would be strange and difficult. I was missing him and I looked forward to his arrival tomorrow.

The picture would be complete.

*

The next day, I went over to the house as soon as Abi had had her breakfast; I was keen to be there, to enjoy the children's excitement. The weather was glorious: hot, piercing blue skies with scudding, fluffy clouds and the forecast was for it to continue for at least a week. Despite the heat, there was a wind and this meant there were waves: a perfect Cornish day. We'd all decided we wouldn't go surfing until Luke arrived.

It wasn't until four o'clock that I saw him; I was on the beach with Abi. The older ones were playing football and Abi was sitting on a rug playing with some plastic bricks. Jen and I were enjoying the sunshine; we'd rigged up a sunshade for Abi but were lying stretched out, drinking in the sun like sponges absorbing water. I remembered how I'd got so bored of the sun in Cyprus; how stupid, I thought now. It was heavenly lying on the beach with my eyes hidden behind sunglasses, my lids closed.

I became aware of a shadow over me, opened my eyes and … there was Luke, looking down at me.

"The sun's rays have travelled hundreds of miles to get to me and you're stopping them at the very last part of their journey!" I laughed, trying to cover up my nerves on seeing him.

"I do apologise, madam," he said, grinning. "You both look very relaxed. Hi Jen," and he bent to kiss her cheek. "Where are the kids?"

I pointed to them; they were now a long way down the beach. "I'll just go and say hello, and then I'll be back. How's Abi enjoying the beach?" he asked, not looking at her.

"She's being as good as gold."

He walked off towards the sea and I watched his so familiar back view disappear into the crowds of other people.

"He looks a little better than when I last saw him," said Jen.

"Yes, I agree. Let's hope this break will do him good. I want to start being able to talk to him properly again without feeling nervous and awkward."

"This will be perfect, I think," said Jen. "But you'll have to work at it. He still can't look at Abi, can he?"

"No, he's just really *odd* around her. Maybe if he spends some time with her, he'll be able to come to terms with it all."

"I'm sure he will," said Jen. "Be patient."

*

Beth arrived at five and the tide was at a perfect point for a surf, so we all got togged up in our wetsuits. What a treat to be able to do it in the house, instead of in a car park or on the beach!

"Tell you what, I'll drag Abi down in the pushchair to the water's edge and take some pictures of you all in the water. The light's just right at this time of day," I said.

"Are you sure you don't want to come in?" said Jen. "I could look after Abi for a while."

"No, I'm fine today, but maybe later in the week. I'd love to have another go."

"Okay," said Jen.

I watched them all walking together, carrying their boards down to the sea. Four adults, four children; Beth with her long board and everyone else carrying a variety of belly boards. This was just to be a fun session. Tomorrow they'd start the children's lessons.

I grabbed my camera with the zoom lens and took several shots of them walking away across the beach; such happy times to remember. I wished I could be with them but then Abi made a noise from her pushchair and I turned around to be faced with her cherubic, happy face and thought, no, there's nowhere I'd rather be.

I bumped the pushchair down some steps and eventually got to the sand. It was hard work dragging it; the wheels kept getting stuck, but I was determined to get there. If I'd carried her I wouldn't have been able to take pictures.

I parked the pushchair near the water's edge; the tide was going out now, so she was safe. The light was perfect and my zoom was long enough to see the kids; they weren't too far out. I could see Luke way out with Beth; she'd let him have a go on her board and he'd just caught a good wave and was standing. I managed to catch a shot just before he fell, but I knew it wouldn't be a good picture, he was too far away. So, I concentrated on the children, whose faces lit up each time they caught a wave. Sometimes, they let the wave bring them right in and would run up to Abi and dripping sea water on her, would shout things like, "Hey, Abs, you'll do this soon," and she'd laugh and kick her little legs. She'd watch them run back in and they'd turn and wave to her.

At one point, I was at the right place, at the right time. I was squatting, so that I got a low angle and all four children caught the same wave and came towards me. I clicked the shutter several times and knew one of them would be a great photo; they all looked so happy and full of life.

When everyone came out I got them to pose together, holding their boards, surrounding the pushchair.

The Atlantic was in the background and I shouted, "Okay, everybody say cheese, on the count of one – two – three!" They all duly shouted cheese and again, I clicked the shutter several times. Everyone was smiling: John and Jen had their arms around each other; Luke had his hand on Charlie's shoulder;

Beth's malibu was standing tall between her and Amy and Holly and Jake were leaning against each other, back to back. Without having to organise them they'd got themselves into a perfect group; it looked like an advert for swimwear or surfboards. Abi was loving it, kicking her legs up and down and smiling.

It wasn't until I got back to the cottage that night that I realised that the picture would have Luke and Abi in it together, for the first time.

*

The holiday continued to be an idyll of sun, fun and laughter. Days passed so quickly and I was beginning to wish they'd slow down. Abi was loving the constant mêlée of people to watch and play with; Luke and I were more at ease with each other and even laughed together. Jen offered to look after Abi one day as promised and I went in surfing with everyone else. Luke and I walked amicably down the beach together and when we reached the sea, we started running at the same time, jumping over the waves and eventually crashing into one together. Through the spray, we laughed at each other and I could feel the tension being washed away.

"Okay, let's wait for the golden wave and see if we can both get on the same one," I shouted, as I jumped over another roller. I could feel its force as it lifted me off my feet and I had to use all my strength to stand on the sand again.

"Right, you're on … and whoever gets the furthest in, buys the drink in the pub tonight," he said. He dived under the next one and came up again looking like a sleek, black seal as he bobbed up.

"Come on, let's go further out. The kids are fine … come on!" he shouted.

I didn't want to go out of my depth but I followed him,

wanting to build on this resurgence of friendship. So I jumped on my board, lay down and did crawl, ducking my head under each wave as it tumbled over me. Luke was further out than me and I was having difficulty catching him.

"Wait for me!" I shouted but my voice was carried backwards to the beach and he didn't hear. When he'd reached some other surfers, he stopped and I caught him up.

"Oh God, I can't put my feet down," I said, trying desperately to find the bottom.

"You'll be fine, Ems," and as he said it, a huge wave rolled over the top of us both.

"Are you sure?" I spluttered, when I resurfaced. "I had a horrible moment once with James; I went right under and couldn't get up. I really thought I was drowning." I was gripping my board fiercely, using it as a buoyancy aide.

"Oh, sorry, I didn't know … do you want to go in a bit?"

"I think I'm okay. Let's get the next one, though."

I looked out to sea; the waves were rolling in consistently, right across the bay. We were far enough out for the waves to be on the verge of breaking, but most of them hadn't yet. If we could only catch an unbroken one, it would be an amazing ride.

"Ems, quick, get ready! The next one's perfect!"

I steadied myself, which was so much more difficult without my feet touching the sand and as the wave reached us I jumped on it, kicking my feet and using my right arm in a one-handed crawl motion to push myself forward. For a split second, I thought I wasn't going to make it, but then I was forced forward by the power of the breaking wave just behind me. I flew down the barrel; it was all I could do to keep myself on the wave and the point of my board from flicking under the surface. Once I realised I wasn't going to plummet down as I had before, I looked across to see if Luke had managed to get on the same one. Through the foam and the spray I saw him on the same wave, next to me.

"Woo-hoo!" he shouted as he used his arm again, to keep

up with the wave. "Well done, Ems, you did it! I knew you'd be okay."

"That *definitely* was the golden wave," I shouted as we swooshed forward together, the wave now smoothing out and slowing down. "That was amazing!" The wave took us so far in that we began to be grounded on the sand.

"I think we've both won that one," I said, as I slid off the board onto my knees.

"Wow, Mum, I saw you two. That was a fantastic ride," said Amy who'd come over to join us. "I watched you right out there, you were miles out. I thought one of you would fall off when it broke but you didn't," and she kissed my cheek with salty, wet lips.

She ran off to join Holly, the two of them immediately jumping on a small wave. That's what I love about this sport, there are sizes of waves suitable for everyone.

I was so excited by the last ride that I said to Luke, "Right, I'm off back out. Coming?" and I ran off, jumping over the waves with a feeling that life, at this moment, was good. My skin was tingling, my body felt powerful, my mind clear. I had a fleeting memory of windsurfing in Cyprus when the board had taken off and everything had come together in a perfect way. I'd felt like this then and I realised that water, whether it was blue, smooth and warm or green, rough and cold, was the thing I loved most in the world.

Water was my home, my environment and what made me feel alive.

*

The children and the other adults had already gone back to the house; Luke and I were walking back up the beach together.

"That was *so* good," said Luke. "It's cleared my head, somehow."

"Me too." I was shaking the water out of my ears like a wet dog. I looked at him and he smiled back. "It's such fun, isn't it?" I laughed.

After a while he said, "I've loved being with you again, Emily. I've missed this." We were walking side by side and he deliberately brushed my arm with his.

"And me," I said … and meant it. In all that had gone before, I'd forgotten what fun we used to have, just simple pleasures. "The holiday's going too quickly," I added.

"It is …"

He stopped walking and said, "Emily … before we get back to the others, could we talk?"

I had almost been expecting this; I stopped walking and said, "Of course, let's just sit here, the sand's dry …" and I sat down. He sat next to me, both of us facing the sea.

"Ems … you know we talked about maybe selling the cottage, a while ago?"

"Yes …" I said, wondering what was coming. I hadn't expected this sort of discussion.

"Well, I'm finding it quite tight, financially, what with the mortgage and the quarters' rent. I think we need to think about what we're going to do …"

"I should have realised, but I've had so …"

"Look, I know you've had a *terrible* time and with the baby coming, but …"

"What do you want to do?"

There was a long pause; he was making patterns in the sand with his feet and was looking at me, studiously.

"Well … this is what I've been thinking … now that you've got the Padstow cottage and it's yours, with no expenses except electricity, why don't you and Abi move there? The children could come down to the quarter and go to school in Devon. I've been asking around and people say the local schools are good and it's a perfect time for them to move; they could start in September, at the beginning of the school year."

I was staring at the patterns he was making. It made sense, didn't it? I'd been wondering for a while why I was living in that house. The children adored Luke, they'd jump at the chance to be with him all the time. And the Padstow cottage was only an hour or so away. I could go up and they could come down …

"What would you do with the Cotswold house?"

"Well, I thought to begin with, we could rent it out … see how it goes and then, if we like living down here, we could sell it and maybe buy another one … down here."

I couldn't help noticing that he was saying '*we*'. Was it 'we' as in: him and the children, or was I included? Did I *mind* if he was including me in the 'we'?

"And maybe, in time," he continued, "we … could start again?"

The upward rise of his sentence made it into a question that demanded a response. I raised my eyes and looked sideways. Our eyes met and we smiled at each other.

"Can I think about it, Luke? It's a lot to take in. But it *does* make sense, the house thing and maybe …"

"Have a think about it," he said. He stopped moving his feet in the sand and stood up.

"Come on, let's get back," he said, offering to pull me up. I grabbed his hand and stood up, our hands lingering together for a touch longer than was necessary. He squeezed mine gently and then, let it go. My hand missed his touch, as we walked together across the beach.

As we approached the house, we saw that the children were building something on the sand. Jake and Holly were doing one thing and Amy and Charlie, another.

We went to see Jake and Holly first. They'd made a pebble circle with four letters inside: three J's and an H.

"That's lovely, you two. Have you shown Mum and Dad?"

"Not yet," said Jake, "we've just got to make it a bit neater, then we're going to call them down. We want to decorate it with seaweed and shells, too."

"Mum, Dad! Come and look at ours," shouted Charlie, who'd run over to us and was dragging Luke by the hand. We walked over; our children had done the same thing: a pebble circle with letters in: L, E, C and two A's.

We stood together, gazing down at their artwork; we were both at a loss as to what to say but with tears in my eyes, I turned to Luke and said, "Out of the mouths of babes …"

I could see his eyes shining, too.

"Don't you like it?" said Charlie.

"We love it, Buddy … we love it," said Luke.

*

Two days later, the weather was grey and stormy. For a change of scene, we all decided to go to Padstow for pasties and then a walk. The kids weren't that keen on the walk part, but the adults felt it would do them good. I had my carrier for Abi and everyone said they'd help.

"Watch out for seagulls, kids," said Jen, when we were sitting on the harbour side with our pasties. "They can be flying thieves."

As if on cue, one dive-bombed and nearly had Charlie's but Luke got there first.

"Wow!" shouted Charlie.

"That was close," said Luke. "Eat up quickly. Then we'll have an ice cream."

"I'm just going across the road to see if Beth's in," I said and I carried Abi to the shop.

"Is Beth there?" I asked, as I went through the door.

"She is … she's with her gentleman friend!"

"Oo, is she? I haven't met him yet! Can I go on up?"

As I entered the flat, I was met by a beaming Beth and Josh. They were holding hands and Grace was playing happily on the floor.

"So, we meet at last," I said. "I've heard a *lot* about you, you know, and it's all good!"

Josh laughed and brought Beth's hand up to kiss it.

"I've heard a lot about you too, from both Beth and Luke," said Josh. "I know all there is to know!" His eyes twinkled, and I knew immediately that I'd like him.

"We're all on the quay, eating pasties and then we're going for a walk. Do you two fancy coming?"

"Yea, that'd be great. I'll just check and see if Mum can look after Grace."

"No, don't worry, Beth," said Josh. "I'll help carry her – let's take her, it'll be fun."

"Okay, give us five minutes and we'll be down."

When I got down to the others, I said to Luke, "Did you know Josh was here?"

"Is he? Cheeky devil! No, I didn't. That's good, though. They're made for each other, those two."

Soon, Beth, Josh and Grace joined us and there were many introductions and greetings. We all set off along the harbour and up the hill towards the war memorial. The sky was even greyer now and the seagulls were being pushed around by the gusts. The clouds varied in colour from steel grey to charcoal black, but there was something exhilarating about the wind. It wasn't cold and the kids loved running with their arms out, pretending to fly. The two little ones were enjoying the scene too, laughing at the older children's antics.

We walked along the coastal path; the tide was going out and we'd be able to walk back along the beach, but for now, we were up high. Looking across to Brae Hill and Rock, we could see a multitude of sails, some stationary and some zig zagging across the estuary. Further along, we could see the surf crashing into the rocks at Polzeath and in the far distance, the outline of Newland Island and Pentire.

We all walked in small groups that frequently changed, as some people lingered, or ran ahead. John took over carrying

Abi; it gave me the freedom to run down the dunes with the children when we got to the part where we could go down onto the beach at Harbour Cove. The sand was so powdery and white and we all rolled around in it, adults and children alike.

Walking across the glistening wet sand that the tide had left behind, we made our way over to the Old Lifeboat Station. I tried to hide my memories from the others; I could see James so clearly here, I expected him to reach for my hand. I could see how hopeful his face had been when Beth told us about our cottage coming on the market; the start of our Cornish dream.

We walked around Hawkers Cove, the children climbing the rocks, the adults admiring its beauty.

"Imagine living in one of those cottages," said Jen. "It's heavenly, isn't it?"

"This was one of James' favourite places. We often walked here."

Jen took my hand and said, "I'm so sorry, I didn't know ... try to remember the good times."

"I do but it's so hard." I looked across the beach and saw Luke helping Amy down from some rocks.

"He's a good father, isn't he?"

"The best," said Jen.

John had taken the carrier off his back and Abi was happily eating sand.

"No, Abi. You mustn't eat sand. Here, have your drink," and I handed her a bottle.

It was a long walk back, so the adults had to keep up the children's morale, by arranging running races and other competitions. I was struggling with Abi who seemed to be getting heavier and heavier.

"Shall I carry her for a while?"

I turned towards Luke, who was walking by my side and said, "Are you sure? That would be great ... my shoulders are killing me."

While we swapped over the carrier, I couldn't help thinking

how significant this moment was. He'd hardly dared look at her in the past and now I watched as he talked to her and tickled her under the chin.

"Come on Abs, in you get. You're going on Luke's shoulder now," he said. He got her settled and then started running and jigging around to make her laugh. She loved it and giggled.

The others were now way ahead of us and we marched across the beach, trying to catch up. We went up the steps to the memorial and stood for a while, to get our breath back, reading the names of the people who'd lost their lives in the war.

Neither of us spoke, as we gazed upwards at the monument; all those people who'd died so many years ago now just names in stone. Life's so precious, who knew when it would end? It passes in a second; we humans are just fleeting shadows.

We walked on and I could see the others right along the path, nearly at Padstow. I knew they'd wait for us back at the harbour side, but for now, by silent mutual consent, we both wanted to linger … to walk slowly, not wanting this moment to end.

"Can we sit, for a while? I'm sure you could do with a rest," I said, smiling across at him.

I sat down on one of the many benches along the way and I realised I was *happy*.

Now, this very moment.

I wanted to forget my past, forget the future and breathe in the air of … today.

"Okay," he said and slipping the straps off his shoulders, he put the carrier down and lifted Abi out. He sat on the bench next to me and put Abi on his knee, bouncing her gently up and down, holding her round the tummy.

"Abi, I need to ask your Mummy a question," he said, now holding one of her little hands.

"Ems …" he said, his expression serious, his eyes hopeful. I looked at him, wondering what he was going to say. I always knew when he was about to say something important; it was the tone of his voice when he used my name.

A feeling of love for them both welled up inside me and I touched the locket that was round my neck.

"Ems … do you remember saying how Abi would grow up without a father?"

"Yes," I said, grabbing one of Abi's feet in my hands. The light caught the diamonds on my eternity ring.

"If you'd allow me to … I'd love … to be her father. I know it won't be the same as having James, but … do you think, sometime in the future, you'd consider it?"

He lowered his head and gently kissed the top of Abi's head.

Looking up again, he said, "It would be an honour and I think James would be okay with it, don't you?"

I swallowed hard, blinking back tears. I squeezed Abi's foot and said to her, "Would you like this man to be your Daddy, Abi?"

Two seagulls swooped overhead, calling and flying towards the ocean, leaving their cries whirling in the air above. Abi smiled sweetly and I leaned over, across the top of her head and kissed Luke gently on the lips. Abi, squashed between the two of us, let out a little indignant squeal.

"Come on, let's go you two," I said. "They'll all be wondering where we are."

"You take this," he said, handing me the carrier. "We don't need it any more. I'll hold Abi."

He stood up, carrying her in the crook of his arm and kissed her cheek.

With his free hand, he pulled me up off the bench and we walked, hand in hand, back along the path to Padstow, to join the others.

THE END

If you enjoyed this book, why not try Sarah Catherine Knights' other books?

Aphrodite's Child - the first part of the Aphrodite Trilogy

and

Shadows in the Rock - the third part of the Aphrodite Trilogy

Love is a State of Mind

Available at www.amazon.co.uk

Aphrodite's Child

(First book in the Aphrodite Trilogy)

When her RAF husband is posted to Cyprus for three years, Emily Blackwell jumps at the opportunity to escape her cosy life in the Cotswolds. Embracing everything the island has to offer, she reinvents herself, only to find that this new life brings its own heartache and tragedy. In a modern take on the myth of Aphrodite, the Goddess of Love, Emily's experiences on Cyprus change her, and she comes to question everything she thought she knew about herself and her former existence.

But the choices she makes will affect not only her, but everyone she loves …

Shadows in the Rock

(Third book in the Aphrodite Trilogy)

In the third book of the Aphrodite series, Abi Blackwell is a young woman desperate to escape her Devon village and start a new life as a fashion photographer in London. The shadows of her parents' past have haunted her life and she needs to break free.

Her new life turns out to be more difficult than she'd ever imagined. On a shoot in Cyprus, Abi experiences both the worst and the best that life has to offer, forcing her to grow up quickly and to learn to forgive.

But has she left it too late?

Love is a State of Mind

Anna McCarthy thought she was leading a good life, but when her husband David tells her he has fallen in love with someone else, she has to re-evaluate everything.

She makes some huge changes, both at home and at work and decides to visit her estranged sister in Australia. Here, she gets a new perspective on her past, her present and her future.

Along the way, she faces tragedy, new love and surprising revelations.

But most of all, she learns to accept her new life without bitterness and realises that behind the Facebook facade, nobody's life is perfect.

www.sarahcatherineknights.com
www.twitter.com/Sarahknights
www.facebook.com/sarahcatherineknights